D1246381

I dedicate this saga
to the maligned heroes
and the forgotten victims of
several fratricidal wars in our century -
men and women, brave beyond belief,
who hurled themselves against the forces
of the New World Order

Copyright © 1998 Ingrid A. Rimland

First publication in March of 1998

Samisdat Publishers, Inc.
206 Carlton Street, Toronto,
Ontario, Canada
M5A 2L1

Cover illustration by Ernst Zündel

Text set in AGaramond Semibold 12

Written and published in the United States. Printed and bound by KNI Incorporated, Anaheim, California, USA

ISBN 1-896006-02-7

This is Book II of a trilogy. Book I and III are available by writing to:

6965 El Camino Real, # 105-588
La Costa, CA 92009

Fax: 760-929-2268

Lebensraum!

The Theft of Land and Peace

A Novel
by
Ingrid Rimland

Book II

Lebensraum! spans seven generations and 200 years. It is a story told to me a thousand times in many different voices: that there was once a place called "Apanlee" that fell to the Red Terror.

A novel is, by definition, fiction against the backdrop of genuine emotions. This novel has been my attempt to grasp and to extract the interplay between opposing ideologies, to find the core of human tragedies that make up cold statistics.

The novel's voice belongs to "Erika" who, in this saga, is older than I was when I experienced World War II. She is, however, of the transition generation, as I am. Hers is the ethnic voice in this novel, trying to find the right words to own up to the pride and courage that were the hallmarks of her people.

She learns to say: "Our history belongs to us. It won't be written, from now on, by anybody else but us."

This family saga was gleaned from the driftwood of history. The people I have tried to show to be of flesh and blood came of a tightly knit community of Russian-German ancestry.

Ingrid Rimland

Lebensraum! - Book I - Chapters 1-39
Reviewed by Michael S. McMillen

Push-button critics and sound-bite sages tell us that the age of the epic is past. They are wrong. Ingrid Rimland has written an inter-generational, moral panorama—an epic in prose depicting what people can be when they embrace both freedom and responsibility.

Like the poets of ancient Greece, she does not evade evil. This author knows the human condition. She illustrates what it takes for man to earn his bread—and what happens when a dash of leaven is added to the whole, wanton cruelty.

Lebensraum! is her trilogy, which traces the lives and deaths, the loves and hates, the hopes realized and the dreams dashed of people from two Russian-German families, the Neufelds and the Epps.

The first book follows them from their successes in the Ukraine during the early 19th century and closes on the brink of the war that tore Western civilisation asunder and the revolution that was Russia's undoing. It commences with a history lesson recounting the migration of peace-loving German pioneers. Early on, one of the epic's tensions comes screaming into the fore. This group of pacifists bases its creed on the Bible—*sola scriptura*—with no need of intermediaries. They refuse spiritual tribute to Papa, and they refuse military service to Caesar.

Hounded, taxed, persecuted, martyred, the sect clings to life with a robust ardor born of pure Scriptural faith. Their tenacious confidence in their ultimate deliverance helps them forge a stoic endurance and determination in the face of furious persecution.

The hounded pilgrims look to the East for living space, the land, liberty and peace needed to survive and prosper. Eventually they find a patron in the Empress Catherine the Great of Russia, who needs people to cultivate the lands along the Black and Caspian seas. She offers the German pacifists free land, self-rule, protection and exemption from conscription.

From the start, the novel focuses on two complementary approaches to the business of living. "Some dug in deep, as Peter Neufeld did, a man with expert hands and fierce ambition." These are the men of active, curious, inventive minds, men of accurate reckoning and rolled-up sleeves who survey the problem, spit on their palms and get to work.

"Others," we are told, ". . . stayed in their covered wagons from where they prayed to Heaven day and night." Among these people is one of the Elders, a man named Hans Epp.

There is a division of labour among these hearty pioneers. Some dig and reap; others meditate and pray.

Eventually the grave and ambitious Germans establish their settlement and sink firm roots in their adopted land. The story moves steadily through that century of progress when even the land of the Tsars felt something of the heady aroma of freedom.

The peace was not to last for long—on the Eastern front or the Western. The protagonists fall prey to the twin snares of those who cling dogmatically to peace: beclouding, complacent pride in the lasting conditions of contentment and vulnerability to aggressors.

Thus, in the very nature of the people who are to enact this vast drama, we see the seeds of later suffering. Why do the innocent often end up crushed in the bloody mud? The search for Lebensraum! is partially the quest for an answer to this moral conundrum.

One of the themes at the heart of Lebensraum! is that virtue is a necessary condition of life, prosperity and happiness. The pilgrims grow and prosper in a community they name Apanlee, which will become the spiritual magnet, the inspirational font, the symbol of life and "Lebensraum" for the good offspring of the Neufelds and Epps.

Yet early on, a smoking fissure is apparent. As the productive and ambitious—represented by Peet Neufeld, Peter's son— hew a cornucopia out of the rich soil of Apanlee, the pious— represented by Hans Epp's son Willy—begin to chastise and warn that the judgment of God must soon descend and crush the pride of the successful farmers and artisans.

These warnings go largely unheeded. After all, doesn't God bless thrift and industry? He's on His throne and the Romanovs—now the Apanlee Germans' staunch patrons—are on theirs.

In a heartrending scene, Peet Neufeld and his wife Greta are entertaining a Romanov prince who says, beaming with gratitude, "Peet Neufeld, see that sun? As long as it hangs in the sky, we of the house of Romanov vouch for protection. Always." Sadly, within decades, the devil himself will smash that pledge to dust, dethrone and massacre the Romanovs and unleash terror and death upon Apanlee and all of Russia.

Living space is the call that the industrious heed and follow. Another of the epic's contrasts opens up when some of the Apanlee Germans decide to seek their Lebensraum on the abundant prairies of America.

The cavalcade continues as new babies are born to replenish the souls of those who have died. America appeals to Peet Neufeld's son Nicky because it offers virgin opportunity to people who are willing to stand on their own and earn their keep. Nevertheless, the American apple is not immune to the vicissitudes of life or the rot and corruption engendered by secondhanders, parasites and outright thieves.

Nicky and his wife, Willy's daughter Lizzy, set sail for America. Nicky is drowned. Upon arriving in America, the widow Lizzy is swindled by a man named Donoghue for a quick buck and left with a piece of seemingly worthless prairie wilderness for her troubles.

Under Lizzie's maternal guidance, however, her strong and noble son Jan leads his community in building a breadbasket of the Kansas wastes that have fallen to their lot. Contempt turns to envy in the mouths of the swindler and his family, who then seek to wrest the land back in order to sate themselves on the achievements of Jan Neufeld.

The Donoghue's goal through the years will be to "prove" that the sale was only a lease.

As the Germans prosper in their new community of Mennotown, Kansas, a word begins to sound faintly like the scratching of a hungry rat among trash and shards: Equality. This word will reverberate and knell throughout Lebensraum!

Eventually it will ignite the flames of revolution, explicitly savage in Russia, bureaucratized and sanitized in America. Indeed, it is one of the negative themes of the story, a counterpoint to the thrift, decency and faith that set the builders of Apanlee and of Mennotown apart from and above their fellows.

In scene after scene and encounter after encounter, our author shows us how those who take responsibility for themselves and face their work tenaciously have no need in the world for "Equality" in the sense that is bruited so noisily, that of income redistribution and uniformity of condition.

If equality has any meaning in a political context, it can only be in the sense that each person is an individual with his own rights and must be governed by the same laws and principles and treated by the same standards as all other people.

The heroes and heroines of Lebensraum! learn to their dismay that the baying wolves about them pervert this principle. Equality functions as a demonic wrench to tighten here, loosen there as the whims of the worthless dictate. It twists and strangles the God-fearing and productive in Russia, as ignorant curs who have half-digested intellectual slogans, try to make milch-cows of their betters.

In America, the cry of equality is heard in the baying of the Finkelsteins, who find it a useful political tool and the Donoghues, who find it a standing meal-ticket. Equality corrodes family structure and banishes harmony from the relations between the sexes. The siren song of the suffragettes is heard in the pages of Lebensraum! as a feisty character named Josie—who eventually marries and torments the dutiful Jan Neufeld—despises the vocations of wife and mother and busies herself among the moneylenders and political malcontents.

Finally, those who establish a state religion on the basis of certain peoples' suffering, while ignoring or denigrating the suffering of others, invoke "equality" while seeking to stifle or out-law even the discussion of truth.

This brings us back to the Revisionist side of Lebensraum! Rimland, who has done so much for World War II Revisionism, takes her mission a step further with Lebensraum!

A movement certainly needs a professional, systematic development in expository prose. Among the many who are providing this are David Irving, Michael Hoffmann II and Ingrid Rimland herself. Nevertheless, if a movement is to gain popular recognition and become part of the warp and woof a civilisation, it must be given flesh and blood, perceptual form. It must be embodied in art. Just as Ayn Rand illustrated her philosophy of Objectivism in characters such as Howard Roark, Dagney Taggart and John Galt, so Ingrid Rimland has given Revisionism a face in the personas of Erika, Jan Neufeld, Jonathan and others.

Lebensraum! is, of course, much more than I have been able to hint here. In its pages are limned the good, bad and ugly feelings of a special band of separatists.

The heroes and heroines of Lebensraum! are in the world, but at odds with it. They are always searching. The allure of productive freedom calls some of them to America; religious forebodings and a misguided spiritual zeal call one group of pilgrims led by Class Epp, Willy's son, on a disastrous trek eastward from Apanlee. The old virtues and customs sustain the good folk, even as newfangled ideas and bold experimental values whistle to them and whisper in their ears.

I was personally struck by the vibrant and cohesive family life that is portrayed in Book I. Rimland's depiction of family rings true to man's nature and potential. Hers is no sugar-coated puff job on the joys and sorrows of kinship. The exigencies of daily life and the social corrosion of a hostile society both take their toll on men and women of the best intentions.

The old ways, however, are always the foundation on which the good folk stand. Indeed, one senses that the robust love nurtured in the bosom of family is itself a vital part of Lebensraum, living space.

Book I ends on an ominous note, as the First World War and the Soviet revolution hover. The reader must realize that the people of Lebensraum! exhibit the full range of human emotions—from the tender to the desperate to the prejudicial.

Lebensraum! does not omit or evade the suspicions and fears—justified or otherwise—of a misunderstood and often persecuted minority. This minority, however, that grows the world's wheat and mends the world's garments has found few spokesmen or defenders.

In the opening book of Lebensraum! Ingrid Rimland establishes the groundwork for that defense."

Chapter 40

The pacifists of Apanlee kept harvesting the wheat, while the rabbis berated the palace. All throughout spring and into early summer, while Hein was busy with the grain, a lot of cryptic messages flew back and forth between the heads opf state of countries to the west of the Ukraine while soldiers ringed the cities.

When the war broke out, it came as a surprise to all but Uncle Benny. It couldn't be. It couldn't happen—the kaiser and the tsar were cousins!

"This nonsense won't last longer than three weeks. You don't make war on family," said Hein, who spoke for all. Up came yet another sunny morning. You did your work, swept out the silos, and readied the crews for the threshing.

"Why not say: bottoms up?" was Dominik's opinion.

He had supped lavishly that day. He scraped the wax off a bottle and smacked the bottom with his palm. The cork shot out and spun into a corner. "Now listen, everybody! Bottoms up!"

The country was afloat with rumors.

The malcontent summed up the situation: "I'm still not worth a thought?" Defiance, that was Dominik. "Why not? What's to stop me now?" He saw a cricket on the steps of Apanlee and ground it in the dust. His eyes locked hard with Hein's. His heart was pounding like a hammer.

"Today is today," he said, leaning forward. "And tomorrow is surely tomorrow." He pulled a German hymnal from his pocket, tore out a leaf, fished for tobacco in his pockets, and rolled himself a cigarette.

"You're wrong," said Hein, and stalked into the yard to saw some wood for exercise. The others sat in silence.

The day the European war broke out turned out to be a milestone day for Uncle Benny and his Dorothy, combining wrenching sadness with great joy, for fate would hand them their first grandchild, a perfect baby boy, demanding that they forfeit to the grave their only, much-beloved child—a girl whose name has been forgotten, who died as quietly as she lived.

So much has happened since that day that her existence seems unmemorable. What can one say of certain lives? She lived, a nondescript. She died with resignation.

Before she died, she bore a son. His name was Jonathan.

"She's turned into an angel with soft wings," said Uncle Benny, laying down his stirring grandchild carefully, unable to believe his lie.

The summer heat sat, trapped, high in the attic. His daughter somehow managed to give birth against enormous odds; now she was dead; fled like a shadow, no more to walk the earth— this on a day as dry as tinder, when all the fields were shimmering with heat and but a spark was needed to set the clouds aflame.

"She searched and found the perfect name," said Dorothy, who tried to hide her tears.

A grieving Uncle Benny stood in silence before the infant's wicker cradle. The winds were whistling fiercely.

"It is God's will. His hand is not shortened, as witnesses this child," said the Elders, for even while the mother died, she bore a sculpted son. And though this sudden childbed death was saddening to all, you never saw such symmetry of face and limb in such a tiny morsel!

This little baby boy whom Dorothy held, weeping, in her arm's crook was blond and firm; its limbs were strong; it had the wished-for large, blue eyes; it had a chiseled profile.

"Weep not, for in the shadow of His hand He has hidden me so far," said Uncle Benny to his little love who shed her silent tears.

He stayed with Dorothy until she fell asleep, and only then did Uncle Benny reach for his pen and ink to write with fine, but shaking hand: "I grope for light as though I had no sight. If war comes to the steppe, death will mow down generations, leaving only stubble."

While the midwife was busily swaddling the newborn, while the Elders launched into their funeral prayers, Marleen stripped the bed while Natasha kept soaking the bed sheets. Dorothy kept dabbing at her swollen eyes while Hein, his big chest heaving with emotion, took his dead cousin to the hill to rest among her forebears beneath a soft carpet of grass.

That's when he spotted Dominik.

"The kaiser's war! The kaiser's war!"

And nothing was ever the same!

Huge rainstorms started racing through the sky. Bugles sounded. Bands hammered marches. Orthodox priests fingered crosses. The Apanlee Elders chanted their psalms. The tsar's army mobilized, and feelings everywhere ran patriotic to the hilt.

"God save the tsar!"

"God save his wife, the tsarina!"

"And blessings on the bleeder child!"

"Bread for his soldiers!"

"Bread or lead! Bread or lead!"

Professional thieves turned eager paper boys, beside themselves with animation: "Blood cousins—open foes!"

Incendiary slogans hung from every fence and blazed across the banners of the masses. The priests blessed everything in sight:

the *kulish* and the *paska*, the newborn child, the fresh, dark grave.
The church bells mourned. People climbed on tables and chairs.
The noblemen twirled mustaches. The Cossacks jumped upon
their small, dark horses, knives clutched between their teeth.

It's strange about a war. A war is like a birthday—to mourn
or celebrate?

Both feelings seemed appropriate. This war was no exception. Forgotten were the bitter quarrels between the landed gentry and the poor. Forgotten were poverty, squalor and shame.
The Russian hamlets—wild with joy. The Valley of Jews—in
chaos!

The frenzied rabbis kept running back and forth; their skull-
caps sliding down. "Oy vey, oy vey!" they wailed, for they could
hear the horses' hard, keen hoofs already hammering across the
boundless steppe, across the sun-baked earth.

At Apanlee, the kettles started whistling as Marleen rushed
her fattest rooster to get him ready for the pot. The twins just
snapped their fingers at each other, ashamed of their pacifist roots.
It was as if the very air was drunken with the headlines.

Shells started whining far away.

Bombs began booming.

The universe shook.

In the vicinity of Apanlee, the little boys kept practicing the
Cossack dance, the *hapack*. The little females kept on curtsying,
to show they had not lost their German manners.

The weather cock spun wildly. The meeting halls were packed
to overflowing.

A fool broke into song.

A cat took to a tree.

Natasha just clutched her umbrella.

"So. Where did it start? How did it end?" the folks told
Erika just recently in Reedley, California. "Who is to say, now
that there's television, controlled by hidden hands, to tell you

what to think? There was a certain scoundrel, too close to the throne, about him the stench of the fiend—"

Imperial servants did his bidding. A crested eagle's carriage took him where he pleased. Of him, it was whispered the length of the empire: a devil in disguise. A blasphemer. A charlatan. A counterfeit and hypocrite. A spy in the pay of the kaiser.

The German empress would have none of that. Now more than ever, she counted on the monk to help the bleeder child. She saw naught but his glittering eyes.

A sainted man, said she.

A gross, crude fraud, said others.

Wastrel or wonderworker—who was to say? Both saints and sinners wear hair to their shoulders. Vagrants and vagabonds like to wear beards, as do prophets, princes, professors.

"Sin is to be used," said the malicious monk, "to drive out sin. The path to repentance—through sin."

At first, he was content to satisfy his needs with giggling peasant wenches. Soon, he cast spells into the lives of swooning ladies of nobility. The empress looked entranced when she but heard his voice.

She claimed he was a saint so powerful and wise that, when he raised his pockmarked hands, he could force streams to run uphill. His eyes had the magnetic light she craved. He told her black was white and white was black, and she believed, not the first to have fallen for folly walking Faith as though it were a creature on a leash.

They say she put her aching head upon his hairy chest. He filled her mind with delusions, her heart with soothing calm. He said to her: "Your eyes—like steamy windows."

She said to her surroundings: "Were it not for this man, a holy instrument of Providence, my little angel would surely die."

"What's on your mind?" asked the tsarina daily.

"Not much," replied the tsar.

A courtier spoke for him. "A bomb can explode on either side of the border."

The Empress fished within her skirts to find her smelling salts.

One word led to another, and in the no-man's land of their emotions, both sought a soothing echo for inconvenient thoughts. Both heard the fire whistle blow. The streets were littered with debris; the alleys, black with people.

She knew she was ordained by God and favored by His grace. The tsar fussed with his dominoes.

The workers, too. They hurt, and they bled, and they hungered; they howled: "A tsar—a war! A tsar—a war! Where is the head of the German tsarina?"

The monk heard that. He laughed so hard he burst a vessel in his nose.

"Let me now pray so the successor to the throne gets well," he told the empress softly. His pupils shrank to pinpoints. His powers flowed into the bleeder child out of the German House of Hesse.

"Saved once again, just in the nick of time," the tearful mother said, and kissed the hem of the pretender's shirt. She had blind faith in him and each day sought his counsel.

He spread ten greasy fingers to show the ministers who came to him, complaining: "See these palms? That's where the power rests."

He said to friend and foe alike: "You cut your father's throat if I as much as wink." His belly shook with laughter. He was carousing with the noblewomen and the court. "This war will be finished by Christmas!" He jabbed another belly with his finger: "When I say 'dance!' a wise man does."

In belted peasant shirt and dirty boots he walked across the steps that Peter the Great had erected, grinding with his heels the revolutionary circulars the wind blew from the gutters.

The monk advised the tsar: "Unless you do my bidding, you will not win your war." Behind his back he boasted: "I scratch the tsar behind the ears, and everything gets done."

He gave the tsar a triple kiss: "Why don't you cast aside despair? You'll win this war. You'll see." As hunger swept the

Russian cities, he played the balalaika and ate with hairy fingers.

"A saint, anointed by the Lord," said the tsar, taking desperate walks through the half-melted snow.

"God willing, faith can move mountains," intoned the tsarina. The glow of self-approval shone on her haughty face. She trusted the monk. She had Faith.

The torches smoked and sparked. The air was foul. The clouds floated, poisoned with rumors. "Dethrone the monsters in the palace!" the angry mob howled from below.

"How can a holy man do wrong?" asked the tsarina coldly, and lit another candle. "Share power with the rabble?"

The tsar replied to no one in particular: "I keep my fingers crossed. The road ahead is dark." He told his ministers: "I cannot see where all this might be leading." He crooked his little finger and kept on sipping tea. His ministers said nothing.

In rolled another sultry summer. It was a task to catch the tsar's swift glance.

"You salvage what you can," the courtiers warned the tsar. "You salvage while you can."

His wife had no such qualms. She turned white and gave a shudder in the sharp teeth of treachery. Her voice rose to a shriek: "God gave us our throne. Only God has the right to take it away."

The tsar began to mutter something about the malice of the universe, the worm in the core of the apple. The monk just held his nose. He flung his arms in a wide arch:

"It's Satan's brood. They are at fault. Each one I know wags several tongues at once."

He also said: "State secrets pass between them involving the entire globe, and all of them are foul."

A cross appeared above Peet Neufeld's grave, but no one saw the curious apparition except Ivan, who told Natasha. Natasha ran, as quickly as she could, to find a broken broom to jump across on her left leg and thus annul the omen.

"I leaped like a hare," she said to Marleen, who gave her a lopsided smile.

For good measure, Natasha consulted a Gypsy. The Gypsy told her it meant nothing.

"Pay no attention whatsoever," the Gypsy said and spat in a fine arc. "Why be concerned with trifles?"

Natasha was not yet convinced. She wanted to be hopeful for the future, because of Dominik, her son and, therefore, in her thoughts. She lit the fattest candle she could find. She lit it for a pouting saint she had neglected lately.

Hein said to Dominik: "Let's stretch our legs. I want to talk to you."

And high time, too. At Apanlee, times went from bad to worse. Hein said to Dominik, while giving him a sidelong glance: "I'd like to send you to Odessa to be apprenticed properly. I will do that as soon as I can. This year has been most difficult."

He spoke the truth. It was as if both heaven and earth had conspired.

Spring had been wet; next came too hot a summer. In years gone by, Hein could have talked most any friend into a short-term loan on less than two hours' notice, but now he learned, to his dismay, that rubles and kopecks were scarce.

The heat wave came and stayed. The springs dried up; the rivers turned to rivulets; the reaping yielded half the yield Hein needed to break even. Worse yet, trustworthy workers were hard and ever harder to engage. The war had pushed them from the fields and out into the soggy trenches; rifle butts kept pushing them into dilapidated barracks and dark factories where firebrands fueled huge, vociferous dissent.

Meanwhile, great swaths of Apanlee's soil went untilled. Illegal price jumps crippled trade. The future lay black and foreboding. Hein knew there would be no money left to pay for next year's harvest.

"Your mother," Hein explained to Dominik, "lived like a mouse before you were born. I want you to remember that."

"So?"

"She has a place with us. She always has her fill of steamed potatoes. She'll always find some hot soup waiting in the kitchen."

"So?"

"A devil drove your mother," said Hein with a small laugh, remembering. He gave his bastard son another sidelong glance. "Look here. Who gave you rides in the family coach? Who taught you how to bait a worm on a hook?"

"But why did you withhold your praise?"

"I did not want to give you dangerous ideas."

"Had I known that," said Dominik, "I would have laughed aloud."

"What do you want?"

"Two names. My own, and my father's. Stencilled in the family Bible."

"I'll give you an answer tomorrow," said Hein, but then that promise slipped his mind as well, and nothing more was said.

Then came the storm. It came with a force not the oldest of oldsters remembered. The winds swept the streets and the porches, and with them came a summons, calling Dominik to war.

Natasha wept with pride and consternation. Her Dominik, conscripted to become a hero for the tsar? Sent out to kill the wicked enemy, perhaps be killed to sanctify the cause? Natasha's heart beat hard with mixed emotions. She knew her son. She knew that any slogan was graven on his memory to stay.

Her grief was boundless, as the Volga. Her pride, just like the sun that only yesterday had warmed the bounteous earth. He could have chosen cowardice. He could have had his teeth pulled and thereby avoided conscription. He could have hidden in Hein's barn or else in the expanded attic—or, better yet, behind the wheat sacks in the granary Hein tried to sell in vain.

"Besides, he's still a bachelor," Marleen was pointing out; she still did not like Dominik. "Who'd miss him all that much?"

That day, the spotlight rested on Natasha, who started biting back. She did so with full gusto, for righteous motherhood shone plainly on her face. No longer need she feel ashamed that Dominik spent every winter on the stove.

She beamed into the crowds. She shouted for the twins to

help her celebrate.

They did not let her down. "Say, Dominik! I'll lend you my sheepskin," said one.

"You can have my watch," said the other.

"Let war not coarsen you. Do not forget to shave," Natasha told her son, to show that she had raised him to good manners.

She gloried in the neighbors' praise. Her eyes snapped with excitement. Her cheeks were cherry-red.

She watched Hein reach deep in his pockets. "Go buy yourself a pair of boots," said Hein, while slapping Dominik on both shoulders, man to man. "And a new uniform. The best is barely good enough. That is my firm opinion."

Hein was at his generous best. War made for generosity. The Faith of his German, pacifist forebears provided a brake, but where was it written that he couldn't harness his best Sunday horses and take the willing conscript from Apanlee in brisk gallop straight to the nearest conscript booth, about him the fields in slow circles?

"And let me know if you need anything. Anything. Just anything at all."

"If there is battle for a cause," said Dominik, and shrugged, "any trumpet will be an excuse."

Hein shouted for his horses, heart pounding with emotion. He was a pacifist; he strove to love both friend and enemy—but in times as heroic as these, that went against the grain.

"Just do your country proud; that is my one request," Hein said to Dominik who slowly licked his mustache. "If you need anything, just call on me. New boots? New socks? Soon enough, the winter will start gnawing on your toes."

"Hey, bottoms up!"

"God bless! God bless!"

And just remember this: that any foreigner who harms my country," boasted Dominik, enfolding Yuri with one arm and Sasha with the other, "is my decided enemy."

Dust puffs rose breezily beneath the horses' hoofs as Dominik set off that day to go to war for Russia—Hein by his side, the twins behind him on the backboard, Natasha waving with her scarf and Marleen nowhere to be seen, glad that the thorn was pulled.

"Just you remember! Bottoms up!" were Dominik's last words. He gave Hein's mares the flick of a whip. Things never yet had seemed so good. He broke into an uncouth laugh while watching horses do what horses do, dropping their steaming apples, one by one, along the quiet and tidy streets that cut through Apanlee.

Chapter 41

As overseas, three monarchies where crumbling, Noralee sat, several pillows at her back, her smelling salts in her pink bottle, her blue eyes round with terror, and wondered where it all would end.

It started with a bad cold in her head. Her illness next progressed to restless sleep and leaky bladder. She lost all taste for dumplings and red cabbage. Her own reflection startled her. It all was bad and getting worse. It was as Lizzy said: "There is no point in waiting for the sky to fall. Go see the Wichita doctors."

"What will my husband say?" wailed Noralee, convinced that she stood toe to toe with death.

Lizzy's tongue didn't curl with her lie. "He'll understand. Besides, it's only temporary."

Doctorjay looked lovingly at Lizzy, for he revered her as a weed reveres the sun. If anybody in this world, his old friend Lizzy understood how much it pained an honest healer—being forced to step aside for diplomas and black magic, making room for men with gold and silver, maybe even meadows in their names, the kind that treated a sore throat and called it laryngitis, diminishing his self-esteem. He still made rounds, as he had always done, his now ill-thought-of stomach bitters in his trousers, to help the neighborhood stay well. Allowing medical pretenders to annex the fame that rightfully belonged to him just went against the better instincts in his bones.

But he had reached his limits. He knew that now. No matter how he plowed his memory to help his Noralee, he could not find an herb to lessen her serious symptoms.

The Hebrew doctors said to Noralee: "By Christmas, you'll feel better."

He nodded, not convinced. "I'm willing to suspend my doubts." He battled his foreboding. He fussed and wrangled with misgivings. "But watch. Watch what happens next. They'll open her. From the neck down to her belly button. God knows what they'll discover."

No wonder Noralee cried out before her husband closed the door to leave her to the scalpel: "I just will have to die, that's all!"

It broke his fleshy heart. He was a helpless man, thus challenged at the core. He treasured Noralee; he stood by her through thick and thin, through varicose veins, palsy and gout, slipped discs, and even diarrhea. But this time it was different. He knew her illness was more serious than even she admitted. He knew Noralee; she did as she said; if she said it was time, it was time.

Lizzy rested her chin in her fingers. "You did all you could, Doctorjay."

He peered at her out of small eyes. He stroked his fading whiskers. "I'm not yet ready to foreswear my happy life with her."

"Of course not, Doctorjay. She will outlive you yet."

"That is my hope, God willing."

Between them was a sturdy bond. They had a solid marriage. As decade slipped past decade, the love between them grew. Together, they had added seven daughters and four sons to the prairie population while he was growing bald and round, much like a July pumpkin, and she was growing wrinkled.

Now he mopped a perspiring forehead. He tried his best to mask his fear, but deep inside there was a knot that wouldn't go away.

"It's been a week. The bandages come off on Sunday. The scar, they claim, is dry and straight. They want to write her up. They urged me to sign my permission. That way not all is lost."

"That's wonderful."

"Her wound is healing nicely, as though she were a youngster."

"Of course. Why not? She's warm and snug inside her quilts. She will be home next month."

"God willing, Lizzy dear. God willing."

"The hottest summer, Lizzy," he said slowly, "must soften into fall." He bit into her apfelstrudel to show how much he valued Lizzy and blinked away his sentiment.

"Yes. That is true. And after fall comes winter."

"She was hurting too bad. It had to be surgery, Lizzy."

"I know. You can still do the finishing touches." She knew where he hurt—on account of his huge lack of schooling. For good measure, she added: "Stop fussing yourself silly. You're the best healer around."

"The nurses thank you for the cheese bits, Lizzy."

"Oh, that was nothing. Nothing."

There were effortless pauses between them. They deepened, and they grew. At last he said: "You know what, Lizzy? You're exceptional."

"Why, you're just saying that."

"I mean it. You're too modest." He still remembered how the ship had pitched and keeled while aiming for America; how Lizzy sat and wept for her young love swept into a watery grave, down at the bottom of the sea. But had that done her in? No. Had that defeated her? No. She'd pulled herself together, married Herbert, bred her cows, adopted electricity, not once mistook a flivver for the devil, placed many hundreds of crisp sheets on beds and couches to welcome far-flung visitors and never wasted time on reading. Never!

He longed to drink to that. He fished in empty trouser pockets. "No, I'm not merely saying that. If anything, you are exceptional—"

If anyone exemplified the pioneer ways of America, the simple and straightforward life, it was this sweet and gentle woman, whose numerous kin were now dispersed throughout the wide plains, improving the country by voting straight Republican. He shot a sidelong glance at her. Did she surmise that, at such trying times, his mind was yearning for the comfort that firewater brought? A drink would do him wonders.

Immediately, she put a soft hand on his knuckles. "No," she said firmly. "You're done with that."

"I know. I merely—"

"No point in even trying."

He studied her discreetly. All members of her family were proud teetotalers. Jan never touched the bottle. Jan shook himself when Doctorjay as much as hinted—just shook himself as if he'd touched a snail.

"Do you suppose—"

She read his thoughts. She jumped into the challenge with both feet. "Why, yes! Of course! Here on the couch. Stay overnight. You know that you are always welcome."

How well she knew his fears! Without his flask, the birds no longer sang as happily. The sun no longer shone as brightly. Drink could turn foe into friend. Strangers were strangers no more. He smiled a rueful smile, stretched out his legs, stared out the window and at the ceiling, hiccuped gently, blew a perfect smoke ring, and rolled an apfelstrudel crumb between thick thumb and finger. "You are a top-notch neighbor."

"That's what you always say."

"By strength of will alone, you helped me overcome temptation, for when I look at Josephine, who nearly died with grief because I lost track of the day—" His voice fogged up, but he kept pushing on. "I know I am a sinner whose duty is sobriety. As Dewey always says."

For the issue was still unresolved. There was still Josephine. While he was warming his round belly, the icy night was feasting on her child. She never mentioned it to him, how he forgot the child, who lost his way and froze to death, but somehow, Doctorjay just knew. Both he and Josie knew; both carried that old scar.

"She has forgiven you."

"I know. But still—"

Of course she missed her son, but it was more. Much more. The loss of her first child, thanks to the elocution lessons, had done something to her. It was as if her mother's heart had lost its special warmth.

She, too, was aging modestly. The accident that took her son was like an ax that fell on a young tree; its blade still clove to her marrow. Her parenting came awkwardly.

There were no words in Mennotown to summarize a thing that catastrophic in a woman. Not since that firstling froze to death because he, Doctorjay, had peered too deep into his flask had Josephine been willing to have children.

She had them anyway. He helped.

He sat all night right by her bed and told her flivver jokes to help her pass the time. And only at the very end, when it was time to yield his chair and let the midwife sit, was he content that he had done his duty. Although a lot of what she said and did still went against the grain of Mennotown, he valued Josephine—one of the few who did.

For one, she hid her pregnancies. She wore her ruffle skirts and said no, no, and no! until she could no more deny the obvious, thus cutting Lizzy's baby preparations right in half. That was Josie; she came with a script of her own.

And little did her husband help, though Jan was attentive, as ever.

When Josie sprained an ankle because she crashed her bicycle, Jan found a maid for her. Jan even dried the dishes. His little Josephine was still the apple of his eye. He never said a word when Josie started ordering: a bread toaster, an automatic cherry stoner, a wooden ice box, more!—all the modern gadgetry a female heart could dream to speed all kitchen chores.

Yet all in vain: that odd, peculiar weariness of spirit just never left her mind. At the rickety bridge where the accident happened, she'd sit, consoling herself with the silence around her.

Girl after girl—and she, more reclusive than ever. It was as if, with every pregnancy that sent the clan's hopes soaring for the son to fill the void the frozen child had left, her innermost essence diminished.

But girls were girls; you loved them, too; they started having boys. Each had more freckles than the other. And all of them won ribbons at the fair. Josie's girls were splendid, without a single mark. They came of proven stock. Those girls could do most anything, for Lizzy was their model—cook splendid Sunday dinners, spruce up the house for holiday guests, milk cows, make cheese, churn butter, raise chickens, weed rose beds, sew nightgowns from Butterick patterns.

Jan loved them dearly, one by one, though he deserved a boy as well with whom to share his willow pole down by the river bank.

"There is still time," said Lizzy, prodding, while having a quiet moment with her son.

"My heart clings to that thought," said Jan, who never gave up hope.

He didn't blame his Josie. He knew it had been tedium that wrought such heartbreak woe. To fight the tedium of life was all, as far as Josie was concerned, embedded in her nature; it wasn't just because his tongue played tricks on the poor little lad who fell into the snowdrift and couldn't struggle out.

His little tongue was silenced for all time. The angels wept that day.

She seemed to grieve extravagantly for many saddened years, but what it was she'd lost, exactly, nobody could discern.

Although her pain had dulled, a sadness had come over Josie, like fog. The relatives sat on the sofa, prattling. They said to her: "Here. Have some decent food."

That cheered her up a little, but not much.

Her spirits barely lifted, no matter what they did. When she found energy to rouse herself and look into a mirror, she said to her reflection: "Well. Now you know. Don't ever claim you didn't."

She would talk to herself as though she herself were the strangest of strangers. She hunted for comfort in books, by the fire, her feet tucked underneath, her nose pressed into yet another paragraph, jotting down her cryptic observations in the margins. If someone spoke to her, she answered sluggishly, as if her mind was far away.

Jan smoked his pipe and watched the Sunday roast sizzle.

A holiday was still a holiday; the wall thermometer said sixty-five; the visitors were flocking to the fair in droves; three of Lizzy's tested recipes were entered in the competition; two stood a chance of winning.

"I wonder what goes on at Apanlee," said Josie next, out of the blue.

"Who knows? Who is to say?" If you believed the anguished letters Uncle Benny wrote from Russia, the riffraff kept on hurling stones to smash the onion domes.

"The letters he keeps sending," said Josie with a toss of hair, "are now postmarked Berdyansk. If you ask me, that's odd. In Russia, all is pandemonium."

"What's that to us?" said Little Melly softly.

Little Melly valued her prerogatives. When she came visiting, which she did conscientiously, she entered through the back door, not bothering to knock. She poured her tea into her saucer, so she could slurp it with more gusto. "Our house is not on fire."

According to Josie, it was. Something was sorely troubling her; she kept glancing at the watch that Jan had given her.

Little Melly started munching on a brownish apple core, while shushing Josie's cat. That cat was diabolical. Some people claimed that it laid eggs—that's why it crouched the way it did, inside the oleander bush.

"And no wonder. No wonder. The newly formed government, chockful of Jews," said Little Melly next.

That wisdom came from Dewey. Most everyone in Mennotown saw eye to eye with Dewey on the matter. If there was mischief in the land, you could be sure it was a Levite, disharmonizing everything. Each Sunday, from the pulpit, that's what her preacher brother hinted before he passed the hat.

"Every bridge," her brother pointed out on many an occasion, "is either named to honor Jews or financed by the Jews, and when you cross that bridge, you have to fork over a nickel."

One day past April Fool's Day, the president of the United States got an excited Congress to declare full-fledged war on Germany. In Mennotown, where you heard German spoken the way it had been uttered centuries ago, deep in the swamps of Prussia, the war changed everything.

The spitballs flew. Nobody wanted to be called Herr Meyer.

Soon, rumors flew like paper bats: the Jews were pouring money into Russia in barrels, to help the country win.

Just what that meant was not at first revealed. Although there was a scary run upon the banks in Wichita, which frightened many folks, that scare passed all too soon. Only the Donoghues cried out, repeatedly, drilling with wooden guns: Bottoms up! Hey, bottoms up! Why, Jesus, Mary and Joseph!

Above all else, the war would galvanize the Donoghues.

First thing they did was shave off every mustache. Next, they put on their snazzy uniforms and stepped up catcalling. So eager were the Donoghues to get themselves conscripted to help America decide the war and make the kaiser lose that they kept stepping on each other's toes before they disappeared in various flimsy barracks, but not before they muttered underneath their breaths: "Watch out! Watch out! We'll get ourselves a Hun!"

The Donoghues had always been against the government, at odds with every rule. Now all that changed. The war made out of them respected patriots. A yahoo could become a hero.

No longer were the Donoghues the butt of everybody's jokes. No longer did the neighborhood accuse them openly of thievery. In fact, the citizens felt such obliging spirits they held a farewell picnic for the Donoghues, who stood there, grinning broadly, provisions, maps and compasses securely fastened on their backs.

"Peacemongers," sneered the Donoghues, derisively, their beady eyes on Mennotown, "are creatures worse than rattlers."

In Mennotown, feelings ran high and crested higher still, but patriotic loyalties to Germany and even Russia were dwindling ever lower. This was America; the folks were Americans, now. Each side on the old continent was driving hard to win, but the outcome of the global struggle was anything but clear. The Jews of Wichita had several anxious moments. The Yiddish signs were taken down because they sounded German.

Doctorjay cracked his knuckles with tension. He had heard it from Dewey, who had it first-hand from a source he had long since forgotten, that the Austrian archduke, who started it all, was pierced in the jugular vein in a knavish, nefarious, treacherous way—but what had that to do, if anything, with banksters in New York?

It must have been as Dewey said: "*Geld. Geld.* That's what it's all about. It's always, always money!"

A broad smile sat on Dewey's face, for he was full of glee.

He fetched his hat and took his leave, leaving unspoken words behind. Jan's pipe smoke swirled behind him.

Little Melly heard the latest news, eavesdropping on the rural telephone. She reported to Lizzy at once.

Both women checked on Josie's calendar, and sure enough— her Saturdays were marked with tell-tale Xs all the way down to July.

"I can't believe my eyes," whispered Lizzy in anguish. "Is there no end to unwelcome surprises?"

"You know what that means. Away from pots and pans."

Those words made Lizzy flinch, for Josie was a relative—no

way around that fact—hence worthy of her loyalty. But did she, Lizzy, know—did anybody know?—a single soul who didn't scoff at kosher diets, bingo games, the suffragettes, the labor movement, and the libertines? The drums beat a long roll. What would be next? Transparent stockings? Penny dreadfuls? Emancipated novelists?

When the suspense grew much too much to bear, Lizzy cleared the tension from her throat to get to the root of the matter. "You're going again to a meeting?"

"I am."

"It would be a Christian meeting, we hope?"

"Hope never hurts," said Josephine.

And to herself: Amsterdam! Oh, Amsterdam! That's how she talked, if only to herself.

But Lizzy was not easily put off. Lizzy gulped air and pushed on, her nose slowly filling with tears. "Their hidden agenda is nobody's secret. I'm telling you. I'm warning you. They'll pull the lead out of your hem."

"My name is mud already."

Those were dark days and darker nights. It was exasperating. It taxed all understanding. But Lizzy got her second wind, thanks to the Holy Ghost. "Not you, Josie? Surely not you? Tell me I am mistaken. You couldn't possibly become a—"

"—a what?"

"I cannot bring myself—" The word stuck in her throat. Only a women disowned by fate—too skinny, too ugly, and hence without a man to keep her calm—could find herself endangered by the suffragettes. Jan's Josie did not fit that mold. Yet still, there was that void.

Still, she was different. Sad.

Sad all the way through Christmas rush and summer fair, sad even though she sat right in the lap of luxury; her kitchen had linoleum. She owned more household gadgetry to help her speed her various chores than any housewife worth her smocking frame could ever wish to own.

Chapter 42

The previous year, a frost had killed the best part of the winter wheat. When spring came, finally, the balmy season did not last; three weeks of rain drowned every seedling; times went from bad to worse.

The road to Berdyansk had the texture of glue. Vast acres lay deep in a mire of mud. Hein had kept grain reserves, in hopes of selling in a pinch for needed rubles, but how to get the burlap sacks to the strike-crippled seaport Berdyansk?

All trains had stopped running. Mills had no fuel. Newspapers died. Rumors abounded. Disgruntled workers stood elbow to elbow.

"The Empress has the evil eye," the workers told each other, crossing themselves in fear. The candle tongues kept licking on the icons.

The banks closed their books on Apanlee, and Hein defaulted on three tractors. A Jew drove up one Sunday afternoon and had them hauled away.

The flies sat thick and silent on the ceiling; Hein's tongue began to run away. He couldn't help himself; the taunt slipped out; no way to take it back.

"That race belongs to Satan," cried Hein, and added, driven by his wrath: "The canker rash on them!"

The half-smile faded from the hunchback's lips. Thrice he tried to find his voice, and when he spoke at last, he said: "I ask forgiveness for the thought. I cannot shake it off. The reckoning is here."

"Whatever do you mean?"

"This is about the haves and have-nots. I've often made that point."

Hein sucked his pipe with force. "I'm sorry, Uncle Benny. But every day I hate it more. I hate what's happening to us."

"It's bad now, and it will get much worse."

Hein looked at Uncle Benny, already sorry for his harsh words. But his anger had not yet been spent. "Do you still cultivate the Hebrews?"

"Come rain or shine," said Uncle Benny calmly.

"Whatever for?"

The cripple did not speak at first. At last, he cleared his throat. "Hein, take my savings. Take it all. Just pay me back when times are mannerly again." The invalid leaned gingerly against the water pump. He leaned against most anything to give his spine support, and this is what he said:

"Times lie ahead, Hein, to make grown men and animals moan."

The war was hard on everyone—hard even on Marleen who still put jam into her tea and butter on her zwieback.

She turned for comfort and assurance to Natasha. "It's cold in here. Go get another log."

Natasha was busy dressing a blister. "I will. I will. As soon as I am finished. There will be frost tonight."

Marleen was in no mood for arguments. This pregnancy was difficult; she hoped that it would be her last. The coal smoked in the samovar. She sat there, shivering, as though within a draft.

"I worry. That is all."

Natasha, too. She worried, fussed and agitated about the measles season, for it was said the princeling was covered with spots. Had she been in the palace, she would have cured the bleeder boy expertly. She knew precisely how: one perfect onion, two gherkins and three thimblefuls of goat's urine, mixed with a bit of spittle. Natasha believed in the curative powers of urine and spittle. A child was a child; a fever a fever. No doubt he was light as a feather. Chances were he needed fattening. She longed to hold him, cuddle him and hum his woes away.

Natasha moved her icons from corner to corner to give them additional light. The priests kept bleating to their saints while the tsar took his leisurely walks through a violent, foreboding spring and an ominous, darkening summer.

As famine stalked the granaries of Russia, the war dragged on and on. There was a serious rifle shortage at the front, while snipers hid behind church steeples.

Entire cities mutinied, and beggars starting rushing orchards, pulling apples, half-ripe, from the trees. Wherever you looked, you saw disorder. Pilfering. Plunder. Food riots flared in many places, and endless bread lines wound around the block.

Somebody shouted suddenly: "The Germans are hiding the flour!"

Another shout, and louder. "Because of the Germans, we're fighting and losing this war!"

Fall came, and brought a rush of blazing colors, predominantly red. The workers stood in knots, the winter at the door.

On the horizon, clouds piled atop the earth. The wind started shrieking. Rumors flew wildly, believed and remembered by all:

"German spies are hiding behind curtains in the palace and stand concealed behind the thinnest blade of grass." Before the year was out, the simplest peasant knew: "The Germans are stockpiling grain."

A chant became a roar. A Hebrew dissident, his hair in curls, his tongue aflame, hurled leaflets into the waiting lines of workers.

Foreigners, all!
Away with them, all!
To the ash barrels, all!

The third winter of the war brought bitter cold and, with the howling winds, the murder of the monk. The fierce, magnetic glance was snuffed by lead and cyanide, and people hugged each other in the streets.

The tsar took walks to calm his shattered nerves. If he picked up a pen, he spattered himself.

The German Empress donned a fluffy dress. She looked as if she had taken a vow: "I shall never forgive nor forget."

The street lamps hung dark in the cities. The railroad stations had no light. The *droshky* drivers disappeared. Factory workers stood elbow to elbow.

Rage fed on rage. Fists rose in hut after hut.

The beggars chorused everywhere: "A piece of wood to warm us. A heel of bread to feed us. Is that too much to ask?"

All blame fell on the foreign-friendly crown—two slow-wits on the throne of Russia, and straddling a volcano. The poorest peasant started shouting: "This war is not our war!"

The angry mob was howling: "Malicious foreigners control the Winter Palace."

Now that the monk was dead, most everywhere reigned pandemonium. The demonstrators waved their flags. The workers filled their pockets with sharp stones. Rifles and bayonets protruded from windows as soldiers rode train buffers. The mob hung out of dirty buildings, swinging banners, shouting fiercely at the masses, who shouted back and waved their placards high.

"Down with the Emperor!"

"Death to our enemies!"

"Shells for our guns!"

The country turned into a kennel. The Russian peasants took their pitchforks and started looking for the tsar.

A balding man, whom history calls Lenin, rolled in a sealed and bolted train across the Russian border, heading north. A dwarfish man with faded eyes, now known to us as Stalin, was heading south out of his icy exile, past the bleached bones of countless beasts, by dog and reindeer sled.

Uncle Benny watched the sun set in an ochre sheen upon the Winter Palace before it darkened all of Europe, just like the lights that dimmed the auditorium before the eerie play began.

"I must go home," said Uncle Benny to a young companion. On previous trips to Moscow and St. Petersburg, he had seen and heard sporadic demonstrations, and his hair had prickled in his nape.

"I know."

"We will not meet again."

"I know."

"All of my people's prayers," said Uncle Benny to the Russian, "will be like feathers thrown into rough wind." His legs were trembling from the strain of a long day on cobblestones. He shifted weight to take the pressure off his spine.

The young man said: "Let the end, then, be our beginning."

Foreboding spoke in Uncle Benny: "For centuries, the land has lain in bondage. The peasants have been wronged. A wedge is being driven deep. Deep down below, a hurricane grows. Well then. Good-bye forever."

His Russian friend stood silent. At last, he touched his hat: "The saints be with you always." He stood outside the train, with worry peering in.

"The saints be with you, too."

"A forest of soldiers, this city."

The train jerked once. The wheels began to move. Hoodlums clung, sprawling, to the roof of every train that roared and trembled between St. Petersburg and Moscow—in olden days, a journey of twelve hours. Now it took several days.

"Find me a bearskin, please," the hunchback told the porter. The porter turned his back as though he had not heard.

"I'm not the enemy," said Uncle Benny softly, but there was

no reply. Night started dropping from the trees. The railroad ties ahead of Uncle Benny ran unbroken to a black horizon.

"I ache for Dorothy," he thought. He closed his eyes to hide the mist that clouded his thick glasses. He listened to the clatter of the wheels, the whistling of the locomotive. And then he started praying.

An intellectual, he was a man who rarely prayed, but now he did; he prayed. "May the Lord be so kind as to grant onto me—" He was ashamed of his covetous prayer. He started shaking uncontrollably, silently, convulsively, out of an atavistic knowledge that even prayers were too late—that all the dice had been long cast by centuries.

The war had turned Natasha's cuckoo's egg into a celebrated hero. When Dominik came home on furlough, he even picked a violent quarrel with the foreman, and no one said a word.

"A spark into a powder keg. Like so. Like pffff!" laughed Dominik.

He liked to laugh at his own jokes. More now than in the past, he spoke of Revolution. He did not seek it out. It came to him as fire comes to cinders. It licked around his youth like flames that lick a log.

He listened closely as a good friend from Poltava explained it all to him, this thing called Revolution, that would set mankind free by leveling the rich and hoisting up the poor.

"War on the past! And peace for the future!" his friend had told him, grinning.

Natasha was there; she laughed. She laughed like a child that was tickled. It happened on New Year's Eve. She knew how to laugh like a child. She couldn't help herself; she always cheered when others cheered, by nature tractable.

A jolly party it had been, friend piled on top of friend in her ramshackle, smoke-laden hut. Natasha melted wax in a snow-drift outside and threw its shadow on the wall to forecast the shape of the future.

"We'll drown the fools in blood," bragged Dominik. His

friend had brought along a loaded gun with which they were wounding the night.

Now Natasha poured oil over porridge. "A headache deep within your skull?"

Dominik picked with a straw in the gaps of his teeth. "Make an important wish."

She felt her feet go numb. "What are you saying, Dominik?"

Just as a juggler showed his tricks, so Dominik. He threw his knife into the air and caught it by the blade. "Just make a wish. I guarantee it will come true."

She studied him at length to recognize him clearly. "Still wishing for instant success? Here, take this piece of soap. And scratch your nails out, too. Tonight, you're invited to supper."

He pushed open the door to the summer room and stepped across the threshold. "Look at me now. On behalf of the tsars and their lackeys, I offered my chest to the bullets."

Marleen gave him a slanted smile. "Don't tell us stories, Dominik. Hot coffee? Tea? Here. Have your fill." Marleen was not impressed. "A hollow windbag. That's what you are. A windbag. Nothing more. Don't tell us braggart stories."

"Two sugars, if you please," he told her. "No, better make that four."

"No waste in my house," said Marleen, but did as he said.

He sat, while sipping slowly, sprawling, watching her. "Hey, you! I always meant to ask: your grandfather was born in Russia?"

"That's right," Marleen said. "My great-grandfather, too."

"Why do you still speak German?"

"Because," Marleen explained, dumbfounded at the question, "the Gospel is written that way."

"Any German in my country," he said softly, "is a spy."

"Any hoodlum in my kitchen," said Marleen, "is unwelcome."

But he was undeterred. He spoke of poison gas and cannon fire and shrapnel pieces burrowing into the groaning earth. "Defending my homeland," he boasted. "From exploiters and foreign intruders."

Here's what he said in Marleen's sparkling kitchen. "I've learned to kill four people with one bullet."

He said to the twins who sat silent: "I rented a girl for a ruble."

"Your mind, as filthy as a horse tail in the spring," said Dorothy at last as firmly as she could, which was astonishing. She seldom spoke like that. Her hair was white. Her face was fine and soft. She sat there, upright, by the window, as clever with her hands as always, while smocking on a tiny bit of cloth to spruce the toddler, Jonathan.

Dominik spun around and fixed her with a cold, mean stare: "Tell me. Where is Ivan?"

"Why, dead and buried in the apple orchard."

He let fly with a choice set of curses.

She sat, and she waited him out. "You know he drank himself to death. You never even liked him, Dominik. He beat you black and blue."

"Well. Didn't he?" asked Dominik, and sucked in the air through his teeth. His glance was now fastened on Hein.

"Did I do what?"

"Did you not beat me, too?"

"I never beat you, Dominik. I only spanked you, reasonably, when your disorderly behavior called for discipline."

"Go sleep off your hangover," ordered Marleen. Her tongue was still sharp, but now she weighed her words.

"A braggart, as always," she said to her husband, who added a log to the fire.

Hein laughed uproariously when he was told by Dominik that Revolution was now right around the corner, or else around the bend. Hein let out a bellow with such force that Uncle Benny's cat took one large, running leap and disappeared around the corner. "And you at the heart of it all? Don't talk such nonsense, Dominik! If there's something rotten, there are maggots to live off the stench."

Expertly, Natasha moved closer. She was proud of her son who was willing to die for the tsar, but forbearance was part of her nature. "There's a toad on your tongue. Spit it out, Dominik! Spit it out!"

She, too, had been molded by the centuries. The serfs had waited for three hundred years. No limits to the patience of the poor. That was her attitude. But Dominik just laughed. "Don't expect me to stretch out my neck for the knife."

The hunchback did not like that laugh. He braced himself before he spoke: "Now, listen, Dominik. Take a deep breath. Just calm yourself. Exactly what does Revolution mean to you?"

"Plenty of everything. Land. Livestock. Watches. Gold." He knew, by then, that Revolution stood for things that challenged everything that centuries had built.

"This, too, shall pass," said Hein, unwilling to be counseled, for skirmishes had flared before, and squads of Cossacks with their whips had always put them down.

All this was ancient fare. Many a dissident had, in the past, tried hard by drawing on complicity and cabala to liquidate the tsars. These plots had always boomeranged. The traitors had been hanged. This time, however, things felt different.

"This time," said Uncle Benny, stubbornly, "the throng swings hoes and shovels. A tidal wave of hate—that's what's out there, this time."

Hein flicked away a bit of ash that had fallen from his pipe. "But why? What have I done? I do not understand. I am rich; that is true. And why not? But with riches come duties. As long as you balance your riches with duties, you are safe and secure in the palms of your Lord."

"Just listen to the slogans. 'The past to the grave. To the peasants, the earth.'"

"—any trumpet will be an excuse," said Dominik again.

That day, he was so angry that not even butter would have melted in his mouth. He drank vodka; his face became redder and redder. He knew what he knew: barracks and factories belched out their hate. The names of the tsars, a sneer and a curse. "If Revolution ever comes—"

He stood no more than five feet tall, but he was muscular. He was missing two front teeth. He stood before his father, his hands deep in his pockets. A hand grenade was slung across his chest; an ammunition-laden bandoleer cut a deep groove into his shoulder blade. The smoke of gunpowder clung to his clothes. In his voice was the growl of the wolf. He was unable to explain why his pockets bulged with rubles.

After Dominik took off to finish the tsar's war, Hein paid a visit to Natasha to talk things over with her. He often sought Natasha's presence to talk of this and that.

"Have you had word of Dominik?" he asked.

Natasha inspected the seam of her apron. "He sent me a picture he drew."

"Oh, really? I didn't know that Dominik could draw."

"He does. He draws quite well." She pulled a piece of paper from a fold within her sleeve. "Look here. He draws for his mother's amusement."

Hein started to laugh. "The rascal! He's right. The kaiser looks like me."

Natasha said slowly, avoiding Hein's eyes: "You better shave it off."

"But why? You always liked my mustache. Did you not always like my mustache?"

She smiled a wistful smile. "In olden days. The olden days are gone."

He shook his head. "Look here, Natasha. Why pretend?" He was at ease with her. "I'm fair. You know that I am fair."

"Whatever do you mean?"

"Have I not always tried to be fair?"

"You have. You have." She gladly gave credit were credit was due. She gently stroked the back of his hand, but that was as far as it went. "I didn't say you hadn't. But times have changed. Remember that."

He wouldn't take no for an answer. He moved a bit closer, an eager seducer. "Look here. I found this ruble in the street. I wonder, now, who lost it?"

She felt a faint burr in her throat. "Just go away. And don't come back again."

He stuck both hands deep in his pockets. "There's more. There's jingling money here. What might I do with it?"

"Marleen is expecting again."

"It's probably her last. She's getting on in years."

"Ha! Don't tell me! Last year you told me such a fable."

He leaned toward her suddenly, a spring about to uncoil. "I did? That was last year."

"And the year before that. Four years ago. Seven years ago. When will it ever end? You want me to swallow your lies? "

"Will you have the boiling water ready?"

"Nine children in the twelve years," she scolded him expertly. "One under each arm. One still around my neck. Three hanging on my apron. The last one, barely older than a tot! "

He liked to tease, just as he liked to tickle. "She has a magnificent husband!"

The Russian servant looked at him with a sober and steadying glance, withholding sharper words, as ever, befitting her station. "I live too close to the margin," she told him, and pushed him away with a small, practiced shove. The universe was fixed. It didn't matter if she planted her cucumbers in an exact crosswise pattern, just as Marleen had done.

What could she say? Marleen bore the offspring. Natasha swaddled them.

Each time Marleen bore another, Natasha found herself so eager for the suckling she kept pushing the midwife aside. A diaper soaking in warm suds, a little pink rump in her palm—that was Natasha's happiness.

Just give her a newborn—she melted. She had that wide, warm lap to rock its fears away.

Hein knew her well. He started petting her. "There was a time," he told her softly, "when I knew all your needs by heart."

"I lament my old shoes."

"Of late, something has changed. What is it that has changed, Natasha?"

She opened her mouth and closed it again. She smiled to herself, only half-understanding. "I don't know what you mean."

She nourished few illusions about the world in which she lived. Her needs were simple, earthy. She longed to hold another baby in her lap and nuzzle its soft neck. She scrubbed the diapers, one by one, until she nearly dropped.

"I want to know. Tell me."

"You know already. Don't you, Hein? Some things just can't be helped?"

But Hein pressed on. "Tell me. I really want to know."

She shook her head. She only knew the furious fits of jealousy were gone. "I have my memories, she said. "And they are pleasant. But I have now enough of them and really need no more."

He reached for her hand, but she pulled back her fingers. "Go back to Marleen. That's where you belong, in the dark times ahead."

He nodded. Natasha was right. No bitterness at all within the soft and aging bosom of Natasha. On good days, Marleen had admitted as much.

Chapter 43

When war broke out, America was not prepared, and there was catching up to do. The shortage of weapons was hotly debated in Congress, but factories sprang into action, new industries appeared out of the blue, corrective laws were passed at every legislative session, and every bird hummed mirthfully, for victory was just around the corner. Young men were drafted from the fields and sent to wet and windy camps where they commenced to exercise with broomsticks, since rifle production was still gearing up.

Trumpets sounded. Messengers scurried. War maps arrived in gaudy colors.

Before the year was out, the war was being waged full tilt. The *New York Times* declared in flaming editorials that the victorious war was knitting citizens together into the fabric of America.

But where was the yarn? And who did the knitting?

A silence fell after the question.

Invisible as spider webs. And dangerous as ticks.

A lot of strangers passed through town and asked, replete with sneer, their eyes grown narrow in hatred: "What's this? A mystic German sect?" They tapped their foreheads several times and smirked derisively.

The Russian-German prairie pioneers felt wronged. It wounded all of them. For it was true; they were still pacifists; they had a higher Lord. But in the meantime, what?

Not one of them had doubts that they were genuine patriots. While their hearts bled for Germany, and Russia as well, their loyalties belonged to Kansas. For decades, they had been Americans.

To illustrate that fact, the menfolk joined in victory parades, and never mind the blisters. The ladies kept on knitting socks, and never mind for whom.

The papers kept up the barrage. The papers hinted: spies! Odd noises came out of the telephone lines.

Spies, claimed the *New York Times*, now infiltrated everything; you couldn't even trust your neighbor. In Dewey's church, the worshipful were circumspect with whom they took communion. There were spies in the pews, it was said.

No wonder, therefore, that many cautious citizens searched out the enemy within. Most people knew that, in most any war, you could find saboteurs and tricksters.

Next on the national agenda was how to deal with them. Uprooting spies became a patriotic duty. The arrows flew. The word was out: you had to be on guard.

Informers working for the enemy recruited help from would-be patriots, the preachers told the flock. The Finkelsteins, for instance, talked Josie into rolling Red Cross bandages for them—and what was in those bandages, to be shipped all the way to Russia, was left for you to guess.

Soon, patriots were thoroughly confused. They wanted none of that. It came to light, for instance, through diligent investigation, that spies had poisoned several batches of livestock feed. Next it was said the Germans were at fault.

The papers kept it up.

The flickers said the same.

The headlines started shouting that German spies were sabotaging factories. Spies filled your ears with pessimistic stories about the outcome of the war, belittling the bravest of soldiers. Spies, saboteurs, and foreign tricksters stirred up a bloody strike at Bethlehem Steel that paralyzed the plant for weeks.

In summary, spies sympathetic to the kaiser were undermining everything. That was the paper verdict.

Here was was corrosive business. Spies saw everything. Spies heard everything. They watched who talked to whom. They took note of the smallest remark. They even checked the mail. No doubt these self-same saboteurs were at the bottom of the outrage why Uncle Benny's letters no longer came to Kansas.

From one world to another, greetings no longer flew. Many nights, this saddening development stole sleep from Noralee and Lizzy. Both of them cherished that soft spot for Uncle Benny and his little love, whom they remembered well, who never turned her back on a deserving beggar. They still remembered how the little cripple looped his letters, but many other memories became a hazy blur.

It took some effort now, for instance, for Lizzy to recall the hunchback boy who stole her heart when she was young and he was small—just stole it with his black and clever eyes, and never gave it back. Now he was getting on in years. She thought the world of him. She thought of him a lot.

Even when he was little, mused Noralee as well, he needed a chair to support him where he stood. His business was thinking and dreaming. His hunchback gave him pain, but he would not complain, just rest on any bench within his reach, his eyes on ancestral portraits.

Because of his affliction, Lizzy knew, he did not have to work the land; he had studied in Odessa as a youth, which was the reason, doubtlessly, that he had started writing on the themes that were of no concern to farmers. He'd grown into a mild and patient man, thought Noralee, who bore nobody harm, who wrote his editorials and sipped his tea and watched his Dorothy, thus making a career of thinking.

All that was long ago. In Lizzy's mind swam faded memories, while she kept tossing through another prairie night, as the moon shone its light through her window.

"He'll write as soon as times are mannerly again," said Josephine. "And in the meantime, let's help Russia. Let's put goodwill to work."

Lizzy took her heart into her hands and sat Josie down for a heart-to-heart chat.

"Even the sparrows are chirping your story," Lizzy gently pointed out.

Josie inspected the tips of her fingers. "They do? What do the sparrows say?"

"They say you help the enemy."

"We're on the side of Russia. America is backing Russia."

"We're pacifists. We're not against this war, but we're not for it either. Why do you have to benefit the Finkelsteins?"

That just popped out. Once it was out, it all came gushing forth. The list was long. The sins were old.

"We've got to watch ourselves," begged Lizzy wretchedly. "Why give the Finkelsteins a hand? No good can come of that."

She had a barrelful of proof. For one, the Hebrews had no sense for harmony. Their conduct was not circumspect. Their Sabbath was on Saturday. They robbed the world through usury. They didn't lend you money, no matter what your urgency, unless they charged you interest that turned into a noose. And some of them wrote poetry that had no rhyme nor reason.

Now that a war was on, their oddities were even more pronounced. Some headed south and disappeared below the Rio Grande, while others, staying on in Wichita, just shrunk into the shade. She knew that Jews were for modernity, which undermined all rules. They kept on snipping at their hems to show not just an ankle but a calf.

The gentle graces fell away: "What's wrong with us? We are your kin. We love you, Josephine."

"So?"

"Must you surround yourself with Hebrews? They aren't on our side. They are against the Germans. They never liked the Germans. They never even liked the Russians. They overthrew the tsars."

Josie took a struggling breath. "If you must know: it's not the Jews. It's not the Unitarians. It's not the Methodists. It's not the Lutherans, even."

"Who is it, then? What plagues you, honey child?"

"Well, it's no secret any more. I might as well come out with it. I've joined the suffragettes. Now, are you satisfied?"

Four shrieks came from the davenport. One faint, and that was Little Melly.

But Josie's temples were now pounding. "Do you folks understand? Do you know what that means?"

"Yes," whimpered Lizzy. "Yes. of course. I looked it up in the fatbook."

"Voting in this country is denied to criminals, lunatics, idiots and me."

"Why would you want to vote?" cried Lizzy, quite beside herself. "I never heard such nonsense in my life! Jan votes for you! You know he votes for you! Is there a better man than Jan who cares more deeply for his wife and for his girls—and votes accordingly?"

"I am no better than a cow. My function is to keep on calving."

"Don't be absurd. Why be so coarse? That's what you learn from them. Don't use such purple language, Josie!"

"I have no legal rights. My daughters will grow up and live and die and have no legal rights."

"You have more rights than you could possibly use up. Why, you can order anything your little heart desires from the wishbook."

Here's what she said, the heretic: "Jan's rights, and nothing more. My rights, and nothing less."

That's it, said Josie, digging in. It's of no consequence to me if you agree or not.

This was too much for even Noralee, who was accustomed to allow for human frailties: Let Doctorjay be whatsoever Doctorjay might be, when push came to shove, she did as he wished her to do.

Little Melly was coming to, whimpering softly. "I knew it. I knew it. The blasted suffragists—"

"It's not the suffragists. It's called the suffragettes."

"Who cares," cried Little Melly hotly, "what name they give themselves? That does not change the facts. Those meetings are a Jewish trap. The goal is to destroy the family."

"They are my friends. This is America. I can have any friends I choose."

Little Melly's face was pitted with blotches. "If I were Jan, I'd be ashamed to show my face at the Wednesday night Rotary Club."

"Hah!"

Lizzy planted both fists on her knees. "Let's have it out. Right now. The talk of the town is that you want to join. You want to be part of the Rotary Club? Tell me that I am wrong."

"Why can't I belong to the Rotary Club? What's wrong with that? What's wrong with me? I'd love to belong to the Rotary Club. That's only one of my ambitions."

"Are you a man? What would you do there, Josie?"

"What does a man do there? They slap each other on the shoulder and tell each other flivver jokes. I can tell flivver jokes."

"If you are undermining your own man, you undermine the family."

"My man," said Josie in a trembling voice, "cannot be undermined by some old flivver joke. Right, Jan? Tell them that I am right!"

In anguish, Little Melly's eyes' sought out Jan's, home from the fields, in need of a cool drink. She thought her heart would break with pain and shame and woe at seeing him diminished. She rushed to his defense. "Jan! Jan! Speak up. This is the moment to speak up."

Jan's eyes went from female to female. He puffed on his pipe and said nothing. His heart was wide and soft. He loved his peace. He loved his hearth. He cherished his niche at the Rotary Club.

"Well, Jan?"

What was a man to do? He loved his wife, but he loved Lizzy also. He loved his sister Daisy, who winced at every clash. And, yes, he still loved Little Melly, by then restored sufficiently from her deep faint so that she didn't have to miss the slightest nuance of this domestic squabble. His females chorused, unified: "Speak up, Jan. Speak your mind."

"Just once," said Josephine in a low voice. "Just once stand up for me." A current passed between them: it was full of sparks. She held her breath. Jan looked from face to face, drew deeply on his pipe, smiled a conciliatory smile, and did what most men do when challenged to decode the psyche of the female. He said precisely nothing.

"Give me five years," hissed Josie, falling back. "We have a plan. Before this decade runs its course, we will have skirt Rotarians."

"Jesus! Jesus! *Jemine!*"

"You mark my word! You people mark my word!"

"Jan! Make her stop. She's feverish!"

"It's now or never, son. You must lay down the law."

"Jan, can I tell a flivver joke?" asked Josephine who never knew when to leave well enough alone. "I have a brand new flivver joke I want to tell right now." There was no stopping her. She launched herself as though she were a cresting wave. "Here's one. Here's one for you. Here's one I heard the other day. Here's one for Dewey, see? You be the judge if that's a flivver joke or not. If that's a scream or not. There was this man, this flivver owner, see? On his death bed, he asked that his flivver be buried with him—"

Jan tried to make the best out of a ghastly situation. "I'm afraid, my dear, that no one in this kitchen—"

"The point is this," shrieked Josephine, "he wasn't sure about

his Faith! But he was sure about his flivver—" She took a struggling breath, but finished what she started. "—he knew there
was no hole so deep," she cried, delivering a stinging blow, "his
flivver couldn't get him out!"

Five stony faces stared at her, unblinking.

Wartime was sacrifice writ large. Wheatless Mondays.
Meatless Tuesdays. Heatless Wednesdays. Porkless Thursdays.
Gasless Fridays. Only weekends were left blank for you to show
your patriotism any way you pleased.

So, here as there and then as now: a unifying enterprise—a
good and righteous war! The politicians had it pat: war business was good for the country. Before the year was in full leaf,
Sedgwick County's war chest started bulging with donations.

Jan's mill kept humming merrily.

The government bought Lizzy's cheese.

Officials out of Washington sent order after order to purchase
brown-shell eggs from Noralee.

The grocer upped his cantaloupes from a nickel to a dime,
and no one said a word.

Bonfires flared in every park; from every speaker, music
roared. Doctorjay ruddered through victory picnics—there were
seven in rapid succession—while struggling down many a demon.

He raised both fists, a patriot. He struggled through a muddle of feelings: he wanted Germany as well as Russia to win,
with the credit adjusted for Kansas. In fact, insisted Doctorjay
when spotting Josephine, he wouldn't be surprised if Jan himself
said: "Bottoms up!"

For such was the spirit of the war.

The only question of significance—the only moral issue of
importance—was where you stood: for or against the kaiser.

The war forced Dewey into overdrive. His task was finding
ways and means. His homilies were in demand as they had never
been before, for old and young relied on him to hunt for defini-

tions in the Bible that spelled the difference between a patriotic pacifist and an unpatriotic shirker.

Before the war, before so many strangers started sneering, before draft officials came to Mennotown to muddle everything and sow dissent by means of innuendo, nobody doubted German immigrants were loyal Kansas patriots. For years, they'd had barbecue pits on the Fourth of July and laid on a band with trumpets and drums. But abstaining from war was the dictum, preached Dewey. To shoulder a rifle was wrong.

He was rolling a boulder uphill.

The young men listened, full of scorn. The war cartoons stung to the core. Now, it was clear, democracy came with a bill—and some folks weren't willing to pay. Could you attend a potluck supper, the males of Mennotown now asked in angry voices, and refuse to bring your own dish? Oh, how they wished—especially the bachelors—to bag themselves a Hun!

"Be steadfast," preached Dewey, perspiring.

"We aren't chicken feed," grumbled the bachelors, just itching to take up the gun. "You want us to bolt from the war and run just as fast as we can?"

The Elder Dewey sat with them behind the gravel pit, where they would gather, scowling, to talk sense into them. "Here's what the Bible says—" He took the matter one step further, philosophically. Why not take Lizzy for a model? If Lizzy had her way, the world would be a dairy!

The youths were not persuaded. "Ha! Aren't we the laughingstock of Kansas?"

The argument taxed Dewey brutally. He knew that, biblically, the dirty business of killing human flesh was wrong; you did that only to the animals; the Bible made allowances for that. But a Hun was a creature apart—subhuman at the very least, demonic at the worst. And patriotism counted, too; he stood in quicksand past his knees; here was the best of prairie towns, packed end to end with blond, hard-muscled sons, refusing to seek shelter in the Gospel. Their faces were red with their shame.

The Elder strove for compromise. He sought a middle ground,

but *jungvolk* smarted from the sting of implied cowardice. The shirker label was like dandruff; you tried to overlook it, pretend it wasn't there. But everybody saw.

"For generations back, we have been pacifists," the Elder argued heatedly. "No matter who the overlord. No matter what the provocation."

"That's just a lot of hooey!" the bachelors replied.

To counteract the mounting pressure to enlist while showing patriotism, Dewey helped uncover spies by ferreting them out of hiding. One foggy morning, he went to the Mennotown Chamber of Commerce and said to the uniformed clerk:

"I'll make the rounds. No one will think it's me."

He trained his ear for suspect accents. He scrutinized the town's assorted flivver stickers. With jutting chin, he stood and watched the kaiser burned in effigy in front of City Hall.

Next, Dewey saw to it that in his presence the government, the president and/or the Constitution were never criticized. Had he not been a pacifist, he would have raised his country's hidden traitors' heads high up on a pike; he was that charged with wrath.

Little Melly made no exception of herself. She felt as Dewey did. She spent her days in an excited flutter. An unaccustomed vigor drove her on.

"You wonder who's behind it all," she hinted sagely to Daisy.

"You do. You do," said Daisy, having no idea.

"We're not yet at the bottom of what ails Josephine."

"I feel it in my bones: where will it end?"

"You tell me that."

"Does it not make you tell that we are in—"

"—that we are in for a surprise," was Little Melly's soft reply, still wagging a smooth tongue while sewing slacks for Archie to grow into.

Which brings us now to Archie. When war exploded across Europe, he was still shedding teeth. He was a laggard academically, but otherwise a paragon of virtue—and no wonder.

When Schoolmaster Menno—still teaching, though barely, loath to let go, though it was time for him to settle in his rocking chair and let the war-torn world pass by—opened a McGuffey reader, asking sternly: "Tell me, children. Look around. Who is the honest fellow in this story?" who else but Archibald? He knew he was the one. He always raised his hand. His source was Little Melly.

His auntie spoiled him wantonly.

Little Melly could not keep her pudgy hands away from Archie's mended trousers; she straightened this and that. She took great pride in making sure he knew exactly right from wrong. "Now, Archie, listen carefully!" admonished Little Melly. "Your father is a pacifist. Your mother is a pacifist. You are a pacifist. You are a little soldier for the Lord. Here. Blow your nose. Blow hard. That's it! Good boy! Once more! Make sure they understand just where you stand. If someone hits you, don't hit back. Our Savior suffered, too."

"Yes, Auntie Melly," sniffled Archie, while contemplating, a sinking feeling in his stomach, the heckling menace of the Donoghues.

"Don't let them frighten you. You don't hit back, no matter what. Just stand your ground. You hear?"

He sneezed a lot. He wheezed. He carried on imaginary conversations with unseen people in the room. He developed hysterical coughs. Sometimes he even ran a temperature at will. Books gave him blinding headaches.

Thus, school was torment magnified. He used up too much pencil at any little task. He was always last to finish up his papers, the first to shoot out through the door. He saw no sense in hunting after commas.

And Josie's girls, by contrast! Those girls were packed with talent. They could do anything. They helped the war along. They made candles out of walnut shells to help raise funds for amputees. They could stuff birds, trap rabbits, raise frogs, and make assorted dolls for orphans out of old, discarded corn husks— all with their right hands tied behind their backs. Josie saw to it

that all her daughters read voraciously, although she had been
warned repeatedly by Doctorjay that certain books, read prema-
turely, impaired the brain and brought on chronic female ills.

By contrast, what could Archie do?

Two years into the conflict, and at the mercy of an aunt who
made no bones about her *Kuckuck* clock and smelled up the entire neighborhood with *Krautrolladen,* he fought a war on his
own shores, not having any other choice. Each morning, before
eight o'clock, he had to cross a school yard—just packed with
schoolyard bullies.

He would have sooner crossed an ocean!

He was one persecuted little pacifist—between a hard stone
and a rock. He had already given up pretzels, his favorite after-
school snack. He had survived a bout of the "liberty" measles.
He did what he could, but it never sufficed. His loyalties were
suspect.

He attended parades; he cheered at patriotic rallies; he volunteered to light the fireworks; he banished his Low German
accent.

No matter! The bullies had singled him out. Each day, it was
terror reborn.

No matter how he tried to fade into the woodwork, as soon as
he showed up at school to cultivate his mind so he could climb
the ladder to success and catch the American dream, the
Donoghues were there, and waiting with their slingshots.

"One hundred percent American," shouted Archie, poor fellow, and ran just as fast as he could, but couldn't shake the pack
that followed him, the anti-German mob that heckled: "Chicken!
Chicken! Chicken!"

The bullies made a ring around him. A howl went up:

"Let's gun the Hun! Spies tell lies!"

Somebody grabbed him by the shoulder and started spinning
him around as though he were a top.

"Kill Kaiser Bill!   Kill Kaiser Bill!"

"Spies tell lies!"

"Gun the Hun!"

He was no match for them. He never had a chance. No matter what he did—no matter how he hunched his shoulders to make himself invisible—no sooner did he show at school and try to blend into the crowd, a bully stood there, smirking, to wrestle Archie to the ground and paint a mustache underneath his nose, and then his, Archie's, ethnic anguish would begin.

So on this fateful day.

Archie thought his lungs would burst as he fled the fury of the mob. But he was small; his legs were short; his heart quite paralyzed with terror. He tried to hide himself, as often as not in the outhouse—no use! "Run the Hun! Gun the Hun!" the cry went up, the moment he pulled up his trousers.

It was survival, base and raw. He decided to brave the first corner. He cringed and tried to duck beneath the bully's elbows, a useless undertaking. The bully lunged for Archie, who staggered from a strong and vicious shove.

"Let's see now. What's that in your brown bag?"

"Just liberty sausage," lied Archie, surrounded.

"With sauerkraut?"

"It's victory cabbage. Victory cabbage. Leave me alone." Huge tears were welling in his eyes.

"It looks like sauerkraut to me."

"It's not."

"It smells like sauerkraut to me."

"It's not."

"It must be sauerkraut. Right? Sauerkraut?" The mob was gathering momentum. The other children hooted.

"Rooshian! Rooshian! "

"Spies tell lies! "

"Kill Kaiser Bill!"

"Run the Hun! Gun the Hun!"

"Rooshian! Rooshian!"

"German chickenshit!"

He started hiccuping. He didn't know why he was singled out for torment. Was he a German? Was he a Russian? Both, the bullies seemed to think.

He gave out a desperate whoop. The Donoghues did likewise.

One of them, coiled, ran his hard skull right into Archie's stomach. The impact brought him to his knees.

"No! No! Please, don't!"

It was too late. Blows started flying in blind fury. Fists started pummeling his cringing body. "I'm not a spy! I'm not a spy!" he whimpered, terrified. Mind paralyzed, his brain on fire, he struggled underneath. He tasted the sickening taste of warm blood.

"Kill Kaiser Bill. Kill Kaiser Bill!"

Somehow, he struggled free. He ran.

Show weakness, and the mob will charge. The end result could have been prophesied—a slingshot, and a rock, smack in the eye, exploding his vision. It felt like the kick of a mule.

Turn on your television set. There's Archibald, your syndicated televangelist, black patch on his right eye, lost to an ethnic hate attack. His left eye sees a mission. He is your basic redneck fundamentalist, vociferous and militant. It's muddle, mostly. Never depth. In favor of the melting pot, yet opposed to Affirmative Action. He preaches love, but hate is what propels. Hate for his roots, mixed up with righteousness. He hates the Huns. He hates them with a passion. The moment he hears "ethnic pride," alarm bells ring; he sees the smirks, he hears the heckling voices, he even smells the *sauerkraut.*

He has no use for ethnic pride. No isolationist is Archibald, and very proud of that.

He has no use for Europe and its bedeviled tribal ghosts—the reason why, when it comes down to helping yet another nonwhite country to its feet, he tells his congregation: "We must export democracy." It's Archibald who prompts them how to vote.

Chapter 44

The flickers were the newest fad in Mennotown, and catching on like fire. A Jew had built a flicker house, down by the Mail Coach Road, before the city fathers realized what was happening and could assess the impact on morale.

"The Devil's workshop, verily!" said Dewey, stepping up the pace of his sermons, but soon his flicker crusade petered out.

Opinions on the merits of the flickers were divided. Some were of such enormous patriotic fire that many Mennotowners came running in to see.

"A fabulous array of razzle dazzle," claimed Josie, by then nearing flicker addiction. Each week, she forked across the five-cent admission the Jews kept raking in.

"The flickers will destroy the peace of the community," Dewey predicted many times, but flicker shows were here to stay; the war forced every Elder to make concessions to modernity and secularity.

Although the Bible warned against the danger of the graven image, the Elder Dewey gave a bit; in fact, he gave a lot. The fires flared; the world perched on the edge of ruin—by sheer comparison, what was a flicker house? War was war; emotions were cresting; even the tomcats were licking their chops. No one raised an eyebrow any more when Josephine, skirts flying, jumped up on streamer-decorated flivvers and roared away with Doctorjay to see the latest rally and wave at US soldiers, all brave beyond belief. The citizens of Sedgwick County, united in their feeling that the war changed all priorities, went every week to watch the flicker actors fling their pies and whack the Huns hard on their skulls with baseball bats for being Huns—hence creatures worse than vermin.

The audience roared and clapped.

The war forced other concessions from Dewey. He learned to close an eye to extra chrome on bicycles, to football games, and even cross-sex conversations on the telephone. What harm a flicker house?

"But only matinees," he said at first. "And only Saturdays."

He closed one eye while keeping open the other.

He set himself beside the door to watch who frequented the flickers. He didn't come right out and say you shouldn't go; he jotted down who went, and if your name was on his list, you knew that there would be a public scolding that only a hefty donation could stop.

His list of flicker visitors grew long, and one of them, to his chagrin, was his own sister, Little Melly.

"Amazing! Amazing!" she breathed. She didn't admit to it out loud, but the flickers did something to her. When Mary Pickford swooned in Douglas Fairbanks Junior's arms—all smiles and rippling curls and dimples—the spinster's heart stood still.

But Dewey pointed out: "The Levites pay her salary!" and that was that; no further argument. She backed away obediently.

That was the last time Little Melly put herself into the path of modern sin. Instead, she waylaid Doctorjay who had a tougher psyche.

"Tell me. Tell me. What did you see?"

"How Bridget Served the Salad Undressed," teased Doctorjay,

who could be crude beyond belief.

Little Melly near fainted with shock. "No! Doctorjay! You're making fun of me. Why are you making fun of me?"

"Look here. Get this." Doctorjay slapped at a fly that lighted on his balding head. "Don't be so dense. The punch line is: she plain forgot to put the dressing on the salad."

"Oh!" exhaled Little Melly, and sipped her catnip tea.

Not five strong horses would have hauled Little Melly inside a flicker house again to watch a film so gross, but she could prod; could she not prod for more details pertaining to the flicker craze and keep herself informed?

"Read this. Read this," urged Josie, still widening her mind.

She kept on clipping articles predicting pending victory. She shared the news with anybody with the urge to keep himself informed.

The other females, too—all of them, patriotic. For instance, Daisy had her cousins in to feast on her liberty patties. Little Melly gathered every peach pit she could find to save for filters for the gas masks. Lizzy sent six cows straight to the slaughterhouse and, with the money thus obtained, began a special savings chest for future amputees.

The relatives stopped coming with their pillows; instead, they spent their energies in organizing charities. Not even Dewey, still staunchly pacifist, dared quarrel with the merits of the war, except in theory and principle—the war filled up his church collection plate as it had never been filled before. When Dewey came canvassing nickels, dimes and even quarters, there were no questions asked about just where the money went. Nobody would have dared refuse an earnest contribution.

The slogan now was unity. The aim was now to win. Even Noralee, still wan from her last surgery, sat straight up in bed and announced with flashing eyes: "Another twenty years!"

Forgotten were the symptoms that had puzzled Wichita's best doctors. She declared that she wanted to live; the war spelled excitement; she now spoke only English to her chickens; her accent practically disappeared.

Only Lizzy was strangely silent. If German was forbidden in America, how could you tell a doctor where it hurt?

"The Lord prefers High German," said Dewey when at first consulted. He soon changed his mind, and no wonder. The war was rough on foreigners.

Who was he? A Christian, naturally. But: American? Or Russian? Or a German? Perhaps a little bit of each?

When he concluded a speech on that challenging theme at the Wednesday Night Rotary Club, there was thundering, roaring applause, though none possessed the answer.

Jan, a first-generation immigrant, felt just as torn as every other Mennotowner when it came to his ethnic roots. His obligations stretched both ways. He longed for victory, yet felt the war was wrong. He hoped America would win, but what about the Germans? And what about his birthplace, Russia?

As a small boy, he rode the creaking wagons into the heart of Kansas. Did he not owe a debt to this rich land that gave him soil the likes of which could not be found the length and width of Russia?

And yet. Behind him stood four centuries of ancestry that had refused the gun. They stood there, and they frowned.

Jan took off his glasses and put them on again, and still his ethnic pride was looming. He lit up his corn pipe, but didn't start to puff. In the end, he went to a Wichita Finkelstein bank and bought fistfuls of liberty bonds.

All was a colossal dilemma. The war machine tore ethnic pride to shreds, and Mennotown was no exception. The Stars and Stripes were in. The papers, the placards, the nickelodeons kept hammering it in: all Germans drooled distinctly at the mouth, and all Americans were heroes.

Before the year was out, you could not find a single home in Mennotown still proud of its old roots.

Everything of German origin fell into ill repute.

All German-language schools were soon declared invalid.

When Archibald saw a small dachshund pup lift his hind leg and let go with a quiver against a fire hydrant, the twelve-year-old paused briefly, stood back, swung wide his leg, and kicked it in the ribs.

"The thrones," cried Josephine, "are now collapsing every-where." Her eyes were wide, unseeing.

"The last time Uncle Benny wrote," said Little Melly evenly, a dimple in each cheek, "did he not mention those diversionists?"

"You mean subversives. Right?"

"It's all the same to me. It all spells bolshevists."

"It's bolsheviks."

"I said, what is the difference? They're all out to destroy."

"Humanity is on the march! A new age dawns! Time for the New World Order!"

Like a storm-tossed sea, Josie's feelings ran high and then higher. It was as if she longed to throw herself into a gale that soon would turn into a storm. "In Europe, all is pandemonium. It's bad! And getting worse! It's mayhem now. Just mayhem. And small wonder!"

"*Ach Gott!* Again? Not now!"

Lizzy dropped several stitches in a row and fell into a soft whimper. If you were smart, you saw the pattern; you under-stood who was behind it all—behind the agitation, behind the labor movement, behind the brand new income tax, the Feds, the suffragettes, all that. Nefarious forces were at work. Why make a bad thing worse by adding oil to flames?

Take Josie, face aflame: "A witches' Sabbath, over there, if you believe the papers. "

"That may be so. It's none of our affair."

"Unless we take a stand and help democracy along—"

Lizzy put on her spectacles to survey Josie better. The edge of her own tongue grew sharp. "I've said it before, and I say it again. It's not our business, Josie. This war is not our war. We've been pacifists since a horse could be bought for three shillings. Stay out of it. That's my advice. Lay off. No need to get mixed up."

But Josie's penchant was to snub advice, no matter how well-meaning. She throve on turmoil more than any Donoghue.

"I want my life to have an impact on this world," she argued heatedly, never at a loss for words. "Next week, I'll join the International Red Cross. Our folks in Russia need our help. We'll help. That's what we're all about. That's what America is all about. I know no better way."

Lizzy gently wiped her fingers, one by one by one. "Stay out of it. That's all that I can say." She no longer had a sigh to spare for Apanlee. She, too, felt sorry for her beleaguered kinfolk there who were in a bad fix, but now she could take it no farther. She was deep into peppernut season.

But Josie was not easily derailed. She claimed she had the facts right at her fingertips—the length and width of the Ukraine, now ringed with the fires of wrath. She swallowed slogans, spit them out again; she didn't even need her index finger to trace a knotty word. She argued herself silly.

The west, claimed Josephine, had broken into full gallop with steam, and electricity, and thunders for equality, but tsarist Russia—a land mass dark, obscure and mostly ice until the summer broke—was still a sleeping brute, unwilling to be prodded, and let nobody try!

She turned into a woman possessed.

Whenever she could spare a minute, she took herself to Wichita to attend her mysterious meetings. She put her stock in Russia. In the old, tranquil days before the war, her book reviews were everything; her novels filled a void. Now books no longer mattered. Her half-finished poems she flung in the fire. She fetched her best taffeta hat, tucked her two braids inside, stared at her face inside her looking glass as though she saw a stranger, and took herself to Wichita, with Abigail in tow, to help the Finkelsteins.

"We're planning ways and means to get relief to Russia," is what she told her family.

"Who's we? Must you cavort with Jews?"

But Josie only shrugged. Not one word more than that.

Three times a week, come rain or shine, she kicked her slippers underneath her bed, put on her heels and stockings and disappeared, behind her Abigail.

The war gave Josie wings. She burst forth like a prairie fire.

No longer did she wait for life to begin; it was here. It was as if a wave had come and washed from Josie's feet the tangle and the slime that had imprisoned her.

She said: "Chop your own wood, and it will warm you twice."

Next thing that happened was: she twisted Jan around her little finger and became a paid lady typist.

"This contraption and I are made for each other," insisted Josie, looking happier than she had looked for years. What thin veneer of modesty and self-restraint she acquired through the years at great costs to her family dropped from her life like ashes from a phoenix.

Before the year was gone, she donned an eyelet dress that showed her upper arms. She bought a blouse that separated from her skirt. She rode her bicycle and bared a rakish ankle. More than one Elder took a stand—it was an aberration.

She even cut and bobbed her hair. She threw away her Sunday corset. She claimed it pinched her in the waist.

"It barely lets me breathe," said Josie, willy-nilly, and threw it in the trash.

At her new job at the Red Cross, she worked long, grueling hours, well into the night. From morning till the moon came out, she sat there, peck-peck-pecking all day long, as though she were a woodpecker. Her family hoped that the novelty would wear off. This, sadly, did not happen.

"I'm having a fine time," smiled Josie. "I'm having a wonderful time. How can a Singer compare?" That was all you could get out of Josie.

So taken was she with her Red Cross job she would forget to eat, even though on more than one occasion Doctorjay would clear his throat and speak gravely.

"Now, Josie, listen. All that pecking on those keys can't do you any good. It will trigger your female disorders. You aren't getting any younger. You know your change of life is just around the corner."

"Don't start on that again."

"I have Jan's interest at heart."

"I said: don't start again."

The healer's Adam's apple danced. "It isn't yet too late. You might yet bear a son—"

But Josie laughed, no, not a chance! She told him bluntly when he nagged: "Oh, hush you, Doctorjay. I thought you were my friend." She outguessed every motive. She tossed her hair and said: "It's good for me. I get my exercise. Three hours' walk. On foot."

No longer was Mennotown dreary. "It's battle with no holds barred," she told him, thus silencing him deftly. No longer did she spend dull afternoons, with nothing to do, with time on her hands, counting the cracks in the ceiling. Forgotten was the ever-present worry of still-unmarried daughters. Not even Dewey's much-recycled sermons were the vapid exhortations everybody, in the past, had heard a hundred times before and learned to endure without falling asleep. Even he breathed fire—blue fire. He held forth on the Gospel zealously. He had his work cut out. "Onward, onward, Christian soldiers!" That was his battle cry. The church pews shook. The dust fell from the ceiling. He made sure—double sure!—that everybody understood he was a Kansas patriot who flew his paper flag stuck on the windshield of his flivver.

He told the folks to render unto Caesar, just as they rendered unto God, and render unto both they did—there was no counter-argument. His Thees and Thous peeled thunder! He told them what to believe, and how strongly, while passing the collection plate—for widows, amputees and orphans.

Chapter 45

Soon after the Red Revolution, after hoodlums had hoisted the hammer and sickle atop the onion domes and put a bloody end to the abuses of the tsars, Natasha had gone to Marleen and told her, fearing mischief:

"I found the garden gate ajar. You better get a lock and chain. The tsars will not sustain you any longer with their bayonets."

Together, they buried the Apanlee heirlooms—the silver, thimbles, coins. Unspoken was the resolution: not even Hein would know. A man was a man, and a woman a woman. If someone put a knife to Hein's left temple and tried to lift an eye out of its socket, she knew that Hein would tell. By contrast, take Marleen. Or take Natasha, for that matter. What was another secret, more or less? A woman's heart, both knew, was used to keeping secrets.

Natasha watched Marleen from the corner of her eye as both dug deep beneath the trees. Each guessed the other's thoughts.

At last, Natasha spoke with face averted and little quivers in her voice: "I'll always treasure that fine samovar you gave me long ago, Marleen, while in a remarkable mood."

"A dented one. I had no use for it."

"Not so. A splendid samovar."

"It did not mean a thing."

"Still good for many years of use."

That was no idle discourse. Both knew the reasons well: of all the places plunder-worthy, not one matched Apanlee.

By then, a band of cut-throats and marauders—their thighs glued to their stolen horses, sharp knives between bared teeth— had fallen into several German settlements where many cousins lived.

First, they had hanged an Elder who resisted. Then they set fire to his church. They splintered the doors; they shattered the windows. They looted, burned and killed all night. Then they fanned out to the surrounding manors.

There they set fire to the barns and mills, the stables and the granaries. They crashed their rifle butts into the gilded mirrors. They ran their bayonets into the burlap sacks that held next harvest's grain. They ransacked cellars everywhere and smashed the cherry jars. They overturned the spindles in the attic. They gutted sheds and chicken coops before they took off, their wagons packed high with their loot. Everything was hauled away: spoons and forks and silver thimbles, samovars. German-brand grandfather clocks. The dead lay where they fell.

Natasha's bosom heaved with wrath. She busied herself with the babies: "Who cuddles you? Who swaddles you? Who puts you on the potty?"

She was a maid; she knew her place. Her people needed her. "Just count on me," the servant told Marleen. She never left her side.

Marleen's cheeks turned a deeper hue. Both knew with growing clarity: one day it would arrive, the torrent of the Antichrist, unfurling its black flag.

Then what? Marleen's palms grew clammy at the sound of the clatter of hooves, the rattle of iron on iron.

Natasha waited patiently for Dominik to come and tell her what would happen next, now that the old was smashed, the throne collapsed, the Winter Palace taken, the ministers arrested, the future bright with hope. Would he come back and tell her what to do with all the freedom she had gained?

She watched Hein and Marleen kneel in the empty granary. She watched old Uncle Benny. She watched his Dorothy. She listened to the Germans pray in unison: "Lord, pity us, for we are trembling. The earth drinks the blood of our kin."

She told no one that she still pined for Dominik, but he had disappeared from Apanlee as if he'd been a rock dropped in a lake—a speck of dust gone with the dethroned gods of yesterday. None cried a tear for Dominik.

Natasha didn't waste her time on speculations either: she was busy—busier than ever. The measles in the nursery were in full swing again. She did what she had always done. She sat guard by the Apanlee cradles.

Would he come back, her troubled son? Or was he dead by now, having given his life for a cause now as cold and as black as the night? And well might he have died! She was sure that the country would always remember. Nothing said about how she might survive.

Natasha looked inside herself and tried to listen hard. She merely heard the silence of the forest.

The day was cold. The muddy streets lay frozen. Berdyansk had hushed to terror and despair.

Torn flags proclaiming: "Freedom! Liberty! Equality!" hung from dilapidated rooftops. The streets were in a pitiful condition—crumbling sidewalks, broken glass along the gutters, sagging fences, gaping walls. Rats shot through potholes in slithering runs. The houses lay in darkness; storefronts were hammered shut.

A bandit stalked about the cobblestones. He wore a pistol in his belt and on his back a rifle with a bayonet. Hoar frost glistened on his collar and nested in his hair.

A hunger-swollen peasant, recognizing him, saluted eagerly: "Dominik! Hey, Dominik! Hail! Hail to the World Revolution!"

"Hail to the World Revolution," the bandit replied, lifting an ardent fist. "We have driven the ogre away. Haven't we? Haven't we? Huh?"

The bandit gave a narrow smile that showed his broken teeth. His boots left indentations on the dirty, hard, packed snow. Four stiffened bodies, swinging rhythmically, hung from the branches of a tree. He elbowed one, albeit playfully, then kicked aside a loose piece of debris.

"Exploiters. Abusers."

"We'll hang them. One by one. What's there to stop us now?"

The muzhik muttered, trying to oblige: "Let's grease the rope beforehand."

"Right. Right you are. Let's grease the rope beforehand."

The muzhik overcame a stammer. "Let's use the new broom wisely."

The bandit licked his lower lip: "What do I smell? A counter-Revolutionary?"

The muzhik clicked his tongue in fear. "Where? Where? Show me so I can beat him."

"Just kidding, Comrade. Kidding."

"Right, Comrade. Ha! A joke."

"Let's hang them, one by one."

"Let's fan the flames of brotherhood!"

"Scurvy and typhoid to the exploiters!"

"Blast the worm-eaten monarchs!"

"Triumph to the proletariat!"

"And power! Power! Power to the people!"

"Rob all that has been robbed of you," the bandit told a ragged urchin next, spotting him beneath a pillar. "It's now or never, son. Just go ahead. This is a free and equal country. The New World Order has arrived."

"You're through?" the urchin asked.

"It's now or never, son," repeated Dominik. "Just go ahead, I said." He turned the corpse beside the gutter onto its belly with his foot. The flags were snapping in the wind as if they were red whips. "This sucker here? Just a damn fool—that's all!"

The urchin scurried closer, like an eager rat. The bandit stood and watched. Now that the Revolution had finally arrived, corpse piled on corpse; there was no end in sight. He'd been a fool, this one, now lying in the gutter stiffened like a mouse, having resisted an order to show his identity card.

"He lived a fool. He died a fool. He will be buried as a fool—that's all!"

"Right! Right!" The urchin grinned at Dominik while emptying the dead man's pockets. This netted a surprising find: two onions, a mildewed sausage end, a gnawed-on heel of bread.

"Give me the onions. Keep the rest," said Dominik.

"Here. Here!"

"Son. Let me show you. Slash his soles. Rip his seams. Cut open both his pockets. Just keep on looking; there is more; he's dead; he won't bite you. Trust me."

The urchin's hungry face broke into a grateful, toothless smile. The bandit watched him for a while, shelling stale sunflower seeds.

"Whatever strikes your fancy is yours now, son. Your property. All yours," he said again, and lingered. The boy reminded him of times not all that long ago: how hungry he had been himself, how thieving and conniving.

"The land is yours," the Revolutionary flyers said. "So are the homes. So are the orchards. So are the rubles the foreigners keep hidden beneath grain."

All his life, he'd coveted what others owned. Here was his chance to settle an overdue score.

A whirlwind summer it had been for anarchists. The mob poured thick into the cellars of the rich and climbed into the attic of the pious, confiscating horses, loading onto stolen carts whatever struck their fancy: livestock, grain, machinery, furniture, clothes, saddles, harness, firewood. Dominik had joined in gleefully, trampling down the cabbage fields and watermelon patches.

Hail to the Red Revolution! The feathers flew. Prayers died on bloodied lips. For Dominik, it was a heady time.

He couldn't wish for more. Any door could be axed open, any window smashed at will. Cupboards, drawers, trunks and boxes could be ransacked, and not a soul to stop an honest hoodlum! Amazing what torture could do! The point of a needle pushed under a pinkie—astounding!

You led a farmer, white and silent, to a corner of his granary, and he came out, once you were through with him, sporting the colors of an Easter egg, his tongue loosened nicely, more than willing to reveal the hiding places for his silver and his gold. A topsy-turvy world—this world brought on by Revolution—where fat, complacent farmers hid in hedges while hooligans could freely walk the streets, now game for any twisted cruelty—rifles on their shoulders, sabers at their sides, pistols in their boot shafts, and mayhem like a sweet, seductive song on their besotted minds.

That's how it was for Dominik.

He scooped sunflower seeds out of his pocket and slowly sauntered on, spitting shells while reminiscing: just why did he hate them so much?

He and the fools of Christ had been friends. He and the twins had shared games. Had they not even shared a spacious nursery? Had they not shared Hein Neufeld's pride when they won foot races against the slower neighbor fry on watermelon days?

That was, he told himself, before he grasped the full extent of avarice. Exploiters, all! To the ash barrels, all!

He didn't even understand how small discords had grown into such major grievances—just bits and pieces here and there, small slights that kept on festering, small, irritating hurts that added up as though somebody slammed the abacus.

Then came the war. It brutalized. The war added teeth to a festering, ill-defined wound.

Small mischiefs grew into a major thievery; that thievery, in turn, had landed him in jail. There he had time. There he could brood. Jail time changed everything. For two long years, all time stood still for Dominik. There were no calendars in the forgotten dungeons of the tsars.

At first, he inspected his past and found it too petty to warrant the hate that he nursed. There was humiliation, to be sure. There was disgrace. Mortification. Shame. All that, and more. His hate just grew and grew.

A cell, seven paces long, three paces wide, that caged eight violent, angry men, had helped him hone his hatred. Filth. Bedbugs. Cold. A bowl of soup but once a day, fish heads swimming in a grayish liquid. A trough outside, a zinc container, where he could wash, but only once a week.

Somebody told him once: "Unless a miracle occurs, you are as good as dead."

No wonder that he listened when, in undertones, the prisoners kept arguing the merits of the Revolution. Some left at dawn to be shot dead; more came in every day. The new arrivals told him—as they lay on the stony floor, exhausted, famished, and embittered—that the tsar wasted lives in an unneeded war.

"A lot of foolish men are dying in the trenches," they pointed out to Dominik, "so foreigners can keep on dunking zwieback in the coffee."

His mind spun in a loop.

The blow had been long prophesied, but when it came, it left the country reeling. One day the prison gates opened and Dominik was told: "Now beat it, Comrade. You are free."

For Dominik, the Revolution was a yellow shaft of light. It came to him as fire comes to dry brush.

"The monk is dead. The tsars have been sent packing. Get on. Get lost. No time to waste on questions."

He looked around. Did peace bells ring in Europe yet? Nobody knew. Nobody cared. The earth smelled of stale blood. Strangers embraced him in the streets and kissed him with wet smacks: "The New World Order has arrived! Look for a new direction!"

He ran. He ran from the past just as fast as he could. He jumped an overcrowded train, hung front to back with streamers. The train raced through the countryside where hordes of people milled about, all shouting hoarsely: "Long live freedom. Long live anarchy."

"Enjoy your freedom, Comrade! Enjoy the birds!"

"Long live anarchy!"

"Hooray!"

"Hooray!"

"Hooray!"

He shouted until he was hoarse. He screamed until he spat blood. He looked about in a daze and knew: the spark that he had nursed within his breast since he had been a little boy had sprung into a roaring blaze. The wind was in his favor.

Now! Fire to the mills! And fire to the manors!

He found himself a peasant's scarf, a rattling cart, a sheepskin, and a pair of skinny horses.

"*Pascholl!*" he shouted hoarsely.

With angry heels, he stomped into the soil of Russia the People's Revolution. He hooted at the burning embers. All this, and more! And mayhem ever since! For the Germans, it was like the end of the world.

In highest spirits, Dominik walked on while contemplating leisurely what he might do for further entertainment. Pride almost burst his skin, for he no longer passed unnoticed. Left and right, a lot of lesser men saluted smartly:

"Let's fan the flames of brotherhood!"

"Scurvy and typhoid to the exploiters!"

"Blast the worm-eaten monarchs!"

"And fire to the granaries and mills."

He sidestepped several queues with great impatience, while cursing softly to himself. There they stood, shivering, the halfwits of Berdyansk, patiently waiting for bread, for salt, for a dozen foul, frozen potatoes.

"Why! Don't you know a better way?" he sneered, and

crudely elbowed one. "Search your heart. Just what are they to you? Just foreigners! Exploiters! Will you miss them, once they're gone? Just shell them with your teeth and tongue. A shower of dead flies."

"No justice, Citizen. No justice," said the man, hugging himself for additional warmth. He had stuffed newspapers inside his shirt to break the force of wind.

"Bring justice with your gun butt," said Dominik, disgusted. "Probe for justice with the tips of bayonets, as you would probe the underbelly of a slug, and see how easily you find it." Instead of bread—bullets! Instead of obedience—bone-rattling fear! "I swear it works. I swear by all Red coffins."

"Sure. Sure. Why not?"

"So. Cast away your past of darkness! March with us into the dawn! Help give history a push! Bring on the New World Order!"

"Yes, comrade. Sure. Right. Let's!" the dim-wit muttered, overwhelmed, and shuddered in the wind.

"Well, think it over. Will you?" Dominik stared at him with narrowed eyes. "Don't say you weren't asked. Come join our crowd. Just ask for Nestor, will you? A voice to chew at sinews. Two eyes to chill the blood."

Chapter 46

His full name was Nestor Machno. He was the king of thugs, the potentate of hooligans. His eyes had the glitter of spite. Where he slept, the demons huddled, grinning. Where he walked, the earth commenced to groan.

He spared neither infant nor saint.

Since he plundered, raped and killed, many years have come and gone. The groans of the tortured have long disappeared; not even the echoes remain. But in the patchwork of most anybody's memory who lived within his thoroughfare, he was the Antichrist who roamed the wastes of Russia, who asked: "What is there to stop me now?"

The Fiend had the run of the land. Wherever he appeared, the cockerel jumped to the roofs and gnawed away the rafters built centuries before. He put the match to every foreign manor house his filthy hands could seize. He hammered down the strongest doors, ripped open every down comforter. He rifled through cellars and attics. He tortured, raped and killed.

No exception was made. No mercy was shown.

And when he fixed his blood-shot eye on Dominik and asked one wind-blown morning: "Just where, exactly, is this place called Apanlee?" the fate of Apanlee was sealed.

Dominik took pride in his precarious footing with this thug, whose name had leaped to notoriety—who shot the priest, who burned his church, and made the rich scrub the peasants' floors. He had come upon him when the battle front was torn to ribbons, the country ripped to shreds.

"I do not beat about the bush," Machno had bragged, and something within Dominik had snapped. He knew he need fear nothing. His new mentor's name spelled protection.

By then, Machno had led his rag-tag army many times across the plains of the Ukraine—looting armories, setting fire to grain, leading his band of dishevelled marauders, searching for places where riches were still to be found.

The spark of mutiny within Natasha's son roared into open thrill. "Your army suits me fine," said Dominik, and joined Machno's black flag.

What fun to see the Germans helpless prey within the claw and fang of Russia! A hoodlum's joy, the German villages—as vulnerable as birds on naked branches. You could rob them and rob them, and still there was enough.

He roared, as others did: "Poetic justice, Comrade, no?"

To see the hated foreigners evicted from their homes with clubs was sweet revenge for Dominik. A country in the throes of civil war—and foreigners still rolling out *vareniki* and dipping zwieback in their coffee?

"What's mine is mine," he roared. "What's theirs is mine as well."

It's now or never," said Machno. "It might as well be now."

Whole armies were sent to arrest him—in vain. He knew no loyalty to anyone, and felt no obligation. His fame spread like fire through sheaves.

Let Wrangel take away his trains; let Trotskys men explode his bridges! An easy thing, a laugh, to catch a fool and smash his fingers on an anvil and thereby learn the enemy's secrets!

Machno was profitable company for Dominik, the dungeons having maddened him sufficiently. The veins in his forehead threatened to burst as he remembered all the full-size portraits of the imperial family that framed the halls of Apanlee.

He'd found his niche. He saw his goal. The Revolution, a satanic mill, designed to pulverize the past? He hooted his approval.

As brother strife fanned out and civil war set manors blazing, to join the avalanche of willing demons in search of loot and spoils seemed natural.

He hated them, the foreigners. On the sweat of the serfs they had fattened themselves. A Revolution was a thing of pain and blood and tears. Let them beware: foul were the times. Into the flames flew every tsarist document and ukase. Down came the hated double eagles.

"Wrest the booty from their hands!"

"Suck the marrow from their bones."

"Loot their pantries."

"Rape their women."

"Triple-check their pockets—and then shoot them in a ditch."

He heard the voices of his New World Order comrades and pushed open the door to their lair with the tip of his boot. There they were, all proletarian heroes, and he was one of them; he felt at home with them; they were his flesh and sinew.

They greeted him with bawdy songs and shouts. "Hey, Dominik! Say, Dominik! What's there to stop you now?"

"That's right. Move over, you. What's there to stop me now?"

He stripped the sheepskin from his shoulders and found himself a place to peel his feet out of the shreds of newspapers he had stuffed deep into his boots to keep his toes from freezing. He turned them upside down and poured out a trickle of mud.

"Say! Hand me your machorka pouch."

"What's that? A German Bible?"

"No finer paper anywhere," the bandit said, and rolled himself a smoke.

God's dictum: puff! and it was gone.

A neat little bullet: a life was no more.

A match: a mansion turned to ashes.

Just aim a cannon at a church—and it became a chicken coop!

Just board a train and travel up and down the countryside of Russia—for free!

Feeling warm and cozy to the core, he stretched his filthy toes and listened to the gossip of his comrades who toasted one another gleefully:

"—you old pig's bladder—"

"—were you born on a manure heap—?"

"—your mother, the old carrion. The ugly, trashy cat—"

Nothing was sacred, no curses off limits. They topped each other's blasphemies: "You rotten horse thief, here you are, and only yesterday, without a single kopeck of your own—"

"Bottoms up! Bottoms up! And freedom to the masses!"

Ah! Bottoms up! Could there be sweeter words?

"What's next?" said Dominik. He was sated with blood, like a tick.

They had already shot the smart and diligent and hanged the rich and massacred the prayerful. The stars, bells, crowns, crosses, eagles—gone! The hapless bureaucrats of yesterday—felled by the bayonet. The power lines were cut, by then; the country all but paralyzed. With his own hands, he'd ransacked many an estate, thrown open every drawer, and thrown the contents about on the floor. And yet there was a gnawing hunger, deep down within, a need that no words could convey.

There was still Apanlee.

He watched them thoughtfully, his tried and tested comrades, munching on sunflower seeds. At his side, he held his bayonet, fingering it now and then. Between his legs he held a dog, and fed it table scraps.

"We're waiting, Dominik."

With one long stroke, he raked the Bible closer. He opened it. He took a pencil stub and bore down hard. "See this fat cross? See these two roads? That's Apanlee. That's where you find this place called Apanlee. They have well-bolted doors. But here's a little side gate the favorite servants use—"

He spit in a long arch. The bandits cheered and hooted. Give us a mansion—like a wolf pack we come! With a demon howl we come.

"—here's where you cut the power lines."

They stamped their feet to show approval. "Where's a stone? We need one to sharpen our knives."

The liquor helped some; no doubt about it. It dilated his pupils. It turned his face as deep and dark as ink.

"Here! Bottoms up! Say! Bottoms up!"

Of late, he was monstrously drunk more often than not, and never entirely sober. How else could he have borne the knowledge that, as judging from his comrades' hoots, in yet another week, a massive grave would cover all—the guilty and the innocent? He spoke in a faint slur.

"See where my thumb is? See where I point my finger? Here's how the buildings are laid out. I do not know who told you. It surely wasn't me—"

The fire water poured its warmth into his veins and clarity into his words. Every drop of blood in Dominik's unwashed body thrilled to the thought of Apanlee.

"How do you know? It it true you were born at Apanlee?" asked one of them, while blowing smoke through blue-veined nostrils.

"Not quite," said Dominik. "I wasn't born at Apanlee."

"Ha! So you say!"

"I was born in a shed," Dominik said coldly. "I was naked. I was cold. I was put into a wooden trough my father's wife gave my mother." He felt remote now, but content. He spoke slowly through tobacco fumes. "My father's wife said to my mother: 'There is a worm in every windfall apple.' And my mother? My mother? She said to the child she had borne: 'You! You! Where are your freckles? Huh?'"

Through a thick haze, he saw Natasha, swaddling them and
cuddling them and cooing to them softly—the twins, her freckled favorites, usurping all her love. He added with a little hiccup:

"If they were snug—why, she was happy. When she was
there, at Apanlee, she was at home with everything." He saw his
mother clearly. Her reign in her beloved nursery had widened
the pond of her life to a lake. He added: "My heart turned as hard
as a nut."

The muffled conversation ceased. The hoodlums listened silently.

"A peasant dipped his finger in his vodka and let me suck on
it. That was the only warmth I knew. That peasant worked at
Apanlee. He beat my mother. Often. He sued to beat me, too.
He beat us both until we started spitting blood—"

He took a deep breath, and his eyes turned to milk.

"They thought that I was blind," said Dominik. "But I saw
all. They thought that I was deaf. But I heard everything. My
eyes and ears were everywhere. Apanlee? What's Apanlee? Its
shadow fell across my cradle—"

The memories of past iniquities now drove the glitter to his
pupils. He stared into the faces of his comrades who had helped
to bring the Revolution, and in his demented soul he knew: "The
centuries will long remember how I helped strangle Apanlee."

He said:

"Watch me. I spit on Apanlee. I'll put the torch to Apanlee.
I'll thaw out my toes in its ashes—"

Natasha had just about shouldered her way through the feverish days, since the measles had come with the fogs. She knew
Marleen was useless; the midwife never left her elbow.

"You go to bed now, hear?" Natasha gave Marleen a nudge.
"And you, with your varicose veins!"

That night, Marleen did not argue. She longed for sleep; she
was not feeling well, and let Natasha have the upper hand for

once.

"All right. All right," she said. Tomorrow was tomorrow.

The many children she had borne throughout the years had weakened her; she did not pick up the implied insult that this would be her last—she might tomorrow, surely, belittle and lambast Natasha. So let Natasha feel triumphant; bed rest was all Marleen wanted, now that confinement was at hand.

"Be sure to sponge them all," she said mechanically, and helped Natasha haul the giant zinc tub from the basement, before she went upstairs to hug her blanket tight about her and try to catch some sleep. "And help them say their prayers."

She knew she need not tell Natasha what to do, and did so only out of habit. She was content and grateful to know Natasha was there, back in the nursery, to lend a hand to Dorothy and lighten the burden of too many voices that whimpered for their nightly lullabys or begged to be put on the potty. Natasha was reliable. Natasha brought to every task extraordinary energy— still scrubbing diapers, wiping little fingerprints off walls and sills, inspecting footsoles, ears and fingernails, snug in her toasty nursery when the hard frosts arrived and didn't go away.

So on this evening.

Outside, the wind blew hard; the night was ink; the trees stood stiff; but in the nursery, the embers glowed as always.

Natasha was just about finished, firmly in charge of the orbit she knew. She supervised the quarantine; she needed every bed.

She had curtly evicted the twins who slept in the straw of her hut, to make room for additional neighborhood children, all covered with spots, head to toe.

Her nursery was packed that night. With Dorothy to lend a hand, she swaddled, scolded, washed and diapered each and every one of them until they shone like apples. She did a final check from bed to bed; with that, her evening ritual was done. She dunked the last one in the suds whose place was second at a row of nine, as counted from the bottom. Her name was Mimi, five years old. She was Natasha's cherished child that night, because

her fever was cresting, and next in line was Jonathan, a little
older than the girl, who had already learned to count, this long
before a mortal taught him anything; he was that smart and clever.
He'd just been showing off a brand new tooth when he, too, caught
the splotches.

"Come, Jonny. Sit here in my lap. Teach me to count to ten,"
coaxed Dorothy, his grandmother, still lovely to look at. She,
too, smiled, lingeringly—smiled at her much-beloved grandson,
a smile that held the warmth of many tiny suns.

"That one is truly special, Dorothy," Natasha said, intent to
please.

"Yes, isn't he?" By all accounts, here was a little fellow so
developed mentally that, as per Uncle Benny, beaming, to count
past twenty was a snap. The secrets of addition and subtraction
would be next.

"He is amazing, Dorothy."

No disagreement there. This youngster still was much too
young for school, but he already knew his ABCs, and when he
stubbed his toe, he was too proud to run and seek for solace on
Natasha's spongy bosom—as did most everybody else, adept at
using any old excuse to be her valentine.

"*Eins. Zwei. Drei. Vier. . .*" said Jonathan.

"*Fuenf. Sechs,*" Natasha finished, proud of her German skills.
She relished the boy's yawn. "Sleep tight now, Jonny. Do. You
can teach me tomorrow."

She looked around. The truth be told, and why pretend? she
loved them all, and dearly. She treasured every one of them. She
loved them like her own. Marleen did not know this—and had
she known, she would have only snorted with contempt and clattered with her dishes!—but did she, old Natasha, need a
bombasting Revolution to get her share of kisses?

Such was Natasha's world.

Chapter 47

Natasha, finished with her chores, next went into the shed to turn the hay. She wanted to sit down with Hein a bit and talk, should he decide to check the horses for the night.

She waited for him patiently. That's when she heard the gallop of the horses.

She threw the pitch fork in an arch. "Machno!" she screamed. "Machnooo!"

She thought her lungs would explode. For herself, she had no fear. She knew that they came for the loot.

"Machnooo!"

She was old and a martyr already: what did she own of worth, what had she ever owned? Her dented samovar? The mare that Hein had let her have—a beast barely able to stand? Ten scraggly, meager chickens? A saucer with some oil? A ragged piece of cotton to which to put a match?

No, she stood blameless—that she knew. Nothing had she ever done to bring dishonor to the Revolution. The tsars? What were the tsars to her? If they were gone—why, they were gone!

She panted in her terror. Tsars or no tsars, they mattered not to old Natasha; what mattered were the folks of Apanlee, whom she had served in loyalty. Her own life had never been of value—if it was lost, so what?

But Susie! Katie! Rosie!

Who else? Her mind went blank, and then recovered: Paulie! Jonny! Rosalie!

She didn't even count the twins, who had long legs to run. But Mimi! Jonathan! All fever-spotted! Upstairs!

"Bozhe moi!" she whimpered, now stumbling through Marleen's bare flower beds. "Run! Hide! Machno! Machnooo!"

The truth at last! It came to her in flashes. All that was Hein's, was hers, vicariously—she never grasped until this very minute that this was so, but now she knew! She knew! She knew, as she had never known before, that she loved Hein's blond, blue-eyed brood as if they were her own. His children were her children, and never mind who gave them birth! She knew!

She ran through the orchards, crept through the thickets, felt her way along the wall and thus reached the back of the grain shed. A dog took off howling; a window on the second floor flew shut. A small hand reached for her; small fingers, hot with fever. She cuffed and kicked it right into the night and deep into the bushes.

She recognized Hein's voice; she felt his hands; he reached for her; she shook him off as well, and headed right into the light that shone from one small window. Not for a moment did she hesitate—she knew where her loyalties lay. Her mind careened. Her voice was no longer her own.

"Hide! Hide!" she screamed. "Machno! Machnooooo!"

A horse whinnied somewhere, sputtering mud. She fell and, spitting earth and gravel, she scrambled to her feet. "Hide out!" she shrieked. "They're coming! *Bozhe moi!* They're here!"

Her shouts swept a small shadow deep into the bushes. She thought, a simple woman: "As death comes, even children cower." There was a roar within her head, but still she strained to hear. Her mind was reeling, boiling, overflowing, yet it was cold as the black ice she felt beneath her soles.

"Machno!" she screamed again. "Run! Hide! Machnooo!"

Would they pass by? They had passed by before.

She waited, paralyzed. She heard the horses, galloping, then slowing to a nervous, prancing trot, right at the gates of Apanlee, next to the lilac bushes.

Marleen heard them as well, but was too thick, by then, with her belated budding life to run. Still drugged with sleep, she stumbled to the shed to quiet the odd commotion, her mind devoid of reason.

A rifle butt crashed hard against a door. The blast of rifle fire tore through the silence and made the snow fall from the trees. Marleen heard the shot, and then another and another and sat, doubled over, each time guessing whose life it might be.

"Machno!"

"Machno!"

"Machnoooo!"

Another shot rang out, and Dorothy, still in the nursery upstairs, cut off from escape, hid her small face in her starched, cross-stitched apron and started praying softly.

"Oh, Uncle Benny! Uncle Benny!" whispered Dorothy. In all his life, his spider legs had never even twitched without a major effort. No way he could have run.

He didn't even try.

The noise woke up a small, forgotten child. Barefoot and blinking, it stood at the top of the stairs, dragging a blanket, thumb in its mouth. A bandit hit it once, full force—and it fell over, dead. Obligingly, another ran his bayonet into the soft and unresisting body to make sure.

Still in a fog of vodka and of fury, the two careened into the kitchen. There they found several measles-covered cousins, in utter terror, huddled together near the door.

"There! There! Another one! Vipers! Viper brood all!"

It was a massacre—no other name is just. The hoodlums

came to kill, and that is what they did. All night long, they killed and robbed and raped and plundered, and when they left, they left behind them several children's heads in saucers on the sill of Marleen's well-scrubbed nursery.

That's part of history. Look at it and find words. And when it happened, where was God? And when the Hooked Cross arrived—a generation later—to stop the Antichrist, small wonder that, at Apanlee, it found its perfect mooring?

Hein was the first to die that night, and brutally.

A bandit pulled him from the hay; three others slid out of the bushes. The four of them kept hooting with their mirth as they pulled down his trousers. They made him run barefoot in circles, first in his granary, across the scattered grain, and then outside, while shooting volleys at his loins until the snow was red. They beat him until they were tired. They egged each other on: "Step on his kulak corns."

Natasha watched it all, too petrified to move. She crouched behind a bush. When Hein went down at last, they knelt on him and slashed his belly open, then filled it with the grain his great-grandfather, Peet, had traded from the Tartars.

"Exploiter! Traitor! Kulak swine!"

For quite a while, they took turns pulling on his mustache, and then they tired of that, too—so, with a slash, they cut it off, a bloody piece of hair and skin, and flung it in the air and laughed uproariously. Hein's kaiser mustache caught itself within the tangle of the dry acacia trees, and there it hung, all winter long, and no one gave a hoot.

And Uncle Benny. He died, too.

He died while shielding Dorothy who lay across the zinc tub, spread-eagled, fiercer than a crab. The zinc tub heaved as though it were a living thing, for underneath that tub lay Jonathan and Mimi. With all her might, she held that zinc tub down.

From the corner of her eye, she saw a hoodlum swing the invalid around and sink his knees into his back, and when her husband tried to ward him off as one might fight a maddened dog, a clenched fist landed in his face. That's when she screamed, for she was not yet dead; she saw—she saw the thug jump up and sit astride the cripple's hunchback, reeking of sheepskin and garlic, and Uncle Benny, panting feebly, went crashing to the floor.

That's how the half-Jew died at Apanlee.

He died, an old and fragile man, entitled to his dignity, clubbed into bloody pulp as one might club a rattler. He did not have a single enemy. Not ever had he harmed a beetle.

"Even your shadow is an offense!" moaned Uncle-Benny feebly to the revolutionary thug, and those were his last words.

"Ha! *Donnerwetter! Donnerwetter!*"

The bandit seized the first thing within reach—a prayer book with heavy silver clasps and sturdy wooden cover. It had been brought from the Vistula Plains. The scoundrel held it in his hands and cursed. A bunch of stupid lies! An old wives' fairy tale! Now, what a fine torpedo!

He swung it wide, let fly. It hit Dorothy smack in the scented temple.

Her valor came from nowhere. She struggled wind into her lungs and wrapped both arms and legs around the tub while terror dug its teeth into her spine and started tossing her about as if she were a bird within the claws of a ferocious cat. She shuddered briefly, while she hugged the zinc tub to herself—a small, obliging woman whose hair was white, whose heart was throbbing still, for what was underneath that basin, now convulsing, was her dead daughter's son. She stretched herself across that basin with all the strength at her command, and there she stayed. A knot.

And thus died Dorothy— the one with pale and tapered fingers, adept at fancy needlework, the one who took the smallest ailment to the doctors. The tub beneath her heaved and rocked as if it were a beetle, but she clutched onto it and would not yield— not to the kicks aimed at her spine, not to the raining rifle butts, not to the threshing flail that whistled down on her repeatedly and bloodied her hair a bright red.

"Please don't," prayed Dorothy, by then a senseless woman.

Why would he count the blows? Why not be quiet?

Three. Four.

She prayed a senseless prayer that faded out before it reached the ceiling.

". . . Five. Six."

A life is short. A death takes an eternity. Beneath her knuckled fists, a small voice kept on counting as he was taught to count.

". . . Fifteen. Sixteen."

Pause.

"Seventeen."

"Have mercy!" she moaned, and then, in higher pitch: "It is you! Let the devil be loose—!" It was a high and choking scream that sent the hoodlum spinning.

"It's me," he said. "It's Dominik." His hands groped for the weaver's shuttle. He kicked it over with his foot. He struck as a man strikes, when blinded by hate. A chandelier splintered. Something else came crashing to the floor. That was the last reverberating sound the Lord would allow Dorothy. She took it in. She knew, exactly, what it was—one of her husband's prized possessions, a stately sculpture and a gift, carved from a solid block of granite, bearing a small, bronze angel at its tip. One hand held the revered cross, the other hand pointed to heaven.

"For all eternity," the gold inscription said.

"For all eternity? Ha!"

A hoodlum ran his bayonet right through the clock, a whirl of wheels and chains and metal. "Eighteen," whispered the child underneath, but Dorothy, we must assume, lest we go mad, now heard the chimes of heaven.

". . . Nineteen. Twenty." Thus counted Jonathan, six years of age, as he had taught himself to count.

The counting drove the hiccups onto his playmate's swollen tongue. "Quiet, Mimi! Mimi, hush!" He put a hand across her face and tried to silence her. They battled with each other in the small space the tub allowed. The boy won out; he forced the girl child down. She had a brand new tooth. She bit him hard, but still he held her down. Against his cheek, he felt her ragged breath. It slackened, and then stopped.

Upstairs, somebody hurled an object through the window.

"Death! Death to all the parasites!"

"And fire! Fire! Fire! To the mills!"

Behold that silver candlestick. Look at that fancy lamp. Smash it into a thousand pieces. That bench? Those portraits of the hated monarchs? For all eternity? Here's how!

Thus silenced Dominik the half-breed, the things he hated most: their scrupulous lifestyle, their slow and strong tenacity, their maddening tongues, their precious racist God.

Now for the aftermath.

The night was clear and quiet. The moon was pale. The stars were gone. The wind kept whistling softly.

A boy's small shadow slid along the stairs, then felt its way along the trampled boysenberry rows. It stood on tiptoes, briefly, to unlock the heavy gate. The clouds sat low. The snow lay still and deep. The windows of the darkened south wing rattled.

The child stared at a pet. The pet stared back unblinking, a bayonet embedded in its spine.

A peasant, passing by, oblivious, stopped by the road to urinate. He did not see the shadow.

"Pascholl!" he said, while hitching up his trousers. He slapped the horse and clicked his tongue, but not before the little shadow climbed atop his cart and crouched to make himself as small as possible.

The muzhik never knew he had a stowaway.

The wheels squeaked away. The silence returned. In a minute, the shaky contraption was gone.

When fine, pale colors tinted the sky, Natasha crept out of the bushes.

The yard lay empty and trampled. A chicken lay, neatly beheaded, smack on the steps of Apanlee, and next to it lay Hannele, eight years of age, a neighbor child, fourth in line as counted from the cradle, beheaded just as neatly.

A little to the left lay Rosalie, Hein's middle child, stabbed more than twenty times.

Natasha doubled over. Natasha muttered in High German: "Have mercy, Lord! Have mercy! Have mercy on us all."

Hein's body lay beside a pile of manure. Beside him, Natasha saw the twins, wordless and rocking. Alive. As she slunk by those two, she cringed as though she were a cur, but did not say a word.

She crept inside. Manhandled and then dropped, all kinds of household items lay strewn across the room. By the still-smoking oven slumped a body, next to the toppled samovar. She knelt to turn it over. She took her time with him. "You? Who would rather read than eat? The skies are weeping, Uncle Benny."

Natasha longed to take his hands, to run her fingertips across the violence, but then she noticed that he had no hands; someone had chopped them off and nailed them to the door.

She searched throughout the house to look for Jonathan. The angry bayonets had slashed and sliced the feather beds. Drawers had been yanked open, their contents strewn about. The little boy was gone.

"My pet?" she called. "My love? Don't hide yourself and cause my heart to stop! Where are you, Jonathan?"

Natasha crept into the barn. The cattle, needing to be watered, bellowed loudly.

"Oh, *bozhe moi!*" Natasha wept, collapsing on some pieces of charred lumber. Deep wails rose from her throat. "You, Mimi? Is it you?" she said at last, and pulled the mute child close. "My little baby girl? Alive?"

A little to her left lay something in the straw.

"Marleen," Natasha begged. "Wake up, Marleen. Now! This very minute I want you to wake up." She reached for her. "Here! Can you walk? Hold onto me and try."

Marleen still seemed to breathe, but shallowly, her face an empty slate. Natasha's eyes grew wide, then frosted as though glazed.

She was a peasant, filled with an earthy knowledge; she bent and bit the cord. She scooped the newborn up and wrapped it in her apron.

She said inaudibly: "I'll swaddle you. I'll cuddle you. I'll put you on the potty."

She said to the comatose woman: "Here is the truth, so help me God. He came because he couldn't stay away." She spoke past a lump in her throat. "He's dead," she said. "Now it's just you and me. From this day on, it's you and me, Marleen."

Thus slid away the past—the hurts of youth, the petty jealousies. The bloody kernels, filling up the cavity where Hein's large, lusty heart had beaten for them both, had evened up a score. She knew that now, as in a fog—it was a strangely soothing thought. She knew Hein would have been a stranger to this unity she felt, this utter oneness with Marleen. Hein was a man, a German, and, besides—for all his charm!—he was a lout who used and then discarded.

Not she. She knew where value lay.

He would not possibly have understood the singularity of loss that brought rebirth. Renewal. Natasha's eyes filled to the brim. She said again: "It's you and me, Marleen."

A stranger he had been, this stately and aloof philanderer whom she had loved for many years, beginning in the fullness of her youth. Now Hein was gone. And she was old. A circle had been closed.

She said to his last legacy: "I'll hum to you. I'll kiss your teeny toes."

She sat in stolid silence, the newborn curled up in her apron. She sat there for the longest time, not thinking anything, not given to unnecessary musings. But then she roused herself. Her eyes fell on the wheelbarrow. She heaved and pushed and pulled, and in the end, she had Marleen—delirious with childbed fever, but fitting snugly in between two boards. All right, now! Here we go!

That cold and bloody morning Natasha wheeled her rival, comatose and manure-coated, right back into the halls of Apanlee.

Chapter 48

Spin backwards a few years. The Lord's sun shone brightly on Kansas—nothing but azure skies spanning a daisy-strewn earth!

The paralyzed streams came to life. The birds built their nests among glistening leaves. The baby cradles filled; the midwife was at hand. Model T's came down in price. Rotarians slapped each other on the shoulders.

Jan beat his previous record—three years in a row, he reaped fabulous crops. He was the town's most trusted leader. All honor went to him.

Josie was wild for that typewriter, truly. Whereas her husband prospered more and more, a model citizen, she still kept secret journals. She still wrote cryptic letters.

Her pad was always in her lap, her pencil always poised. She kept on clipping articles for Uncle Benny to have them at her fingertips the moment mail to Russia was restored. She kept them in a shoebox.

She read the nights away, and often slept all day. For years, she had poured all her energies into the final push to get the female vote, which no one thought would pass.

Her blue eyes flashed with challenge.

"This club today—that club tomorrow," insisted Josie nastily and plunged her nose into another novel. She read one book that had five hundred pages.

When Lizzy begged: "Explain yourself. Explain the whys and hows—" Josie preened herself before her looking glass and did not have an answer.

Her gaiety was mocking, and it hurt. She vexed her soul with this and that, and was fond of peculiar notions. Midstream, the tone of her arguments hardened. An alien in Mennotown, she never found her niche. Between Josie and the clan, there yawned an unbridgeable chasm.

She wore her skirts two inches off the ground and kept cavorting with the Finkelsteins. The source of all of Josie's mischief and maneuvers was her astounding intellect. The Articles of Faith that Dewey proffered as an antidote brought no relief to Josie. She battered and destroyed.

And yet, there was a void.

The neighbors watched her standing by the window—yearning, hoping, saddening—but what it was she grieved was a deep mystery to them.

She often spoke of matters philosphical. She claimed she longed to set right what was wrong. She pined for an ass' sharp jawbone, like Samson wielded on the Philistines.

Once Little Melly spied a piece of carbon paper, held it up against the light, and drew her own conclusion. "The Chosen ones again," she said, and relished several shudders.

"Gold! Gold!" the anxious townsfolk said.

It wasn't deeply rooted, nor was it a controlling ideology. It was just there. It was an understanding.

So let the Hebrews claim the lofty banner in hard-hit, bleeding Russia was universal betterment. The driving force, they knew as members of a creed that had a German history to fall back on—a history of hard work, diligence, self-discipline, and thrift—was money.

If you had ears to hear and eyes to see, the city fathers told themselves, you knew, behind the social unrest everywhere around the globe—and that included Russia—were still the sidelocks and yarmulkes.

"Please, lovey. Just don't you encourage these people—" begged Lizzy, but Josephine, ignoring her, had tea with them, right on the sidewalk, out in the open.

"There's a New Order waiting in the wings. The world will be our garden."

That's what she said. With Josie, all was drama. There was a slant in Josie's eyes that said: "Just wait and see. One step at the time. One day at a time. You haven't seen anything yet." Excitement fueled her embers.

"I think," cried Josie, shrill as the overseer's whistle, "Jews are the smartest, most progressive people in the world."

An Elder let fly a guffawing laugh: "Oh, yeah? Yeah? How come, then, they missed the Messiah?"

That made but little difference, as far as Josie was concerned. Steeped in rebellion, she throbbed with impatience, mad for any action, contemptuous of chapter and verse. The female vote was within reach—and she at center stage!

Jan never tired of watching her. He cherished Josephine. But, on the other hand, he also cherished harmony. He treasured peace of mind. He valued family. His eyes were bright with pain.

The day came when Jan cleared his throat and said to Doctorjay: "I came to ask for help."

At once, the healer sat back, lit his pipe, and smiled attentively.

"She craves too much excitement," Jan began. He would have been much rather in the fields than within range of the old Lutheran's cunning wink. "What's happening in Russia looks like deliverance to her."

"Harrumph!" said Doctorjay, restrained. "Your wife's the talk of Wichita. As odd as a blustery Christmas."

"Her heart warms to most any ideology that's new."

Doctorjay spoke from instinct, seasoned by a lifetime of experience. He nudged his friend along: "There is a failproof answer. Put yet another baby in the cradle."

That would have been nature's solution. Both Noralee and Lizzy said as much. They pointed out the neighbors gave long stares.

"I don't think so," said Jan, unwilling to confirm the rumor.

"But how can you be sure?"

"Not even God," said Jan, his temples white by then, "can alter last year's harvest."

The village healer stroked his stubbled chin. He flashed the bright sunshine a lopsided grin. "It only takes a couple and a bed."

"Yes. Health permitting, health permitting," said Jan with a small laugh. He trusted Doctorjay as though he were his father. "Discounting that, is there a remedy?"

"Don't give me your excuses. Just take my old gal, Noralee, and me. Almost four decades, son! And look at us! Each hoping to outlast the other! She's healthier and plumper than ever. That's surely my good fortune—"

He briefly lost himself in happy reveries. His earthy marriage to the deacon's widow still yielded joy and comfort. She hugged him and kissed him in obvious delight when he returned from Wichita, unharmed.

"Don't you forget it, Jan. You run the show. You are her husband. A female's point of view is not that hard to understand—"

"To understand a woman such as Josie," Jan told his lifelong friend, "a man needs second sight."

But Doctorjay had good advice to spare. "Take it from me. There's trouble brewing. Trouble, son. Real trouble. And I mean trouble with a T writ large. Watching Josie is like watching Lizzy's milk pots coming slowly to a boil. That one has fire in her belly. Fire, lad! She's got to be contained. You're her husband, aren't you? You've got to calm her down."

For weeks, the healer plowed his well-scored groove, determined and precise.

"She still has a waist as slim as a wasp's. Is that not a temptation? What do you say? Why not give it a try?"

"I know. She's beautiful."

Jan still loved Josie as the apple of his eye, and Doctorjay was not yet willing to give up. With the help of ten fingers he helped Jan along:

"Wasn't she sixteen when you and she married?"

Jan lit a pipe with work-gnarled fingers. "Yes, she was just a little girl."

"She can't be more than forty-two."

"I do not know her age."

"What? Why not? Don't tell me it's impossible. Why, just the other day, your mother saw her feasting on a plate of dumplings, and all her hopes soared to the sky—"

Jan said with an uneasy laugh: "Let's call it a day."

But Doctorjay was rolling downhill now. "She's still remarkably preserved."

He left in highest spirits to share his hopes with Noralee who kept her fingers crossed. "

She's still remarkably preserved," said Noralee to several friends, to get full use from that fine phrase.

All females in the neighborhood agreed: a pregnancy would put a speedy end to short hems and rolled stockings.

But Josie kept on saying "no" when prodded for specifics. "There is no way," said Josie, fighting back as best she could to even the indignity. And each and every book that came her way, she read.

Doctorjay liked Josie well enough and tried to see her side. She was as fond of Wichita as he, where every taxi driver was his friend. He had been in her camp for many years—and she in his, no matter what the gossip. But this was a couple in conflict, and both of them his friends.

Both shoes were pinching him. He loved Jan dearly, too. His

heart thumped with his love for Jan, who had done more than his fair share by buying bonds and yet more bonds to push the foreign war to victory. Here was the end result: Doctorjay could not hold two opposing points of view—not without getting dizzy.

"This so-called female freedom business," he therefore counseled Josephine next time he crossed her path, "if I were you, I wouldn't take too far—"

At once, she was on guard. "What do you mean by that?"

"As I just said, if I were you—"

"You aren't," she snapped, curtly, and turned her back on Doctorjay. She said little, but did as she pleased.

Doctorjay, however, was not that easily put off. He started stalking her activities. He knew that almost everyone in Mennotown agreed with Dewey Epp—this business with the suffragettes was an affront to any male, and had to end somehow.

That's how things stood when word came from the wilds of Russia: the tsars had been dethroned.

A tremor went the length of Mennotown. All paled with rage and wrath. The culprits were well known. For decades, they had flung their bombs against the Romanovs. And here was the result!

You did not have to say their names. A baby in the cradle knew their guilt. By their own signatures, they gave themselves away. They snared, and they deceived. Most shared that attitude.

Not a few oldsters still remembered clearly how those who called themselves the Chosen had feuded with the tsars, who tried to weed them out in pogrom after pogrom. The Cossacks came charging; the rascals hid themselves in cellars, under beds, in closets, and in attics, but still, the Cossacks pulled them out and meted out what they deserved by bloodying their heads.

Now this?

"Dreadful news! Dreadful news!" yelped Doctorjay, gunning his flivver, breaking every speed law in the county—and he a fellow with no reason to distrust the banner of equality!—"the tsars—all gone! The Cossacks—gone! The Winter Palace—gone!"

It was a nasty jolt. What would be next?

"The female vote will destroy everything," concluded Dewey angrily, who needed no survey to tell him the shape of the future. Would he, a healthy male and the dispatcher of the Lord, hold still while watching Kansas females riding roughshod over both the spirit and the letter of the law?

"Just ask yourself," snarled Dewey Epp while waiting on himself—since Josie didn't seem to notice that his coffee cup was empty—"who benefits by toppling governments?"

All six of Josie's daughters paled beneath their freckles. The Elder was no weathercock. He was no coward when it came to his convictions. He spit it out. "The cunning of the serpents is well known."

Noralee stared at the wall, out the window, up at the ceiling, and down at the floor. Little Melly started squirming in her seat. Daisy's stocking grew longer and longer. And even Lizzy muttered wretchedly: "Sure. Sure. Today. Who knows about tomorrow?"

"In our days," chimed in Noralee, as ever practical, "the tsar's dragoons would have arrived and bloodied a few noses—"

She relished memories. She still remembered the imperial eagles—their outspread wings, their haughty beaks, the Cossacks with their uniform of blue and red and gold. She carried gaudy memories of lavish life designed for kings and courtiers. Her glance fastened firmly on Josie's.

But Josie was Josie—she just squared her chin. She rolled words on her tongue as though she were running for office. She knew precisely where to park her loyalties.

"The Russian people are the ones who work the land. No wonder they insist on putting their own profit in their pockets."

Doctorjay next took the issue by the forelock, so to speak.

"We know who engineered the Revolution, Josephine. If nothing else, that much we know. The tsars tried to tear them out by the roots—"

"What do they want? Why is enough never enough?" wailed Lizzy, desperate.

"What do they want?" cried Josie, furious. "Equality. They want equality. Equality for all. That's what they want. Equality. Why not? The Russian people are entitled to equality. Like everybody else."

Lizzy begged when she had wind again: "Let's wait for detail. Let's not panic." If it was serious business over there, at Apanlee, she knew she could depend on Uncle Benny to give her the straight facts.

Yet all the while, her knees and elbows locked with fear. Something was odd at Apanlee—but what? Daisy whimpered quietly to herself. Little Melly kept sipping her tea from the rim.

"Democracy? Don't make us laugh. That doesn't work in Russia," said Dewey.

But Josie's ears were closed. She was running the liberal fever full tilt; she was blazing with anger and fury; she kept tossing her head like a horse.

"If we're so democratic around here," cried Josephine, "how come we have no woman preachers? How come there's no woman governor? No woman senator? No woman president?"

All stared at her, aghast.

"Don't let me interrupt you in your thoughts—" said Josephine, and lit a cigarette, shaking. By then, she had taken up smoking.

Jan told her then and there: "Enough already, Josephine. I think you'd better put a padlock on your tongue—"

All heads went up. All eyes turned into searchlights. Was this the long-anticipated turn of tide?

"Had I been born a boy, you would not speak to me like that," said Josie after a long pause.

Exhaling. Falling back.

Jan minced no words. "Well, you were not. Just do yourself a favor. Calm yourself. Just calm yourself."

It was unusual to see Jan that upset. He hardly ever chastised

Josie. In fact, so much in love was he—this after all these years!—
that barely had he said those words, he went and bought his wife
a poodle. That's how upset he was.

An unarticulated dread became a sharpened spike that went
through every heart in Mennotown. Just what was going on in
Russia? The old and trusted order shook and trembled overseas
and, at long last, collapsed. Sharp editorials in several east coast
publications, which Josie ordered for herself to keep herself informed, applauded heartily.

It was clear the Hebrews had taken an axe to the legs of the
Romanoff throne. The result would be thistles and weeds. Some
people even claimed religion had collapsed, while others held
the lesser view: no, just the Christian holidays.

For weeks on end, the conversation always turned to Josie
and her Hebrews. There was no need to point it out: her new
friends at the Red Cross, mostly Jewish.

All, since the Middle Ages, money changers. Each one of
them, up to his ears in politics. All liberal to the hilt.

To be a Hebrew lover during peace was bad enough; in war,
where every sentence counted, that kind of thing was just like
wearing knickerbockers. It was too much. It was imperative to
wean her from her hazards.

Which now became the plan. The preachers said as much. In
Mennotown, you knew that Jews were useful citizens in times of
peace. In war, you had to watch. They all knew secrets of trading in grain they wouldn't reveal to outsiders. They had always,
it was understood far and wide, a devious, hidden agenda.

Besides, it wasn't easy being German in America. The
Donoghues' heckling just never let up. And where did they get
their ideas? From the Second Street Wichita Jews!

Although the war had worn down for some time and now the
aftermath was here, to be of German origin was still a shameful
stain. A Hun was still a Hun. That's what the papers said. They
shrieked that, with gallons of ink, tons of paper.

The only counter-weapon was neutrality and silence and keeping all your thoughts and your opinions to yourself.

Most citizens of Mennotown made sure they had a Hebrew
pal or two with whom they did their deals, and never mind the
curls. You treated them well, and why not? You liked them well
enough. You did whatever business came your way, with all your
cards out, open on the table.

But you tiptoed around them. Regardless.

You didn't bring them home for dinner, unless you were out
of your head. Just as you left your overshoes outside when you
had tracked them through the mud, so, too, you left the Jews
outside. The slowest dimwit knew that Jews had never liked the
tsars. If Jews deposed the tsars, what would be next? Wide skirts
in City Hall?

That's how it was in Mennotown where, after forty years of
life in a democracy, the good Lord and His German-speaking
Russian monarchy were still, if not synonymous, at least on
friendly terms.

But not a few of Josie's Jews in Wichita felt an ecstatic admiration for what was happening in Russia. Their battle cry was:
"More power to the Soviets! Land to the toiling masses!" She
called that sort of thing progressive. She talked things out with
them. She shuttled back and forth to Wichita as though she were
a weaver's shuttle.

"This Lenin guy," cried Josephine, while eating standing, too
high-strung to sit down. "A hero! A real hero!"

"Not so loud! Please! Keep your voice down!" Lizzy begged,
who had ample cause to mistrust any suffragette backer.

"You hear me? He will make rest homes out of palaces. He
plans enormous scholarships for poets."

Josie followed all political developments with eager energy,
thumbing through the picture magazines. Her beak did not snap
shut. She started stabbing with her pencil.

"See? Sweeping Russia of the debris of yesterday—that's
what it's all about. Planting snapdragons. Freeing peasants of
their bondage and freeing women of their slavery—"

Lizzy hardened herself on the spot. "And who'll do the cooking and baking?"

"Why not take turns? What's wrong with that?"

"A man on a sewing machine?"

"Free health care for the elderly. A savings bond for every new-born child! We ought to learn from Russia. Here in America, do we have benefits like that?"

"We live in Kansas, dear. It's different in Kansas. We have our choices here. We're mostly citizens relying on our families—"

"Right. That's my point. We have our choices here. The Russians never had a choice. Now it's their choice. It's Liberty. Fraternity. Equality. That's what it's all about."

"Okay. Okay. I said okay. Just leave me out."

Nobody quarreled with democracy. They had helped to forge equality out of the fissured soil of Kansas. If all the fuss on the old continent pertained to things like justice and equality, they were sure that their struggles would sort themselves out. At least that was their hope.

But Lizzy knew not even Doctorjay could hold his own when Josie started arguing equality. He'd scratch his head. He'd start to waffle dreadfully when Josie started serving up democracy by palming off the rights of the downtrodden.

A genuine American like Doctorjay agreed: less power to elites. More power to plain folks.

But Lizzy also saw the other side and couldn't close her eyes. It was enormously conflicting, this business of equality. The Donoghues already thought they were entitled to a life served on a silver platter, yet thought nothing of snoring a Monday away. Was that equality?

"For every toddler, Lizzy dear, a cup of milk," claimed Josie, looking sly, while battering already sore emotions. "Fresh from the udder, Lizzy! Foaming!"

Lizzy punched several pillows while making a bed for a visiting uncle. "Okay! Okay! I said okay! Just leave me out, I said!"

Lizzy was nearly blind, by now, and had some trouble hearing, but when her dogs brought in her cows, old Lizzy's heart still sang like a canary.

"The lowliest herdsman, nowadays, can draw a salary that's equal to a judge's salary."

"That's just a rumor. Nothing else."

Regardless of birth. Regardless of gender."

"Hold it. Stop it right there. Don't use that dirty word."

Chapter 49

The constant wailing of the suffragettes, as Dewey pointed out, for rights they didn't need and wouldn't win, was hard on everyone. The issue loomed large in the papers.

Meanwhile, the Methodists and Unitarians were warring over membership and cutting into Dewey's flock, but that was small potatoes compared to a portentious development: Jan's Josie was up for election. She was running for president of the regional suffragette club. She kept tacking up posters everywhere—even on fences, on barns and on trees.

"I do it as a public service," she argued herself ill. "The female vote will change America. Just wait and see. Just watch and wait and see."

She ran for office brazenly. Her plan to have a hand in politics showed up in telling ways. It was a chore to get her to sit down. She still was eating standing. She had her eye fixed firmly on the Chamber, which was the prelude for the kind of mischief everybody feared: to throw a monkey wrench into the power lunches the town's Rotarians put on.

If Lizzy said beatifically, attempting to distract her: "Looks like it's going to rain—" Josie would outguess her small maneuver on the spot and counter haughtily: "Don't get your hopes up, Lizzy dear. We're planning a rally tomorrow—"

It was time the deacons laid down the law. They had glued themselves to her heels; consensus stood behind the Elder Dewey like a mountain, solid.

By then, he was near comatose with wrath. He knew she couldn't be budged. Her eyes were beaten gold. She preened herself, oblivious to the heartache that she caused, as if she personally had a hand in Russia's Revolution, and Kansas would be next. All that came out of Russia. Taffeta hat and all, a rooster plume atop, she followed all developments in Russia as outlined in the papers.

"Do something! Do something!" begged Lizzy, who wouldn't let go of the bonesetter's sleeve.

Doctorjay, at his wits' end, racked his brain. A week went by, two weeks, before he found a wedge.

"You're at that age now, Josephine."

"Whatever do you mean?"

"You're triggering female disorders, including melancholia."

"Oh, just be quiet."

"What will be next? Tap dancing? Table tapping?"

"I don't see that I'm doing anybody any harm."

"Harrumph!"

"And I might do myself some good. To have a purpose makes me happy."

It was all clear to her. The long-suppressed, long-suffering peasants had finally cried out and overturned the old, established order. They made a Revolution on the old so as to build the new. She understood that cry. She sympathized with the oppressed. Had she not weaned herself on Uncle Benny's editorials?

She went to meeting after meeting and saw a sea of upraised faces. Here was excitement. Here was progress. It mattered little that the struggle raged on overseas—it was the ideology, the principle that counted. She launched her loyalties in turn.

"I do the things my conscience tells me must be done."

She clenched her fist. She wore a fiery scarf. "Oh, how I wish I could do more!" sighed Josephine. All of Jan's small change went straight into her purse and, not a few guessed angrily, from there into the pockets of the Jews.

She knew, she next confessed to Abigail while swearing her to secrecy, that many Jews of New York City were sending money, blankets, and rolled bandages to help to reinforce the Reds.

"We're rich. They're poor. This is about equality."

"That's what it's all about," said Abigail while standing at her elbow.

"Right. You can't ever do enough to lend a neighborly hand to the poor."

"Some go so far as to donate their wedding rings," suggested Abigail, but Josie shrank from that.

"I cannot bring myself to take the leap," said Josie wretchedly, who knew whereof Abigail spoke. She would not dip into Jan's bank account behind his back and write a hefty draft. She stopped short there, but she came close. She burned to be of aid. She was still powered by her memories of Apanlee and all that she and Uncle Benny had discussed so many times, the ins and outs, in reams of correspondence defining social justice.

"For, after all," said Josephine to Abigail, while glowing like a fireplace newly stoked with firs, "in many ways, this Revolution has to do with Apanlee. I still remember Apanlee. I clearly see the gap."

"That's right. The gap. Between the haves and the have-nots."

"That's what I always say." Josie spoke from personal authority. She still remembered everything. She still remembered being *herrenvolk*, devouring berries by the fistful while Russian peasant children stood and watched.

"Well, then?"

"I'm racking my brains for a simple way out, but all I have is mostly Jan's and Lizzy's money."

"Sure. Doubtfully acquired," said Abigail, whose sons still

sought that missing document that would have transferred title.

"We don't know that," said Josie, reddening.

"But we suspect," said Abigail.

When odd, disjointed stories started trickling into Kansas that Russia's earth was turning red, Josie put on her dark glasses. Not true, said Josephine.

"No doubt," she argued lamely when word came of enormous ethnic suffering, "the country is cleaning the house."

The dream for true equality, she amplified, punching a down comforter with both fists, could never be corrupted—although, admittedly, the government of Russia was now beset by foreign intervention and counter-Revolution.

It was a languid afternoon. Five visitors had come for coffee and were now sitting on the porch.

"That's leadership? You call that leadership?"

"Yes, leadership," insisted Josephine, a fine sheen on her face.

They watched how she painted herself into a corner. Remember her *papa*? He, too, was afflicted with tongues.

"The kind of leadership I speak about," said Josie, practically shouting, "knows how to court the power of the people. It pays attention to the wishes of the populace. It will curb the almighty power of monopolies. It will not tolerate fat bureaucrats."

"You wish to help the Bolsheviks?"

She was rocked back on her heels. She claimed she had no wish to help the Bolsheviks, but neither did she wish to stop them.

"Their females count as well. Their women can be anything that they decide to be."

Closed eyelids, that was all.

The Elder Dewey led the way. The Elder knew that it was now or never. He had laid siege, successfully, to many crusted sinners in the past.

Clad in his Sunday best and wielding an umbrella to brave whatever weather, he was determined not to leave until he had a firm solution in his pocket. It had been many years since he'd gone on a mission quite as clear.

Behind him, single file, walked Lizzy, Daisy, Little Melly, Doctorjay, Archie and Noralee. All came well fortified with Truth. So what if Josephine had on her side the force of learned argument—which was already hardly possible!—they had experience on their side, and common sense, and unity, and best of all, the Gospel. And they had strength in numbers.

"We need to have a talk. A smooth but long talk, Josephine."

She heated, reddened like a stove. Her forehead rested in her hands. She hardly looked up, but the sheen on her face became deeper.

"How are you, Josephine?"

"Much better than could be expected."

"Still working in the Red Cross office?"

"I am."

"What are you doing there?"

"I'm speeding social victory."

"I'm glad to hear that. Mighty glad. I called a special prayer breakfast for next Saturday to help speed social victory. I'm sure you'll want to join us."

"I'm having trouble with my goiter."

"Coming to prayer breakfast will do wonders for your goiter. You take it to heart and let it bear fruit."

"My goiter?"

"Our prayer breakfast, Josie. What's the matter? Are you sick?"

She wouldn't even rise to shake the Elder's hand or take his overshoes. She sat there, by the window, defiant and alone, while Lizzy, Noralee and Little Melly marched past her chair into her kitchen to start the hospitality.

The Elder Dewey put his felt hat on the hat rack, his umbrella in the corner. "Now, Josie. Pay attention. We have come to check on certain facts—"

"The facts are no secret. I am up for election. I'll probably win. I'll be happy to give you some facts. We have twenty-seven chapters. Five hundred and thirty eight members. Besides Kansas, we embrace Colorado. Nebraska. Missouri. Oklahoma. We are a political force the House and Senate can't ignore. Our platform calls for—"

"Where will it end?"

"What's that supposed to mean?"

"Out with the truth!"

"We have ambitions, Dewey. Legitimate ambitions."

"To be elected governor?"

"Why not? What's wrong with that? The day will come when we'll have female governors."

"Look at yourself. Is that a wedding ring that's on your finger? Does that not mean a thing? Someone spied you in the Workers' Hall. By going there, you undermine your spouse who has a payroll of three hundred workers. You give the enemy support. Has all good sense deserted you?"

She raised her chin. "With little standing in my own community, I am invited everywhere in Wichita."

"I heard you talked Jan into buying stock in airships, Josephine?"

"I did."

"These thoughts come straight from Satan."

"I am a human being."

"We're human beings. We're not birds. We aren't meant to fly. My flivver's pulling forty miles an hour." The Elder deftly changed his strategy. He started shouting angrily: "If God had meant for Jan to fly, He would have grown him feathers!"

She shouted back: "If God had meant for you to have a flivver, Dewey, He would have grown you rubber wheels!"

To say that he was shocked was putting it politely, for never within living memory had anybody ever spoken cheekily to any preacher, mediator between man and God.

"That's blasphemy!"

She would yet eat those words in public, if Dewey had his way. He kept on chewing furiously, while pondering a comeback.

"An air road," announced Josephine, triumphantly, "is in the works, and it will make all flivvers obsolete. It's true! It will stretch all the way from Washington to Apanlee—"

"She's looney. Like her Papa," the clan concluded silently. Their eyes were round as saucers.

"Who," ventured Dewey slowly, "would want to fly to Apanlee? You hear these horror stories—"

"I would," chirped Lizzy, desperate, a master at diffusing. "I never quite lost hope of visiting with Uncle Benny, and to embrace and kiss him joyfully."

But Josie, being Josie, was on a roll, and would not be restrained. She curled her tongue around another argument. She said, maliciously: "Don't get all hopped up, Dewey, about a thing you just don't understand. In Wichita, there is another world. You might as well inhabit caves, for all your backwardness. You're out of step. You plain have no idea! No idea! The world is changing, Dewey. It's changing for the better. A speaker at the Workers' Hall predicted just the other day that workers' wages soon will double, and next in line—"

"Fine pickles. Fine pickles," said Little Melly, crunching noisily. "Is that a special recipe? Do you mind sharing it?"

"I do."

Ear to ear, that was the spinster's grin. "Is that Sears coffee, Josie?"

"It is."

"Oh, hi there, Jan. Come in. Come in. Come in and join us, will you? Guess what? We're visiting with Josie. How is the weather treating you? Still fighting the jackrabbits?"

Jan nodded warily, while standing in the door. "What's up? What's going on? Are you folks ganging up on Josie?"

Jan was a tired man; he had been up since dawn. The previous summer had been short and searing, the winter full of ice; the hungry rabbits came from nowhere, eating everything that grew. His eyes went from one caller to the other.

"What has she done this time? Another Bolshie plot? Move over, Little Melly. Let me sit down. The rabbits are a pest.

They're simply everywhere you step." Lopsided smile: "Just like the suffragists."

That's how Jan put a stop to almost any argument—he pulled the stinger out.

But Josie was, by then, beyond the bounds of reason. The laughter was at her expense. She turned a fiery red. "Jan, will you please not trivialize—"

He gently shushed a puppy that was gnawing on his shoe-lace. "What's up? That's all I asked. I need some peace and quiet. I just don't understand—"

"If Jan can't understand, who can?" asked Dewey righteously. "We have an argument that's begging to be settled."

"Well, fill me in. What do we need to settle?"

"For one, this airship business, Jan." The Elder felt a rush of blood; he saw Jan flinch and knew that he struck near the truth. "Out with the truth. Is that a Hebrew deal? How much did you invest? The church is still unfinished."

"Travel by airship all over the globe," coaxed Josie, "is only a hair's breadth away. Right, Jan? Am I not right, Jan? Tell them why airship bonds are now considered prime investments."

"You're right," said Jan, still looking puzzled. This was a weary argument, with more miles than his flivver's. "We've been over all this before. It's very simple, really. If you put all your savings in a jar, it doesn't grow. It stays the same amount. Whereas investment in a bank that deals in stocks and bonds—"

"No doubt the money grabbers put that idea in your head by using Josie as a decoy to pull your dollars from your pockets. Where will it end? The usurers again! They'll be your downfall, Jan. They're using Josephine."

"Not so. I never—"

"That's not how we do business." The Elder spoke past Josie. "We know the value of an honest dime. Our money does not grow on trees and is not meant to multiply through wrongful in-terest in stock of dubious value. Remember how our Lord went out and broke Himself a switch and drove the usurers right out of their own temple?"

You could have cut the tension with a knife. To break it,

Lizzy spoke a bit too crisply. "Look. Look. It's just a little airline."

"That's right," said Josie, flaming now. "It has a board. It has a nice portfolio. I had this tip. A friend of mine gave me this tip. I merely passed it on. I mentioned it to Jan. It is an excellent investment—"

Dewey kept on slurping thoughtfully. "Sears coffee, huh? A bit expensive, no? Add just a little bit more milk. Oh, thank you! Thank you kindly, Lizzy! I like my coffee pretty strong. But not that strong. What friend?"

"One of the Finkelsteins."

"I see."

"He knows a lot about the stock exchange—"

"You bet they do. You betcha! The banksters will yet be the downfall of your husband, Josie." The Elder Dewey shifted his pale gaze as though it were a timid searchlight and let it rest on Jan. "Speak up. What do you have to say in your defense? What is the sense of flying? Why not keep both feet firmly planted on the ground? The airline's just a cover, right? This business about Russian aid is just a cover? The money really goes to this—this silly drive to get the female vote locked in place? You know that that is only the beginning. Away from pots and pans!"

The treacherous pink that Jan knew so well, the color he loved and feared, ran slowly into Josie's neckline. She took a trembling breath, but she restrained herself. She spoke as calmly as she could, which was no small endeavor. "It is the future, folks. Before this century is out, the sky will be awash—"

"I think that your wife, Jan, is running a fever," boomed Doctorjay. "She needs to be cooled down." He poked his elbow in Jan's ribs. "What did I tell you just the other day? Remember?"

"Excuse me," said Josie, "but it must be said. What Jan does with his hard-earned money is none of anybody's business. It's not your business, Dewey. It's not your business, Lizzy. It's not your business, Cousin Melly. It's private. Private. It's just between my husband and myself—"

"Not quite," said Dewey Epp. He studied her with bitter joy.

"One thing we know with certainty: our good Lord calls the shots. The Lord gave Jan his riches. Lavishly. Our Lord may well decide to take them back if you dilute your husband—"

"I'm not diluting Jan. I'm not diluting anyone. I'm not diluting anything. I am giving the future my best—"

"Are you being paid for all that pecking that you do, down at the Red Cross quarters?"

"Male wages! Here. Try my watermelon rind."

"And do you really need the money?"

"Not really. No. Do you?"

Jan shifted with discomfort. "Every penny of her wages, Dewey," he apologized against his will, "goes straight into the Red Cross kitty. She donates every penny."

"Sure. And from there, straight into Hebrew coffers."

"Come on, now. You exaggerate."

"You know the Red Cross is a cover for all the Jews' shenanigans. They like to hide behind those tax exempt foundations."

"She's merely rolling bandages and keeping track of the supplies. She's doing nothing wrong. She doesn't cause anyone harm—"

"Jan, I can surely speak for myself—"

Jan started puffing on his pipe. "And here I was trying to help."

He started buttering a roll. He stretched his legs and turned to Doctorjay: "Let's change the subject now. The jackrabbits are ruining me. I've set a hundred traps—"

Here's where the story should have ended, as it had ended every single time with every single argument before. Jan's veto should have settled it. He still had veto power.

At least they thought he did.

But not this time. Josie's collar grew hotter and hotter. She looked like a goose about to be plucked. She leaped from her chair as if launched like a rocket.

"All right! Let's have it out. Once and for all, let's have it out. I feel proud and privileged to help build a better tomorrow by fostering equality today. Equality for all! For myself! For my six lovely girls! For the women of America! Right here in my own country. Right here at my front door!"

"If you have extra time and extra energy," suggested Dewey Epp while flicking dust specks from his trousers, "after having done your household chores and charities and place cards for the Chamber, why don't you knit your bit?"

"Knit my bit?" shrieked Josie, trembling.

"Knit your bit," repeated Dewey, leaning back, exhaling softly.

"Knit your bit," said Daisy, dusting herself with a napkin.

"Knit your bit?" said Lizzy, pleadingly, and placed her old and wrinkled hand on Josephine's left knee. "Yes! Knit your bit. That's good advice. That's excellent advice. Just knit your bit, and in the meantime—"

"Knit your bit—" said Little Melly, too, who couldn't help herself. "—why, any woman worth her salt should surely feel both proud and privileged—" She herself had spent months knitting woollies for those handsome Kansas boys while they were sitting in wet trenches. "Jan? It's your turn. Tell her. Tell her! Tell her that she should knit her bit."

"Yes. Knit your bit," said Jan, who liked to tease and tickle, who always made a joke to ease the tension in his kitchen when females worked each other into a serious funk. He threw his hands up with a laugh that had an edge in it. "Why can't you knit your bit? Just knit your bit. That would solve many problems."

It was oblique, yet it was like a shot. She took a trembling breath and reached for something deep within.

"Look here. Let's put our cards out on the table. This really isn't about airships, is it? It really isn't about money, is it? This isn't about knitting, is it? This is about the fact that Jan has only sired girls—"

"Six times," thought Lizzy wretchedly, "he heard the midwife say it was a girl, and not a single word!"

Jan twirled his mustache thoughtfully while stirring sugar in his coffee. Daisy expelled three sharp little cries. Old Doctorjay kept swiveling his red mane side to side as though he were a lion. Beside him, Noralee just held her breath and hoped she wouldn't faint. Little Melly inspected a hangnail, which triggered a series of thoughts. A slow, triumphant light seeped into Dewey's eyes. Doctorjay gave a guffawing laugh. Noralee squirmed in her seat while craning her neck, and no wonder. For now the Elder Dewey had the scent, and it was sweet and righteous in his nostrils. He knew nature's ways; he was getting the Biblical drift. He knew where it said about being a man and having a surplus of daughters while lacking a boy to pass on a fine family name.

"It isn't yet too late, is it?" He surveyed Josephine appraisingly. "You're not yet old enough to mothball your last diaper?" The Elder lurched forward. He went for the jugular swiftly.

"I must ask a question that is of a personal nature. You aren't exactly a spring chicken, Josie. How much time is left? How old are you now?"

"Meanwhile, eat. Meanwhile, eat," Lizzy practically wept.

This was a hand grenade. He carefully pulled out the pin and let fly: "How many daughters, Josie? Five? Six?" You couldn't blame Dewey for having lost count, for the birthdays of females were seldom recorded. "But where, Josephine, is Jan's son?"

She fished a cigarette from her pocket, and a match. She lit that cigarette, and she filled her lungs. She filled them just as deeply as she could. She stood before her husband now, on tiptoes practically, a flaming female anarchist, blowing smoke in his face and shame into his heart.

"Health permitting. Health permitting," said Josie with icy precision.

It was as if sharp lightning struck and broke a tree right down the middle. At her words, a silence fell. It numbed. It withered everything. According to family legend, that is how Josephine, near the end of her childbearing years, pierced the heart of a very good man. Time would erase most any other trespass Josie had amassed. These words would never die. They stored within the clan's collective memory. No choice was left. She brought it on herself.

About the matrimonial sequel, both partners would be silent, and we can only guess. But the outcome was this: She lost, and he won. His nails tore away, but he won.

Chapter 50

As the war on the Old Continent drew to an anguished close, Josie gave birth to a fine baby boy.

She lay in her pillows, gray and exhausted. Her age didn't help; it would be her last, it had been a difficult birth. The global flu that claimed its victims by the millions nearly did her in as well. It hit so hard in certain parts of Kansas, no room was left in church for all the funeral wreaths.

It was a somber time. The relatives sat in respectful silence before the mystery of death, while Dewey passed the plate.

The globe still turned. The seasons came and went.

A war was winding down; several monarchies had fallen; democracy had proven superior to other forms of government; all wanted to get back-to-normalcy, as Little Melly put it.

Lizzy slipped on a watermelon rind and was laid up for weeks. Dewey said successful prayers over an afflicted child. Little Melly settled wisely a dispute between two feuding neighbors—one owner owned a goose intent on nesting in an outhouse, the other owned the outhouse chosen by the goose. The cataclysmic question: who owned that set of goslings?

Two simultaneous weddings were announced—two sisters marrying two brothers. Two houses were duly enlarged. Two rooms in the attic were added.

The oldsters passed quietly on. New babies arrived. The darning needles flew; the ladies of the Sewing Club conversed at length about the merits of the Savior.

The church still held the universe in place. The porch steps were for gossip.

The relatives from Saskatoon, Saskatchewan, who took advantage of the spell of harmony that came with Josie staying in the hospital much longer than the norm, departed finally with many hugs and kisses, but not before they telephoned; that was the ritual.

"The menace of the suffragists," they told the folks back home, "did not cause havoc quite as much in Mennotown as we had feared at first. Our folks are stout in Faith."

Lizzy waved them off, relieved, and poured herself a cup of strong, hot coffee before she stripped the sheets. By then, she was waiting for guests from Vancouver who had announced their coming. Before they came, they telephoned, and here is how that went:

"It's your turn, Lizzy. Really."

"No. No. You first. I visited last year."

"Won't we be in the way?"

"Please come and stay. Please do! At least a week. A month?"

"Don't go to any trouble."

"I won't. I won't. Please. Come next week. If you don't come and visit me, my heart will burst with sorrow."

Lizzy's world was restored to acceptable rules. So what if she was still up to her ears in household chores, in cleaning up post-Saskatoon? She glowed with blessed fervor. She knew her relatives, knew all their wiles. She knew that they'd show up when she was still arm-deep in suds, the better to gossip craftily behind her back and think they were not heard.

"Please come before the icicles begin to drip, " she stressed, to show that when it came to extra guests—why, she slept soundly.

Always. She was her neighbors' better any day. She set a lavish table. Lizzy wasn't like some folks she knew, who didn't even sweep. Her sheets were crisp, her recipes flawless, her household staples locked in place, to the last jar and bucket. Come summer time, her cows walked past their ankles in the lushest grass imaginable—no lack of butter, cream, or cheese.

Ach! Gossip about Mennotown telephonically? Just let them only try!

The relatives might drop in, claiming they would stay a week and then stay for a year: but she was well prepared. Her milk house and her smoke house, too, now came with electricity. In olden days, there was the added chore of dipping candles, but no more—with modern electricity, you pulled a string or flipped a switch; that's all there was to that.

By then, the telephone was commonplace. The world was changing drastically. Modernity was on the march. Not even Dewey hinted any more that it was Lucifer that ran along those wires.

Jan Neufeld was a happy man; he had a brand new son. He even took a day off work, smack in the middle of the week. He donned his finery and visited his wife at Brookside Hospital.

It was late afternoon. The air was chill outside, but inside all was cozy. In his gnarled fist Jan held a bundle of forget-me-nots made from crepe paper and starched twine. Across his face, there stretched a smile as wide as the Kansas horizon.

There was a screen in front of Josie's bed to cut down on unhealthy drafts. A sign said she preferred no visitors.

Jan pushed it aside and sat down on the edge of her bed.

She did not drop her gaze, but it was blind. It held no love. It held no anger either.

The flames kept leaping in the charcoal pan the nurse had set up near the bed to toast the mother's cheeks a bit, but not a glimmer of the dancing fire reflected in her eyes. For quite a while, Jan looked at her in silence.

She veiled herself as closely as she could. A force drove her into herself.

In the end, he tried to tease: "What am I in for now?"

The silence filled the sickroom, floor to ceiling, wall to wall. No fire could melt it away.

"Say something, Josie. Please."

She faced her husband fully. "You pinned me. Like an insect."

He took her hand and held it lovingly between his hardened palms. He cleared his throat. "I used to think that Dewey knew more about heaven and hell than I did. Now I'm not so sure."

There was no fury now in Josie, only a silence, thick as the fog that veiled the chimneys in November. She looked at him, but she was far away.

He told her awkwardly: "That's some baby, Josie. Beautiful. Like you. Look at his tapered fingers."

She spoke at last. "He will be first in all his classes. He will grow up to be an artist and a dreamer—"

And the writing was plain on the wall. But she said it lowkey, almost hushed, and Jan was clearly in no mood to challenge her; he never tired of her whims; he was, in fact, quite overcome; it was as though a gloved hand had been clopped right across his mouth; the words she might have longed to hear just wouldn't come.

"The war is over now," he said, instead, and that was that. He thought that that sufficed. The baby boy stirred gently, and Jan's eyes clouded over.

"I ask for your forgiveness. If it makes a difference."

"It doesn't. It's too late."

He looked as though he had robbed and plundered. She looked as though she had taken a hammer and driven an icicle straight through her heart.

But greater, vastly greater than his shame and sorrow was his joy. He had a son. He loved her as he always had, and knew he always would. She was still there, for all to see. But she no longer struggled.

Jan patted her hand and said nothing.

After giving birth to Rarey, Josie was laid up for weeks, remaining weak and feverish. When she could stand again, she leaned her face against the window and wept briefly.

When she was finished giving way, she said with a small smile: "Don't expect me to change overnight. I'll always mix debit and credit—"

Jan placed her chair beside the stove. "A blanket? A cushion? A book?" Still a devoted husband, he shielded her. He petted her. He loved her to excess.

"For Josie, books and happiness are one," he said to Doctorjay, who slapped him on his shoulder, man to man.

In the decade that followed, Jan was increasingly active in public affairs. Three years in a row, he was voted the fundraising chairman of Mennotown's Chamber of Commerce. He presided at the Rotary Club and became its District Governor, high honor indeed. He rounded out his generosity by supporting the Needle Club Temperance Drive, which Little Melly chaired.

No doubt in anybody's mind that Jan was Sedgwick County's most respected leader! If a small grandchild skinned a knee, Jan knelt and soothed it.

The president of the United States announced a visit to Topeka to cut the ribbon for the annual state fair. He predicted a progressive future, and everybody cheered. All of Jan and Josie's daughters wore ribbons in their buttonholes for Lizzy's splendid calves. Those girls took after Lizzy—between them, they milked sixteen cows.

Old Lizzy groomed them carefully. All practiced their *vareniki* with marriage in mind, though one of them—her name, quite tellingly, was Wichita!—was clearly on the plain side. No wonder Josie spruced her up. With a mouthful of malice, Little Melly dropped dark hints.

"The right man," Little Melly hissed behind her handkerchief to no one in particular but loud enough for anyone to hear, "will have to come along, then close his eyes, before he marries

Wichita."

A few folks raised their heads.

"It's now or never, Wichita," urged Little Melly, who spoke from hard experience; her chance had slipped between her fingers. "Don't sleep away our luck. Don't clatter when you set the table. Don't trample on your chances. Be nice to Archibald."

The girl blew her nose in her apron and fled while shedding tears. The spinster shouted after her, firing her parting shot: "You hear me? Pay attention. It will be touch and go."

She told bystanders: *"Ach!* Does she think, foolishly, that fellows grow on trees?"

That was a malicious remark. As such, it was open to challenge. But Josie let the dagger pass, unusual for her. Her thoughts were somewhere else.

Jan ran his fingers through his earth and felt it crumble in his fingers.

He bent down to the newborn, and told him: "The times are bright with hope."

In his Bible, Jan Neufeld wrote with trembling fingers: "The Lord has shed his blessings. His name is Peet. Peet Neufeld, named after a respected ancestor."

Josie did not contradict him openly. She said as softly as she could, glancing at her lap: "You name him what you will. I'll always call him Rarey—"

In weeks to come, she systematically surrendered all that she had cherished in the past. She parted with her looking glass. She gave her parasol to Abigail. She mothballed her red scarf. Her yellow pad flew in the fire where slogans turned to ashes. At Doctorjay's insistence, she wrote a long poem to spruce up the Fourth of July, and she didn't mistake a lake for the sky, nor vice versa.

Not that the change was all that radical. No one changes overnight, and Josie didn't either. The best that could be said of her was this: she tried. She genuinely tried.

She might take Lizzy's rocking chair, but did she rock it?

No. She sat there, motionless, and stared into a void.

The flu postponed the female victory, but in the end, they had the vote; yet life was still the same.

Jan bought a brand new traction engine plow to add to his Goliath fleet. He built a bigger barn to house his mother's cows.

Churchgoing. Childbearing. Funerals. Picnics.

"To each his own," decided Little Melly evenly.

She knew a woman's brain was not as capable. She knit. She mended. She embroidered a shaving container for Archie, who was a bit foppish in manner. The relations of the sexes were still a mystery to Little Melly, but even she could see—her Archie was rather a sissy.

Romantically speaking, you had to call him slow. He had a girl's soft cheeks. A Donoghue had noticed his emotional delay and scribbled "queer" across his jacket. The snickers never stopped.

For Little Melly, prim and neat, that was a nasty shock. Now was the time for forming proper habits. She knew she had to have a first-rate talk with Archibald—but how? The words just weren't there. She still was largely virginal in thought. Experience was missing.

As time went on, she worried more and more. So much did Little Melly worry over Archibald she once milked the last drop from a cow and let its calf go hungry. But what she lacked in first-hand facts, determination rounded out. In the end, Little Melly put down her needle and put on her hat. The prairie seethed with rumors.

A letter came from Russia. A second. Then a third. She did not even open them. They caused no stir in Josie. No longer did she thirst for news that had to do with politics. All that was now behind her, thankfully.

When visitors arrived to see how she was doing, she filled their empty cups. She did her best to cook acceptable *vareniki*. She cultivated interest in cupcake recipes. She stirred her pride into her mashed potatoes and smiled while doing so, a castle ghost.

But the Finkelstein pamphlets were gone—hallelujah! The female aggression was gone—praise the Lord!

When she and Lizzy now conversed, they did so calmly, without shouting, and once an argument was settled, they always hugged each other.

Now very old and nearly blind, old Lizzy went limp with relief. She knew that all of this was wondrous beyond words.

"God mend you, child. God mend you," she said to Josephine, now sporting many wrinkles, like any other woman of her age.

"No prayers are in vain," she added for good measure, thus gently nudging Josephine, who still did not reply.

Most striking of all was this silence. She had run out of words.

As August gave way to September, a doctor came from Wichita, pulled out a dangling instrument, stuck it in both his ears, and listened to her heart. She sat there like a shell, forgetting to button her blouse, until Lizzy, peeking through the keyhole, rushed in and pushed the *medicus* aside to help her back to modesty.

In essence, she had given up the battle.

The decade that historians later called the Roaring Twenties did not stir Josephine. Time and Old Lizzy's sour cream took off the edge of sadness in the end. The townfolks took her pessimistic moods for granted and ignored them. The trick was to outlast them.

She still backed mild, progressive causes, and every now and then, she went to check on friends in Wichita. By nighttime, she was back.

No longer did she see the need to speak those sharp and hurting words that wounded relatives. No longer did she buy a paper when she could borrow one. And best of all, no longer did she argue irritatingly that if you traveled long enough, the west became the east.

Not even the Rotarian lunches meant anything to her. Her husband had his proper place, and she had hers, and that was that. The neighborhood relaxed.

For Christmas, she bought Jan a compost tumbler, and he bought her a butter churn, identical to Lizzy's. As season followed season, she even joined the Doily Club, without a doubt the most prestigious female enterprise in town, because she realized the cash raised from the annual fair booths that Little Melly ran would help bring Christ to erring heathen in Borneo.

"Why not?" she said, and shrugged.

When Dewey pushed his luck and told her: "Josephine! Good deeds alone won't do. Your Savior died for you—" she said in weary resignation: "I know. I know. While writhing on the cross—"

He knew when to back off. As a guest on her davenport couch, you showed your respect by eating and drinking. Dewey inspected his plate and found there no cause for complaint. Ham, cured with the finest corncob smoke. Peanuts. Raisin bread. Crisp gherkins from ripe brine. Everything in right proportion, daintily arranged.

"Harrumph," he said at last, half-grudgingly.

"Bless you!" said Josephine.

Once she was overheard to say: "It's people who invent the gods; it's not the other way around," but Dewey checked that out against the Scriptures and said that that was progress.

"That's progress. Real progress," said Dewey.

He was glad to let bygones be bygones. He kept an anxious watch on her, on call to help her in her struggle against sin; he even told her so, but that was mere formality.

"Just call on me. Call anytime. Just anytime at all," said Dewey.

She thanked him for his offer with a dilapidated smile.

"Not even God," said she, now echoing her husband, "can alter last year's harvest."

Glad for the hard-won victory, the Elder Dewey nodded soothingly. Here was a lukewarm Christian, but that was better by a mile than to see Josie strut through the entire neighborhood the haughty Hottentot of yore.

"Be sure to remember my work in your prayers," he told her, and gave her a pat on the cheek.

For pray she did. She said she did; she told Jan so; she said she genuinely tried, and since she never lied—not her worst enemy could claim the Devil ever made her speak the smallest lie!—the Elder Dewey was relieved.

No need to boot her from his church and thus shame Jan, more generous than ever.

Chapter 51

After Satan's hooves had clattered eastwards at the break of a stunned dawn, numb neighbors crept out of the bushes: *"Bozhe moi! Bozhe moi!* At Apanlee, did anyone survive?"

Some did, but many died. The earth took them back, one by one.

A mass grave, shoveled with the help of grieving neighbors, enfolded the remains of Hein, the hunchback and his gentle Dorothy, all of Marleen's beloved progeny except the twins and Mimi, and dozens of ill-fated relatives who happened to be visiting. No one found a trace of Jonathan, although Natasha kept on keening for the little boy long after the others gave up.

She was like a desperate cat in search of her favorite kitten. "Who'll cuddle you? Who'll sing to you? Who'll tuck you in at night?"

The twins tried to comfort their Baba. "He's asleep in God's mercy, Natasha—"

Sooner the sea will give up her dead than a survivor will give up his Faith. Why else had they been spared? Why two of them, alike?

By the grace of a merciful God; that was why.

Everything was gray on gray: the earth, the sky, the people's faces. The only thing that shone was Faith. It shone in the twins like a beacon. Engraved upon their inner eye remained a night beyond the grasp of human comprehension—and now, before them, what?

That was the question mark.

Behind them, stiffening their spines, lay centuries of persecuted piety that had carved as a prime theme this: all suffering was pre-ordained. All tears were meant to wash one's eyes so as to better read the Ten Commandments. That's what they now believed.

For centuries, Faith yielded ready warmth. Now it sprang into flame.

Never keener on the Gospel than the rest of Apanlee, two young survivors found themselves now on the threshold of maturity, drenched with their Faith, consumed by Faith, enraptured and enthralled by Faith. Faith suffused every thought. Faith sustained and controlled them completely. Faith had become the critical ingredient. Without it, nothing balanced.

How else could they have borne the knowledge that they had lifted not one little finger to stop the slaughter of their kin? They had hidden themselves in the chimney.

They knew survivors' guilt before that phrase was coined. With Faith locked into place by tragedy, the earth rotated on its axis—and right around the earth, the sun. A wobbly earth—but still.

It's strange with Faith and those it wins by soothing woes the likes of which no animal can feel. Faith will not grow a leg. It cannot make the sun set in the east, nor make a river run uphill. And yet, the laws of nature, grim and rigid, will matter not one whit to a survivor who needs to set his guilt aside by reading travesty as meaning.

For two young men, their forebears' Faith, until then largely ritual, became a thing apart. It cast its iron roots into the bloody soil of Apanlee—ghost country now, where those who managed to survive lost every other earthly gift of reason.

Faith spoke its litany hypnotically—the kind of litany you hear at any funeral: "And who am I to question Thee? Thy will be done. Forever."

That's Faith. It softens, and it blurs.

It calmed the twins. Had it not been for Faith, they told themselves, could they have faced a mirror? They clung to Faith with a defiant loyalty. Their eyes were smoky suns.

Faith helped Marleen as well. Faith spoke to her with velvet tongues. Here's what Marleen kept hearing, and what she fervently believed: those murdered children, one by one, once put into her loving arms to live a long and fruitful life, fell accidentally into the Lord's soft palms like beads from a cut string.

That was her Faith. She had no other choice. It was as if she knelt before the smallest of all flames. She put both hands around it, cupping it and shielding it, knowing that if anguish quenched that tiny source of warmth, she might as well be dead.

"He'll dry all eyes, and ease all pain," Marleen said many times in years to come, and who would have the heart to call that sham? To call that travesty? She needed Faith far more than doubt—how else could she have lived?

She shuddered, now and then, as if from cudgel blows, but she echoed her psalms as she should. Thus did she lean on Faith—not for those she had lost, but on behalf of those who still clung to the margin—her twin sons and her only daughter, Mimi.

She didn't even add into her sad equation the whimpering small speck of life for whom, tomorrow, if not sooner, the grave was waiting, too.

Faith was not all that potent in Natasha. She was a realist.

She saw no choice at all, she keened—as the days faded slowly and Apanlee faced its first winter without grain—but to assume that her favorite youngster had choked on the flames, along with the chickens and ducks. She only hoped, she wept, while dab-

bing at her swollen eyes, her little darling's agony was swift.
She hoped, but she knew better. And little difference did it make
when the twins tried to soften her grieving. "Where little Jonathan
is now, there is no sorrow and no pain."

She was not easily deceived. If he was dead, death had come
hard. If he was still alive—as well he might be; who could
say?—would days to come be any easier for a small and gentle
boy used to his honey spoon?

She hoped and feared, she wept, that he was still alive and
one day would return. Where might he be? Had the assassins
carried off her valentine?

With trembling hands, she carefully inscribed the missing
youngster's name on the back of her favorite icon.

"His name was Jonathan," she wrote in awkward letters. Let
not the saints forget! She kept that icon hidden in a jar behind
her onion strings.

"These days," she told Marleen, "you cannot be too careful."

"Yes. Many hazards. Many hazards." Marleen just nodded,
sparingly. "Particularly for the twins."

The thugs had run their bayonets right through the spine of
every handy Bible. The government had since declared that God
was dead, then added injury to blasphemy by labeling His help-
ers parasites, and her two sons, now yearning to serve Faith by
tending to the vineyards of their Lord, could find themselves en-
snared by faceless shadows, hidden hands, if they did not watch
out.

"Where will it end, Marleen?"

No one knew. No one could even guess. The New World
Order had arrived. Both dreaded the knock on the blood-spat-
tered window: "The censor wants to see you."

The night light barely flickered. The frost clung to the au-
tumn leaves. The halls of Apanlee, still hung with many ancestors, were dank and drafty as though overcast by fog.

"He who gave us our blessings lavishly in richer times,"
Marleen said to Natasha, "can also take them back."

Natasha only shrugged. The anarchists? Hell belched them up and took them back! That was her own opinion. The dreadful tsars were gone, the government proclaimed repeatedly the saints were dead as well; the church stood dark and mildewed.

"Red forever! Red forever!" came the shouts of visionary leadership that kept on rolling over corpses as though they were but logs. The pentagram flashed gaudily from many grimy collars.

Marleen kept hugging her knees. Subdued—but not destroyed! For she had Faith! She wore it like a purple heart— that faith of hers that told her suffering gave meaning.

Her former life, now altered beyond recognition, lay in sad ruins at her feet, but Marleen did not point a finger at Him who set the pride of centuries aflame. It was clear her spirit was breaking; almost all of her children were dead; but still, she said nothing; she never once questioned the Lord.

She kept cradling her Faith—that was that.

A potent elixir.

It numbed the blinding mass of pain where once she had carried a heart.

All was survival now.

Most earthly wishes had fallen by the wayside. More than just the woe, the guilt, the sorrow, and the loss—this was a trial, a test. Marleen was bowing to the will of God as though she had been knighted.

"We must have Faith. That's it." This was her litany. She came from an unbroken line—ten generations of martyrs. She drew on Faith and fortitude; she said not one rebellious word against God's bloody handiwork. He had taken her children by bullet and hatchet and had softened the earth with their blood. He wounded, then healed. He gave, and then withheld.

"It must be true," Natasha countered softly, not in the mood to argue.

"It's true. He is the staff on which we lean—" Such was Marleen's despotic Faith, abiding and relentless.

"All right. All right. It's true."

Now, as before, Natasha was merely a nanny, a maid, but when she sat next to Marleen and watched her reach for Faith as though for food and drink, she had no choice; she had to ask herself, a realist: "Marleen's God is a God of love? What kind of love would drink that kind of blood?"

Natasha and Marleen no longer quarreled with each other. All that was yesterday.

Natasha cast shy glances—Marleen looked brutally abused, all bent and crushed, a collapsed butterfly, her wings pulled from their sockets. There was no point in making matters worse.

As for herself, she would have liked a fierce and crafty argument. Instead, Natasha parlayed several wonder-working saints. She lined them up and scolded them repeatedly.

She read them a long list of pressing needs. She launched into brisk common sense. She liked to keep her irons in the fire.

She asked for many special favors while slowly sucking on a crust. The crust was meant for dinner, but she would have it now. "There's five of us still left," she told her vacant saints so they would not forget. She paused, then added, swallowing: "Well, six, to be exact."

The pygmy child was still alive and stirring. She kept it in the half-charred wicker basket and hummed soft lullabies.

It had been a game to cut down the old—terror and fury had helped. Now came the end result.

The plow was dull; the treasury empty; the granaries put to the torch. No meager bowl of cabbage soup, the hungry muzhik wailed.

Where was the sauerkraut? No boiled buckwheat dripping with bacon. Not even a salted cucumber. Nothing of substance was left for the starving. The destitute peasants kept shaking their heads, refusing to climb out of their blankets.

Instead of freedom—fear.

Instead of bread—hunger.

Instead of clothes—rags.

Instead of discipline and pride—despair.

"Seize what's before you," the muzhik was told, while the New Order was strangling the old, but once you shot the ducks and chickens, they were gone; and so were the eggs with which to raise a flock.

"Give us the land," the muzhik had shouted, but now that he had it, what good did it do? The tools were still lacking; the will to rebuild the Old Order was gone.

"We haven't seed enough to fill a single bucket," Marleen said to her sons, who answered back in whispers. "Though in good time, the Lord will surely provide. This He has promised us."

It was no secret that it wasn't safe to speak of God, now that the country had a million eyes and ears. Most people learned to whisper early.

Only Natasha paid little heed. She spoke her own mind, now as then. She said what she wanted to say.

"Not even God," Natasha said, who knew most German proverbs well, "can alter last year's harvest."

Natasha did not tell Marleen that she had chanced upon a drifter, who brought her word that he had seen her son.

"I saw him. It was Dominik," the drifter told Natasha.

"He is alive?" she cried, as any mother would have cried, but did not tell Marleen. Right then and there, Natasha thrilled to several possibilities that might ease everybody's lot. "Can you be sure? Don't tell me lies—"

"Why would I lie? I saw him with my own eyes."

"Why, years slipped by, and not a single word!" Natasha chatted with the drifter while helping him to prick a blister. "What is he doing? Has he become a ticket counter? A useful bureaucrat?"

"Step by step and rung by rung, right up the Party ladder," the drifter said and spat.

"Don't tell a soul," she begged, shame burning in her face.

Though Comrade Lenin was believed to be a perfect man who would do wonders for her country—bring to the Motherland vast benefits—Natasha cradled many doubts. Natasha rocked the baby. She was a servant still, as loyal now as then, though posters told her otherwise.

Enormous posters, painted red, all told her she was free to walk through any door she pleased. She still preferred the back. Old habits were deeply ingrained. No matter what the Party said, as far as she could see, not all that much had changed.

What could have pleased her more, back in the days before the Revolution, than yet another baby to whom to coo and sing? She had one now. This one was pitiful, but even so—a baby was a baby. How could her heart be stony to a baby?

Marleen gave it nary a glance, so busy was she to hold fast to the soil that was still hers to ready for the grain.

Marleen walked the fields with her tormenting thoughts, an aging beggar woman, gray and grim, where once her martyred husband's grandfather had walked a king of wheat.

To grow another harvest would take three hundred workers. Tractors. Fuel. And rubles. Lots of rubles. The banks now belonged to the people—but where, dearest Lord, was the cash?

There was dearth in the heart of her country. There were holes at her elbows and knees.

Factories idled. Piers rotted. Granaries, put to the torch, stood black and desolate. Mice gnawed on the grain in the government bins. Yet power to the proletariat! And freedom to the masses!

What could they do with it? The country's treasury was empty, the peasants stuck in moral rot, but slogan after slogan kept sprouting from the rooftops. No matter where Marleen walked, they kept on mocking her.

Behind her lay a winter without snow and a bleak spring without a drop of moisture. Few seeds were stirring in the ground, for little had been sowed. Acre on acre of the finest soil lay bare, for death had plowed the fields. The harvest, she knew, would be famine.

The call of soil stirred in her blood. The days grew long. A farmer started spading. The twins sprang to her side. They worked until they dropped.

Before the year was out, Marleen was sure she'd wrought a meager edge against the looming winter and the growing scarcity of food with her small vegetable patch, though it had not been easy. The plants were spindly from the start. They sprouted, then shriveled and rotted.

By September, hail had pelted down behind her bedroom window, destroying all her efforts. Even the potato harvest was pitifully poor.

Both friend and foe were fainting in the streets. The countryside lay in ruins. The prison courts stood empty. The court house was destroyed. The countless victims of the civil strife lay silent in their unmarked graves. All day, the death carts rumbled.

Survivors faced another woodless, foodless winter. The fields were trampled and torn. The fruit trees were broken and dying.

As the thermometer plummeted, food prices shot up to the sky.

Still: Power to the proletariat! And freedom to the masses!

The peasants in the depth of Russia knew long before the winter storms arrived: not all the slogans in the world could buy a heel of bread.

Chapter 52

Some people would drop everything, including knitting stitches, as soon as the mail sacks showed up—not Little Melly, though. She had more self-restraint than that.

When she spied the arthritic postman walking up the porch steps, gingerly—for he had told her in strict confidence just where he had that painful bunion—she slowly dried her hands. She raised one eyebrow, archly. "More Jeremiah letters? Just put them over there. Behind that apple crate. As soon as I have time, I'll sort them out for you."

"Another batch." The postman threw the bundle in the basket Little Melly had readied for him. "Well, there they are. More work for you. Do I smell apfelstrudel?"

"Cream and sugar? Just say when. Here. Let me have the lot."

"Are you going to steam-open them?"

"Why, have I ever?" laughed Little Melly, while filling his cup to the rim.

"You have. You have. We all know that you like to get a head-start on the news."

"Just hearsay. That is all." She dimpled at him coyly. "What's new these days in Wichita?"

He knew precisely what powered the spinster. "The suffragists mean business."

"You're telling me?"

"Now that they have the vote, they'll all vote libertarian."

She set her chin but chose to let that pass. She had all afternoon. "Is that a fact?"

"Don't say you weren't warned." He leaned into her face. "Say what you will, there is no stopping them."

"Well, you know me. I have my work cut out. The vineyards of the Lord come first. It's critical. Here's how we counteract."

She hauled three baskets to the fore. The special pamphlets advocating fire trucks with curfew whistles had all been printed and bundled up in Hillsborough. "I personally sorted them—with Archie's help, and Daisy's. Be sure to get them out by Wednesday."

"I will. I will."

She chewed her lower lip. She wanted to say more. In general, she stayed away from politics, but whistles were a worthy cause; she wanted whistles; that was it! For three long years, she and her brother had campaigned for fire trucks with whistles to reinforce the curfew. She'd bent Jan's ear until it practically fell off to make sure that the fire truck committee Jan chaired while sitting on her porch wrote that into their minutes—that fire trucks required whistles; the Donoghues, hot from the war, careening at all hours, were still a bunch of thieves.

The mailman relished his break in routine. "What do we have here? My-my-my!" His smile stretched, ear to ear. This was like feasting on a rooster. "Another letter out of Apanlee. Addressed to Josephine."

She, too, was savoring the moment. "Surprise. Surprise. And so, what else is new?"

She had her own priorities cut out. This distant relative, Marleen, kept writing practically every week, ibut who was she? No one could remember. Not even Josie did, now that her memory had holes.

And who could still read Russian, this after having lived in Mennotown for decades? Not anyone she knew. This was America.

"Give it to me. Here. I'll take care of it." She quickly snatched the letter. Doctorjay was practically the only one still left of the old immigrants who could decipher Russian, but he was known to be a blabbermouth. She couldn't take that risk. If there was something in that letter to jeopardize the fire trucks, he wouldn't keep it to himself. He never kept a secret.

"The Devil is ringing their bell." The postman was not about to give up. "If Lizzy knew—"

Little Melly beamed as expansively as a lower lip fever blister permitted. "Here. Have another slice." Old Lizzy, too, might get much more excited than was good for her doddering heart.

"A lot of hungry, angry people."

"Apanlee. Apanlee. That's all you hear these days. A hornet's nest. That's all that I can say."

"Well, don't you think—"

"No, I do not. Nobody hates a body without reason."

"That's what I always say."

She spoke in a low voice: "I've had it with this *Rooshian* business. We shouldn't stress this ethnic stuff. That cost my Archie one good eye."

"I must agree with you. These radicals. They like to bellyache."

"All of them, redskins. Gangsters. Why do we trouble our lives with Russia? Don't we have plenty problems of our own? Right here in our own country? Right here at our front door?"

"That's right. We need some law and order around here."

"We need those fire trucks to set a decent curfew, or else the Donoghues—" She kept on knitting furiously. "I've had it with those *Rooshian* friendship rallies! I've had it! Just plain had it!"

"Well, you know Jan. And you know Josie. They have this thing about the past. They keep this warm spot for the *Rooshians*—"

"You're telling me?" Jan might be mum about his plans, but Little Melly had her social service blueprints, too, and was not coy about them. You took an aspirin before you had a headache. You cleaned up your own porch before you started pulling weeds in someone else's yard.

"Give her a leftist cause," the postman kept on needling, "and watch him leaning left."

"What's it to me?"

"He still is putty in her hands. Whatever Josie wants, she gets. That's what folks say."

She was as naked as a sparrow in the spring. She was a cloud that started dripping. She practically choked, but managed to say this: "The Lord works in mysterious ways. That's all I have to say."

He still had several arrows in his quiver. "Last Wednesday, the Rotarians voted Jan head of the Ukrainian Emergency Food—"

She didn't duck. She didn't even flinch. She caught that flying arrow in mid-air.

"I know. I know. It isn't yet every day's evening, is it? Another cup of coffee?" She gave an enigmatic smile. She boasted a secret or two.

"They want to send him off to Russia. They say he'll take her along."

"By airship, right?"

"Your blood boils at the thought?"

She took her slipper off and threw it at the cat. The matter with the Hebrew airline stocks and bonds still rankled. She cleared her throat and launched herself.

"So. Someone has to go. I'll grant you that. They are our relatives. You help your relatives. We've got to send relief. That's what we're all about. To help the needy elsewhere from our abundance here. So let somebody go. Why can't my brother go? Why not let Dewey go? He wants to go. He's willing to do witness. He feels it is the Christian thing to do. He could take Archie, even. Those two don't have this foolish sentiment about the past. They'll see things with impartial eyes. Why must it be

Jan Neufeld?"

"Well, you know why. This *Rooshian* thing is Josie's private nettle."

"In Mennotown," said Little Melly pointedly, "the cause of Russia is popular with some and not at all with others." She blew a speck of dust off her thumb. "This stuff is decades old. We're now Americans. Can we fix everything that's wrong in this big, wicked world? It's none of our business. An ocean lies between us—"

"Some papers claim the Soviet government is slaughtering the people in great numbers—"

"We have no business helping Soviets. They've done some butchering themselves. Haven't they butchered the Lord's Holy Day? They're heathens! Atheists. They exist in a world that we can hardly conceive of—" She and Dewey had discussed the sorry state of Russia at length. No services in Russia. No bells. No prayers to give thanks. "Is that a country worth our money? No wonder our Lord is running out of patience."

"Can you imagine living like that?"

"Can you imagine Sunday without church? A proper Christian takes himself to church to take in an uplifting sermon—"

She loved her Sundays dearly. She cherished every one—the fragrance of coffee and bacon that drifted through the open doors in the early morning hours, the clatter of a milk pail, the smell of the hot iron with which she gave Archie's starched collar a final once-over, the quiet patterns of the pews, the men on one side, the women on the other, their youngsters sleepy in their laps—that was the proper Sunday attitude. All else was blasphemy.

The postman had run out of arrows except one. He now let fly his parting shot. "No word from Uncle Benny yet? What do you think that means?"

"Well, who's to say? It could mean anything."

"Right. Anything."

"Remember what they said about him? If he would only write, we'd know what's going on. Why did he stop? Your guess is as good as my guess. He wasn't ever really one of us. He was half-Jew, half-Christian. Here. Take this last one. For the road. Come on. Take it. There's more where this one comes from."

"Don't you suppose you should at least let Josie know that there's this bunch of letters that keep on raining from the sky—"

"I'd sooner help the Unitarians," said Little Melly smoothly— and never mind it was the Unitarians who had thrown a decided monkey wrench into her calendar with their malicious Orphan Drive. "If she gets wind of this, you know what she'll do? She's going to head straight for Wichita, try on another hat, and traipse from door to door until she develops large blisters." The shaking palsy that the doctors talked about came out in times like these. Her mouse-colored bun was a-tremble. "I don't want the responsibility. Do you? A letter from this relative, Marleen, whom we don't even know, could push her right over the brink. I'll safe-keep it until she's well again. That is the least that I can do, considering—"

"Tsk. Tsk."

"Don't tsk you me! I count on you to keep your lip zipped up. You hear? We don't want Josephine right on the edge of lunacy. Remember how her *papa* snapped?"

The postman winked at her while standing in the door. "Tsk. Tsk. A gentle thing like you?"

She did not reply: let the silence speak for itself! It wasn't that she had no heart; she did; those letters vexed her soul. Those letters all but shouted. *Chleba!* Bread! She still remembered that one word. She had deciphered it. She gave what she could, but enough was enough. She emptied her purse to the poor and the needy—always had, and always would! But if you went by human nature—and she did!—you wanted something back.

A little bit more gratitude. A little bit more piety. There was no reference whatsoever to the mercies of the Lord in those appalling, Russian letters—not even if you used a magnifying glass. And if those letters meant what she assumed they meant—why, then the outcome could be anybody's guess.

That's how it was in Mennotown. Each time another letter came from Russia, the spinster stuffed her conscience with some cotton and put it with the others. She kept them all well-hidden in a box. That box was stored beneath her bed, and she had padlocked it. She knew what she knew, which was plenty.

Jan contracted for several up-to-date, steam-powered harvesters. He kept some for himself to benefit his fleet; he planned to ship the others overseas to give the needy Russian farmers a needed helping hand.

He made the purchase on favorable credit. He had the fattest bank account in all of Sedgwick County, but still he bought on time. The reason was: it was a package buy, and that reduced the rate. Jan knew he couldn't wait. He was immersed in serious labor struggles that cost him sleep and cash.Some people thought that odd, for Mennotowners estimated Jan was worth more than a hundred thousand dollars.

The aftermath of war was gain; the price of wheat went up; the price of feed went down; life was more lush than ever. You could buy fine-tuned flivver jokes at bargain-basement cost: ten dozen for a nickel. Doctorjay used them to cheer up his elderly patients and help them forget their arthritis. These jokes included jokes about three Methodists, two Lutherans and a Jew, all trying to do business with each other.

These stories made the rounds. Sometimes, the Donoghues were thrown into the story line, which weakened the punch line but added in glee. When Doctorjay shared one such joke with Abigail, both laughed until they gasped.

As year piled up on year, so piled up Jan's worries: the Donoghues still eyed his property with eyes of bitter envy.

A bothersome crowd were the Donoghue kids—all more tenacious than weeds. When they were angered by a whim, they started throwing stones and bottles.

A constable arrived periodically and hauled them off to jail for trading stolen property, but before sunset they were back. The Donoghues loomed large, what with their matches and their threats. Some folks had their suspicions about peculiar prairie fires. That's where the fire trucks came in. Let Russian troubles wait. The fire trucks came first.

Even in the best of times, the Donoghues were difficult, but now the war had coarsened them; they were insufferable; they needed brakes and limits. Not one of them knew how to carve a farm out of the grass of Kansas.

They often stood and stared, comparing. They kept on singing loudly at all hours. They teased poor Archibald to death for lacking facial hair.

The Christmas fund included them—not that it made a difference. The list of their needs kept growing. They claimed they needed this; they needed that—beds, kettles, chairs, and coats, along with socks and toweling. They wouldn't let their children be inspected. They suffered from a lot of city-bred diseases. They even fancied peep shows. Little Melly caught one spying on her, crouching down below the window sill, while she was changing her chemise.

She filled her lungs with air. They were impossible!

Jan, too. He had his grievances. He told her more than once they made a lot of noise about what they called Benefits. They claimed that they were underpaid and overworked. They thought that they deserved the fleshpots of the pharaohs. They hoped that Jan would hand them all their extras on a silver platter—and some, no doubt, to spare.

They asked for twenty-minute breaks. They kept on whining that Jan was exploiting their labor.

One wore his hair down to his shoulders.

Another flashed a fake gold tooth.

They smelled. And they attracted swarms of flies.

A dish lay broken on their porch for weeks.

In summary, it was impossible to rehabilitate a Donoghue. It was hopeless.

The end result was always this: comparison. Jan's flivver— purring like a tiger. Their sorry vehicles, just wobbling at the touch.

They were the parasites of Mennotown, and tempers would run short when efforts to reform them came to naught—for red was their favorite color.

Chapter 53

"Red equals beautiful—synonymous words," proclaimed all the Bolshevik poets. No other color was permitted in their gray and wretched country.

Red soldiers sprung up everywhere, like toadstools after rain. Trains overflowed with troops who wore red bands on sleeves and caps. They dangled legs from rooftops painted a bloody red. They rode on buffers draped in crimson flags. Blood-red was the denunciation box set up at the end of each street. Red was the rubber stamp now needed to visit a neighboring town.

Plain everything was Red! Red! Red! And yet still more Red!

Marleen surrendered a single tear: "A countryside that has been ruled by bullets cannot grow grain on soil so soaked with blood—"

She said this to Natasha. The two sat on the crumbling steps of Apanlee, gray in dress and gray of heart, and knew: the Reds had more in mind than just the end of war.

Natasha and Marleen would often sit like that, intent on sharing warmth, preserving energy while plotting for survival, absorbing the fading rays of the sun. Now worry piled on worry.

The stables were empty; the bandits have taken the horses. The cow that pulled a plow all day could not give milk at supper time. Marleen stared at a crimson poster that flapped in the lame wind.

"The Earth to the Peasants? The sky to the birds?"

"Shhh! Have you lost your mind?" Natasha cast quick glances. Since they were having a defeatist conversation in the open and anyone could listen in, you couldn't be too careful.

"Our Comrade Lenin is the perfect man," announced Natasha in a strident voice, this for the benefit of passersby.

Marleen still clutched her bitterness. "You hate your neighbor? Denounce him. Report his words to the authorities—"

"I know, Marleen. Be quiet!"

Two hungry women, wrinkled both, now sat together, plotting for tomorrow. Their thoughts were bitter gall.

"We're filled with Faith, and may our hollow faces testify," Marleen wrote every week, painstakingly. She had dozens of cousins in Kansas. She knew they were swimming in riches. She kept on writing—letter after letter.

"Why don't they answer back? Could our letters have been lost?"

"I sent them weeks ago," Natasha said, while touching Marleen's cheek. "Maybe next week? We'll manage until then."

Marleen was gnawing on a wormy apple. She still owned four medium potatoes, obtained through a decided miracle. She carefully saved up the peels.

"I cannot imagine what happened. They're family. Were they in our place and we in theirs, would we neglect to speed our help and prayers?"

"There are spies everywhere."

Natasha watched Marleen write missive after missive with trembling, unaccustomed fingers, as food diminished by the day. She did no longer bother masking what she knew—what everybody knew: Once they had eaten their reserve, there was no food left anymore. None. There was no margin left for hope.

"Please! Please! In our dearest Lord's sweet name—let a large vessel full of wheat speed across the ocean."

Instinctively all turned toward Natasha. "Maybe tomorrow you can go and gather thistles from the field—?"

"—maybe that hen has still an extra egg?"

"—maybe a real surprise is waiting at the barter market?"

"—a neighbor might be willing to share some edibles?"

Natasha's hands moved furtively, begetting the sign of the trustworthy cross. Natasha's raised three hunger-swollen fingers: "Let help come soon, oh Lord," she echoed loyally, though she was Orthodox and hence committed to her saints for timely intervention. "Let it come from America—"

Nobody had explained to her where this mysterious country called America might be that would speed grain on Faith. But she aligned herself with Marleen's Faith; she liked to keep all irons in the fire.

"It can't be otherwise," she said in a low voice, and briefly patted Mimi, a shadow child by then.

The little girl kept chewing on her lip. She was a feline child, starved to a skeleton, already cynical. She asked herself, while small, brief shivers kept tumbling down her spine: what would the Party say? To pray for alms sent by Imperialists was dangerous.

She was seven years of age. She knew the Party rules. To plead for help from overseas Imperialists as if she were a beggar child instead of a proud citizen of Russia, equal to any former nobleman, was treason of the highest order.

A government official had come to Apanlee the week before and taken her by her left hand to ask some pointed questions about the prayerful.

"Now tell me of your brothers," the official said, her spindly fingers in his claw.

"Help will arrive," her brothers said. "Help will come soon," her brothers promised, kneeling in daily prayer.   "Say amen, Mimi. Please."

"Come with me. We will have to talk alone."

Her eyes grew big, but she went willingly. Since then, her head felt light. The neighbors kept her in the corners of their eyes. By then, she was already training for the future and Comrade Lenin's property, already first in class and up for a promotion.

"Now tell me everything you know."

She hung her head, pretending she were deaf.

The famine took its time. Two raw, wet winters in a row turned crops across the land as black and gummy as tar. The fences, one by one, fell down. The tractors stood in disrepair. Bolts, nuts and screws were missing.

"Some people still trade wheat," Natasha volunteered.

"So try," Marleen said, while giving her free hand.

Piece by piece and box by box, most everything that had survived the looting of the anarchists was bartered away for handfuls of food on the thriving thieves' market. That's where Natasha wrote her rules. Few there matched her bartering skills.

Natasha took the inlaid sewing box that had belonged to Dorothy to trade in for a cup of mildewed flour.

She took the silver-coated cane the cripple used to carry and traded it for seven turnips and three medium potatoes.

She helped the twins trade a good bottom plow for fifteen pounds of wizened beets. They told her, barely audible: "If we get caught, it's chains at state expense."

But feed the cow, or feed the clan? Of course the cow must go. But once the cow was gone, so, too, was the milk for the baby. It kept toppling sideways as it tried to take a few steps.

This was the child, born on the slaughter night. It never smiled, and hardly ever cried.

It knit its brow. It barely stirred. It chewed the air as oldsters do, and swallowed with reluctance. Natasha looked at it and knew, a realist: in olden days, it might have grown. The olden days were gone.

Still, she fought hard. A baby was a baby.

To live and die, and not a single dimple? The heartbreak of it all!

She did not give up easily. The others in the nearby Russian village jeered at her; she didn't care; she owned an infant once again; she kept on feeding it potato water and dried its diapers by the stove.

She muttered dolefully: "Who pampers you? Who swaddles you? Who bites your teeny toenails?", while salty tears fell on the baby's wrinkled face. She pleaded, feeding it a pallid carrot broth: "Drink just a little bit to please your old Natasha. For if you drink a lot, you little worm, you puny little miserable worm, you pee. And if you pee—why, watch Natasha swat your little bottom and scold you lovingly—"

She chanted to her saints as loudly as she dared—the more obscure a saint, the better she rated her chances. She had found one in whom she still believed—a dusty and neglected saint dug up from underneath old manuscripts in one of Uncle Benny's crates he used to keep behind his shelves to store important thoughts.

Natasha spoiled that saint with her attention day and night, and swathed him with an old handkerchief she had lifted from Marleen. Thereby, she hoped to soften him. She bowed before his sullen countenance. She arched her back as best she could to make him feel important.

"Don't disappoint me now," she told her saint, and shook her bony finger in his face. "Or else, you will not get that extra candle—"

So let him think she still had lots of candles stashed away!

The truth be told: she had a few still left. She used them sparingly. She knew precisely why.

In months to come, she said a lot of tested prayers to that saint. She pleaded first for Yuri, then for Sasha—if strength was left, for Mimi. She told the saint they were the last, those three, to keep the creed alive, but then she waited for the miracle to come—and when it didn't come, her negligent saint was in for a tough, angry scolding.

She yelled: "You! You! You try to bend my nature!"

All she could see were empty eyes, dumb lips.

Regardless! She took him everywhere. He nestled in her pouch.

Thanks to Natasha's chants, born centuries ago, the infant girl survived two long and bitter years. It survived by the smallest of margins but did not live, regrettably, to grow a single tooth. Natasha kept on dragging it to her own stove where it was dry and warm, but its glance stayed dull; its forehead was damp to the touch—just like the year to come: cold and damp and gray and desperate.

Spring took its time arriving.

Death took its time arriving.

The infant was expected to succumb most any day, right from the start, but it kept struggling on: amazing will in such a tiny body. It lived just long enough to learn to call Natasha's name, until the great Ukrainian famine, after all, came stealthily and hushed it for its grave.

Natasha strapped the little body to a board. She pushed her shoulder underneath and took it to the orchards. "You ought to be ashamed!" she told her dusty saint, and did not speak to him for weeks.

Still, he was credited for helping her endure the queuing lines, where she would start a lot of petty arguments to lessen the pangs of starvation.

Three still remained—the twins and Mimi, not yet a Pioneer but soon, who was shedding teeth belatedly to grow a second set.

While Natasha stood there in the cold blasts of winter wind and shivered, expressing her frustration as loudly as she could, her borderline saint in her pocket, small bits of hope fell on her mind like sparks.

One bleak and drizzly morning, early, Natasha saw a half-grown piglet rooting outside in the mire. Her eyes became two narrow slits. She didn't know whose animal it was—a piglet was a piglet; this here was half a pig.

Natasha took a club and hit it on the head. It shrieked piercingly before it toppled over. Natasha beamed in triumph. She kept on hitting it and hitting it until it was so weak that she could straddle it and dispatch it with a sharp knife.

She took it by its hind legs and dragged it in the shed, then ran to fetch Marleen. "See what I have here! See?"

She helped to scald and scrape the stubble, and when Marleen probed for details as to this wondrous find, Natasha squared her chin and started lying brazenly. "I traded it for something I still had tucked away."

"For what? What did you trade, Natasha?"

"You really want to know?"

"What was it? Tell the truth."

"A pair of boots. That's all."

"You stole them? You're telling me you stole my dear departed husband's boots—"

"Think what you like. What's it to me?"

"Did you not promise me," Marleen was shouting angrily, forgetting for the briefest moment that now Natasha was her equal, "that you would never steal again? Did you not promise me?"

"He who did that, and foolishly," philosophized Natasha, "can also take it back."

Ach! Almost like the olden days. Natasha dabbed her eyes.

Because Natasha was Natasha, hence loyal to the core, she did not fully see the brutal sky, the broken earth; she kept her eyes turned inward. Faith brought her to her knees repeatedly. Faith came in waves of hope.

She tricked herself to think her heart was stone—how else could she have borne the knowledge that He, whose very name was Mercy, kept slashing wounds into her heart that time would never heal?

She could decipher but not read, but she hid Marleen's Bible. That hidden Bible, said the twins, was now the key to everything. They claimed it could restore sight to the blind, sound to the deaf; it made the lame walk sprightly and raised the dead from their chill tombs—all that and more, just Faith and yet more Faith. Could Faith not, therefore, feed an eight-year-old as well—her sugar baby, Mimi!—the next to die? Unless help came—and soon?

"Ask, and Ye shall be given—" the twins prayed fervently, while pushing Faith uphill as though it were a boulder. "—are Ye not much better than sparrows?"

"Your turn, Mimi. Please. We're waiting."

"I can't," said Mimi softly, obliged, by government decree, to do away with Faith.

"You must," Natasha ordered, and gave her a soft nudge. "Among us, we don't cry."

Which was much easier said than done. Only yesterday, for instance, Natasha came upon the youngster, sitting huddled in the loft. She thought her heart would crack like glass at what she saw—for there was Mimi, sitting hunched with matted hair and glowing eyes while sucking on a harness strap. Once upon a distant time, that piece of leather had been greased.

"You can depend on me," Natasha told Marleen.

Marleen did not waste extra words. She only said: "I know."

Her shoulders were sloping; her heart was a-flutter; her breath came in gasps and her mind swam in blood—but her grief mattered not, her pain counted not: He who in richer times poured blessings upon blessings could also take them back.

"It's so," Marleen insisted, not tolerating any counter-argument.

For there they sat, two hunger-swollen women, together, side by side, both pondering the glorious Revolution. What had it yielded them?

The snow melt had collapsed Hein's grave, and with it, all ambivalence.

"I know. It's true. Of course." Why argue what was now on everybody's tongue? Natasha shivered and said nothing to challenge Marleen's Faith.

All that was strong and good and clean and sane had turned to dust and ashes. Their country writhed in hunger's claws, in poverty and misery—weeds higher than their shoulders!—this, now, was happiness? Faith grew its iron roots at Apanlee. It grew roots where nothing else grew.

Natasha knew that, for herself, it wasn't Faith that kept her pushing on against the blasted wind—it was, above all, fatalism and persistence, bred into her strong peasant bones by centuries of woe.

So let Marleen depend on Faith to heal herself to where she could draw an easy breath again, not choking on the blinding mass of pain where once her heart had beaten for her children! Natasha counted on her elbows. Faith or no Faith, she used her elbows, too.

She stood in line for days on end and waited for her share. Without a word or order from Marleen, the servant took her place in any queue to help sustain the pious clan—though had she had a choice, she now said to Marleen, enraged with a betrayal she never fully understood, she would as soon be dead.

All this—for Liberty? Fraternity? Equality?

Natasha often rode in open lorries to hustle for edible treasures. She shivered in the wind, but nothing kept her back.

For flour, two days.

For sugar, one night.

For a pair of used boots, as long as a week.

There were long lines at every store, and there Natasha stood, wrapped in Marleen's discarded shawl, and here she pushed, and there she shoved; she was vociferous. She argued expertly and didn't stop shouting until she got her share. No one argued as fiercely as she. That was the margin now by which the clan survived; Natasha's arguments and elbows.

If there was a queue, Natasha stepped in line. She didn't ask what might be sold or bartered; chances were it might be edible. For days on end she stood, patiently waiting, her feet in the debris the Revolution left behind.   She stood there, her mittenless hands in torn pockets, fingering a stolen coin, perhaps a hoarded silver thimble, still hoping for a chance to buy that piece of bread. Aching in muscle and bone, she queued and she shivered, hoping for a heated brick at night to warm her tired feet, while pondering the past, a sad ruin! the present, a sham! and the future?

The future belonged to the people, no argument there!—but to whose good?

Free rides on trains—with windows broken out, upholstery ruined, and thugs and murderers now riding next to her.   Free postage stamps—but danger in receiving letters.

Four hapless people had been executed, willy-nilly, deep in some broken orchard, for correspondence with some relatives, suspects of having plotted to undo the gains the Revolution wrought.

Those people, shot for having sabotaged the government, were Germans.

Chapter 54

The neighbors raised their eyebrows when they heard of Jan's plan to give a helping hand to the scoundrels running roughshod over Russia, but most agreed: Jan was enormously successful; he could do as he pleased. At testimonial dinners, it was an honor to sit next to him. Besides, there was no rush. He might yet change his mind. Jan had agreed to teach Men's Bible Class, with schedules well past Christmas. And Josie had her troubles; she wasn't well; her stockings were still sagging.

Despite her former Red Cross job that might have speeded paperwork—for through her former friendship with the Finkelsteins she had connections that would have helped Jan's travel papers past every rubber stamp—Josie was still lethargic and subdued and, hence, of little use. Her hectic energy of yore had never quite come back.

That's where things stood.

As it turned out, to get those harvesters to Russia turned out to be a bureaucratic nightmare. It was no wonder, therefore, that Russia became a low priority, though Lizzy moaned and fussed.

"Look, if they really needed help, they'd write and tell you so. Don't you agree?" said Little Melly, deftly weaning Lizzy from her apprehensions.

Now that the war was over, finally, the world was turning back to normalcy, as she would tell her neighbors. And high time, too. It was as Dewey said: "Our own community is battling with the weeds."

"Street order has to be restored," said Dewey Epp. "Or else the rabble wins."

The Donoghues grew ever more rambunctious, and it was time to put some distance between them and proper Christians. Why bother with the Russians? The town had its concerns. The bullies had returned. They were out in the streets, carousing at all hours. And Archibald, albeit grown by then into a gangly youth—though not yet shaving properly—still bore the brunt of taunts. He turned up black and blue. It was high time for Mennotown to blow the whistle on the wicked. There was no other way. That was her battle cry.

"Until we have those fire trucks and funds to staff them properly to reinforce the curfew, we have no business raising funds for Russia—"

That's where her preacher brother's gospeling came in. She was ashamed to have uncharitable feelings, but truth was truth, and she must speak the truth—the more that money was drained off for Russia, the less the coins dropped into the donation trays the ushers passed around.

As Little Melly tidied up her cluttered drawers, so Dewey tidied up his flock. He drew up a checklist of hazards.

The Perils of Pauline. Houdini and his sorceries. Transparent sleeves. Round robin letters. Fire crackers. Flush commodes—particularly flush commodes!

"No need to dress up nature," decided Dewey firmly; he spoke for everyone.

By then, most folks were used to electricity and even elevators, but water toilets down the hall from where you breakfasted were something else again. A certain Unitarian, who had installed one such device, would go so far as to stand back, pull the string, and glory in the gurgle.

"And don't forget the dance bug. Hear?" admonished Little Melly, close by her brother's elbow.

"I won't. I won't. That's where I draw the line."

When it came to the dance bug, the Elder Dewey and his deacons stood united. Episcopalians were jitterbugging openly; no doubt the Methodists were not that far behind. One-two-three-hop! One-two-three-hop! Couples vaulted, leaped, pranced and gasped. It was the height of decadence. Some even danced the polka. All danced the Bunny Hug. The Grizzly Bear. The Turkey Trot. The Crab Step. The Kangaroo Dip. The Chicken Scratch. The music never stopped.

Broad was the road to hell!

"Those trucks are critical," the spinster therefore said to Josie, whose actions were no longer frivolous. "What if Jan has a fire at the mill? The union folks are restive."

"If you say so," said Josie listlessly.

Her mind was far away. She seemed bereft of feelings. A gossip once observed her walking in her nightgown in the moonlight while talking to herself.

Little Melly watched all that, while acting blustery. Her heart was singing like a nightingale; she had already given it to Jesus, but somehow, social energy remained. Things were progressing nicely. She often had to hum herself a soothing hymn to keep herself in check, for Jan would sit out on her porch each Thursday evening, surrounded by the Fire Truck Committee, to plan his ways and means.

"Any day now. Any day—" giggled Little Melly coyly, leaving open what she meant.

Not only did she giggle more than ever, these days she even laughed out loud. When she would hear an oft-repeated flivver joke of Jan's, she laughed as hard the seventh time around as she had done the first. And when she intercepted yet another missive out of Russia that made her think that someone tried to inter-

fere with getting those much-needed fire trucks, and planted herself on the evidence—why, nobody asked her to move!

Still, folks did not give up. People kept nagging Dewey about
the folks at Apanlee. Some of them were peskier than the worst
Jehovah's Witnesses whenever Apanlee came up, and that included Lizzy.

"Our folks back home might need a hand from us" fussed
Lizzy, nagging Dewey morning, noon, and night to make sure
Uncle Benny was all right.

The Elder Dewey wanted to forget.

"Sure. Sure. Why not?" he stalled. "Say, what about the
bake sale? Have all the ladies signed? We need their contribution, too, to get those fire trucks. By nine o'clock, the town lights
should be out."

Dewey had it from firm sources that the new government in
Russia was to the left of everything. Himself a staunch Republican, he made sure that his deacons voted likewise. The Russians
were the least of his concerns, what with the creeping unions.

"So let them now enjoy their workers' paradise!" was Dewey's
point of view. Politically, things could be called fishy in Russia.

His sister quickly backed him up. "Right. Right you are.
Some people never learn."

She felt no loyalty and, hence, no obligation. She had been
small when she left Apanlee; her memories were faded. She had
no use for Apanlee. None whatsoever. None. America was now
her country. She called herself an isolationist, like everybody
else.

Old Lizzy looked as though she hemorrhaged inside when
she heard talk of corpses piled around the Kremlin. Little Melly
had sturdier emotions.

"Don't pay attention. Hear? You can't believe the scrib-
blers. Such stories are always dressed up in the press."

"Perhaps a bit, but even so—" said Lizzy timidly, but in her
nimble way, the spinster cut her off.

"One's charity begins at home," decided Little Melly firmly.

"Unless we get those fire trucks, the Donoghues are bound to overthrow morality and decency. And then what? Well? Say! Have you ever thought of what the consequence would be?"

"But don't we owe—"

"Those fire trucks are critical. And I mean critical."

"Has Uncle Benny written lately?"

"Not since the Middle Ages. Remember how he used to write five pages to explain a single word."

"But what if something happened?" cried Lizzy, giving way to panic.

"God, no! It couldn't be! Who would touch him? He never harmed a beetle. Don't you agree he'd write to Josephine and ask for her assistance? He would. He would set pride aside. Those two were thicker 'n thieves."

"That's true. You're right."

"Of course I am. I'm sure that everything is fine."

"You're positive?"

"I'm positive. Now, settle back and take a little nap. You'll wake up quite refreshed."

Thus Lizzy shelved her fears. Besides, there was the fair. The country fair was in full swing again, and Lizzy's cows, still nurtured on the principles of Apanlee, were as acclaimed as ever. She knew every cow and calf by name. She didn't care if people smiled; the buckets that she carried all the way from Apanlee, now almost half a century ago, still gave her ample status.

The weather turned balmy. Then hot. And then chill. The bells kept on pealing. Seasons revolved, as always, around the wondrous holidays.

Spring came again and left, then June, July and August. September arrived. Next in line was Halloween.

When an aggressive Baptist minister took ill, the Elder Dewey filled his shoes admirably and finished off the pumpkins.

The postwar flu had ravished many families and left young children needing mothering. Little Melly, to her relatives' delight, received three serious offers of marriage.

Little Melly was flattered and charmed. She practically threw off sparks. But all the same, she coyly shooed each suitor from her door the way she shooed the tomcats—her life held sufficient excitement.

"Look at my hens," she pointed out with several pearly giggles. "They keep on laying eggs without the benefit of roosters." She saw no need for matrimony at this point in her own earthly voyage. She might have, in her younger years, but certainly not now. Her hips kept spreading; her gout gave her trouble. She had her starched, white curtains; she had her potted plants.

To round out this brief life in preparation for the next, she had begun to minister to several shut-ins, a dwarf, and two blind diabetics. These causes put lumps in her throat.

"No need to be someone I was not meant to be," she pointed out, her eyes on Archibald, who was her pride and joy. She still trimmed his hair with the help of a dish pan. In church, they hit high notes together.

Archie proved a moral challenge, seeming romantically delayed, but she was up to it. First she smacked him, then she petted him to help him grow into another trusted citizen America would need.

Of all of Dewey's children Little Melly raised, Archie was her favorite. She had high hopes for him. While Dewey clattered round the country in his flivver as eagerly as ever to track down sliding sinners, she sat amid her pillows tranquil, plump and plain and pious and content, and with no need to burden her imagination with anything except the Second Coming of the Lord.

She nursed a private fantasy. She did not tell a soul. She would not even tell her preacher brother, but she often dreamed of what it would be like when Jesus finally appeared. She was His bride; that was the grand design; she hoped to see Him first. She counted on His Coming.

No one, of course, could foretell His arrival—she didn't even try. But she could dream, and dream she did: before she fell asleep each night, she toyed with variations of her favorite dream that made her feel as though she had taken a shower with plenty of suds and hot water.

Her visions made her feel scrubbed clean. They made her

feel relaxed. She knew that it was vain and probably heretical to want to know the date—so as to be prepared!—but still, she hoped against all hope He would announce His visit to her privately. She ached to show off her town—the joy and the sparkle of Kansas. She hoped there would be time to have the main road sprinkled. To settle all that union dust, mused Little Melly, caught dreamily in that delicious interim right between wakefulness and sleep, one needed fire trucks.

The new acoustics Dewey had requested so as to bind the Devil with his zeal had cost a fortune and a dime—but every dime was carefully inspected and well spent. Now, Dewey relished his new voice in his expanded church—it bounced from beam to beam as he called sinners to conversion, undercutting the rapacious gains the Baptists and the Methodists amassed.

The folks were pleased, but even so—the church funds had been drained. Three hefty notes were still unpaid, and Jan still talked of shipping harvesters to Russia, and called for volunteers to help him raise the money.

Though Dewey was a trusted expert at turning conscience into cash, he and his deacons huddled weekly. He worried at his church's monetary pinch. There was an upper limit to what people were willing to give to the needy. The Elder Dewey knew that if he crossed the safety line between glad nickeling and risky quartering, the members of his flock would become quarrelsome. And if he pushed them into dollaring, they all tensed up, like Lizzy's cows, with too many hands on their udders.

"The *Rooshian* brethren curse their lives, no doubt," he preached repeatedly, so that there was no doubt where he stood—fair-square with Mennotown and its own social needs. "They must have sinned, however. Now let us pray to do what's right by our own folks at home, so that we learn humility. So we don't follow Russia."

The congregation shuffled restlessly. Most people scratched their heads.

Still, Jan spoke up, his own brow furrowed with ambivalence, and Doctorjay backed him at every meeting, his nose getting redder and redder.

"They are our kin. They might be in serious straits."

The Mennotowners, house by house, palavered their responsibilities at length. It was decided at long last to send a scouting expedition, as in the olden days, to find out what was what. The plan was to find out, once and for all, so there could be no doubt, what improvements, if any, the Red Revolution had wrought.

That happened the following fall. The church fathers met after services. They met in the augmented basement where Dewey had, by then, installed a row of built-in kitchen cabinets, the newest rage, to please his volunteers. He still had plans to renovate the sanctuary—an elevated platform for the choir, a gleaming basin, to the left, for baptisms.

"A pie is a pie; it goes only so far," argued Dewey adroitly, while dusting off the abacus.

It was incomprehensible in any case to think of Apanlee as needing their assistance—in every oldster's memory, a place blessed gate-to-gate, and wall-to-wall, with riches beyond words.

"Of course we'll help. Why not? But first things first. Let's finish what we started. Let's clean up our own yard."

The issue boiled down to two choices: to have a huge spaghetti feed to raise enough hard cash to ship those harvesters across the great Atlantic and all the way to Apanlee—a place now shrouded in a fog of godlessness, if you believed the rumors!—or to buy fire trucks to bring some law and order back to town.

"I'll check into the Apanlee matter. I'll do so as soon as I can. I'll have my sister pack my cardboard suitcase, in the meantime. As soon as I am getting used to my new spectacles, I'll volunteer to be His eyes and ears."

"But don't you think—"

"As early as next year," said Dewey Epp, and changed the subject deftly.

It was hard to sustain the momentum. The fire trucks won out.

Chapter 55

There had been murderous famines before, leaving both peasants and gentry exhausted, but nothing compared to this famine! Not within the oldest peasant's living memory had there been ever such a want, such utter desolation.

Life emptied out. It was as if the world had ended. The length and width of the Ukraine, those who still clung to life were eating grass and roots.

Bleak days and bleaker nights—and scores of ashen villages.

It was as if a hand had wiped a chalk board clean; it was as if the locusts came and stripped the fields and left bare earth and nothing else. Now it was springtime once again; but where was the seed, and where were the workers? The torrents of blood had abated, but where was hope for betterment—or food?

Natasha lifted a weak hand.

"In olden days," she told the twins, "a peasant would elect to starve to death before eating the seed set aside for the following year—"

Had it not been for them, those two, still clinging to the brink, tomorrow would have died. Two hardy striplings in the olden days but now two rattling shadows, the twins had grown into their meager manhood as hunger struck with virulence and it appeared that what the anarchists had failed to do, starvation would—lure those two to the grave.

"Why two of us?" they asked, in voices barely audible.

The twins chafed like two mules. They had failed once. If tested one more time, they would not be found wanting. The Lord had turned His gaze on them; they didn't know what lay in wait to test their Faith in Him, but this they knew: before them, a relentless mandate.

"Be it His will," said Yuri, "to send us either calm or storm."

His prayers, still in German, were benchmarks of grit and endurance. The famine stalked him like a wolf, teeth bared and fangs exposed, but all the same, there was still Faith—the kind of Faith that reaches for the Gospel, blinded, as for an elixir as sweet and overpowering as sleep.

"He walks forever by our side," said Sasha, too. Between him and eternity stood Faith. He whispered, barely audible: "He will provide. I know this for a fact."

By then, the faithful did not even have the luxury to speak of Him by name, for several people had been shot at dawn for having done just that. The twins, however, trusted Faith, for nothing else was left. They trusted Faith as though it were their father's *bashlik*—the sheepskin Hein had worn in his own youth with careless nonchalance to keep his burly body toasted happily while, outside, blizzards howled and peasants yelped with cold.

"—we'll suffer not in vain—"

"—He'll spread a cloud for covering—"

Across the dried-out fields flew tumbleweeds. The gusts of wind kept licking at their cheeks with dry, persistent tongues.

They still had this: a trunk, the width of a small apple crate, filled to the rim with seed, the safety valve between a miserable existence and the grave.

"The government—" Marleen tried speaking, and let the sentence drop.

"Shhh. Hush!" Natasha was saving her strength. It was not

wise to speak with disrespect of leadership, but though she was so weak that she could barely stand, she had strength left to spit against the wind, and why not do that now? Her thoughts curled like poisonous smoke. She razed the fields for roots; sometimes she hunted down a rodent. That bought another day.

The government? The government had done away with the official gallows, only to unleash the terror in the streets. The terror ran its course; the land no longer crawled with anarchists; the dregs of war lay dying in the hedges of causes not recorded. Each day, the corpse cart came and threw the corpses on the lorry.

Marleen spoke up. "Hein used to say: 'A beggar is a messenger from God.'"

"The olden days," Natasha said, "are gone."

Still, duty sat on Marleen's tongue. "Hein used to say: 'If you are asked to share, you share. It will come back to you tenfold.'"

Natasha gazed into Marleen's dull eyes reproachfully. "Don't be a fool. Quick! Lock the gates! Don't be a mollycoddle, you! Be sensible. What's there to share? There's nothing left to share."

She stuck by her own instincts. So let a beggar die! A beggar was a beggar—a nuisance, and no more. That was Natasha's point of view. She shared it often with Marleen—in fact, at every opportunity.

Natasha started ordering Marleen about as though she had no *umlaut*. She barricaded every window, every door. She saw the vermin crawling on the beggars' collars. "Just go away! You hear? *Davai! Davai!* Away!"

"Please. Anything."

"No. Go away. Why don't you go away?" She knew of the diseases they would bring. Spotted fever. Typhoid. Cholera. "Now scat! I told you! Go away!"

The larder was empty. The cupboards lay bare. And through the crumbling gates of Apanlee still poured the ghosts of yesterday as famine emptied Lenin Square and Trotsky Street, and more arrived, and more—a torrent of the starving—as hunger emptied cities and drove the people to the land, as famine emptied every hut and factory and sent the hungry masses out into the countryside to grub the earth for food.

These human ruins with wan faces, hollow eyes, swollen hands, were tapping on Marleen's masked bedroom window. At Apanlee, they claimed, there still was golden bread.

In the ditches they sat, by the mulberry trees, their feet wrapped in the slogans of tomorrow. "Just a morsel," they pleaded. "Just half a crust, maybe?"

Natasha never faltered for a moment. "Go away!" she shouted angrily and swung her reedy broom, but they would not; wild rumors glued their hollow faces to her panes.

Natasha made a fist repeatedly and shook it at the beggars. She hollered, and she cursed. "There is no food. No food at all. Why don't you go away?"

She watched them move into the shelter of the hedges, where they would sit, sometimes behind the empty chicken shed, nursing ugly frost bite that exploded on their toes, waiting for a change of heart, waiting for something to happen. String parcels in their hands, they held out a few meager possessions for barter: nails, matches, thread, perhaps a comb, a handkerchief.

Natasha shouted until she was hoarse: "The olden days are gone!"

From prayer to prayer, the twins learned their lesson—that there was yet significance in suffering the likes of which a monster might dream up. They were cowards, they knew—when the anarchists came, they should have fought back. Instead, they had hid in a chimney.

When they emerged at dawn, the Lord's Prayer on blue lips, and found the earth thick with the ancient martyr blood that ran in their own veins, they knelt and solemnly committed to a life of sacrifice for any test, for any task the Lord would set before them.

That's why they asked right from the start, two stubborn lookalikes: "No food. Why two of us?"

To that, there was no answer. They learned that life did not snap easily. The orchards still had apples.

Their hands soon were covered with blisters. They chafed from dawn to dusk. They pulled the plow, large ropes tied several times around their shoulders. Soaked through with rain and shivering with cold as rain turned into sleet, they tried to plow the acres to bury the last winter wheat before the storms arrived.

"—why two of us?" they panted. They worked like beasts to pull the blade to feed themselves, their mother, Mimi, and finally Natasha.

"Thank God there's two of you," Natasha said, for she had eyes; she saw that hunger had so weakened them that one would not have had the strength to pull the blade that cut the earth alone.

Soon the October winds were whining through the gaping holes of Apanlee. Another spring arrived and left, and summer came and went. Marleen stared at Natasha. Her eyes were dry and burning.

"I found a pair of Hein's old spectacles," Natasha said at last. "I'll trade them for a dozen fat potatoes."

Natasha nudged Marleen in hopes of coaxing a small smile— four small potatoes, at the most. Natasha liked to boast. In the old days, Marleen would have been jolted. There would have been some cuffs. The old days were no more.

Marleen responded listlessly. "Do that. Why not? It cannot hurt to try."

"I'll try. You know that I can argue heartily—" Natasha nudged Marleen a bit more forcefully. The bartering in the old days—the energy it gave!

Marleen sat silently. She was so weak she couldn't cross her legs. "God preserve you. God preserve you. If we manage to live through the year—"

"I'll go and gather thistles. We'll grind them up, and mix them with potato peels—"

"All right. Here's a canister."

Natasha gathered thistles. Marleen ground them up and mixed in the potato peels. Which made ten crumbling cookies. Which bought another day.

Many died, but some survived. A ghastly winter followed. The wind howled through the broken chimney. Next came a rain-clogged spring. The mound that held the dead of Apanlee became a muddy cavity. Outside, the dead lay on the frozen ground and in the melting snow. The village street grew empty; the corpse cart came and went—and still a few lived on.

Those who survived ate fish heads and potato peels, and that's how they survived. They ate such weeds as cows eat and survived. If need be, they ate mice, rats, ants, and earthworms—and survived. Those who survived lived on because they willed survival. Not many, but some did.

The story is told of Larissa.

Larissa survived—a distant cousin from an obscure branch of relatives who, in the landless days, had sought a fortune in the east and settled in Sagradovka. One wind-blown day, the twelve-year-old arrived at Apanlee as if pulled there by a powerful magnet.

The twins stared at the visitor. "How did you know how to find us? Apanlee is not on any map."

"Nobody knows. Nobody knows—"

The young girl was foot-sore and gaunt. Her skinny legs were trembling with exhaustion.

The twins sprang to her aid. Natasha scurried for a heated brick. Marleen found an old blanket with which to wrap the relative.

"I walked on wooden clogs," Larissa said in a low voice, "while eating dandelions, burdock, bluebells, willow roots and nettles, and that's how I survived—"

"Here! Here, sit down—"

"I picked my way across the dead. Where I collapsed, I slept. I rode a train until that train stopped running—"

A story emerged, by and by. It took many months to complete it.

"I just walked on and on—" Larissa said repeatedly. "What could I do? I walked—"

The cold rains fell on her; the stars above recoiled; the woods stood dark and shadowy. Raw courage and defiance, bred there by centuries of hardened forebears, drove Larissa on.

"I walked," she said. "I am telling the unvarnished truth—"

She said she walked on wet, then icy cobble stones, through pelting rain, through freezing sleet, hands buried deeply in her pockets. "I walked," she said, still speaking in a monotone, "into the melt of yet another spring—" A raw will drove Larissa.

"I picked my way across the dead," Larissa said, oblivious to release.

She sat there in the kitchen, by the oven, very straight and very still, just staring at her folded hands. Not since the days before the Revolution had there been anyone so mannerly.

"Faith drove you," said the twins.

"Somebody," said Larissa softly, "would hand me, now and then, a piece of wet, black bread—"

"Your prayers, surely, made the difference?"

She did not echo that, but neither did she differ. "I walked. What could I do? I walked. The sun's rays grew thinner and thinner—"

Hunched hard against the coming winter—across the frozen land, through howling blizzards, on and on, into a second spring, a third—that's how Larissa walked.

Luck, said Larissa softly, next led her to a workers' dormitory. That's where she found a cot. "I stayed there through the coldest days. When it turned warm again, I walked—"

She kept on talking, softly, recounting how she begged her sustenance from passing trains while walking on and on, past the untidy heaps of frozen bodies, her skin a dusty gray that folded into many creases.

"One day, I bit into a naked sparrow," Larissa told them, twitching. "I felt it moving in my mouth—"

"On wings of prayer, surely—"

And when the thaw set in again, Larissa said, she walked again: across a land now bristling with barbed wire. Her skin erupted. Festering sores formed on her heels.

"I walked and walked," she said. It seemed she could not say another sentence.

"The Lord brought you to us," said Yuri. His voice was husky with emotion.

She stood, her shoulders bowed, in the dilapidated halls of Apanlee, her mind filled with the knowledge of the dead who had lain everywhere, stacked up in piles, like wood. She spoke so softly they could barely hear. "Why me? Why two of you?"

A hush fell over the twins in the gathering dusk. Larissa stood, wasted, before them. Their glances met and locked. The instinct of a hiving bee—that was what drove Larissa.

No one ever came to claim Larissa. She simply stayed at Apanlee and no one said a word. She huddled by the stove and kept the fire going with dry leaves, sticks, straw, and underbrush while snowy gusts of wind kept rattling the rafters.

For weeks on end, Larissa's memories would keep her shivering as if there were no warmth in her at all, and finally, she wept. The slightest effort caused fatigue and nausea.

"It felt like an ax," she said in the end. "Just parting my head from my body." That's how she cut clean to the bone.

Yuri and Sascha heard that with relief. They kept their Bible hidden in the straw. They pulled it out for her. Her heart was pounding like a hammer. She kept on pushing it aside. She would have none of that. She sat and rocked and shivered, but finally a story fell in bits and pieces from her lips. The day came when she said: "Somebody pushed me through a window. There was a dugout in the garden, and that is where I hid."

"Your father? Your mother?"

"Dead. Dead."

"Your brothers?"

"I saw them fall and not get up again."

"Your sisters?"

"Four. Four sisters. Raped and bayoneted." Larissa rubbed the pearls of perspiration from her forehead with her sleeve. "What could I do? I walked."

The twins did not give up. "He washed away your sins like footprints in wet sand."

"There's two of them. There's still a chance," Natasha said, and hobbled painfully.

Chapter 56

The war had helped Jan make a paper fortune from what he called his airship stocks, with Doctorjay hard on his heels, although the latter didn't trust the usurers who still swarmed about Josie.

Doctorjay fancied nickeling.   He kept his savings, wisely, in a can. When one filled with coins, he found another.

A tooth no longer cost a quarter; the price went up to fifty cents; Doctorjay kept stashing cans filled to the brim, on which he would fall back in case of rainy days. His Ready Relief now sold wholesale; his herbal business was brisker than ever. His acreage stretched past Hillsboro, all of it free and clear.

"You can't stay behind. You must keep ahead of inflation," boomed the bewhiskered Doctorjay, his Low German accent thicker than ever.

Now that the kaiser was no longer everybody's favorite punching bag, he knew Jan was renewing hope to ship those harvesters. Fat chance he would succeed!

While Jan was still entangled with the bureaucrats and their shenanigans—the sermonizers of the president in Washington insisting wordily in reams of clever but confusing rhetoric that Russia was sorting itself out as to the kind of democratic government it wanted and deserved!—wheat stood at seventy cents a bushel, and Jan held onto several shipments in hopes for even higher gain.

Jan struggled through enormous paperwork to get those tractors shipped, but it was red tape fore and aft. There was no way, Jan finally admitted, to get equipment overseas to Apanlee.

All that his efforts netted him was just a shoe box full of bills, now gathering both dust and interest, while fifteen tractors stood there, waiting to be shipped.

"Why not just pay for them? Be done with it?" asked Lizzy. Her lips compressed, that's how she sat and watched how Jan conducted business Hebrew-fashion. Every time a bill was left unpaid, she heard her heartbeat hammer with foreboding.

"There are enormous tax advantages to doing business on credit," Jan tried to ease her mind.

"We never sanctioned debt."

"Look, Mom. I'm watching it. If I don't borrow now, I drive my taxes up. Machinery is property, to be used for collateral."

That, too, was new. It made no sense at all. The government taxed diligence and punished thriftiness. The more a farmer worked and earned, the more the government knelt on his spine and tried to weaken it.

She summoned every ounce of courage. "I don't like buying things on time. It's wrong. It says so in the Bible."

"Don't worry, Mom. I'm careful. I had to buy the harvesters. I could not let that kind of bargain pass me by."

A frightening amount, by all accounts, thought Lizzy anxiously, her shy glance on Jan's whitened temples. Was this her son who, in the olden days, would have been anxious and alarmed if Lizzy owed a quarter to the grocer?

She tried to hide her worry beads but couldn't help herself; she kept on venting her opinions. "This Russian tractor business does more credit to your heart than to your head," is how she summed it up. Her son had cash on hand. He had a checkbook, balanced. There was no need to yield to usury, while interest piled on interest.

How she despised the word!

Some people started hinting that Jan should run for governor, because he had a noble heart to go with fat pockets and a benevolent spirit. For quite some time, he even entertained the thought.

"How would you like me to involve myself in politics?" Jan queried his wan wife.

He was teasing, of course, but she cracked no smile; she just sat and inspected the tips of her shoes. Both knew he was only half-serious. To take on politics would have cost Jan his harvests. He still worked the land, and his grain spikes were sharper than ever.

"There's nothing that you couldn't do," she said to him, obediently, but then forgot the matter. She was too numb to bother. In effect, she agreed that the Rotary Club was designed for the male of the species.

Jan was so taken with his matrimonial truce, his systematically upgraded flivver, and his precocious baby boy he just about perfumed his beard. He let the toddler sniff the flivver fumes until the little fellow all but swooned.

That made the town folks laugh. "Is that a boy, or what? That is no ordinary child. Are you taking him hunting and fishing?"

Jan smiled a pensive smile. He let the challenge pass. The boy-child was sedate and pretty; as quiet and pleasing as the breeze. Jan did not nuzzle his soft neck unless he was clean-shaven. And Josie, too; she cherished him; she plain outdid herself; she treated her small son with reverence and awe. If there was joy at all in Josie's curtailed life, it was joy in the smallest of doodles.

Before the little fellow even learned to speak, she knelt in front of him so that their eyes were level: "Did you do that? All by yourself? That is just beautiful!"

It was soon clear to all that Rarey, true to parentage, was a decided prodigy. Never once did little Rarey, still teething on his silver ring, chew on his fingertips like normal youngsters might.

"The little fellow tidied up your life, correct?" said Dewey, genuinely pleased, and slapped both Jan and Josie on their shoulders.

"He did. He did," said Jan, while Josie merely sagged.

Still, there was Apanlee. The topic dragged through meeting after meeting. Jan might as well have tried to hurry up a snail, though Dewey said repeatedly that he would go and see, if for no other reason than on account of Noralee.

"My sainted mother would have wanted that," he told the congregation while passing the collection plate to save up for the passage. "She would have said, had she been still alive: 'You help when you can. While you can. Without neglecting your hen house, of course.'"

The congregation hushed with reverence. Those words were vintage Noralee. The neighbors all missed Noralee, now safely gathered to her fathers. Just as the war was winding down, she had developed water in her lungs. Doctorjay, who had made light of her complaints and thought it was the foreign flu and, hence, a harmless ailment, learned to eat every word.

The day came when she shouted suddenly: "If you don't pay attention to your wedded spouse, I will just have to die, that's all!"

He refused to believe it, however. "You look rosy and fleshy and fit."

She sent for her children to warn them.

They chuckled and patted her hand.

Therefore, she seized the matter by the collar and carried out her threat. She up and died, triumphing over everyone, including Doctorjay who, in the end, came running. That's how she lived and died, with zest and spice and drama, and never out of character.

The congregation carried her to her eternal rest through sheets of drifting snow.

"*Von der Eh-he-herde reiß mich loß,*" sang the shivering funeral singers.

The coffin was lowered. Noralee sank away, out of sight, as dressed up as the unfortunate *Titanic*. The shovel brigades started shoveling. Most of the mourners wept.

"Could she have only seen herself," said Doctorjay a few hours afterwards while thawing out in Lizzy's toasty kitchen, his red nose full of tears, "she would have been so pleased!"

"You were the best of husbands. You gave her every honor."

"I tried." His sniffles were luxuriant. He had done well by her; he even underlined his love for her by ordering the most expensive coffin he could find—with ribbons, laces, paper flowers. That was the least the Lutheran could do for Noralee—the lusty deacon's widow who gladly snuggled up to him, no matter what the season.

For quite a while, he grieved and wept, well-anchored in the knowledge that his beloved Noralee would rise to heaven without blemish when the Lord's trumpets blew. He looked enormously distressed—and then, before the decade ran its course, he up and married Abigail, who was a heartless flirt.

With Noralee, the sturdiest link to Russia was gone in that branch of the family. Except for Doctorjay, voluptuously teeter-tottering between temptation and restraint, no one was left in Little Melly's home who could remember Apanlee and, therefore, neither she nor Dewey felt as pressured any more about the tiresome refrain of living up to Old World sentiment right under their own roof. Old Lizzy barely counted; her years of youth were shadowy. By then, the tooth of time had gnawed most every memory.

That left the house across the street, where Josie sat and stared.

Would knowing of those letters from the wilds of Russia that Little Melly kept, padlocked beneath her bed, restore her to her old, defiant ways?

Could be. Though hard to say.

For now, she was still docile. The pall on Josie's life did not lift. The neighbors hardly noticed her, she was that quiet and meek. She sat beside the stove, her shoelaces loose, her blouse hanging out of her skirt. All her torrential energy was gone. The chip on her shoulder was gone. The mad dash to Wichita—gone!

When, in the end, the Elder Dewey volunteered to go to Russia as soon as the siding was stripped and repainted—maybe take Archibald along and teach him by example precisely how to witness for the Lord in heathenland—the Kansas farmers were relieved. Far better it be Dewey than Jan Neufeld—or, worse yet, Josephine! The last thing anybody needed was for Jan's wife to snap out of melancholia and jump back in the liberal ring. From sad experience, the neighbors knew how quickly Josephine, when at her fiery best, could throw a monkey wrench into the city plans to reinforce the curfew for the Donoghues, who still gave Mennotown scarcely a moment's peace.

The mischief-causing Donoghues still agitated at the bottom of the heap, while nursing their leftist ideas. The folks of Mennotown thus took each other's measure and found themselves in full agreement before they left in single file to take their Sunday naps: there was no rush at all. If you inspected any map and saw that Russia was a country larger than America—now sprawling half across the European continent and spilling into Asia!—why pull the fools out of their self-created hole?

When Josie started writing, finally, to find out for herself just what was going on at Apanlee, her letters all came back.

They grew into a little pile. She held them all together with a little rubber band.

But there was hope for her. She was well on the road to betterment. As per Old Lizzy's last report, her taste was back, her sleeplessness was treated intermittently with garlic milk, and she no longer burned her food. Best yet, no longer did she take herself to Wichita with Abigail in tow—the two of them in hat and gloves, with deviltry in mind.

That town was Babylon!

In Wichita, there now was dancing every night; some of the

seedier places even sported colored waiters. In olden days, Josie would just have fetched her parasol and gone to check the action. Not now. Those days were gone; the olden days were gone. She was learning to carve up the turkey in the time-tested Thanksgiving manner.

One odd, disturbing letter slipped by the spinster's vigilance and fell into Josie's hands by accident, bearing no signature but hinting that Russia was hungry, exhausted; that people were tortured with fear. It was a letter oddly sapless—containing lofty words that spoke of Russia on the mend thanks to the brilliance of its leader, Comrade Lenin, It was a missive, Josie sensed, concealing hidden howls that issued from a sinkhole. It made no sense at all. The stamp was two years old.

She tried to compose a reply, but her body grew weary; her eyelids were lead; her words turned into marbles that rolled away from her.

"As soon as I feel well again," said Josie, resting her spine on the spine of a chair, "I will check up on them."

She made up her mind to do what the letter was asking, but then she forgot what it was. She felt relieved and grateful when Little Melly took the letter gently from her lap and let it slide into her apron.

"Look. It's a fake," said Little Melly, softly. "It isn't Uncle Benny's hand. Somebody's tricking you. If there were something wrong with Apanlee, he'd write and tell you that."

"But what if—"

"Just don't you vex your feelings, dear. Just try to heal yourself."

"But don't you think—"

"First, try to heal your wounded spirit. You have not yet bounced back on your feet."

Josie the pen woman, infected with liberal thought, was Josie the invalid now. At the slightest toil and trouble, she took to her cushions, still pale and wan, and there she would lie—quilt over her ears!—refusing to come greet the neighbors.

"Another year," the doctors promised Jan. "This time of life is hard on every woman—" When an imported doctor finally arrived to remedy the situation, he took one look and narrowed down his forecast:

"Familial melancholia."

Just like her *papa*, people said. Remember the madman, Claas Epp?

What was most striking were her silences. Known as a witty talker in her youth, she had run out of words. She had covered her fire with ashes.

She forgot she supported a marginal Wichita poet. She lay in her bed or sat on her couch and said nothing. For years, there was a leaden cast to her that only lifted now and then when she looked at her youngest offspring, Rarey, with the eyes of a slightly mad cat.

Had it not been for Rarey and his astounding talent, she might have slipped away into her inner world entirely. This lastling did something to Josie. He was the thread that bound her to this world. Her love name for him was still Rarey. It was as if she had passed on her icy flame to him. She spoke to him in code.

"It is all humbug anyway," she told the little fellow. "To me, the mind is all."

And Rarey proved to be the wonder of his age. As he shed all his baby dimples and turned into a pleasant toddler, she developed a fierce, focused joy in the smallest of scribbles he made, while his father became more reserved.

Some people were fond of fooling themselves, but not Jan and Josie; that was not in them. The life they shared with one another was now as somber and as satisfying as a funeral feast— the pillage of time did the rest.

And yet: the moon was still full; the breeze was still gentle; and fragrant were the blossoms of each season. Those two were not a matrimonial couple any more, in the strict Gospel sense, but yet, between them, they had Rarey whom they loved equally, who showed an early calling.

As he grew up, he painted in oils. He won one award. Then another. Soon, Josie had a wall full of plaques. Her son's artistic talent became the talk of Mennotown.

Jan grew more faithful in his visits to his church, where Little Melly led the choir as though her heart were bursting with accumulated sentiment. Most of the time, Jan came alone; on rare occasions, he brought Josie. Before the sermon ran its course, his arm supported her.

The word was now on every tongue: the Lord had silenced her.

She was so strange! Her tongue was strange, her manners strange. The look in her cat's eyes was strange. She kept an hour glass beside her bed and, pensively, from time to time, she turned it over and watched the sand grains settle in a pile.

"Ach ja!" the neighbors said.

Her violent rebellion had burned itself out. Her arguments no longer struck a nerve in Mennotown. The hiss the length of Mennotown was gone!

Jan cultivated Faith. He frequented devotions at least three times a week. He came and sat, surrounded by his daughters, holding his newest grandchild gently in his lap. At night, he read the Gospel to himself, snow having settled permanently at the temples, turning page after page of the Gospel with stiffening hands.

Just what it was he hunted for, not even Lizzy knew. It used to puzzle her. She couldn't help herself.

"Why add—or worse, subtract?"

The glow of Lizzy's Faith was deep; there was no need to probe. The Lord's Commandments were as natural to Lizzy as breathing in the air; the Bible was not something she would have spent her energies dissecting.

"Why hurt yourself?" she chided lovingly. "The Lord knows every nook and cranny of your heart."

"Does He?"

"The state of Kansas knows you live to benefit your fellow man. So don't you think He does? He who counts every star?"

"I give and sympathize. Is it enough?"

"It is," she told him firmly.

She ran a double check and came out satisfied. Jan had been baptized properly. He was careful to set an example. He did not have a single serious vice. Not even Doctorjay, not one to give up on his silly bet about the fire water, could make him have that sinful sip out of that flask he still kept hidden somewhere.

She added for good measure. "You tithe. You're generous."

Jan kept on giving lavishly to every church event; in fact, he went so far as to champion the Episcopalian Temperance Drive. He also supported the Annual Bake Sale the Baptists put on, and the Methodist Orphans, and even the Salvation Army.

In summary, Jan was his town's most trusted citizen. Without unnecessary words, he put his wealth into His service, quietly. Old Lizzy knew beyond a shadow of a doubt that Jan lived in accordance with the Holy Spirit; he felt it; he respected it; what more was there to say?

"You set a wonderful example for other congregation members," she told him lovingly, and Jan gave more and more.

"Say, would it help to make you feel a little better," Jan asked, when all else failed, hoping to spark his wife out of her melancholy mood, "if I went back to Apanlee and took a look myself?"

She said while rising feebly on one elbow: "Well, can I come along?"

That would have terrified the best of husbands, but Jan was as patient as ever. He lowered the boom of his voice. He kept tucking her into her sheets.

"You are still weak and out of touch with your own body, dearest. I promise I will keep an open mind. I'll watch out for an opportunity. No one knows what's going on in Russia. It might be dangerous."

She did not argue that. She hardly ever argued. Jan could no more have touched her heart than he could have touched the horizon. The closer he came, the more she retreated. A famine of the grayest kind had settled on her spirit. It seemed as though something of devastating avarice had sucked the marrow from her bone. Her appetite left much to be desired. No stick-to-the-rib food for Josie. A bean soup lunch was all.

She knew in a vague way that Jan kept trying to break down the bureaucrats in Washington to ship those needed harvesters, and she approved of that. The papers wrote it up. That's where the matter stopped.

"It is as though I forgot what to make of myself. Or of others," she said to Little Melly.

The spinster just tiptoed around her. "Whatever you want. Whatever you say."

If reproach she must speak, it was gentle, and patience was her middle name. "Try to remember, Josephine. It's critical. One ounce of cloves. Two tablespoons of cinnamon—"

Ladle after ladle full of Little Melly's patience finally paid off, for Josie, who had loved her reds and lilacs over every other color, no longer spurned the somber hues that Lizzy recommended.

No longer was she mocking providence with high heels and lofty proclamations. Gone was the way she flung apart that napkin in her lap. All knew she had diminished powers, and since she did not seem to want to heal—checkmated thoroughly by menopause and melancholia!—the drive to get those harvesters to Apanlee quietly petered out.

Chapter 57

Mimi knew there were dangers in prayers. When the feverish family prayers began, she stepped aside to sit on an upturned milk bucket. Her eyes were on the floor. Her heart began to race. Who could say who was watching? You had to be sure.

"The Lord will protect you. The Lord will provide." That's what her brothers said. Her teacher, gaunt and famished, had lectured her repeatedly: "Do not destroy the Party from within."

The teacher said each morning, her hungry eyes on her: "One of my brightest and my best. A keen and critical intelligence." Her brothers said: "Your turn now, Mimi dear."

"I can't. Say what you will. I can't."

Bewildered eyes turned anxiously on her. "We're praying for relief. Don't risk what we are praying for by angering the Lord."

She listened to the wind outside, soaked through with rain, rattling on the windows and whining through the gaping holes. Relief was coming? Well and good—but what if, with it, arrived menacing foreigners and tricksters? Forewarned was better than forearmed. That's what the teacher said.

"Behold the fowls in the air," prayed Yuri, Faith shimmering, small drops of mercury, in his wide-open eyes. "For they sow not, nor gather unto, yet your heavenly father feedeth—" His husky voice broke from the strain of duty and conviction. "—your heavenly Father feedeth—"

Sasha obediently took up the chant, perspiring with his brother's lie. "—feedeth us all."

"It can't be otherwise, for He hath—"

"—promised us!"

Larissa's hands touched Yuri's first, then Sasha's. The words came by themselves. "No news as yet?"

"Not yet. Maybe tomorrow?"

"Our time is running out. Relief is overdue. Thus we—"

"—thus we beseech Thee, Father—"

"—our Father of all creatures—"

"—to help us in our need!"

The little girl watched the deception closely, taking slow and shallow breaths. She leaned into the shadows and wiped a furrowed brow. A spasm fluttered in her chest. Faith? Easier to force down a pebble.

The twins, who had been spared, would credit Faith with widening the margin between a sorrowful subsistence and the grave—for it was up to them, they realized with ever sharper certainty, to hold their Faith aloft until the testing time was done.

For this they knew: The testing time was now! The alms were coming; they were coming! But Faith was needed; prayers, too; the Holy Ghost was quickened morning, noon, and night—and though they knew the seed was coming, verily! as per a thousand prayers—why, if the weather intervened and stalled the shipment from America, they might not live to benefit.

"Next week for sure," said Yuri, full of hope, the gentler, calmer of the twins. "If not next week, then soon!"

The adults linked their hands. For her own safety and protection, the child was left outside their prayer circle. She was still small. It drove the salt into her eyes. She knew that, by refusing to be part of the old ritual, she sabotaged the Faith, important to her family. But, on the other hand, could she impair her country's beaming future by yielding her young mind to superstition? That's what the teacher said.

Her head spun with confusion. Her shoulders slumped with misery. The soil beneath her thoughts was slippery.

Good folks in faraway America—a place where wheat stood tall and thick, where all the streets were strewn with gold, where many cousins lived a rich and haughty life, where supper tables bent with riches—were sending food to feed her. That's what her brothers claimed. She was so hungry she felt dizzy, but on the other hand, she knew that spies were watching and reporting.

She could not bring herself to say a single word to further Faith, but she held up her face, as though by accident, to be touched by Natasha's benevolent icon.

Marleen had written once again, as carefully and poetically as Uncle Benny used to write. Despite a wobbly pen, she looped the smallest letter, as Uncle Benny used to loop, but where was the reply?

"Send us your grain, for otherwise we perish," Marleen wrote, tearfully, while Mimi stood and watched, alone with a child's thoughts.

Here was her crime: she still had half a crust, of which her family knew nothing, an unexpected windfall straight from the barter market. Nobody knew that it was there, deep in her ragged coat. One of the argumentative, recruiting Pioneers had given it to her.

"We need your help," he had said, winking knowingly.

She owned that crust. She kept it as an iron ration in her pocket. She fingered it for reassurance now and then.

"—in the name of the Father—" chanted Yuri, his burning eyes on her.

"—and the Son—" muttered Sasha, whose face took on a purple sheen each time he prayed like that.

"One little word. Just one. Please, Mimi? If no one knows,

what harm is there in prayer?"

What harm? How could they ask?

If she reneged, she sabotaged her family. If she obeyed, she yielded to dishonor.

"Take tiny bites," said Yuri, parceling the meager rations, "to make the taste stretch out—"

Natasha poured some heated water. "Here, drink this, child—" She said in a low voice as she had done already a hundred times before: "Among us, we don't cry."

That, too, was Faith—that hunger would diminish by illusion.

"No one will know," coaxed Sasha. And Yuri, bringing up the rear: "What is a little prayer, said in near-silence if you wish, as long as no one knows?"

She was like any child. She longed to please and placate. What if her lack of Faith stalled the important shipment? But what would be the end result if someone told on her?

She heard the teacher laugh. She heard the children tease her without mercy. Where was this entity called Holy Ghost when good, kind people—dearth in their very sinews and vermin in their hair—now needed Him the most?

She squirmed with her divided loyalties. She wanted to shut out their glances; she wanted to plug up her ears. Faith? Prayers? Holy Ghosts? Old wives' tales, all. She wanted none of that.

She knew smart people had stopped praying to free their minds for reason. She knew, because her teacher told her daily in words too big for her small heart, that reason was the only way to pull her proud, defiant country from the depths of devastation.

She knew there was no God—no heresy among the learned.

"Clear thought," the teacher said, "will choke religion. All religion. Does anybody disagree?"

The teacher had explained to her the dangerous deception in lesson after lesson, while purging from her pupils' mind all thoughts of Jesus Christ.

"There is no God," the teacher said each day. "The nightingales are gone."

This teacher told the government inspectors who came periodically to stamp out Faith among the young: "This little girl?
One of our brightest and our best. I set great store by her."

"Don't slip on a rotten tomato—" the teacher said each day.
When the teacher spoke up to praise Mimi, all the children fell
quiet in the room. When the teacher mocked Faith in the foolish,
the classmates howled with mirth.

"There is no God," the teacher said repeatedly. "I have your
best at heart." And if that teacher had the smallest inkling that
Mimi, up for promotion to the rank of Pioneers in just a few short
years, still practiced her appalling prayers, she would have called
her to the front of the class. The guilty bench was waiting. That's
where the dunces sat.

There was no God—that much was clear, no matter what her
kneeling brothers claimed in their repeated, furtive whispers. She
was resolved she would not stain the future of the Motherland by
yielding her clear mind to noxious fables.

But all that—easier said than done!

When she looked at her brothers, imbued with burning Faith,
the old-fashioned prayers just flew to her lips. She had to bite
down on her tongue to keep them from jumping like frogs. Besides, might she receive another crust? When they saved up an
extra crust, it always went to Mimi.

It all came down to this: she had no choice; she had to stay
alive to help in the regeneration of her country. She would grow
up to bring great honor to the Revolution. She would plant birch
trees everywhere. She would bring pride to Russia.

All that lay burning deep inside, where she kept several other
similar deceptions against the people she loved most—deceptions much too ghastly to reveal.

Word came at last: it came over the telegraph poles. If Mimi
held her left ear pressed to the pole, already slippery with hoar—
why, she could hear the message hum.

Joy rushed through every nerve end. America was sending food! The miracle was here!

On the spot, she decided to meet it half-way.

Soles flapping, the chill of raindrops in her nape, her small hands red and glassy, she walked on, resolutely. She needed to make sure. Her feet, bloated grotesquely with hunger fluid, no longer fit into her shoes. She knew she had to last—somehow she must survive. She knew that food was coming—she knew that for a fact and with the instinct of a very hungry child.

Against her will, she started chanting guiltily: "In the name of the Father—" which seemed a small concession, since hunger gnawed her belly like a rodent, but in her hollow gut she knew: At last! At last! Good food was on the way. Where was the harm in drawing just a little bit on superstitious magic as long as no one knew?

"—and the Son—" This for Sasha!

"—and the Holy Ghost." For Yuri, whom she loved best of all!

Although she felt so faint she had to sit down several times, she kept on, leaning hard against the rain, determined to make sure. She drew on Faith against all better evidence.

She swallowed and then finished: "Amen!" This for her mother's sake who grieved the dwarfish child.

This baby sister, born of the horrid night, had died some time ago, but still her mother grieved. Dead, but not lost, her mother said, without a single tear. That was her comfort now. Her baby girl sat hand in hand with Him, the King of Kings, the Emperor of all the heavens, now free of hunger, without pain.

"Safe," said her brother, Yuri.

"Forevermore," said Sasha, crediting the Lord.

She, Mimi, was no fool; she saw the gaping earth. No God. No Son. No Holy Ghost. The hungry sparrows chirped that message from the roof. The baby girl was gone.

But still, she liked the story.

Now that the infant was no more, Natasha once again was cradling her in murky moments in place of that small baby girl,

now cold in death and dark beneath its fingernails, and not a budding Pioneer, alive, and first in all her classes.

With blue lips she carefully nibbled her crust. She softened it
with spittle and sucked the moldy taste. She had to be careful;
there were three loose teeth in her mouth.

She took a deep and trembling breath. Death sat in wait.
Natasha had told her that death, in the end, came to all. The baby
died, just toppled over sideways, and kept one eye still open as
though it had been tricked. Natasha had no explanation whatsoever why it would look like that.

The dead lay everywhere. Just this morning, she had counted
thirteen bodies lying scattered in the hedges—lying everywhere,
in fact. By the roadside they lay, underneath the mulberries, out
on the crumbling sidewalks, along the unused railroad tracks.
There they lay, the dying and the dead, poor devils from the cities, swept here by foolish rumors, wrapped in their rags or sacks,
in their pockets the last peels, perhaps, of a shriveled and stolen
potato.

"At Apanlee, there's wheat," they said as if a wish for miracles could make a miracle come true. Faith or no Faith, they
died. That was the bottom line. They died in the hedges; their
skull-like heads on a bundle of rags. This much was clear: the
dead did not look happy.

She took a greedy gulp of air. She knew she had to last,
somehow she must survive. The teacher told her every day she
had to stay alive to help regenerate her country.

She would not put her stock in Holy Ghosts unless she checked
the source and evidence with her own vintage eyes.

"Amen!" she said again, this time defiantly.

Some people died. Not she!

Death would not take her by the neck without a struggle first.
She would fight good and hard. She, only yesterday a child of
privilege and position, would swallow ground bones! Seeds of
weeds! Dust! Rodents! Anything!—why, she would eat the
very earth of Russia!

"—in the name of the Father and the Son and the Holy Ghost.
Amen."

A carriage approached from the distance, spattering soft mud.
The harness jingled merrily. Two men sat on the lorry.

Mimi hid what was left of her crust in her coat. No need to
arouse anyone's envy.

"Hey there! Say! Tell us! Quick! Which way to Apanlee?"

She saw at once—those two were professional looters. They
sported boots that gleamed, and they wore furs, with not a button
missing. Both wore new caps, along with woolen shawls.

"Huh?" Mimi stalled, while narrowing her eyes.

The older was a man with beefy hands and yellow teeth; the
younger one looked strangely faceless, ageless, and remote.

"Hop up. Can you give us directions?" the older of the two
said sharply. He had a round moon face. Though short and
paunchy, kind of squat, he looked well-fed indeed. His belly
spilled across his belt and sat there, like a watermelon, on his
knees. The lanky youth beside him peered at her out of one milky
eye. "Hey, you! Cat got your tongue? Where's Apanlee?"

"Huh? Apanlee?" Fear showed on her forehead in droplets.
The rodent in her stomach gnawed raw flesh. What were these
people doing here, all dressed as for a carnival? Their voices had
a queer, peculiar twang. They looked disdainful yet familiar.
She lifted her small chin. She felt her jaws lock firmly. She had
practiced her untroubled gaze. There was no room at Apanlee
for strangers.

The fat man raised his voice. He had a nasal twang. "You!
Are you deaf? Where's Apanlee?" He started pelting her with
tricky questions. "You don't live here? What are you doing here?
Alone? All soaking wet in this cold rain? Have you no sense at
all? Where is your family?"

He was smooth-shaven to the point where she could see his
pimples. She noted reddish hair, a freckled face, a fleshy nose,
fat, curling lips. He probably kept company with other thieves
and gangsters. Behind him piled huge burlap sacks. She swal-

lowed hard. Her instincts did a somersault: had he arrived to
rob? Would he start dumping drawers?

"What do you want?"

The older gave a cackling laugh. "What do we want? Why,
not a thing. What do you people want?" He turned his face and
told the younger one. "Just think of Little Melly's fire trucks.
For this?" He fixed a wintry stare on her that shot through the
rags of her coat like a sword. He leaned forward and gave her a
poke in the ribs with his finger.

"We've come to visit Apanlee. Now tell us. Where is
Apanlee?"

Her eyes grew wide with alarm. "Keep following the road,"
she said, now forcing cheer into her voice. "That way. That way
to Apanlee."

"That way?"

"Right! Right! That way."

"You're sure?"

"Yes. Pretty soon you'll reach a shack. The road will fork.
Turn right there. Keep on going—"

Apanlee lay to the left. You couldn't be too careful. No
margin left for error.

Chapter 58

"Well, look at that. That must be it. That must be Apanlee."
The Elder Dewey's Adam's apple danced to the oscillation of
emotion. He stroked his temples thoughtfully.

"You're right. That must be it," said Archibald, his chin in
one of Little Melly's furs.

"That's it!" said Dewey, forcefully. "That's it! That's it! I
can't believe my eyes!"

His earlobes had turned scarlet. He stared, and there was
unrelieved disgust and loathing written in his face.

This was ghost country here and could not rightfully be called
by any other name. It was late afternoon; the rain had stopped at
last, but it was cold and dreary. His kidney stones shot rays into
his groin. "Where are the people, Archie?"

For days, he and his son had traveled over muddy and, at
time, half-frozen roads in search of needy relatives. Pushed into
this endeavor against his will—for Jan had given him no peace
until he packed and went—the Elder Dewey went, expecting an
emergency. But ruins instead of homes? And weeds instead of
vegetables? His voice was strangely slurred; he sounded as if he

were drunk.

"They must have sinned," he said. "This is God's punishment."

"Well, there you have it, Dad," said Archibald. "It looks as though the hoppers have devoured every single blade of grass."

He, too, had reached the last stage of exhaustion, for as he passed through village after village, he who had come to bring both food and gospeling, thought that the populace would greet him, overjoyed, but no! They shrank away from him.

He had expected hats to fly into the air at his arrival; instead, wherever he encountered people, they stood with eyes downcast.

"Just what is going on?"

"Well. You tell me."

Way back in Washington, while being briefed on what to say, what not to say, because the government was touchy regarding certain views, the Elder Dewey had been told that Russia was a country savage, poor and insignificant. But this? He had been told that rubles were counted in millions while bread would be counted in crumbs. He had been briefed on hunger, terror and despair. All that made little difference.

His inner eye saw landscapes all his own. Some deep and lasting pictures out of his past told of a bounteous time. He had grown up with fairy tales of yesterday from Noralee, from Doctorjay, from Lizzy, from old neighbors. He knew of Jan's ancestral home, for Noralee had chiseled out for him the serene world of Apanlee, where children and pets were petted and pampered, where troikas parked with arrogance in long and lofty lines to unload the nobility of yesterday, while humble footmen, one by one, stood waiting for their orders.

"Ah, Apanlee," said Noralee, who in her youth had scrubbed and bleached its linens, agog and smitten with the glamor and perfection. While he was still a child and unwise to the wiles of autocrats, he had absorbed it all with veneration mixed with envy.

Now this?

Where was the trodden goose path for the barefoot neighbor children who came to play at Apanlee? Where were the sun-

drenched haystacks? The cozy summer kitchen where generations had assembled to drink their scented tea in peace and harmony on languid summer afternoons?

The Elder Dewey sat atop his lorry, staring. He sat there,
wating, but nobody sprang to his aid. In the end, he made a fist
and gave his son an energetic punch.

"We might as well—" he said, and cleared his throat for added
volume, while his mouth twisted in a grimace of distaste.

"Yes. Yes. We might as well," said Archibald, and started
pulling on a hangnail. "There go our fire trucks." His missing
eye, his right, was itching in its socket. His face took on a purple
sheen. He, too, had his priorities. He, too, had his opinions.
Could he forget that day—half of his vision gone, shot out by
racial ill-will? For this? All fences hung in disrepair. The paint
was flaking from the windows. Three doors were ripped from
rusty hinges, and there were glass shards everywhere. This was
the place the sentimental oldsters in his hometown longed to see?
Jan's haughty forebears, once upon a time, had ridden through
this gate, a bunch of unrepentant autocrats? A selfish Emperor-to-be
had leaned against those crumbling steps? Where was the endless sea of wheat, just swaying with the songs of well-fed peasants? Where were the men of fortitude and strength who would,
all summer long, be heartily engaged in never-ending races
against the sinking sun?

For Archibald, it was a milestone moment, for something dark
and murky and unspoken came to rest. For what he saw while he
sat, staring, made for its own conclusions.

This was far worse than anything the Donoghues might have
dreamed up to tear down ethnic pride and vex and aggravate the
town. He, too, was but a human being, as Little Melly always
said; he, too, had hoped the fire trucks at home would clean the
town of heckling and give him breathing space.

"This disaster could never have—"

"—would surely never have happened in Kansas!"

"A travesty. A shame."

"The magic," said the Elder Dewey harshly, "has run out."

"Right. Man proposes. God disposes. This here is taking charity too far."

"Why!" Dewey cried out then, and rage built like a thunderstorm. "Look who's here! That little double-dealing viper that managed to lead us astray! We'll teach her a fine lesson!"

What Dewey saw at that triumphant moment was not a hungry child, forlorn in a weed-infested alley against a drab, dilapidated edifice, so famished that her eyes bulged in her face, but Josie! Josephine! In her defiance and contempt and brazenness, upsetting and unruly, unwilling to be gospeled. "Hey! You! Come here!" His moon face twisted with his loathing. "You lied to me!" he shouted. "You soiled your mouth! Come here so I can smack you!"

"I didn't know you, Citizen!" the youngster stammered, stumbling. "I didn't recognize your face!" She came running as soon as she saw she had made a mistake, but now she stood still in her tracks. She shuddered as though from the blow of an axe but she didn't back off; she stood holding her ground; she tilted her head to the strangers, and her eyes filled with great expectation.

"I am ashamed," said Dewey to the youngster, while fixing a bilious eye, "to be vaguely related to you."

"You aren't," said the child.

"What? What?" He eyed her balefully. Fat chance he'd swallow that! He had grown up and old anticipating trickery from Josie, repeatedly a menace to the plans and wishes of the Lord. He was still making count. Was he not wearing Kansas clothes? How could she miss his brand new hat, though soggy now from rain?

The child spoke very softly. "You are a foreigner. You came to see the changes the glorious Revolution wrought."

"We're all related to each other. Related over centuries."

While she stood, waiting, watching him, all but on tiptoes, verily! he kept on looking for a hitching post on which to tether his two horses. He barked: "Here. Hold the reins! We must be cousins. Or else, I am your uncle."

She kept her distance now. She did not offer help.

"We are your cousins from America," yelped Archibald, whose voice had not yet found its bedrock. "We've come to help. Where is your gratitude? You lied! Why did you lie? Why in the good Lord's name did you decide to lead us astray in this rain?"

She did not reply. She was small; she was cold and she shivered; she kept staring at Dewey, who now sensed a chilling reserve. This was no agreeable female!

"Here. I said hold the reigns." He kept her in the corner of his eye. He knew her kind. Here was the cause that drained those nickels from his church he needed sorely to throw a monkey wrench into the Methodists. He spat. He was settling a very old score. "You're a liar! That's what you are. A brazen, shameless liar!"

He could spot her ilk without trying. She was the kind who, numb to Faith and all its benefits, would tell him before long, unblinking, as soon as she grew old enough to face him, toe to toe: "I have no use for you." He arched damp eyebrows, furious. "My, what a place! What is the matter with you people? Where is your pride? Did you not know that relatives were coming? Did we not write to you? Why did you not clean up?"

A wave rose deep within. The curfew he had sacrificed to keep the Donoghues in check—for this? This landscape, bleak and bare?

These frightened and emaciated creatures who now materialized from the bushes, who stretched out bony hands to him yet shrunk against the wall?

He took a deep, deep breath. He flexed ten angry fingers. For once, he saw the truth. For once, his judgment stood redeemed. When German farmers starved to death on the world's richest acres, there had to be a moral failing. Here's where his role came in.

The more in need a flock, the stronger was his ministry!

He reached for his stilted High German, turned into a hickory stick. "Do not be mistaken!" he hollered, now shaking his fist at the shadows. "God is not mocked, nor is He deceived. For whatever a man sows, that he will also reap—"

At that, the youngster backed away as though she were attacked by wasps.

"But praise the Lord," hectored Dewey, now swinging. "It's never too late. You liar, you! You cheat! But I, for one, shall do my best to shed the Gospel light on you."

"You will. You will," said Archibald, and put a soothing hand atop his father's twitching knee.

"I will!"

"Calm down! You'll teach her things. You will."

"That's right. I will. You bet your bottom dime I will!"

The Elder Dewey flicked a smart, determined whip across the horses' bony shanks and rolled into the gates of Apanlee to do the Lord's strict bidding.

The Elder Dewey checked his brand of Faith into the halls of Apanlee as though he checked a hat. He knew his own Faith's worth. He knew it to the penny, and it was not for free. It came in thirty burlap sacks packed seam to seam with grain. He also had with him, deep in his cardboard suitcase, the one-and-only Gospel, as rich as lentil soup.

By evening, a crowd had gathered, all stretching out their trembling hands to get the food that Mennotown had sent. Night fell, and still more came.

They climbed out of cellars and down from their ovens; they materialized out of the bushes. They would not shake his hand, nor would their eyes meet his. They tried to rush the bags.

He culled their faces, one by one. They were a ghastly sight. They looked as though a ghost would come and snatch them on the spot. They exchanged anguished, significant glances and ducked when he tried to take pictures.

His anger belched like lava. He had arrived to bring them charity; where was their gratitude? Here was bread; here was seed; but it came packed in sensible rules. It came with appropriate conduct. It required the Lord be praised loudly.

He asked for bright smiles to display on the bulletin boards in the churches back home. He asked them to join hands to form a prayer circle.

The shadow people never raised their lids. Not even the oldsters seemed willing to join. All stood with downcast eyes.

Before he started parceling the goodies the volunteers back home, all squealing with devotion, had readied for the voyage, he read them a timely Bible verse first, expertly navigating through the Gospel while showing off agility.

"As we have opportunity, " he hectored, glowering, a pencil in his teeth with which he started checking off their names, "let us do good to all—"

This was symbolic only. How many qualified?

No easy task to get a handle on a number. He could not feed them all. Not having any better gauge, he went by their *umlauts* and freckles. He gave them extra helpings—he could be sure of them. He launched himself more firmly. "The power of the Gospel is much stronger than the power of the state," he lectured. Might as well.

They stood in silence. Shivering. They stared at him, wordless, as though he were daft. He had never felt so out of place. He couldn't wait to head back home, shake hands with folks in Mennotown. He knew that, once he told them what he found, they'd witness properly and boost his missionary kitty.

He made the shadows walk right underneath the church insignia that Little Melly had cross-stitched for him, her face all vague and dreamy. "You, there! You lead us now in grace. You speak your prayer thanks," he chided the dishonest child, ambitious to make an example.

She shook her head. Her lips were quivering.

"Repeat after me: 'Let us give thanks'" It was clear that she wanted his food; it was equally clear she was scared to admit she was hungry. He saw the subdued terror, but he saw this as well: her bulging eyes were glued to his fat burlap sacks, and that gave him his margin.

"Well? We are waiting."

She had no words in her defense. Her brow was damp with

sweat. Her nose looked pinched. Her eyes were wide. She did seem pitifully starved.

Still, could he let this opportunity pass by? He had to come right out and demand forcefully: "Somebody needs to witness. Openly. Without it, there's no food."

"I can't." She backed away from him.

He followed her and bore down hard. "Look, here! I know you're hungry, aren't you? I know you need some nourishment to fill your little belly. But first things first. You lied to me this afternoon. Why did you lie to me?"

"I did not know you, Citizen."

He held a piece of bread aloft as though it were a trophy. "See this? I want you to apologize." Against his better judgment, he felt a stab of pity for the girl, but that did not alter his purpose. She was unwilling, clearly, for not one word came forth. The crowd looked on in silence.

"I said apologize!"

Her face started twitching. Her shoulders contracted as though under blows. He hovered over her.

"What did I tell you? Huh? Are you sorry you lied? Are you sorry?"

"Just say you're sorry," coaxed Archie, who understood the sting of being singled out for punishment. "Come on. Say sorry, honey. Say pretty please and sorry."

She spoke up then. She spoke so softly that he could barely hear.

She said: "These alms are not from love."

Dewey let go of his ladle and stiffened his spine. Here was his evidence. This here was Josephine who argued everything. This one would not bend short of breaking.

He, on the other hand, knew what his calling was, or else there was no soup tureen. "Now listen here! Young lady!" Much as a train was building up steam, so Dewey was building up anger. He told her, thick with rectitude: "You played fast and loose with the truth. Will you apologize? Here is my hand. That's all I am asking. Just say you are sorry. Come on. Say you're sorry—"

She lifted herself up on tiptoes.

"Just say it. Just say you are sorry," prompted Archie. He was nervously biting his hangnail. "Look. Look. Why not apologize? You know lies have short legs—"

The child glanced at her calves, confused. They were swollen from unhealthy fluid. "I didn't know you, Citizen—"

"You heard me. You heard me loud and clear. Just say you're sorry, and all is forgotten." He was rapidly losing his patience. "Why did you lie to me?"

She stared into his wind-shot eyes. She saw he had hair in his nostrils.

"Well? Do I have all afternoon?"

She spoke between clenched teeth, but loud enough for the last bystander to hear. "I would walk many miles," she said, "just to avoid you. Hear? You have no place in Russia. You are a foreigner and trickster."

Rage twisted his shoulder and shot through his chest like a bolt. It was clear that she wanted that fat slice of bread that he held in his hand, out of reach—she wanted it so desperately her eyes protruded from her skull. Her need was as raw as the weather.

He stood on tiptoes, for his part, while holding it aloft. "Hey! Hey! Do you apologize? Or not? I expect you to say you are sorry!" It seemed to him the hive was humming angrily, but he was not afraid. He knew he had the upper hand, for he had rectitude. He had that piece of bread. He held it up with his right hand while he spread all five stubby fingers of his left to count out the rest of her sins: her cheeks unwashed, her hair untrimmed across her brow, the vermin crawling on her collar—a sullen, unkempt youngster in need of stricter discipline. America wept with the weeping, but on the other hand, nobody spared the rod in Mennotown.

"You won't say you are sorry? You won't? All right. So pay the piper. Have it your way. You asked for it. It looks like you'll just have to go to bed without supper!"

For Dewey, the issue was settled. A modern century was on

its way, and in this heathen country—or so he was instructed while being briefed in Washington, D.C.—the most recalcitrant, vagabond, worthless of children were seen as a national resource. In atheistic Russia, you couldn't even spank them with your horse strap any more!   Conspiratorially, he winked at Archibald who kept track of the names on the list.

"Too bad! Too bad!" winked Archie, who read his father's thoughts. "Looks like we're running short. Looks like there is nothing left over for liars. You will just have to wait. You have all night to think it over. And if you come, tomorrow morning, and tell us you are sorry—"

He and his father, Dewey, were cut from the same cloth. This here was a showdown of values. Bad habits must be trimmed, and they had the gardener's shears.

The forces that shape history are splinters, left deep in martyred flesh. This story is now many decades old, but Mimi still remembers it as though it happened yesterday—and so does Archibald.

That day, they eyed each other, and they knew. They still do, to this day.

For on that dreary, hungry afternoon they glimpsed a flash of savage hatred in each other's eyes that neither one would ever manage to forget—and to this day, God speaks to Mimi sneeringly through Archie's mealy mouth.

Here is what followed next.

When all had finished eating, he went to look for her. He spoke about redemption and salvation while holding food aloft.

"See this fine piece of bread? I've saved it up for you."

He, Archie, would not easily give up. This bread came on the wings of Faith. This bread came back to back with rules.   He hadn't come this far to spread the promise of the Gospel to get all soft-bellied with pity. He had to trim her claws, for if he didn't, here and now—why, everlasting hell would not be hot enough.

"This is for your own good. If we let your defiance go unpunished, you will develop a strange character." Here was his chance to step into his father's preacher shoes, to force a timely lesson.

He took her by the shoulders. "This minute, you apologize! You will! You will! You will!"

He spoke not only for himself; he spoke for Dewey who was wet and chilled and tormented by kidney stones, who knew full well that, in his absence, the Methodists would make the rounds and snare the undecided.

"I won't."

If nothing else, he could still pinch. He pinched.

She twisted, and she ducked. She slipped out of his fingers.

He asked himself: "What kind of child is this?"

She did not ask herself—she knew.

He watched her face go slack. She saw his lips snarl odiously. "What's it to me?" said Archibald, and laughed derisively.

It was a nasty laugh. The devils danced in it for quite a while. They danced and didn't stop.

She heard that laugh and stored it. That laugh held many things, but mostly this: he owned the food; she owned her hunger. Both knew there was bad blood between them, and it would never go away.

That, too, is history. He knew that she had stared the Devil in the eye as he had not, and never would, for she was hard as nails; she came of tested stock; her pale, set face told volumes. And he was pulp—a worm without his Bible.

That day, she was so famished she felt faint, but still she sensed the weakness that was central to his character and message. She knew that on the pulpit, it came out, revealed as sleazy staple. How did she know? She had been witness to the empty burlap sacks that fell around his ankles to the floor. She knew forevermore that nothing coming from America—or from the Gospel, for that matter—would come to her for free.

Chapter 59

They ran in packs, the mangy children of the Revolution, frostbite softening their toes, hunger shining brightly in their eyes. They roamed the dying city of Berdyansk in search of food and prey.

They came upon the freezing boy who huddled, knees drawn to his chin, within the shelter of an abandoned cattle box. He tried to shrink into himself, but they surrounded him. "Look here! A kulak boy! Hey, you! Hey, kulak boy!"

They emptied his pockets: a pencil stub, a cross-stitched handkerchief, three little wooden animals. "Your name? What is your name?"

He shook his head. They did not press the matter.

"How old are you?"

"Ten. I am ten."

It was the first lie of his life, born of the instinct to survive. To demonstrate his nonchalance, he broke off a dirty icicle and started sucking it. They pointed to a cat. He understood at once. They were the mob. He was alone. He saw and seized the opportunity. He stalked it patiently all morning. In the end, he threw a well-aimed rock. A little jump — he had it by its hind legs.

Triumphantly, he took it to the horde. They howled with glee and slapped him on the shoulders. They skinned the twitching animal. They terrorized a beggar woman, until she relented and fried it for them.

He watched what they were doing and learned their tricks from them. He sat with them on many a street corner, begging. He followed vague rumors of food.

He slept his afternoons away, for then the sun shone warmest. He slept by the roadside, in tunnels, in doorways. The dead piled up so high he couldn't see the fence. He knew that they were waiting for the thaw to have a burial of sorts.

At night, he slithered from lamp post to lamp post. He ate whatever he found—a frozen potato, half-rotten cabbage, the heel of an old loaf of bread. In a pinch, there was always a handful of earth.

He spent his mornings near the rails where foreign journalists passed by sometimes, their pencils poised like lances—all gullible, all easily deceived. He held them in contempt. He told them many lies.

Once, through a sudden streak of luck, he found a bag of onions. He sold them, one by one. With the money thus obtained, he rented a small child.

"Shhh! You!" he expertly scolded the infant. "Who cuddles you? Who tickles you? Who gives you tiny kisses?"

He took good care of it, knowing that its warmth was as comforting as a baked brick out of Natasha's oven. He still saw his Baba's face clearly. He no longer remembered the others.

He liked the small child casually; it was his life insurance. It never failed to melt the hearts of foreign passersby so that they rained their kopecks into his waiting hand. He warmed it, and he rocked it. He worried it would shrivel up on him while he sat— waiting, begging. It kept on whimpering beneath the cold and cheerless rain until his patience broke. He put it in the gutter carefully, face down, did not look back, and stealthily moved to the other end of town.

He spent a night in jail for panhandling excessively on a street corner where foreigners passed by. He did not mind at all. It was a quiet, dry place, much warmer than out in the streets.

In the morning, he was given a broom and a pan and told to sweep the floor. He was a quick study. He knew how to drive a sharp bargain.

"If I can sleep here every night, I'll spy on foreigners and tricksters," he offered himself to the guards. They roared and slapped him on the shoulders.

It was on such a wind-blown corner, where Dewey Epp of Mennotown, on his way back from Apanlee, saw lifted from the rags and filth of anarchy a face that made him stop.

"My God," he said to Archibald. "Look at this boy. That's one of us. Could that be one of us?"

A bony arm stretched from a threadbare coat. An urchin, straight out of the gray of the gutter!

"Bread! Bread!" the urchin whined expertly. "I haven't eaten anything for days!" His instinct told him to use German.

"That boy," said Archie, staring, "looks just like Auntie Josie's Rarey."

In the gaunt face, there was a sharp alertness, in his blue eyes the blueprint left by centuries. The youngster wore good boots— expensive leatherware, but worn to shreds, cut off at the heels to facilitate running. The soles were tied with string. A bird's voice kept on pleading: "Just half a slice of bread—"

The Elder Dewey cleared his throat. "Say, guttersnipe. Do you know of a place called Apanlee?"

The urchin flinched as though he had been hit. "I don't know what you mean."

He started shuffling, sullenly. He watched both strangers from the corner of his eye.

The younger man, the pimply one, said swiftly: "Well. Listen, little fellow. Just don't be scared. We'll see what we can do." The older one, who had a pumpkin belly and wore a pair of horn-rimmed glasses, still scowled with indecision, whereas the other one reached out for him and tried to take him by the hand.

The ragged street child shrank away. He wouldn't let himself be touched.

"All right. All right," said Archie, irritated. And Dewey added: "We won't bite. Follow us."

The urchin followed meekly, head lowered, fists buried deeply in his coat.

"Dad, don't you think—"

"No. I said no."

"But Dad—"

"I said no, Archie. No! Forget it. In Mennotown, we don't need kids like that. We have the Donoghues."

But Archie understood a misfit's needs. He understood them, achingly. "He has no name. He has no memory, it seems."

"He's probably deceiving you," ventured Dewey.

"He says the State is his father, the glorious Revolution his mother—"

"Some jokester. Some jokester we picked up." Disgusted, Dewey took the youngster's cap and flung it in the fire, while Archie stripped him of his rags. "Stand right there, by the door, so I can measure you. How old are you?"

Archie took a pair of scissors and cut the matted fringes from his brows. "See, underneath that filth? My, what a handsome boy." His voice was strangely gentle.

The urchin bit his lips.

"I'd like to take you home," he said to him in halting German. "I'd like to take you to America. The Boy Scouts will be good for you. They'll clean you up. They'll know how to straighten you out."

"No, you do not," said Dewey, in sharp English.

"But I—"

"I said no, Archie. That's my verdict. That is it."

"Perhaps—"

"Don't blow against the hurricane. He knows only the filth of the streets. What would he do in Mennotown? We don't need vagabonds like that. We have our own. As I already pointed out, we have the Donoghues."

But Archie's heart was pounding painfully. He ached to bring some light into those ancient eyes. He took the urchin by both hands.

"Your Savior died for you," he told him eagerly, not knowing what else he might say.

"Who shot him?" asked the child, and pulled his hands away.

"No one shot Him," said Archie, sharply. "Why, what a horrid thing to say! You need to have your mouth washed out with soap. Our Savior died for you. For me. For all of us. For our grievous sins."

The urchin had a smooth reply. "To kill is easier than to convince."

"Did you hear that? Dad, did you hear what he just said?"

"Some wise guy," scolded Dewey. "A real smart aleck, huh? Say, guttersnipe. What happened to your hand?"

The boy backed up. "No! Nothing."

"What do you mean, nothing? It's all red and infected. Here, let me soak it clean. It looks like something bit you. Did you tease a defenseless animal?"

"A dog? Let's see," coaxed Archie, too. "That is one ugly wound! Was it a dog? If so, we'll need some turpentine."

"No. Not a dog. A girl."

Archie backed away as though he had just touched a rattler. "A girl? What did you try to do? Come. Sit here by my side. Sit here with me, right by the window. I'll tell you all about our Savior Jesus Christ—" He tried to pull the urchin to his knees. His hands were weaving distressed circles. "See? It's like this. No matter who you are, no matter what you do, your Savior stands there, waiting. He'll wash away your sins. The choice is up to you—"

The urchin listened sullenly. A faint, pleasant memory stirred. Had he not heard it once before, this tale about this so-called

Savior, who would arrive in thunderbolts and darts of fire and still all hunger, dry all tears?   He leaned against the stranger gingerly while something deep within turned drowsy and contented, while something inside broke, much like a helpless wave.

"See? It's like this," said Archibald, while tightening his arm. "The choice is up to you. No one can choose for you. It is all up to you. You can choose to hear the message, or you can choose to live with both your fingers in your ears. Now look me squarely in the eye and tell me this: would you not rather go to Heaven—"

The urchin snapped sharply to attention.

"Heaven," said the urchin nastily while pushing against Archibald, "is now a place for birds, for angels, and for fools."

There was no reaching him, though Archie did his best. He had an extra blanket; he would get up at night and try to cover him, but even in his sleep the urchin jerked his arm away as though touched by some poisonous rattler.

"Look, I'm your friend," said Archie, pleadingly.

"I do not need a friend. I've never had a friend."

"Well, now you do."

There was no soothing him. He rolled himself into a ball and slept with his back to the wall, his face to the door, refusing to lie next to Archie. "I'm hungry."

"But you just ate," said Archie.

"So?"

"Don't scoop the food up with your fingers. And don't tear the bread with your teeth. There really is enough left over for tomorrow."

"And fold your hands," ordered Dewey. "I taught you yesterday. No progress yet?"

"No progress yet," admitted Archie sadly. "The more I push, the more he's digging in his heels. The more his conscience hardens."

"A blunted conscience," Dewey found, and heard no contradiction.

The urchin stayed with them for several weeks, while the two preachers waited for the bureaucrats to reach the bottom of their pile of papers and straighten out a mix-up with their travel papers, still needing signatures and several red stamps.

They did not like the street child much; nor he them; that was mutual. By then, he had become a burden. He took, but didn't give. He didn't give an inch, no matter how they gospeled.

He ate. He slept. He heard their admonitions, his ancient eyes on them. He hardly ever argued back. He did exactly as he pleased.

He often escaped, but he always came back. His comings and goings were secret.

His pockets were bulging with flyers. At night, he emptied the last marmalade jar that Little Melly had packed.

"That is one guilty little thief," said Dewey Epp, not easily deceived. "What did I tell you, Archie?"

"Poor child. Poor child," mourned Archie in great pity, and at a total loss. "No matter what we do or say, he finds the Word of God revolting. A pity, Dad. A pity."

"He's hopeless. Did I not tell you from the start?"

Archie gave a long and bitter sigh, now speaking more from duty than conviction. "At least he's willing to sit through devotions. That's progress. Don't you think?"

If he looked hard, he saw some progress on good days, but it was slight—it was so slight that one might call it imperceptible.

"Why do you hate us so?" asked Archibald.

"Because you're spies," the gutter child said angrily. "You're harming Mother Russia."

"Why, that's a laugh. That is preposterous. We are the Lord's dispatchers."

"You're spies, and maybe worse."

"We are Americans. We are ambassadors of love. We're vassals of the Lord. We've come to heal the spirit."

The urchin shrugged and bit his lip. "If I were you—"

"Why? What is going on?"

The boy spoke up with quiet authority. "You better leave. And fast."

"What do you mean?" Some evil lay in wait that had no name, no focus. The aftermath of the triumphant Revolution had turned into a war of shadows.

"What are you saying, guttersnipe?"

"Five foreigners have disappeared at point of bayonet."

"But we've done nothing wrong!"

"That matters not. That matters not one whit."

Dewey looked at Archie, worried, and Archibald stared back. Neither one could force a smile. Before them stood the found-ling, sullen.

"Just leave," he said. "Get out of here. Don't say you weren't warned."

A child might speed the paperwork; that was the Elder's reasoning—and, lo, it worked; it did. Between those two, the urchin crossed the borders amid the last small troop of foreigners who had come to see for themselves what the glorious Red Revolution had wrought.

The moment they arrived in Germany, the Bible smugglers vanished, as swiftly as they came, just ruddering with flying arms out of the chaos of the east and aiming for the safety of Kansas before another country, Germany, exploded like an overripe to-mato and splattered everything with red.

"We'll send you two letters a year," shouted Archie, while Dewey gave him a powerful shove: "Jump! Jump! The train is slowing down."

The boy stared after them. He stood beneath a gray, indiffer-ent sky—a gray louse in a cold, gray land he knew instinctively would show no mercy either.

He sat down in the snow and wept briefly, relieved to be free of them. He was glad to be done with their prayers—as violating as a body search, as exhausting as a night filled with mosquitoes. He knew he would not miss them.

The day was gray on gray. The only speck of color was a garish poster displaying the hammer and sickle. It kept on flapping in the wind, torn and defaced. An angry hand had scrawled on it a hooked cross and spelled out in sharp, angled letters: "Events begin to favor A. H."

A question mark inside him grew. He hugged it to himself.

"Hey, there! Hey, you!"

Several children, no older than he, huddled forlornly in door-ways—a rag-tag lot, in looks not all that different from the mangy pack he'd left behind in wind-torn, starving Russia. He hoped to strike up a friendship. He missed his little comrades with their hard eyes and nimble feet from whom he had learned to survive.

He gave them a tentative smile, but they did not respond; they sat, silent and hunched and defeated. He kept them in the corner of his eye. They watched him but did nothing.

"All right. If not, then not." His head was swimming with fatigue. His hands were cracked from cold. His belly hurt with hunger. He had sprained his left ankle when Dewey pushed him from the train—now every step he took shot knives into his groin.

He roused himself to action. He tried to jump onto a moving railroad car, but a gaunt brakeman took him by the ear and threw him back down on the asphalt.

Next, he followed an arrow that pointed to a shelter. It was a hovel, little more—a leaking roof, a foul-smelling latrine. He had lived in such hovels before. He looked around and found a corner. The bunks were filled with gray, defeated people. Their blankets smelled of urine and accumulated dirt.

"Have all good ghosts deserted you?" asked one. "Here. Share my stall with me."

His hands were moist and smelling sour. He had a cackling laugh.

A few weeks passed. A month. A year. Another. And an-other.

The sun was cold. The moon was silent. He emptied his eyes and his heart.

He lost all track of time. He felt as though he had no weight. He knew that he was young, yet he felt ancient and depleted. He slept badly; he stared into the darkness and listened to the rough and brutal voices that wafted back and forth. He heard the thuds of anarchy. Despair gnawed the depth of his being. He was a struggling speck of will in this abysmal sea of dying flesh; he felt relief at last when someone came and took him by his collar, depositing him, none too gently, in an orphanage clear on the other side of town.

Again, it was a makeshift edifice, a former stable, boarded up, that had been built for sheep. A metal bar was laid across the gate. The padlock snapped shut with a click.

He claimed a bunk next to the oven. He defended that bunk with his teeth.

He felt ill. Foul. Confused. He hardly ever spoke. The winter kept on moaning through the broken door. His eyes were on the floor out of necessity—to find a cigarette stub was bliss. He hoarded butts. An intact butt could be exchanged for things that had enormous use: a box of bolts, a rusty knife, a crooked nail, most anything at all. In an unhinged and shattered world, you kept your eye on butts, the best of currencies.

He was a stubborn youngster; no one forced him to do anything. He rarely cried. He never laughed. He knew no one who did.

His thoughts were thoughts of stone.

He often ran away. No matter where he went, about him was the rancid smell of unwashed people who stood in queues with sullen faces, carrying barrels full of worthless money while waiting for a bowl of lumpish soup dispensed by the Committee of True Democrats to Aid Suburban Poverty.

He shook off every memory of Apanlee as one shakes off a slug.

That's how life was in Germany for many youngsters such as he before the light burst forth that poured caressing warmth onto the smallest insect, all struggling to survive.

From where she came, nobody knew. She was a slim and fragrant thing, almost a girl, yet many years a woman, wearing red patent leather shoes, a short blue skirt, a blouse so white it blinded, beneath an open coat.

It was as though a shaft of light fell on that blouse and straight into the gutter. Her hair was the color of wheat.

She huddled next to him. "Hey, little one. What is your name?"

He shrugged. His memories were vague. The fat pretender preacher was the last who had called him by name. What was it? Guttersnipe.

She poked him gently with a rosy index finger. "You must have a name. Most everybody I know has a name. You cannot live without a name. Now tell me yours. What is it?"

The words came of their own accord. "I am not sure. My Baba called me Jonny."

He tried to tell her more, but his voice was no longer his own.

"I have the honor, Jonny." She smiled to give him courage. "Now that I know your name, I'd like to know how old you are. When was your birthday, Jonny?"

"I don't know that."

"Come on. Don't be afraid. How old are you?"

"Fifteen?" He squinted at her shyly.

She saw through his lie and straight into his heart as though her two cornflower eyes shot rays through a series of thin sheets of glass. "Nobody could be fifteen years of age, as handsome as you are, and not in uniform. Now, let me guess. Eleven? Twelve?"

He nodded miserably. "I think so. I'm not sure."

"It's not that bad. Is it? It could be worse? You will be fifteen in no time at all. Trust me. It doesn't take that long to grow into a man."

He swallowed. A wave started cresting within.

Her voice was warm, caressing. "Consider me. Compared to you, I'm practically Methuselah. My age is twelve times two plus one. How old is that? Is that some age, or what?"

He roused himself. "You're twenty-five?"

"That's right. My, you are smart."

It took enormous effort. "I think my name—my name is

Jonathan."

"My name is Hannelore, but everybody calls me Heidi." She resembled the heather—small and resilient, sun-baked and scented, attracting bees and ladybugs. She tugged him by his thumb. "Where are you from? Do you have any family at all?"

His head hung on his chest. "I am alone. I've been alone for years."

On each lapel, she wore a tiny pin that showed a hooked cross. She wore her coat wide open. "Who's taking care of you?"

"I don't need anybody." He saw her blouse had every button sewn in place. That blouse had not a single crease. It smelled sweetly of soap and hot iron.

"We all need friends. We all need family."

He scowled to keep her at bay. That part of him was dark and violent. His memories about the people he once called his family now danced and echoed through the space of many empty years.

"Might someone be looking for you?"

At that, something astonishing happened. The faces that he couldn't bear remembering rose from within as though from murky waters. They were still there. Each one of them. His grandparents. Marleen. Natasha. Sasha. Yuri. A little cousin, Mimi. His shoulders started heaving.

Her voice was low and thoughtful. "I have a hostel, nice and warm, for youngsters just like you."

He shook his head and thought his heart would fly apart. "I better not. I have too many enemies. They might just follow me."

She took his fists and put them both into the pockets of her coat. She started unfurling his fingers, slowly and methodically. She put both of his grimy hands, flat, on her spotless skirt.

"There. Feel that, Jonny. That is the future, Jonny. Right inside me. Below my heart. It's growing inside me."

Marleen! Heavy with progeny! That gesture was so achingly familiar, yet clearly from another world—he stood, his shaking fingers on her belly that was ballooning gently.

"See? Now you found me out. I'll have a little baby," she said with a small laugh.

He would have slunk away with shame, had she not nailed him to the spot with both her arms that snapped about him suddenly, just like a safety belt.

Those arms. That warmth. The trembling wonder of her presence. It held the universe in place. He felt his tears collect upon his chin and fall onto her shoulder while she stood, silent, waiting, pretending not to see that he was crying now, in heaving sobs, as he had never cried before, and never would again.

She let him cry it out.

When he had emptied every tear, she told him, friend to friend: "I have three sons already. I'm hoping for a girl. If it's a girl, I'll let you pick a name. If it's a boy, I'll name him after you. What do you say to that?"

He said, when he could speak again: "I am absurdly happy—" and did not know those were the very words that Uncle Benny kept, cross-stitched by Dorothy, for years atop his dictionary.

That's how it all began.

She had a ledger where she noted name, date, place, size, weight and comment: "Found wandering. In need of scrubbing, discipline and schooling."

She took him by the hand and up two flights of stairs. She handed him a cake of soap. "There, take a shower bath. The water's nice and warm." Goodness and patience shone from her face. She was of his blood. Of his sinews.

She said, a little later, while he sat in her kitchen, overcome: "Here, have a cup of coffee." She kept on refilling his cup, putting in sugar and cream. "What's this? You've stopped eating already? You have no respect for my food?"

Such were her gifts. She was a miracle. Obedience and worship were bred into him by his kin. He had not thought a human heart could hold such rapture as he was feeling now. She was like a flower that sat in a vase, just smiling and smiling at him. He could not yet smile back. He tried, but each smile crumpled.

As though she read his thoughts, she said: "The outside may be pillaged. The inside never changes, Jonny. Never. It may be buried, but it's there. You have a mind. A heart. A soul. There's work to do. Let's start with honesty. Where is your birthplace, darling? I can't endure another minute of this mystery."

"It's Apanlee," he said.

He told her more. He told her all he could; the rest he still held back. There was no way that he could tell her, yet, how Dorothy had died. Supine. Clubbed dead by anarchy. For being of the clan. Atop the old family tub.

The bed that Heidi pointed to had not been slept in yet. She handed him a bundle. He stared at it, not comprehending.

"Those are pajamas, Jonny," she said with a small laugh. "My husband's old pajamas. He'll have a fit when he comes home tonight and finds out I gave his pajamas to you." The day was done; she still smelled fresh and clean. She bent to him. For a brief, breathless moment, he thought that she would kiss him— as Baba used to do, a long, long time ago.

She did not do that, though. She covered him from head to toe with a fat feather comforter and, daintily, she made a little cushion for herself and perched there, like a bird.

"Are you too tired for a little talk?"

He shook his head. "Of course not. No."

Had she but asked to have his ears, he would have cut them off and handed them to her. Had she pined for the moon, he would have brought it down with silver arrows. Had he known how, he would have serenaded her; he would have put her on a pedestal and knelt before her, humbly.

"I'll pay you back," he told her, choked. "I will grow up and pay you back. I promise."

"You do not owe me anything," said Heidi seriously. "This is about moral perfection." She took a picture from the window sill and handed it to him. "Here. Do you know this man?"

He shook his head.

Her voice was shy and reverent. "We call him our Führer."

Chapter 60

To this day, loving legends are told of Natasha. The best, perhaps, recalls how she went out and stole that special bin of grain so that there would yet be another yellow harvest.

You hear this story everywhere the clan of Apanlee has settled—in Mennotown, in Winnipeg, in Waterloo, in Reedley, in Vancouver. When oldsters tell it, haltingly, watch how the hair will rise on withered arms, much like a tiny forest.

"That was Natasha," they will say. "Ah, what a sturdy Baba. When she was young, she raised a lot of eyebrows. But when the Revolution came, why, she displayed a serpent's tongue. It hid a heart of gold."

Each morning, rain or shine, Natasha went to scavenge—a sly and cunning peasant who somehow hung onto her donkey cart, her proudest, still private possession. By a sheer miracle, she had procured it from an enormous pile of rubble in the ransacked neighborhood. Now she pulled it by two ropes the twins had slung across her shoulders.

"I will be back," she promised every time she disappeared.

And back she came, night after night, with something she had traded for, to help the clan survive.

Once, she was gone for several days. She wasn't lost, however. Home she came, staggering beneath a burlap sack. She said, collapsing by the fire: "Don't ask, and you won't know."

"You stole it!" cried Marleen, and quickly pulled the shutters.

"What? I confess to nothing," smiled Natasha, radiating pride, and it was plain that she enjoyed the stir. "Guess what you like. No one can stop you guessing."

Natasha's conscience didn't pinch her in the least. Her nerves no longer hung in tatters.

"Straight from the government bin? You'll be shot, you fool!"

"Who? Me?"

Natasha did not feel the least bit worse for watching Marleen work herself into a mighty funk. "Look here! It sat there, at the station, smoking from combustion. Could I help spotting it?" Her hands were cut and bleeding, but she was in fine form. "Ah, what a night! What opportunity! A pile of grain, in big fat sacks, unsupervised! Let all those riches go to waste?" She savored stretching the suspense, while Mimi and the twins pressed closer. "I couldn't resist. I stood between anvil and hammer."

"You didn't!"

"Did you really?"

"Natasha, no! My God!"

Natasha looked triumphant. "Surrounded by a bale of wire! Somebody had twisted it open already. Would I let such a stroke of luck pass by? Fail all my lucky icons? I made a fist and pushed it through. With pounding heart, I filled my apron. Here. Pinch my arm to know it's really me."

All pitted with pockmarks but shining with purpose, enjoying an immense—and growing—reputation: that was Natasha now, as useful and as capable as anyone they knew.

Sometimes, she went so far as to start bullying: "Where is my heated brick? Quick, get my footstool. Run!"

They loved her; they esteemed her; in fact, they needed

her—they couldn't do without her. Content with her station in life, she was serving the Germans, as always. Her heart was set on being useful, and it sang like a bird.

For weeks, Natasha preened herself before Marleen, whose nose was full of tears. Natasha made the most of it. She could not get enough of praise and recognition. The story grew and grew. She garnished and dressed up her pluck as word spread of her daring deed. Her tongue had a life of its own.

"There was this guard, this scoundrel, see? He tried, the rascal, to restrain me!" Perhaps Natasha should have felt ashamed for her un-Soviet deed, but Natasha had never felt happier—and never mind the famine cost her every tooth.

"I bit his hand. I bit it hard. He fled!"

She smiled as widely as she could, as often as she had a reason. What harm another little lie as long as it bought smiles? If she walked down the street, the German farmers stopped to chat. She basked in rays of glory; she could not get enough.

So let the village council visit her and tell her, frowningly, that it was now her solemn duty to hound the people's enemies, to help unmask destructive plots, to find a broom and sweep away corruption.

"It is a crime against the government," he said to her, "to violate the quota laws. On fear of punishment, the quotas must be kept."

To show she was a realist, she hummed the *"Internationale"*. It would not hurt, she told herself, to keep her ears wide open and keep her two feet firmly planted on the ground.

The twins paid her the finest compliments.

"We'll make it, thanks to you—" said Yuri many times, and Sasha added seamlessly: "—and to our dearest Lord."

"I know. I know. I just lucked out, was all."

"We'll have a new harvest," said Yuri, love shining from his eyes. "Had it not been for you—"

"The bitter days are gone!"

She watched them thoughtfully. She had hummed to them both in the cradle. They were a joy still, spare and thin, though filling out, developing some muscle. Thanks to the grain she stole for them, her faith in Apanlee and in the twins was of the deepest dye imaginable. She had high hopes for them.

But in the meantime, how to keep their stolen treasure from being plundered by the government before it had a chance to sprout? That took a lot of cunning.

With the help of the twins, Natasha conspired and plotted and schemed. The Pioneer lay face-down in her pillows, her fingers in her ears.

Marleen and Natasha were melting down the last two of Natasha's iron-ration candlesticks. In the dark of the night, they deftly sealed bottle by bottle. The moon shone bright and cold. The air was like a diamond.

Then came the prayers, by government decree forbidden yet proscribed:

"—Thou settleth our furrows—"

"—Thou maketh them soft with rich showers—"

"—as smoke is driven away, Thou driveth the devil away—"

"—let us rejoice exceedingly—"

She linked her hands with them. She lowered bottle after bottle into the waterhole the twins had hacked into the ice, but not before she tied a string to each and fastened the ends to a rock.

"—as in the olden days, oh Lord!"

"Be it Thy will! Fat crops!"

As long as there was seed, no one could destroy the seasons. No hoodlum could divert the force of spring. No government could stop a grain from pushing up toward the sun, come spring again, and summer. No slogan could improve the riches of the Bible, fatter than any other book.

Now stood Natasha solemnly within their prayer circle, an equal in the eyes man and God. She knew the Lord was on their side. No mind the missing psalter words the hooligans had torn away—she knew them all by heart. She trusted them. She knew the German farmers' hearts beat hard with Faith and certainty, as bottle after bottle sank down beneath the murky waters, beside the age-old oak—a little to the left, where, in the bygone days when serfs were serfs and masters, masters, the Elder Willy used to baptize marriageable couples to keep the progeny within the ethnic fold.

Marleen sold on the thriving black market what little the new Soviet leaders allowed her to grow. She sold cucumbers, beans, tomatoes. She raised and sold a goat. She still owned six decrepit chickens whose eggs Natasha traded for a spool of thread with which to mend a jacket, a piece of string with which to tie a sole.

These days, Natasha wore Hein's boots with nonchalance. They were too large and rubbed at the heel; therefore, she tied some string around the tips to keep the soles from flapping.

Natasha proved to be an arduous ally. She was a recognized authority on queues. She went out early every morning and came home late at night. When everybody else at Apanlee gave up, Natasha stood in lines, right through the muddy season.

Sometimes the others heckled her: "Still serving the exploiters?"

"Why, I have nothing else to do. So what?"

"You'll learn. You'll learn," they sneered.

Natasha only shrugged. The Soviet bureaucrats wrote brand new laws in bold red ink, but she paid no attention. Nobody had Natasha's patience in spotting bargains as she did, outlasting rain and cold. She knew that if she waited long enough—if luck was on her side!—fine items could be traded for, with items from the past.

She traded off from Apanlee whatever she could find; she carted off to Apanlee whatever she could hoard, heaving hard with triumph and exertion, tramping through the falling snow.

Was anybody craftier?

Sometimes Natasha spoke her mind; she was an equal now.

As often as the opportunity arose, she launched herself into a heated argument to round out the rest of the day. She clung to her opinions with tenacity. She stamped her feet with rage.

"Let bygones be bygones!" she shouted. "He who stops, rusts! That's what I always say!"

Natasha still believed that it was true that he who stopped would rust, as she had done for altogether different reasons before the old life toppled in the streets and sprawled into the gutter.

She had horse-sense, and brawn, and copious spit, as well as proverbs by the bushel. She repeated them often, between clenched teeth, as she swept from the sidewalk the glass shards of the Glorious Revolution.

"Why keep your head right in the lion's mouth?" the field inspectors countered, taunting her. "Why not, instead, help usher in the future?"

Natasha lacked the words to find an apt reply. She was a simple woman. "Just leave me be!" she barked. "Every day has a sunrise and sunset."

Deep down, she had her reasons. She kept Marleen in the corner of her eye. A small geranium, red and sassy, blazed on the window sill, out to the west, that no one dared to touch. Marleen was tending it.

The twins survived, two somber men with burning eyes and hungry hearts, whose daily task it was to concentrate their energy to help the land renew, and to beseech the Lord to let them live so they could carry on the double task of piety and propagation.

"Which one of us?" they asked. Between them stood Larissa.

Each night they climbed the ladder to pull the Bible from the straw. Sometimes the Pioneer, whose German name was Mimi Neufeld, would watch them, sitting on some half-charred girders, knees drawn tautly to her chin. She liked to sit like that, close to the twins, for reasons only dimly understood, yet deeply felt within, where things were warm and soft and painfully for-

bidden. Her brothers did not think it odd to ask the Holy Spirit to
help enlighten them. She watched how they devoured the Gospel, a bourgeois fairytale.

"The spirit of Lenin, the spirit of Stalin suffice," she corrected them gently, but she was small, not yet ten years of age,
and hence indulgently ignored. When Yuri stroked her hair, when
Sasha told her of the Holy Spirit, the Pioneer, in training for the
Soviet future, grew goose bumps on her spine.

Yet, day by day and week by week, she sat with other children of her age in four neat rows, three to a desk, discussing how
torture, deftly applied, could unmask the prayerful Germans.

"Now find a synonym for Faith."

"Superstition! Superstition!" shouted all the gutter children.
They shouted with such lustiness that Lenin's bust leapt on the
window sill.

Their teacher smiled with glee, small bubbles forming in the
corners of her mouth. "The Bible? Answer me!"

All eyes were riveted on Mimi. If there was laughter, chances
were it was at her expense. She had no choice at all. She said as
firmly as she could: "Slime! Filth! All Bible stories, just a pack
of lies."

She took top honors in her class for an entire year. She knew
that she would never be possessed by that brand of deception.
All that was yesterday! The future was tomorrow!

She still had years to grow.

Thus was a young girl caught between the twins, on one side,
and the demanding doctrine of the Party, on the other. She walked
on stilts eternally. She tried to sit between two chairs. If she
reported what she knew, the Party smiled on her. If she kept
secrets from the Party, she felt the tongues of guilt.

She tried to please both sides without surrendering. She felt
as though she had two eyes of different colors—depending on
which eye she closed, that's how her world appeared.

"Faith can't be trusted. Ever!" said the teacher, and put an-

other star beside her name, to signify her growth in Party doctrine. "To be of use to us, you have to be on guard."

"Trust in the Lord," her brothers said, and put warm hands
upon her wind-blown face, "and nothing will befall you."

"Make up your mind," the teacher told her daily. "You cannot please both sides."

"Now fold your little hands. Give thanks to your Lord and
Provider—"

She did so, furtively, her two eyes darting left and right, still
hoping against hope the Holy Ghost would come, just as her brothers claimed, and give her peace and certainty and fill her aching
heart. And since that didn't happen—hope as she might, wait as
she did, all but on tiptoes, verily!—she slammed the door behind
her.

She was not burdened, as her brothers were, with surplus sentiment of gratitude to God because she had been spared. She
knew she had to live. For life, one had to pay.

Here's what she saw, a hardened and cynical youngster: Some
lived—but many, many died. She did not link one faulty notion
with another.

And so she stood before the class and pledged: "If I hear
someone pray, I will report that crime."

She knew it would sadden her God-fearing brothers, that ex-
pedient little lie, but the treacherous words just jumped from her
tongue. She had been spared, and she knew why: the Party needed
her. If one put duty before pleasure, the end result was worth.

These things were done to little children as Stalin did away
with Faith to launch the New World Order. Against the backdrop
of the past, that dictum was not difficult to see for youngsters
such as Mimi: Faith was a tool meant to deceive and dupe; Faith
was the obstacle that stunted thought. She wanted none of that.

Faith warped the mind and slowed down reason, she told herself repeatedly, while climbing up into the attic to watch her brothers pray. She could not stay away. She knew she was duplici-
tous. Not even a pup would be licking her nose. She was a proud
and confirmed non-believer. God was a myth, for science had

unmasked the scams of yesterday with the triumphant Revolution. Forward-looking citizens of the progressive Soviet Union discarded such fables for good. She did not need the murky Faith of yesterday.

She did, however, need to be comforted. Her brothers had caressing hands. They smelled of earth and hay. When Sasha said to her: "Come join our prayer circle, darling," she melted. When Yuri coaxed: "Here, little love. Here is my lap. Curl up!" her nose commenced to drip with sentiment.

What was a child to do? She sat between them, modestly. If she could manage to forget the twins and their incessant prayers, her future lay before her, like hills in a blue haze. If, on the other hand, she did as she was told by them, the likely end was grim.

"Thou maketh lightning for the rain—"

"Thou maketh wind out of Thy treasures—"

Sasha's prayers blazed like flaming torches, but Yuri's prayers! Yuri's prayers! They flowed like seasoned wine.

"No evil shall befall you, darling," whispered Yuri. "For He shall give his angels charge over you—" She shuddered at the force of their whispering voices, before the task they had set for themselves.

Softly, her mind began to wander. To Mimi, the Gospel meant naught. She barely recalled celebrating Sundays, Christmas, or Easter holidays with prayers—comforting, happy times now swept away with brand new brooms the Revolution had supplied.

Forever! was the boast.

Her glance went through the window, furtively—and when she saw a shadow move, she felt her tongue go dry.

Chapter 61

In Mennotown, the Hebrew grain and cattle buyers came and went, periodically, as did the winter relatives. Brick was in keeping with your station. Wheat, barley, peas, oats, rye, and cucumbers in season were in keeping with your instincts. Moderation in all matters was in keeping with your reputation—you didn't treat your verandah to curves. If you were worth a housewife's salt, you kept a modicum of secrecy around your recipes.

It was a placid time. The Lord was good. The wheat stood rich and lush. When it rained, you slept into the day. When the sun came out again, you pruned your cherry trees.

Perhaps you planted yet another orchard. You watched the food rise from the soil or hang in clusters from the branches, and there was glory in your belly and your soul.

No matter where you looked, everyone was linked by kinship, and everything was orderly. The tailor tailored shirts. The mailman brought the mail. The chairman had a chair.

Doctorjay had many friends in Wichita where, lately, formality was now a habit of the past. Most people had a nickname, preferably one-syllable. He was on courteous terms with all—

even progressive folks such as the Finkelsteins who walked through Wichita in long, aggressive strides with arms about each other.

Sometimes, he joined and talked. Sometimes, they did the same.

With Noralee now dead and gone, he felt as if an engine had uncoupled from a train and, Prohibition in full force, the bars of Wichita were hidden well behind facades. Not that that stopped the healer. He had his inner maps. They steered him faithfully. He knew that Little Melly had discriminating nostrils, and what she smelled when he came home, she did not like one bit. In fact, she nearly had a fit each time he came home singing.

Little Melly could smell a Jack Daniels from afar, just as she could predict, from the aroma of Josie's scent jars, that she was heading off to Wichita again to visit with the Finkelsteins in open-air cafes.

One topic of discussion there remained the wonders of the Marxist Revolution. Now, voices lowered guardedly, the Hebrews started talking about the exploitation of the masses here at home. Their one absorbing interest was now the Labor Union.

The healer drank to that.

That was his way of making cheer. He missed his Noralee. To forestall lonesomeness, the bottle filled with fire water was always within reach.

Doctorjay was imbibing again. He drank to the most obscure elections. He toasted the Catholic Pope. It was cheers to good health, to good-byes. He toasted Lizzy's sauerkraut. He toasted her *vareniki*. He did general toasts, specific toasts, and even toasted several quasi-anarchists, although by accident.

He kept slapping his thighs with delight.

Before another year was gone, he drank to absolutely everything. He toasted the sunshine; he toasted the rain. He toasted Carrie Nation! He even toasted Lucky Lindbergh, a rising star and just about as close to perfect as they come, although the Hebrews had their doubts and spoke about them openly.

Here was a national celebrity on account of his air ship endeavors, still of enormous interest to Jan. Was Lindbergh, thus, a genuine patriot and four-square for equality? Or was he flirting with the Right and, hence, a man of perfidy?

That's what the Hebrews asked.

"We'll never meet this young again!" the healer cried, embracing the trunk of a tree. He was a Lutheran and, therefore, unrestrained.

Once, when he spotted Abigail returning home from Wichita—where she had gone to see a judge to help explain to him why her two youngest sons had managed to disturb the peace by shouting union slogans through a loudspeaker—he followed her, determined.

"Abigail! Say, Abigail! Wearing out a brand new pair of shoes?"

"You can say that again."

He leaned across his flivver door to get a better view. "What's going on? Why are you all spruced up?"

"What do you want from me? " asked Abigail. "A glass of sugar water?"

She talked like that, in question marks. She was a tease; she had a feline malice that gave him pleasant jolts. This meeting happened on the day the sparrows started feasting freely on the peaches, pears and plums on trees his now-departed Noralee imported many years ago from Apanlee.

Black galoshes glistening in the sunshine, Doctorjay decided to go check how Abigail's cucumbers were growing, right after a good rain. His household was in tears, but all was light and air within his fleshy heart. He was toasting the Army. The Navy.

He shouted when he spotted her: "How are you, Abigail?"

"Much better than can be expected."

Her hour glass figure was long gone, but on the other hand, she had no bony corners. She had a round behind and a face that was dusted with sun spots. She wore her hat on her left side. She wiped her lips with the back of her hand. "What's on your mind? I'd like to know. Precisely."

He chuckled happily into his double chin. No fly could ruin his appetite.

"Spare me," cried Abigail, but with a knowing smile. "Why, you old sinner, you!"

No one tracked sinners like Dewey, right into the heart of a Catholic stronghold. By this time Dewey, too, was getting on in years, but he was still his old and eager self. He saw no choice. He had to act. He knew that it was now or never.

"It's now or never, folks," he said, a master at the close.

The preachers in his family had come and gone, all undiminished. Dewey could have long ago retired pleasantly, leaving someone else tend the vineyard of the Lord, but who dared even hint to Dewey Epp about retirement?

Besides, there still was Archibald, to lend a hand as needed. Archie had precisely what it took to keep the members of his congregation on the straight-and-narrow path: he hammered at their sins as though he shooed a horse.

The Great War had ended a decade before, but for Archie, the war was not over. He still collected every week to help the orphans and the amputees. He still went house-to-house, collecting for the war graves. "All in the name of Christ," said Archie, a bit shrill.

He knew, as Lizzy did, that Faith grew best in graveyards, and who could prove him wrong? For weeks on end, each afternoon, he went to visit folks. Tea was at four, supper at eight. At the heart of all talk was the Savior.

Modernity, preached Dewey Epp, one eye on Josephine and one on Doctorjay, was still a Serious Social Problem.

The neighborhood agreed. The Donoghues claimed, wantonly, they were entitled meat for breakfast, lunch and dinner. They wanted longer holidays. Their eyes were glued to those reformers whose speeches ended in a question mark, who looked for allies everywhere to strengthen their own ranks.

A case in point: Jan's Josie.

She still bought things she could have made herself from portly Jewish merchants down on Second Street. She still shunned the heart of a picnic. She absolutely didn't do what every other woman of her status did to keep herself informed: push back her curtains and her flower pots to get a better look at what was going on with Abigail and Mennotown's determined healer.

Ah! Life in Mennotown, where gossip was the beam of scrutiny! No matter how dark or how cluttered a closet—in a roundabout way, you found out!

Lizzy would have liked to have relied on Josephine to keep her gossip up to date, now that her legs had given out, but Josie, looking fit to be a queen, albeit full of tiny wrinkles, had scarcely time for that.

"It's all about the liberation of humanity," chimed Josephine, at last recovering.

Once more, she dressed herself in rainbow hues, preferring fiery red. Reverting to her former self, she spoke poetically of this and that, chiefly of social justice—this time at home, right in her neighborhood. Whatever she did, she did exceedingly well, but she didn't draw back her hair in a bun, and she didn't share gossip she heard.

She arched her brows. She was like a cat. Softly purring.

In Wichita, she kept all sorts of friends of every kind and hue. She introduced them everywhere and even brought them home at supper time, without announcing it, instead of giving Lizzy time to find out for herself whom she might want to know.

She burst into loud laughter when salient tidbits about the twosome's budding romance came her way. "What? Doctorjay and Abigail? Whatever gave you that idea? You've got to be pulling my leg."

Gossip was useful, sniffed Lizzy, offended. As good as rich milk, still warm from the cow. Lizzy proffered her own point of view for Josie to consider—after all, was Doctorjay not family? He needed to be warned.

"Why wait? Why not find out before it is too late and give him useful hints?"

"So what if he likes Abigail? It's none of our business."

"It's good to keep yourself informed to forestall worse to come. Just sound him out a bit. And let me know so I can tell the neighbors."

"He's a grown man, entitled to his privacy."

"But if you live in Chinatown, you bow. She isn't one of us. She isn't orderly."

"But do I live in Chinatown?" was Josie's deft reply.

Ach! What to do? Old Lizzy relished sorting out romantic details before she spread them to her neighbors, but to get Josie to sit still for gossip about Abigail and Doctorjay for any length of time was as hard as unloading a cartful of piglets.

At first, Abigail pretended Doctorjay did not exist for her, but not for long. She relented and planted a kiss on his pate.

"You wouldn't want to waste your life," teased Abigail. With those words, she embedded herself in his heart.

He nearly burst with sentiment. His heart had lost its gallop but nothing of its warmth. Old age was as light as a feather.

"Just wait and see," said he, replying instantly, returning a resounding smack.

"You shouldn't have," squirmed Abigail, and toyed with the bands of her hat. She whispered her romantic wish list; he gave her a poke with his elbow; he had a peacock's pride. Returning home, he had to pause at least five times to wipe his eyes, he was that overcome.

"To the kaiser in exile!" he shouted.

In weeks to come, Abigail gave Doctorjay a lot of long and curious stares. She knew her powers well. She read him like a book. His temples throbbed with May.

They eyed each other carefully, from every single angle, and found each other fit. In a village where nothing was private, soon it was known that Doctorjay had made himself a frenzied fool who polished his belt buckle. Poor Noralee, revolving in her grave!

Old Lizzy was incredulous. In memory of Noralee, whose big and noisy sobs were legend, she kept wiping her eyes with her apron.

"How could you, Doctorjay? What's this I hear? For practically fifty years, you walked with Noralee in harmony. Now this?"

He was the world's worst liar. "Whatever do you mean?"

"What do we know about the Donoghues? The papers call them elements, prefixed by undesirable."

Weeds to their knees! Flies on their ceiling like sesame seeds on a bun! Not that that mattered to the geezer. "I'm not yet feeling sluggish. She has a round derriere—"

"And you, in your old age!" gasped Lizzy.

In fact, she gasped twice and had to sit down, while Doctorjay hooted and couldn't stop laughing: "What's that? Are you claiming I'm over the hill?"

"Just where is it going to end? You'll be the laughingstock of Mennotown before the year is out. Her noodles swim in grease—"

All that fell upon stony ground. All that occasioned only shrugs. The healer showed no signs of cracking. He even spurned the timid tailor's widow whom Lizzy pushed into his path, to forestall worse to come. Instead, he dug a pointed elbow into Little Melly's ribs and needled her for days: "Stay home? With weather fit for love?" The more she argued with his choice, the wilder he became. He was enjoying his own jokes, and Abigail was one of them. He aimed his flivver down the nearest street, his flask inside, snug in a leather pouch, while taking corners, tires screeching, air horn blowing, spraying behind him large fountains of dirt.

He went to visit Abigail each day, his straw hat full of apples, five hairs fluffed up on top. The summer was still winding down when Abigail agreed: "I do. I will. What else is there to do?"

He wore his shiniest trousers for the wedding, for Abigail

had costly tastes not only for herself. "I miss the matrimonial warmth," he said, and marched his Abigail right into Dewey's German church and married her, for better or for worse.

Jan's daughters, on the other hand, of a younger generation, were not at all alarmed. They were a jolly lot, like leafy and well-rooted plants, who drove each other into fits of laughter when they watched Doctorjay salute another tree.

"He claims he saw a Zeppelin," they screeched while collapsing with mirth and elation.

Such joy, to share in a gossipy windfall!

Fine quilts and fluffy pillows everywhere, that was their happiness. Each one of them was dutiful and punctual, more than content to stay within the bosom of their kin. When it came time for them to take a husband, these maidens had no trouble finding nice and solid citizens of proven German stock. Their wheat stood tall; their cows' tails switched away the flies. Before the decade ran its course, all six except the youngest were married well and gone from Jan's and Josie's home except for visits on the holidays. The youngest was still making up her mind between assorted suitors.

"My zwieback, like the foamy sea," she bragged to them, and to the neighborhood, and that was poetry.

Lizzy was very proud of them but kept her feelings to herself, for fear of showing vanity. Jan's daughters were her joy. The little fellow stole her heart, however, and never gave it back.

When Rarey won first prize for doodling, his mother combed her hair with individuality in a decided sweep. Photographs show Josie ravishing way into middle age.

One of her refrains ran: "He'll be a first-class artist." Josie parted her hair on her left, while most matrons wore parts in the middle.

Since she had modified herself, however, in more important ways, this was a small concession. Her appetite was better now: she scarcely left a crumb. Growing plump and rosy over time made for a more complacent disposition. Rare flashes of the younger Josie were dismissed. No matter that she still cavorted with the Finkelsteins! As long as Josie took her turns in brewing coffee in the basement of the church where Archie kidded with the volunteers with such enormous verve and energy that spittle flew in sparks, all was not lost! There was still mileage left.

"Repent! Repent!" was Archie's battle cry.

Most did; she didn't; but you could only push Josie so far.

She never quite became the middle-of-the-roader that everybody wanted her to be. She lived with books; she lived for books—and treated them like people.

And she taught Rarey likewise.

Maps. File folders. Binders. Pens. Pencils. Notebooks and looseleafs galore. There was no end to it.

She bought him a globe, she bought him a microscope, she bought him leather-bound encyclopedias. Before Rarey even started school, the shrimpkin was a fluent reader.

"Too good for this world," said the neighbors.

Modernity was moving in on Mennotown as well; artistic children were the rage; crowds gathered around Rarey to admire. His drawings were passed on from hand to hand and hung in people's parlors. So proud was Jan of his small son and his exceptionality he practically did somersaults, and Josie was beside herself each time her last-born finished yet another sketch.

This youngster, their familial train's caboose—a perfect progeny in every way, without a single birth mark, although not made for football—was destined to change everything. Or so old Lizzy's hopes.

"Why, he can have as many brushes as he wants, plus several extra sets," bragged Josie. No one checked on how many she bought. She never made apologies for doodles.

Deep in her soul, she nursed ambitious plans for Rarey. This child, whose origin still loomed as though it were a stony mountain whose tip was shrouded in white fog, showed early signs of independent judgment—this long before he shed his baby teeth.

Josie smiled with approbation, silently watching him. She watched him with a focused, strange intensity. It was as if the talents of her daughters didn't count.

Let all those blinkered people plod to church on their flat feet, in rolled-up socks, and then plod home again to homemade noodles! She knew that Rarey would succeed where she had tried and failed.

He did not have his mother's prickliness, her acid anger, her rebellious thoughts. He was her compromise. And yet, he had inherited complexity: that was her gift to him. He shared her love for well-wrought poetry. For symmetry. For silence. This little fellow was the best that she and Jan had managed to bring forth. He was her flesh and blood. He had her hair. Her skin. Her shimmering sheen of eye.

But he was also different: accommodating, yielding.

"Come. Sit here by the window," said Josie, softening, when she saw hurt wash over Lizzy's face for a rebuff she had not meant to slip across her lips.

"Sure. Sure. Why not?"

Old Lizzy peered at Josie, squinting. She was entitled to some rest. Well over eighty, she could no longer feel her fingers or her toes. Her eyes were dim; not even glasses helped.

"If you don't mind my saying so, you're overdoing it."

"Whatever do you mean?"

Old Lizzy bit her lip. Her heart just melted at the sight of little Rarey. She felt pride, too, mixed with vexation. No doubt a lovely little treasure, his chin cupped in his hands, a favorite with everyone, the hub of his adoring family—but why a telescope sent all the way from Washington? Why not leave well enough alone? Why clutter up his mind?

Old Lizzy fussed and squirmed. She had a silent battle with herself before she gave vent to her worry.

"Say. Please forgive me, Josephine. His reading doesn't give him headaches?"

"That theory," said Josie smilingly without the slightest rancor, tucking a hand-stitched quilt around Old Lizzy's knees, "went down the day the *Lusitania* was sunk."

"He takes after you?"

"I guess so. And why not?"

"None of your girls took after you."

"No, Lizzy dear, they all took after you," acknowledged Josie peacefully, and let the matter drop.

And she was right. All Jan's daughters were alike in looks and manners and demeanor, as though they all had been cut carefully from Lizzy's cookie cutter.

Chapter 62

Marleen grew silent and subdued when she was told that she must now work hard to meet her quota yield.

"Set an example as a model citizen," the quota agents told her.

How to accomplish that? The masses that had howled the *Internationale* now chafed in mines and factories. It was hard to find hands for the harvest.

"Our little father Stalin," the snoopers said, "is clicking glasses with the humblest citizens of the Soviet, toasting peace and friendship with his workers. We expect you to show proper faith in his genius."

All that was written in her Bible: she knew exactly where. The Gospel of her forebears instructed her precisely how she must render unto Caesar. It also told her she must render unto God.

She struck a middle road. The quota rules were merciless, she soon discovered, but the Germans were bred to obedience; they did as they were told; they shared all that was safe to share, and quietly withheld the rest.

"I'll do my best," she therefore promised solemnly, and did

not tell the agents of the gherkin patch behind the chicken coop, well hidden from the eye.

She did not think that wrong. She saw no need to blush. She had lived to witness renewal. Her babies had sprinkled the road with their blood.

Marleen grew potatoes, onions, watermelons, sugar beets and cucumbers on the secret plot behind the hen house, well-hidden behind some boards. The food the plot produced was grown in stark defiance of the law. It helped her and her family to make it through another bitter winter. The frost sat on the cherry trees. For months on end, the snow lay on the hedges.

When finally the sun came out, a well-known Party deputy arrived at Apanlee and started asking ticklish questions. He shouted himself hoarse.

"We know it all! You can't hide anything!"

He kept searching the building from the eaves to the cellar, and when he was finished, he started again.

"Well, are you all through now?" asked the little Pioneer, hoping to bewilder him with clever diverting maneuvers.

The agent stepped around her and started fumbling with a lock. "What's this? A trap door? Huh? What are you traitors hiding?"

The Pioneer said airily: "*Kapusta*. That is all." Her flanks heaved with distress as though she were a foal, but she controlled herself. She knew the bucket had a double bottom; she quickly sat on it. She knew inside the double-bottom bucket were coins her brothers had set aside to pay for a small plow.

She was cunning past her years. She smiled her brightest smile, and gave the Pioneer salute. "Now that you haven't found a thing, why not report our innocence?"

"Ha! Sauerkraut! You are found out. What else? Potatoes? Young potatoes?"

She did not argue back. He was already opening the cellar door to find the brine that bathed the precious food grown from Larissa's secret cabbage patch. She tried to look angelic.

"Oh, nothing much. Not much at all. See for yourself. But be forewarned. Down in that hole are lots of big, fat spiders—"

"You profiteers," the agent spat, "are worst of all. The scum of the earth! Traitors, all of you! Saboteurs! Counter-Revolutionaries. Just vermin. All of you. Just vermin."

He kept abusing her until he grew tired of her. She sat there, and she smiled.

At Apanlee, a foolish sentiment prevailed: the government leaves you alone if you leave it alone. She knew that that was incorrect politically. There was no doubt in Mimi's heart of their collective guilt. She knew her mother and her brothers were obedient citizens; she also knew that they were hoarding, desperately.

Worse yet, and much more dangerous: at the Pioneer club, several friends hinted slyly that they knew.

The meddlers and kibitzers didn't go away, though even Natasha made herself as smooth and pleasant and agreeable as possible. She learned to nod with vigor to what the agents said, while keeping her opinions to herself.

She did not marshal ammunition with which to meet the argument that it was more efficient now to milk a cow with a machine; that a plain box, if wired right, could hatch an egg as well as any broody hen. Let any fool believe that!

The principles the Party spawned to pauperize the rich were of the loftiest kind—in practice getting there from here was different. The agents' homilies were convoluted. Reality was plain. You needed fodder for the cow. You needed rye and barley for the chickens. These all had to be grown.

Her reasoning went thus: The people knowing every secret as to how to raise the grain crop needed to restore the herds and flocks of fowl had to be practiced farmers, experienced at coaxing the seed. The clan shared all this knowledge; the twins knew every secret.

Yet plowing, hoeing, digging - except in service to the state - were now considered felonies. This made the twins near mad.

Natasha knew they cocked their ears toward the soil as though it were a living, breathing thing that needed to be treated with respect, esteem, and courtesy. The twins were mum about their plans, but she had eyes to see; she saw that spring drew them to their acres like a magnet.

Natasha cast an extra cunning look and saw that they were optimistic for themselves and venturesome on how to turn the tide. Though good workers were hard to come by, the twins had still hope for the seed. Once buried, the kernels would grow.

Natasha backed their hope at every opportunity. It was unthinkable that they should fail the land. It had sustained the family for five abundant generations; chances were it would again. There was no room for any other sentiment. The string of sparkling spring days following the latest agents' raid was like a rich and heady wine.

"You! Vermin! Scum!" the next one sneered, while trampling down the lush geraniums that cleverly hid five tomato plants. "Why not pool strength in a commune? Why work for selfish gain?"

At that, a spring gave out. Natasha was shrieking, a woman possessed: "I'll scratch your eyes out, you!"

Her shrieks did not intimidate the lout. It only brought the neighbors running.

The agent hectored them while climbing on a chair. "We live in challenging times! The old rules no longer apply!"

Her eyes misted over. The old rules were gone; the wind blew them down.

But here is what she saw, as clearly as though written in bold ink: the earth had its own mandate. The past was still the past, but the abused and plundered clan was slowly moving back into the well-worn ruts they knew so well before the Romanovs had lost their lives and throne.

Thus, while the struggle for survival still was grim, the looming question mark seemed gone. Endurance had won out. The sun was out again; the Germans started spading.

No longer thin as hay rakes, thin to the point of vanishing, the twins were filling out. Their shoulders started widening. Each morning, Natasha pinched their muscles. Each night they climbed the ladder to leaf through the Gospel and pray.

"The girl? The church? We'll have to split our duties."

Larissa kept pulling her apron for answers. "Even a turtle must stick out its neck," she said in the end, producing a very small dimple.

"Why two of you? What is a girl to do?"

"Look at this pretty girl. Everything is carrot red—"

"—her hair—"

"—her eyebrows—"

"—her lashes—"

"—her freckles—"

Marleen, too, caught her breath in awe. Here was a young woman of prim, tidy habits, suitably modest, taking the string bag, patiently waiting in queues. She ironed her bed sheets both sides. She knew how to darn with precision. She practiced her loops with an eye to the shortage of yarn. What better evidence that they'd exist in harmony? They shared each other's values.

She, too, saw the girl through mist in her eyes: a chance seed, brought on by the wind.

When Marleen saw the youngster standing in the wind-blown halls of Apanlee that dark, raw November morning—trembling, hungry, numb with cold, and blinded by the whirling flakes of snow—and saw her sons gaze at the ragged visitor in wonder, that's when a mother knew, deep in her wounded heart: "They're still intact, the ancient laws of love."

The twins had surrendered their male drive to famine, but now it stirred anew; Larissa stood by smiling.

"I came to claim kinship," she said.

"Here is your apron, dear," Marleen said to the willing girl. "Now go and help Natasha in the kitchen."

Larissa, for her part, did not waste words herself.

"Help me decide. Which one?"

"The fitting thing," Marleen replied, "is for the human heart to let the Lord decide."

Her answer was pleasing to all. Who else but the good Lord, intent on propagation, had steered Larissa stealthily through all the ice and snow to kindle the anemic blood of the two heirs of Apanlee? All credit be the Lord's.

That was the sentiment. Marleen knew then and there that those who had been spared would live, that she would live to see the coming of a future generation, and that the year to come would bring a measure of relief.

In the following weeks, Larissa spoke to several neighbors without prompting. Her claim was this: she could not take her heart away from one to give it to the other. Her mind was in a muddle.

"Why are there two of them? Alike?"

The neighbors had a ready answer. "What else are prayers for?"

But they made sure as well that no one heard such sacrilege against the leadership of the Soviet which had outlawed the Lord.

The twins stepped up their efforts, their voices growing husky with emotion. They tossed a windfall apple. Larissa reached for it. They held it, teasingly, just out of reach, to coax that distant smile.

A pale pink seeped into her young and fragile face. "You're so alike. How is a girl to know?"

Their glances were like water running through her toes. Their thoughts! The coals of junipers.

"The Lord will choose," they told her, quick as lightning.

She nodded, satisfied. She was a willing pupil. She kept them waiting, hoping, while both kept courting her with ardent constancy to help her heart decide.

The day came when Larissa flung her braids. Her heart swam with the scent of the acacias. She closed her eyes and started drifting. The sun streamed golden ribbons. Deep in the meadows, in the damp, five fragrant violets grew.

" Yuri? Sasha? Yuri? Sasha?" she said to Mimi next, who
was, by then, just weeks away from leadership in the coveted
Komsomol, the next step up the Party ladder.

"What do you mean?"

"There's two of them. What is a girl to do?"

The Pioneer was jealous of Larissa, who walked between the
twins along the twisting goose path. "I don't want to torment
myself with that riddle. Don't ask me. Ask Natasha. She knows
them best. She cuddled them. She swaddled them. She put
them on the potty."

"Which one?" Larissa asked Natasha. "You always boast
how you can tell the two apart. So. Why be modest now?"

Natasha's heart swelled up like a balloon. Her face shone
bright as Easter. "What's that? You ask an old donkey like me?"
With red, raw hands she counted on her fingers: "Yuri. Sasha.
Yuri. Sasha."

Larissa's face grew pink. Her moves became quick, impul-
sive. "Speak up. They are identical. I can't make up my mind."

Natasha had a high opinion of herself. The sun tugged at her
heartstrings. There were shimmering beams in her soul. Gone
were the days when all the gutters ran with blood. Her raspy
voice turned motherly:

"Just take your time, my little love. Those two won't run
away."

Larissa knew the worth of modesty: "I have my faults."

"What faults?" Natasha felt expansive. "Did I hear faults?"
Had the choice been up to her, Natasha would have said: "It's
Yuri. Definitely Yuri." He was the gentler twin. She wet her
middle finger with her tongue and stroked across Larissa's brows
to make them dark and shiny. "Just take your time. There really
is no rush."

Unbidden memories came in a flood. She knew precisely
why she favored Yuri over Sasha. He was his father's replica—
blond, burly, stalwart, strong—but with his honor still intact. He
had a lively mind, a genial nature and a ferocious appetite for
spring. Hugging the earth with his manhood and youth, that was
Yuri.

It was far from decided, however.

Once Larissa stepped on a rusty nail; Sasha put his lips around the puncture to draw the poison out. She said to him, her eyes on his bent head: "Why two of you?"

"The day will come when I will ask to kiss your cheek," he ventured in a bold endeavor. "Here is a daisy, girl. Let's see. She loves me, or she loves me not? Let's let the petals tell—"

She saw his face was red. She saw smoke curling from his eyes.

She started stammering. "Please, no. You frighten me."

When Sasha looked at her like that, Larissa felt as though she missed her footing. By contrast, every feeling Yuri stirred in her was deep and powerful and sweet.

His love for her was like a rainbow mounted on black marble, while Sasha's eyes shone with an inner fever, not gleaming evenly as Yuri's did, much like the sun that shone in May.

She was fond of them both, but Natasha was right: she tilted a bit toward Yuri.

"Well, think about it. Will you?"

Larissa thought of nothing else as she hung out her towels to dry.

Natasha's deepest needs were rooted in the nursery, now empty for too many years. There she attacked the spider webs, in her time off, just to be sure, as she had always done.

The twins were men. They had a girl. In good time, there would be another baby.

That baby had to have a lap, two arms, a lullaby. So ran Natasha's argument.

She resumed some of her boisterous ways. "Run, Mimi! Run! Put on the kettle for some tea to warm your silly Baba!"

She bullied everybody shamelessly. What need had she for centrally decreed equality? She was content with her station in life. The Party added nothing to her stature.

Natasha rose before the sun was up to shove herself into another queue, her heart set on a special deal; whatever might be sold was of no consequence to her; a bargain was a bargain. She knew the clan could use most anything—why not get busy now? Natasha stepped in line and waited, patiently, while trembling in her threadbare overcoat, a discard of Marleen's but still with some life left. She bargained long and hard, stretching Marleen's last kopeck.

The government inspectors of the nascent Soviet state arrived repeatedly.

"Say! Do you know of anyone in your vicinity who could be called a traitor?" They taunted endlessly. Natasha watched as they rolled flint after flint into new cigarettes, lit them with testy fingers and stubbed them out on the old German portraits that still hung in the halls of Apanlee.

Their questions never varied.

Who was maliciously withholding corn needed to feed the workers in the city factories?

Who was intent on undermining Party goals?

Who was involved in sabotage against the reconstructive efforts of the nation?

The answers grew louder and louder.

The counter-Revolutionaries. The nation's enemies. The foreigners. The kulaks. The restive, recalcitrant Germans.

"You! Little Citizens! Speak up and answer boldly," the teacher told the class. "Who's hiding surplus food?"

"I know no one that wicked and corrupt," lied Mimi, cunning past her years. If she withheld her information, what would the Party say? If she reported what she knew, what would they eat tomorrow?

She stared out of the window. The wind outside was tormenting the trees. Rumors were rife there would soon be a village-wide, house-to-house search.

Now it was spring again and time to seed; the land had already been furrowed. If she reported that the twins were plotting on the sly to seed so as to harvest for themselves, she sacrificed the family. If she refused to sacrifice the family, she sacrificed herself.

"Now, little Citizen. Stand up and speak the truth," the teacher demanded, loath to let go. "Who is filling his belly with government food?"

"If I knew that," she muttered, miserably, "I would run to report it at once."

The children stared, two with their mouths wide open. The teacher hovered close. "Your conscience twinges, Citizen?"

She shrank back in her seat. Last night, when all the family had joined around the supper table, the curtains had been drawn. Had anyone peeked in? Bright color streamed into her face. She muttered wretchedly: "I cannot imagine such treason—"

"You'd better not—" the teacher said. She knew how to punish, and did.

For weeks on end, the teacher fixed her eye on Mimi and and watched for any slip.

"Some of you merit Party scholarships," the teacher told her, probing for her underbelly. "Is there a secret that you have to share? Do you need to confide?"

The youngster shook her head while finishing an apple core to show her nonchalance. At every opportunity, she struck a docile stance. She didn't care to have the German taint; the task was to outfox the teacher.

"Think hard. Who still prays to a non-existent God for extra, unearned favors?"

She shook her head. She felt like a pin cushion; the teacher kept sticking sharp needles into her.

"I don't know anyone."

Her brothers prayed. Her mother prayed. Larissa prayed. *Ach Gott!*

"Who grovels still before a silly icon?"

Her Baba did! Natasha! Natasha never ate the smallest morsel without crossing herself with three fingers. The candles for Natasha's icons were long gone, but still she spoiled her saints. She was incorrigible. She covered her dilapidated saints with bits of discard cloth to overwhelm them with attention, and to protect them from destructive dust. But tell the teacher that?

"And who is sabotaging wickedly the reconstructive efforts of our Soviet Motherland?"

The twins! She knew they had hidden three buckets of wheat in the church, now an abandoned edifice, thick with chicken droppings. From the outside, the building looked deserted; the floor had not been scrubbed in years; the sparrows nested in the gables. The plan was, Mimi knew, to keep it thus, for there they kept their kernels, between some double walls.

She had young eyes and ears; she could not help but know. That's where her brothers prayed in strangled tones: "We are in mortal danger. We ask Thee for deliverance. Deliverance! Deliverance!" What if that guilty secret managed to slipped out? Guilt came in waves of heat that swept across her face. *Ach!* How they prayed! How desperately they prayed!

"Lord, we beseech Thee! We beseech Thee! Deliverance! How else can we survive?"

Day after day, she picked her way with cunning. Night after night, struggling for sleep, she blessed and cursed her background. As tales of Stalin's reforms spread, encircling every citizen, the teacher told the class:

"In the collectives, no one starves. And those who foolishly refuse to help rebuild the land collectively will soon be forced into the cattle trucks with rifle butts and clubs."

The teacher had thin lips, sharp eyes and was expert in giving Marxist diatribes. "Now, little Citizen, be careful with your words. Who serves the ruling class? Who's undermining teamwork?"

"I don't know ," Mimi whispered wretchedly, still first in all her classes. By then, she knew things of enormous value to the Party.

To wit: that Sasha, Yuri and Natasha had slaughtered a grown pig. This was a horrid crime. Marleen had salted it away and now was parceling it out at intervals for just the six of them—her family, and no one else! Not even closest neighbors!—instead of sharing it communally for all to partake equally.

"—who still owns flocks of fowl?"

Larissa did. *Ach Gott*! Two ducks still left. Three chickens. And the rooster!

"Just you remember: if you obey, our Comrade Stalin smiles on you," the teacher said, and scribbled something in her notebook to pass on to her betters.

"I will."

"He is the perfect leader. He knows what's best for you. Poets compare him to sun and moon and stars. Don't let your comrades down. You must report all hate crimes. You must tell who hates whom."

"I am reliable. I do what is correct."

The words came of themselves. Outside, the raindrops were gargantuan. The spring earth soaked up moisture. The seedlings pulsing with life.

"I can be relied on absolutely," she said in a low voice, "to carry out every order."

"Do not forget you are a merit child, the youngest one on record," the teacher said, while snapping shut her notebook. "Dare you risk everything? I look at you and think: must I spell out the rules?"

"I know my duty, Citizen." She still was proud she came from Apanlee, but as day followed day, her pride grew in her merit badges. She loved to show them off. She did not want to be a disgrace to her Motherland. She strove to please. She wanted to placate.

But on the other hand, could she turn in her Baba?

For instance, just last night, before the latest storm moved in and started ripping from the clouds such rage that the acacia tree tops started trembling, Natasha saw a shooting star and took it as a timely omen. Natasha's candles were long gone, but still she crossed herself!

"Your harvest will be blessed," Natasha told the twins.

Ach, Baba! thought the Pioneer. Your Faith and love and loyalty, as rich as bacon fat!

Chapter 63

Soon afterwards, the Pioneer brigade leader gave Mimi a white blouse, red scarf and three sugar cubes, along with firm instructions: "Here is a notebook, a pencil, and a ruler. D is for duty. K is for kulak. I expect you to distinguish yourself by reporting to us what you hear."

"Of course I will," said Mimi, cut from the cloth of her obedient clan.

She lived among pariahs. Their Christian dogma was corruption's germs; their monarchist views were well known. She was impatient with their ways. Their thoughts were tiresome and silly, composed of little else but useless sentiment. She knew their furtive sermons and quiet servitude to by-gone days and folkish views were foolish leavings of an outmoded way of life, and dangerous as well—more so as time went on.

The Party, on the other hand, lent Mimi graphic images she could respect and wield. A giant squid, religion! Like slime on naked flesh!

She kept her tongue in check, reluctant to offend. Since she was lithe and limber, she learned to walk on egg shells all the time. Submissive in her character, she did not like to cause her family unnecessary hurt, but on the other hand, she felt a high regard for Party goals with which to mold herself.

So did a child grow up, torn between family and Party.

She knew that the slogans, sing-songed just right, would earn her a star and a badge, yet on the other hand, however, the words her brothers spoke were sweet and low and kind. They loved her, for she was still small. She loved them because they were handsome and smelled of earth and hay.

She sat between them, small and silent, absorbing what they said. So what if they were praying freaks, imbued with superstition? She loved them still, regardless. She watched them carefully.

When Sasha was angry, the tip of his nose would turn white, but Yuri seldom angered; Yuri quieted; Yuri saddened; his gentle counsel pushed her to the brink of tears. When she came home from school and told them in detail how she would help reform humanity, provided all followed the rules, Yuri always put aside what he was doing and took some time with her.

"We have a higher Lord. There is a higher law."

She argued back: "There's order in the universe. Why else would water run downhill?"

She loved them both, but Yuri more than Sasha. He always scooted over to make a nest for her. If she made herself happy, she displeased him. She felt glum when he was joyful in his Savior, in whom he placed his trust.

She pushed her reddened fingers up inside his sleeves, and there they rested, all curled up, like two small, toasty pets.

"I know what's going on behind the hay stack in the dark," she told him softly, swallowing a lump.

"Don't tell," he cautioned her.

She held her breath. She had the guile and patience of a cat. "I won't. But I don't understand—"

"You're much too young to understand," he said, uncurling each of her small fingers and holding them in his warm hands,

"We have a higher mandate—" He gently stroked her pinkie with his thumb, and when he did that—*ach!* what bliss! She almost offered up her belly to have it scratched as well, but then restrained herself.

"Let that be our secret. Mimi? Can we depend on you?"

She nodded, feeling faint. At such times, in communion with her brothers, the country's functionaries and officials—already stringing wire, camp by camp, to fence the kulaks in—just vanished like dark shadows from her mind.

The teacher raked thin fingers through her graying hair and asked repeatedly: "Who's our model? Who's our hero? Who is the most beloved man who ever walked this earth?"

"Comrade Stalin! Comrade Stalin!" chorused Mimi, along with forty other children, paying homage to a cagey,pckmarked bantam, a man who, though he stood a mere five feet in height, had energetically replaced the sluggish tsars, bewhiskered and corrupt.

Pupils like Mimi were at a premium. She was like a blotter, absorbent.

"We thank thee, Comrade Stalin, for a happy childhood," recited Mimi, striving to be mannerly. She filled three notebooks on that theme. She wrote with even hand:

"Our little father Stalin must be our prime example. He wants a New World Order. He does not wish us caged by outdated beliefs. He is the magnet; we are the filings. He will level the rich and raise up the poor. He strives for a state built on reason. He is getting ready for world Revolution. He is tomorrow's universal ruler of the globe, the master of the masses. The fate of every Soviet citizen rests in his clever hand."

Lest she forget how much she owed to him—the man who chased the past away and spelled it out for her precisely whom to hate and whom to love—she had installed his picture over her bed, to be reminded of her duties daily.

"He and the Soviet citizens are one," she finished with a flourish, although the ink was watery, the blotter soaked with blotches.

"We will never betray one another."

The teacher gave her several sidelong glances: she looked like a stork that was digging for frogs.

"Now, little citizen. Yet one more time. Speak up and answer boldly. Where does the Bible now belong?"

"Atop the compost heap."

Mimi, at ten, was earnest and quite well-informed. She knew who harmed the country, who was above reproach. The God of yesterday had been a tyrant. A forward-looking citizen was free!

She signed her name to everything, for she was eager to do battle for her Party. She sang the Party songs as gustily as possible, believing all people were brothers.

Her body grew muscle from handstands and backflips. She fastened her eye on a proficiency medal. She wrote: "From each according to his skill, to each according to his needs." That was her slogan now, but only one of them.

Aware of her own taint—for she came from exploiters—she wrote long, ornamental essays against her ancestry. She knew that Soviet Russia, in future years, would grow four-season grain.

"Oh, what a man!" she wrote of Joseph Stalin many times, while hunger gnawed her innards. "Each day, he combs the beggars' alleys to rescue gutter children." She wrote five pages on the topic that she, for one, held Papa Stalin's enterprise in very high regard. "He is the kindest friend imaginable—" she wrote, and added after thinking hard: "—much like a kindly uncle."

She took enormous pride in her smooth penmanship and silky sentences. She took great care to loop the smallest letter. She still remembered Uncle Benny in small, odd, idle moments that made her bite her lips. A dwarf-like creature. Guileless. Ancient. Now that she pondered, hardly a man at all. Had he not spoken of the dream that there would come a brand new order? To sweep away all Faith?

On whose side had he been? She wasn't sure at all.

She winced a bit and shushed an inconvenient memory—a memory filled with small specks of bliss out of another time, when life seemed ancient. Guileless. As fancied and predictable as a familiar fairy tale shared by a sparking fireplace. Nice. Cozy. But believable?

"The page on which all that was written," went the song, "will soon be ripped from history."

Her brothers claimed repeatedly: "You work. You pray. You trust the Lord. You do your duty always, and happiness will come."

"You don't concern yourself with your own happiness," the teacher lectured, daily. "You do your duty, always, and happiness will come."

The words were practically identical. The difference was in action and belief. She knew her duty now—to keep alive the memory of her own forebears' criminality.

She knew the Bible was a fairy tale, not worthy of a thinking mind. She wanted none of that. Regrettably, and to unending shame, she was a German child, sprung from exploiting, vile offenders.

She, too, somehow survived. Her eyes sat in a face so utterly transparent that one could almost see her skull, but she survived because she willed survival with the strength that will come to a desperate child.

She survived with the help of the Party. When she strolled down the street, people walked quickly and had nothing to say to each other.

Still standing on starvation's brink, young Mimi made herself into a worthy Pioneer, who never shirked a meeting. Her sense of civic duty was the key.

Each day, the Pioneers broke into song, all lyrics modified to praise the Soviet leadership Red commissars, poised to destroy the last small shred of bourgeois decadence that had enriched the strong at the expense of the abused and anguished masses.

Hatemongers! Racists! And exploiters! That was the battle cry.

To find hatemongers, racists and exploiters and flush them out of hiding was now the task at hand.

"The Party needs your eyes and ears," cried the Pioneer leader, guidebook in hand. "The morning mists are gone!"

By then, the government officials had decreed that worse than plunder, spoilage, mayhem, monarch worship and corruption— even killing!—was a seditious spirit, a crime against the Soviet Government.

Hatemongering—the crime that made all others pale! Tipping off the government to those hatemongering against the Party's reconstructive efforts was now the foremost task.

At Apanlee the winter seeped through walls and ceilings. The halls were dank and chill. The wind kept slamming doors.

"How else, but on the wings of Faith?" her brothers urged her on.

Those two still banked on Faith, which was foolish. Her brothers had forgotten how to laugh but clung to their belief that they were singled out to resurrect the past. Her eyes were clear. Her mind was fixed on duty.

"You pray. You give yourself to Jesus. You do your duty, always, and happiness will come."

That's what her brothers claimed, but was it true? Did that make sense? It did not sound convincing. Faith was for sluggish minds.

And yet, no matter how she tried to struggle free, it was the one consistent message her brothers wrapped around her heart as she was growing up: their Faith was intertwined with past ordeals and present strife and future safety valves.

She knew her family invested every ounce of energy to spare into this thing called Faith and, hence, into the earth to keep the seedcorn safe. Empowered by their prayers—that was their firm belief!—their wheat would sprout again.

All well and good. But was it true? Or was it air and fluff?

Faith was like poetry. It made the heart feel tender but served no useful purpose. It warmed your soul, perhaps, but did not fill your belly.

"Remember our Christmas songs? Remember how at Easter—"

Whatever for? She memorized the two important Soviet goals, twin tickets to the future: Kill off the old. Salute the new. She knew the formula by heart. She was up on the sorry tricks of kulaks and hatemongers. She merely shrugged and deftly changed the topic.

"Good riddance! Finally!" said Mimi to her classmates, who had their slogans pat.

Uppermost in all their minds was the collective spirit; its vehicles were deference and zeal. The future was the goal. Her classmates were already way ahead of her; they could barely remember the past. She did her best to follow their example.

If she was honest with herself in odd and quirky moments, she found herself admitting that the color and the scent of Christian holidays had not quite faded from her heart, but she could do without remembering, for it took an enormous effort to forget.

She desperately wanted to forget. She knew she could. She tried.

Yet floating up came memories, unbidden, all the time—so brutal and so bloody that they still gouged her soul.

"The Christian holidays? Just relics of the past," she said, and watched her mother, who remembered still the patter of small feet, just slump and bump into a wall.

There was no choice for someone such as Mimi. Unless she re-designed herself according to the Soviet plan and edict, she would forever be detested and despised. She bore the same last name engraved on all those crumbling headstones, but she was different; she was young. She was ambitious. Smart.

Best yet, she was no racist.

She knew that she belonged to tomorrow, while they belonged to yesterday. She barely knew her ancestors by name and had no wish to be contaminated by faulty, bourgeois ways.

She knew, by then, as did Marleen, as did the twins and even old Natasha: the shortest way to global unity was over a dead body.

All her friends were Pioneers. She knew nobody of her age who had not turned himself into a worthy Pioneer.

At home raged struggle, want, fear, and despair. Her father was dead; her mother numb. Larissa was still a bit daffy. The twins were still busy surviving. Rare were the moments, verily, when someone would remember her and tiptoe to her bed to give her one last hug.

She made an expert survey to map her strategies. She was agile in mind and in body; a gymnast's career was her goal. She was not ready to be laughed at by her classmates without reason. She was ashamed of her land-gobbling, racist forebears, who had been praised and honored by the tsars.

Where the Party-loyal Pioneers gathered, no one was in rags, nobody suffered hunger. Life was still threadbare, filled with hunger pangs, but at the very least, no longer did she have to fill her stomach with earth or with water to trick it.

No longer did she have to swallow grass as she had done that grim, wet day when those two Kansas foreigners arrived with burlap sacks and quackery and proved to her forevermore Faith was a mockery and sham.

The end result was this: she did her best to hide her thoughts, but even so, her brothers had a way of looking wounded and distressed that made her knee caps soft when she told them, repeatedly, as soon as she had her own arguments down pat, that they were clinging to a brand of superstition that was unworthy of two forward-looking citizens.

"Salvation comes through Christ," they told her, looking sad. "Born in a virgin night."

She shrugged to show contempt. A strange Messiah who claimed that he could walk on water, sprung from a married woman who had cheated on her husband and blamed the consequences on the Holy Ghost? It was grotesque and lewd—not worthy of another look, much less an argument. The factor that would usher in the New World Order, she believed, was rationality. All forward-looking citizens now had to do was put their shoulders to the collective wheel and shove. There was no conflict in her heart about the dusty deities of yesterday. Thanks to her preacher cousin Dewey, that toady from America, she knew forevermore that, in the name of Jesus Christ, no morsel came for free.

Mimi still remembered Dewey and his lisping son, who checked their sallow brand of Faith into the drafty halls of Apanlee with loathing and contempt. That day had left a painful wound— an injury never forgotten.

She understood from personal ordeal how strangers from the outside world meant harm to Mother Russia. She had no doubt about the toxic motives of such racists, opportunists, swindlers, and connivers who used the Bible as a tool to force humiliation on a child so weakened by starvation she couldn't wipe the tears out of her vintage eyes.

For years, she felt nothing but hatred for Faith. Good riddance to that loathsome hoax—the sooner gone, the better! Once and for all, those two Americans had helped her cleanse herself of harmful old wives' tales. She knew that she, for one, put solid stock in evidence. The key was rationality. It would deflate all yesterday's mistakes, prick them like a balloon.

She only need recall those tufts of hair she saw in Dewey's flaring nostrils as he stood, feet splayed, and gave his bleated offerings to God, to double up with laughter.

The New World Order was her Faith. She would not fail her country. And so she shouted back, as loudly as she could: "Religion is their poison! Their Gospel is sheer filth!"

The teacher hovered. "Preachers? Priests?"

"By definition, fools!"

"Close," said the teacher. "Try again."

"Provocateurs and saboteurs—"

"We'll have to free the country of this menace," said the teacher.

But there was Yuri. There was Sasha. And how they tried, those two, like spindly, gentle beasts, to nudge her with their noses and try to win her over to their world!

"You are His little lamb. He cares for you," they told her, and she quaked. "Here. Fold your little hands." From her scalp to her footsoles ran tremors.

Her brothers had flames on their tongues, a mystic hand upon their shoulder blades—a hand that no one else could see. Mimi knew they saw themselves as chosen by their past to be honed to perfection—and that included Faith, and that included ancestry.

"Just where do I belong," she asked herself repeatedly.

To that dilemma, sadly, there was no happy ending, since she was not a Russian and never could be one. She was a German child.

Her brothers were her private world—a small, forbidden luxury. They were the only adult males she knew. She worshipped them; when they came home from having worked the soil from dawn to dusk to coax it to regenerate, they smelled just like a warm and sun-baked pumpkin in July. She was tired of winter and want. She sat down on a footstool to listen.

She watched them all the time. She longed to curl up in their arms where it was soft and warm. She liked those Gospel stories best that had to do with harvests.

"You make your bed, you lie in it," such was Natasha's wisdom.

She, too. Wherever Natasha bustled about, there was still that odd whiff of her icons.

For Mimi, so it was for years as she grew up—years emptied of all pride in her own German ancestry.

She marched in parades; she carried the flag of the future that snapped like a whip in the wind, aware that she did not belong in the groove of her family's desperate prayers. There were times, however, when she slipped in quietly because she was sleepy and small and longed to be cuddled a bit.

She would pretend that she was dull and sleepy; she needed tucking in. She kept her eyes downcast, her heart in firm control, as they besieged her from both sides with their sweetly-told stories of Jesus.

"See? We are certain of our Savior's love for you, " they told her many times, and heaven knows what else. They fancied themselves in alliance. They seemed to know Him well; to her, all that was mystery; she never even caught a glimpse, but He was there: they sensed His godly presence.

She, steeped in evidence and reason, did not like Him at all—this so-called Savior and his repeated peek-a-boos in response to their scandalous prayers. They called that partnership? It promised more than it bestowed. All that was bothersome and sick—like a sty in the eye or a cold in the nose! She longed to see clearly, breathe deeply.

The teacher noted on a form that her star pupil, Mimi, was growing in awareness. She told the youngster constantly: "You must set your sights high, and then higher."

So Mimi did. She had her eye on speedy advancement, her ear on the slogans that worked. The other children watched her with curiosity and, sometimes, jealousy. When her conscience started pinching, quickly she soothed it by checking her noteworthy ideological chart. She made sure she was noted for her loud, emphatic songs. She applauded in all the right places. She cheered at every rally. Mastering nausea took swiftness and practice and skill. A squeamish stomach was a liability. She filled a notebook on that thought; her essay received the five highest possible marks.

She hid that honor from the twins, whom she was yearning to impress.

Both Yuri and Sasha insisted that the Party's methods of farming were faulty. The twins would shoe a horse before taking it out on the road. They would lovingly rub it down after making it pull a large load.

"If they keep doing what they're doing," said Yuri, for exam-

ple, "they'll ruin the land, they'll ruin themselves. They'll have
to face the music—"

At the newly formed *kolkhoz*, people quarreled and bickered
and clashed. They beat a mule until it fell dead in the furrows.
They cursed the workers until they spit back: "Why work ourselves to death?"

"For if the state takes our gains, what is the use of it?" the
sullen workers cried. Already there was talk of nasty, raucous
confrontations between an angry Soviet foreman and a crew he
chased down from the ovens with his stick.

"You will be fined! Or whipped!" the angry foreman yelled.

"So be it," cried the peasants, shouting in one voice. They
had seditious counter-arguments. "What good are our collective
acres if we can't plant the crop? What good is our land if we
can't own a horse?"

The government inspectors warned: "Here is a list of do's
and don'ts."

The peasants merely sneered. They gave it brief flicks of the
tongue.

The quota agents yelled: "Here, Citizens! Here are your
quota charts."

The peasants took them to the outhouse. They spat against
the wind.

The peasants dug in deep. Dissent was seething everywhere.
It was soon clear to all that something had to be planted, and
soon, but what? How? When? How much?

"Why would we want to climb aboard a ship that's bound to
sink tomorrow?" the workers asked each other. When they heard
sudden footsteps, all conversation stopped.

This, now, was Mimi's world. She stood between two boulders that moved on one another, a fragile ladybug.

The twins belonged to "them"—hatemongers! Foreigners!
exploiters!—as she did not and never would. Yet "they" were
part of her—the only family she knew.

And what a stubborn creed!

You could bend them, you could snarl and tangle them, you could burden, curse and frustrate them, you could even try to snap their spirits—a German stood his ground. In the dead of the night, the recalcitrants took to the streets, paint pot in hand, and covered every slogan the dutiful, enlightened Pioneers had painted on the fences.

Before another year was gone, Mimi knew the twins were being shadowed. Not that it softened them. She hung her head in silence. It was painful to sort herself out. Her brothers had that mysterious wellspring that gave them certitude and strength. They were older and wiser than she.

She knew that she was growing in awareness. Already she was tall and lanky, and boys gave her long stares.

"Call me Tamara, " said the teacher, a grim-looking female, whose long face was pitted with acne. "We don't need class distinctions. We are all equal now. The New World Order has arrived. Repeat after me: the future will bathe us in light."

The youngsters all chorused: "The future will bathe us in light."

The teacher hovered close, her glance on Mimi's nape: "It's all for one, and one for all. Why do we run our prison vans—?"

"To weed out harmful elements." For instance, take last week—a string of circumspect arrests for sabotage.

She thought of the twins, sick with horror. They never left her mind. Her fear was as sharp and as sudden as a knife, but it would never do to show anxiety before the teacher and the class.

The teacher hovered close. "What do we do with traitors?"

"We send them to Siberia."

"Don't let us down!" the teacher hectored daily. "We count on you. You are the link. The country needs your vigilance."

A few forgotten leaves whirled in the gusts of a departing year. The tree-lined roads grew dark.

"Where there's a prison, there is also redress. What is that, redress?"

"A petition to visit, perhaps?"

"Don't lean on your elbows. Straighten your Pioneer tie. What similarity is there between a parasite and preacher?"

"Why, both exist without producing," reported Mimi, eyes downcast, thus stabbing her beloved brothers in the heart.

She could not bring herself to go that far, to turn her preacher brothers in to the authorities to be corrected and reformed, but she came close. She hedged and stalled. She lied, deceived, and cheated.

She needed stars to go to camp; she needed extra points to qualify for honors. To be a racist child of German ancestry, to have that branded on her soul—while struggling with a whole array of slick avoidance tactics to keep a measure of control—was not an easy matter.

Chapter 64

A Donoghues had found a mildewed document stashed in a rusty tackle box and claimed, by quoting an attorney—who promised him with many silky words he would not charge him any fees unless he won the case—that the old homestead Lizzy had acquired from the cheat with the elastic conscience, the cad who'd left her sitting high and dry amidst the weeds of prairie land, belonged to the Donoghues instead.

"It was a lease and not a sale," they claimed repeatedly, still eyeing Mennotown's prime property, expertly riding roughshod over both the spirit and the letter of the law.

"Fie! Fie!" cried Doctorjay, torn between Abigail and Lizzy. Not even Doctorjay could close his eyes to worsening reality. The have-nots were eyeing the haves.

He tried to be a go-between. His tongue grew raw from trying. Things went from bad to worse. His in-laws were mixed up in secret goings-on. Life was to come to them, that was their aspiration, served on a silver platter.

The next week, Abigail went shopping, attired in blue smock, white socks with colored borders, and flaming red bandanna. She, too, was drunk with victory.

"Every star in the sky within reach!"

Her words would make the rounds for weeks. The leftists kept shaping her values. She had that broad clan of her own; most of them, now as before, looked still as unkempt as the streets of Wichita. They were slapping and kicking each other, rough-housing. Their geese and their chickens ran wild. Their doors came unhinged. Their window panes stayed cracked. They squabbled with their neighbors. Bareheaded and barefooted, all! Ignoring the foot scrapers, even!

The Donoghues kept everybody's feelings in a turmoil. Soon, Doctorjay was trembling with confusion.

They had their counter-arguments.

"It's not a hand-out. It's our due. Equality. Fraternity. And Liberty. We'll take whatever's not willingly shared."

There always had been gaps between rich and poor, but now there was venom mixed in. Some people went even so far as to see Doctorjay as prime example of values being watered down—those self-same values he had brought along when he came sway-ing all the way to Kansas atop his prairie schooner to marry Noralee.

He argued himself hoarse: "When we came here to farm the land, the one thing all of us had was our honesty. *Ach*, were we poor! Not yet a single team of horses in all of Sedgwick County! But nobody expected a handout!"

Ah, for the olden times! With opportunities galore! When you could make your own way, step by step and day by day, by pulling people's teeth and lancing boils—and stash away the sav-ings!

The Donoghues grew increasingly audacious and ever more tenacious. They never gave up hope of settling an old score. It was clear they were up to no good. They telephoned excessively. They reeked of unwashed life. In three words: they were trou-ble—writ large.

The neighborhood watched in alarm.

The saddest part for Doctorjay was the estrangement his marriage to his garish Abigail had wedged between himself and Jan, whom he loved more, respected more, and wanted more to please than all of Mennotown combined.

"Jan! Here's to you! To the caboose! Here! Have a swig! Don't be a killjoy. Bottoms up!"

Jan answered brusquely and with irritation while puttering about. "That stuff is not for me."

"How can it hurt? Just once?"

"You cured me with that wisdom tooth. Remember? Now leave me be. I said, just leave me be!"

It was a rare moment of tension; it had passed in a flash. But both men sensed it keenly.

The healer tried to catch Jan's eye to find the old-time friendship there. That was no longer possible. Autumnal days had come; the gardens began to look bare.

"I'll get him yet," swore Doctorjay, while trying to devise a game. He felt he sat, bare-backsides, on a tight clump of nettles. He itched all over, dared not scratch.

He spread his strategy in front of Abigail. He wanted both Jan's friendship and Abigail's lush love.

"Jan's getting stuffy. He's no fun. He's lost his sense of humor. He needs to loosen up. Pass the potato pancakes."

It was all right again in Mennotown to fry potato pancakes. The German language schools had never quite recovered since the war had come to an end more than a decade ago, but most of the Muellers and Meyers were back.

"Don't waste your time," said Abigail sarcastically. "He'll never have that drink and toast to friendship, love, equality and brotherhood."

"What do you mean?"

"Jan's reputation as a teetotaler is known all over Sedgwick County."

All kinds of bets were riding on the outcome.

One positive by-product of advancing age was, luckily, that

Josie didn't bicker Lizzy into corners any more and hardly ever raised her voice to parlay socialism. Weeks, even months, would pass in silence, without a single argument. She only dabbled in black magic when she and Rarey talked.

She talked to him in code. She lost herself in him.

And Rarey, a responsive child, was still her little wonder. He did not disappoint his mother. He was her wonder child.

A pencil stub and a small scrap of paper were all that Rarey needed to keep himself content. His brush strokes were as smooth and even as a slim boat's prow cutting quietly through tormented waters. His mind was as alive with images as the Arkansas River was alive with trout after a hefty rain. From the day he was born, he showed talent—talent in buckets, and genius to match.

Rarey's every picture throbbed with magnificence and meaning. His mother shone with pride and ownership, her eyes like molten glass, sipping her lemon tea.

While Josie grew ever more still, Lizzy grew ever more shrill. Advancing age had taken Lizzy's benign nature and sucked it into a black hole. She never noticed. She had progressed from youth and middle age to old age the way she walked the neighborhood—just step by step, and stair by stair, her eyes and energies and concentration fastened firmly on her goal, which was to live correctly.

Now life was almost finished. She knew her end was near.

She made the most of it. She had already suffered through a serious kidney problem. A Wichita doctor had predicted her heart would be next, but Doctorjay had sneered away the city slicker, and handed her his own supply of stomach bitters.

"Five drops three times a day will forestall early death," he said to her, and that came true; she still was here, on earth, right next to her geraniums, both just as spry as ever.

Lizzy stuck by Doctorjay's advice. "Oh, thank you. Thank you kindly. And my bill?"

"Don't even mention it."

"No. I insist."

"If you insist."

"I do. You heard me. I insist."

"Let's say three and a quarter—"

"Well. Hm. A bit steep, don't you think? Last time you charged two-seventy-five—"

That was the ritual. She trusted Doctorjay with her last dime, but she still watched her pennies. He knew what he was doing; she knew what she was doing. She knew he would not make the same mistake that he had made with Noralee: ignore her serious symptoms of palpitations of the heart, while mocking them as evidence of jealousy.

"Five drops," she told her visitors with pride, one foot already in the grave, "will forestall early death."

"And still so many teeth," they marveled.

Old Lizzy surveyed her realm in triumph. She came of hardy stock. She took it all in stride, even her kidney problems. She was just like her hardy neighbors, appreciative of health.

She kept fanning herself with excitement. She was still plagued by a stubborn cough, but she still wasn't finished. Her work on earth was almost done, except for Josie's last-born.

There was still Rarey, to be sheltered from a mother's untoward ambitions and worldly vanity that had already cost one child. For what a jewel, Rarey!

"Before it is too late, I must make sure," she said to Little Melly.

Lizzy knew she must imbue this precious child of Jan's with her own bedrock values—and not a day too soon. "Run, Rarey, run! Fetch Dewey Epp and tell him I have hunted through my prayer book and found the quote he needs—"

That's how you drew a line—by finding tasks to do that tied into the Bible, to keep a child from straying off too far.

Time passed.

The acorns started falling.

Jan never gave up hope he would win Josie's love—at least win back affection. He was not blind, nor was he deaf, nor was he totally unschooled in matters of romance. His hair, by then, had turned to snow, and Josie, still the same! Still haughty and aloof. He could no longer hope she would grow out of it.

"I love her," said Jan Neufeld. He loved her, whims and all.

His love for her was hard in grain, a wonder to behold. Her feelings for the man who gave her everything—a splendid home three stories high, the widest fireplace in all of Kansas, as many greenbacks as her fists could throw into the social whirl her trendy friends in Wichita stirred up—were intricate in hue.

An ocean lay between them.

She had some hidden scarring, deep inside, she never touched upon. It was as if she had thrown the key to her heart in the river.

Not all was lost, however. Between them they had Rarey—a new life sprung from a violent night. It was as though that night had wedged an opaque pane of glass between them. She still saw the man who had looted and plundered. He knew there was ice in her heart.

He also knew she hurt. He was not made of stone. He knew there was the mocking side of Mennotown that Josie, being Josie, would never manage to live down, though Lizzy helped defy the biting tongues in every way she could.

Josie, over time, was wilting undeniably from sheer exhaustion of the spirit. Without her husband, she was nothing. She seemed to have accepted that. She glued an odd, obliging smile to her still-pretty face, suppressed a sigh or two, snapped shut her book, served zwieback topped with homemade jam, and did as she was told—at least, most of the time.

Hence, Lizzy was in her full glory.

From her corner window in the kitchen, where Jan had bolted down her chair so it didn't slip when she staggered and had to hold on—since worsening glaucoma now seemed to be an added problem—Lizzy savored sovereignty. She was the undisputed matriarch of a clan whose pride and joy was Rarey.

When the caboose read things to Lizzy, when he explained the world of art to her, the hours just slid by!

She watched him sketching things from his imagination. He

had a perfect eye and small, precise, slim hands. His mind was sharp yet flexible, expansive, much like a rubber band, his fingers as nimble as ten little, fluttering birds.

"Come. Lean against my knees," Lizzy begged, so she could put a trembling hand upon his head and savor generations.

She wished she could live on and on to see him to adulthood but knew she asked too much. Why, any moment now, she knew with virtual certainty, the Lord would come and smother her in His embrace—in fact, send several angels to come swooping down and lift her to those meadows evergreen of which the heavens were composed.

Lizzy was too bashful to admit this selfish thought, but she kept wondering if there were tubs of butter where she was going next. Although the Bible didn't talk of butter tubs, it definitely talked of meadows.

She knew she would find out, and soon.

She liked to speak of her impending death, as though she were fixing to go to a wedding. "Now I shall lay myself out," she'd told her grandkids more than once, and all of them had gathered. She made the most of her recoveries. Her kitchen was, as always, a haven of comfort for all. That's where the village females congregated, once a week, to do their backlogged darning.

She launched herself more thoroughly. She reveled in her role and status, entitled as she was to all the deference and honors she deserved. By then, she was too rheumatoid to navigate the smallest step across her icy porch without the help of Josephine, who always lent a hand.

"Run, Rarey! Run! Get me my peppermint drops. You, too, Josie! Hurry! Get me my footstool and bring me two pillows—"

Josie rose obediently. She pulled a wooden face but did as she was told.

Old Lizzy looked around, exulting, to see if her lady friends noticed. They had, and they nodded, impressed to the hilt: Old

Lizzy merely snapped her fingers, and all her wishes now came true. She started glowing head to toe as though a flame had kindled deep within her.

"Fetch me my glasses also, will you?"

The neighbors watched Josie rifle through every last drawer. This was as good as life could get, like eating sunflower seeds: once you shelled one, you simply had to shell another.

"And let the cat out, too."

"All right! All right!" Josie practically sprang from her seat, and Lizzy leaned back and rocked herself, thus savoring her triumph.

"You didn't close the door," she pointed out, unable to let up. "I seem to feel a draft—"

It had taken a lifetime of struggle and the proverbial patience of Job, but Lizzy had won in the end. Her left leg could not quite support her body any more, but if the weather was decent, she still took her walks to the neighborhood store, where people mentioned her longevity and asked: "What is the secret, Lizzy?"

"Fresh air, firm prayers," smiled Lizzy.

Death would destroy her old and useless body, but she had plans to waft her soul into eternity on the wings of Dewey's prayers. That was her plan. What medication couldn't do, a prayer could accomplish.

Her cuckoo clocks kept cuckooing. She was as ready for the final curtain call as she would ever be. Meanwhile, let all the neighbors marvel.

In preparation for her death, Lizzy often went to visit Herbert's grave, where all was sweetness and decay. When she returned, she shared her happiness with Josie.

"Oh, I cried. I cried. It was lovely."

Even into ancient age, Lizzy's spirit shone as brightly as the Kansas sun shone in July. "Death could come tomorrow," she told Josie, who had little to say in reply.

"Next week. Or next month."

"Well—"

"Next year?"

Lizzy kept rocking herself in contentment. She had nothing to fear; she awaited the blast of the trumpets. Nobody knew when Rapture would come, but that it would happen—and soon!—was already a foregone conclusion.

"And when that happens, dearest—why, I'll just close my eyes, draw my last breath, and melt into the arms of my Savior—"

"You would. You would," said Josephine, with emphasis on *you*.

This after all these years!

Some quirks of Josephine's just wouldn't go away, no matter the veneer. Old Lizzy pondered that reply and other oddities, searching for a fitting comeback but always ready to excuse the frailties of people whom she loved.

"Have yet another glass of milk," she said. She took firm hold of Josie's shoulder to give her counsel emphasis. "There's nothing milk and prayers can't heal."

But drinking milk, fresh from the udder, still brought on vertigo in Josie.

"My Rarey will be first in everything," said Josephine to Little Melly, next, filling up her cup.

The spinster blinked with puzzlement. "A Pomeranian prince?"

"You can say that again."

This was another nice development of getting older, growing mellow. No longer did the two hold hidden grudges in their respective bosoms like two old boards with rusty nails. Now all was unity to every naked eye, which was the right deportment and to Jan's benefit.

"He never throws a tantrum? He never breaks a pencil?"

"Not on your life. No. Never."

"Amazing. Just amazing."

"Yes. Isn't it? He's just like a sapling, extending his branches to take in the blue of the sky."

"You don't want a lopsided youngster." Little Melly said that to survive and with Archibald in mind.

"What's that supposed to mean?"

"It wouldn't hurt to give him a newspaper route before school."

"Whatever for? We don't need the cash. We can afford most anything. His daddy is one of the richest men in Kansas."

"He needs to be out in rough winds. That way he'll grow up rugged."

"Hitting home run does not make a man," said Josie, full of charity, since she had private guesses about Archie.

"And what is that supposed to mean?" Little Melly kept stitching away.

"Why, not a thing. Why, Little Melly! Nothing!"

Jan raised his voice sometimes to chide his son a bit, to add a dash of influence, but never once his hand. He even took the little fellow to watch sunsets. The result was a near-perfect child.

Day by day and step by step, both Jan and Josie walked their last born a little deeper into culture and urbanity. They did not fear that they would overheat his brain, while piling books on top of books, ideas on top of ideas. They thought he was a potted palm; they had only to water it.

Little Melly, by contrast, had Archie.

She still mothered her nephew, doing this and that. He was grown now, an eligible bachelor. He looked upon her, he respected her, as though she were his mother and he her favorite son; he did as she had taught him; he kept his prayer book atop a dainty doily, his sheets without a single crease.

Archie was gawky, not to say ugly, but was very fond of her, and she of him; it was a mutual thing. When she and Archie were alone, she still kissed him goodnight, with soft lips, moist with spittle. He liked her to button him up to his neck. She hated it when he was gone.

Best of all, Archie confounded all the neighborhood with an astonishing and pleasing piety that centuries had wrought. Before he even came of age, he packed the church with worshippers.

No one was as sure of the Gospel as Archie. Today, you can still see him prancing on the television screen, but even then, he liked to play to audiences. Give him a pulpit and a prayer book, and Archie danced and pranced; he whispered and he shouted; the windows shook; the congregation sobbed.

If Archie couldn't find a girl who pleased him well enough to stop him from pulling his hangnails, then maybe, reasoned Little Melly, her dearest Archibald could Christianize the world?

Little Melly was certain the future would even a score. Archie was no romantic catch, but quite an ardent Christian. He had only one eye, and that eye had a film; girls shied away from him; and sometimes even Little Melly would wake right in the middle of a dream and toss and turn with anxious thoughts that lacked a proper focus. On the practical aspects of love, she was hazy.

She took her worries about Archie, one by one, to Doctorjay, after she had gathered evidence enough to make a case for them.

"He swings his legs. He licks his fingers. He crooks his little pinkie as though he were a girl—"

The healer agreed: those were the symptoms of a warning. "I must admit I saw it coming."

With resolution, she pushed on. "He blows into his soup with puckered lips so that the droplets fly. Is that still normalcy?"

The healer checked on every clue that she laid bare for him. He even lectured Archie:

"Don't swing your legs. Don't lick your fingers. Don't crook your little pinkie as though you were a girl. Don't blow into your soup with puckered lips—"

"Mind your own business," Archie said, this in a nasty undertone.

Chapter 65

A month before the acorns started falling, Jan first had serious trouble at the mill.   Labor unrest had been there before—friction during lunch breaks, grumbling as the pay was handed out. From there, things went from bad to worse.

Jan bought a dog from the police in Wichita to help his night guard make the rounds, and yet the Donoghues became more boisterous; their heckling never stopped. He heard them shouting slogans for Equality, Fraternity and Liberty through several loudspeakers that they had mounted on a truck. More than once, it even came to blows between the Donoghues and neighbor youths, whose ire they'd aroused.

Each time the constable arrived to separate the rowdies, Jan hoped they would pack up and leave, but they seemed in no hurry. The Donoghues were there to stay. The deacons hinted daily that worse was yet to come, and they were right; the greengrocer told unbelievable stories.

All this caused great discord in Mennotown where people slept as they had always slept, with every door unlocked.

Jan blamed himself for these developments. He needed to be

firm, lay down the law, enforce the rules, and that, for him, was difficult. Of late, his mind was simply not on business. Faint sparks of light danced in his brain, and more than once, to his surprise, he carelessly miscalculated numberwork and found he had to borrow money from the bank.

He paled when he learned how dear such money came. The interest on his needed loan was high; it killed his appetite; he started having splitting headaches.

He lost his mood for other people's woes. "Not now," he said to Dewey, when Dewey came a-canvassing.

"What do you mean, not now? You are a ten percenter."

"I overspent a bit. I need an extra grain insurance policy, and grain insurance policies are dear."

"You don't need grain insurance. God watches over you."

Insurance was the Devil's latest scheme. You only bought yourself disaster policies when you stopped trusting in the Lord.

"Your profits are slipping? And who would be surprised?"

"I'll make it up to you next year."

"Grain-rich, cash-poor, huh? Right?" mocked Dewey. If Dewey saw a business wobbling, he saw the hand of God. He launched himself politically: "This country's going to the dogs. This is no game of dominoes."

Dewey chaired the Hoover-for-President Club. Here was a candidate to almost everybody's liking: a deeply pious fellow with broad shoulders, a round chin, hair neatly parted in the middle, a stickler for detail. Rich meals were part of his daily routine.

"With a new congress voted in," predicted Dewey confidently, "hems will drop. Markets will go up. You don't need grain insurance."

"I signed some legal papers—"

"You mean to say you're willing to pay interest to the usurers?"

To Dewey Epp, the usurers were maddening—all in pursuit of Mammon. Here's what they did: They took the cash out of Jan's pockets and put it in their own. They wore carnations in their buttonholes to advertise good will, but sidled up to every rabble and canaille.

"Where is your conscience, Jan? The riffraff is gathering strength. This labor union business will be your ruin, and when the unions move in, you watch it, buddy! Watch it!"

"As if I didn't know."

"Some people could get hurt."

"I know."

"Those blasted Donoghues grow ever more rambunctious."

"You're telling me?"

"You must lay down the law. Now, are you still a ten percenter, or must I strike your name?"

Two of the Donoghues came visiting. They had hard, fevered eyes, and each one wore a triangular beard.

"Why should a foreman get more money than we do? We want equality. This is America." They stared at Jan; they looked unkempt and insolent. Jan's patience was down to a trickle. It was a muggy afternoon. He felt a strong revulsion, an almost visceral nausea that rose in a gray wave of bile. He struggled to focus his gaze: something hummed in his ears like a bee.

"Your foreman earned his place. You haven't."

"We work the same long hours."

Jan didn't add: "He's family. He is my daughter's husband's brother." The unions harped on that.

"Paid holidays," said one.

"Paid sick leave," said the other.

Jan spoke to the opposite wall. "Pay you for loafing? Absurd."

"We are entitled. It's either that, or else, the unions."

"That's out of bounds. That's unacceptable." The glare through the window kept blurring Jan's vision. He longed for his cool bedroom. He struggled to keep his voice even.

"Isn't your mother ashamed of you two? Don't you know the harm you do to her? Your mother has a reputation to uphold, now that she married Doctorjay. Did your mother raise you savages?"

The Donoghues took turns. "It's criminal, the way some people keep on hoarding riches, whereas their workers grovel in the dirt."

"We want our share."

"No more. No less."

You're exploiting us."

"That's un-American."

Between long silences, Jan studied the two. His heart was leaden with foreboding. He looked at his own hands, gnarled long ago by heavy labor.

"I worked like a donkey," he said at long last. "Call me anything you like, but don't—don't call me un-American."

The roughnecks stood their ground.

"We want our share."

"No compromise."

"We need a union here."

Fixed pay, Jan knew, was next. Why pay a worker costly summer wages October through December when all work slowed and coffee breaks were extra-long? It made no sense at all.

"I'm not without a heart. I do my best, and I am fair. Ask anyone. Today, I pay you three times as much compared to what my mother ever paid you folks, before we had machinery that helped us husk the corn and stack the sheaves."

"We want what's fair."

"What you call fair would ruin me." Something inside Jan's head was throbbing. Although it was late afternoon and almost time for supper, the Kansas sun outside baked every cobblestone.

"I'll look into this union business," said Jan, against his better judgment, for he felt strangely vulnerable, sitting there behind his desk this brightly-lit, aggressive afternoon.

"Time's running out."

"There's been a slump in grain sales. A serious slump. As soon as our exports bounce back—"

The prices of almost all products had fallen; oats sold a dime a bushel; corn brought two paltry pennies more. Not even Lizzy

knew about the chattel mortgage on that special piece of land Jan
had bought for cash on Rarey's birth, after a truly exceptional
harvest. It was indebted now.

"We're giving you fair warning."

"I'll see what I can do."

Jan knew he could have taken out another loan to ease his
workers' grievances, but his commitments to the church, his family and his town lay on him like a sack of stones. And Josie was
dreaming of art school for Rarey.

One of his tormentors now settled back with a sarcastic squint.
"We want an answer. Now."

"What's that supposed to mean?"

"Some people, you might say, are in the mood for fun."

Wrath rose in Jan—much like a cresting wave—for this was
cheeky talk. "Look, if there's work that must be done because
the seasons push, I say it must be done! I can't have artificial
schedules. The Chamber would be furious! This country wasn't
built on sloth—"

"The winds of change—"

Jan cut them off; his patience had run out. "Look here, you
two! Don't push me past my limit because your mother married
my best friend. I pay my workers what they've earned. I don't
cheat them; nor do I work them harder than the task or the seasons demand—"

"—the winds of change will blow your flivver off the road.
Right off the road, Jan Neufeld."

Jan's neck grew thick with the implied insult. "Get out," he
said, "before I throw you out."

"A match," they told each other, smirking, still lurking between door and jamb, "can make our argument much better than
we can."

When word spread far and wide about the possibility of arson, Jan's mother begged: "Fire them. Just let them go! There is
no way to please the Donoghues. No way! The night guard has
already spotted a suspicious stranger twice—"

"They need their jobs," said Josephine. "What's more, they need a raise. Estella's once again expecting."

"She no longer says 'pregnant,' however," said Lizzy to herself.

Out loud she said: "Again?" She put both elbows on the table, for being old gave her advantages and privileges she savored to the hilt. She coughed, and Rarey ran for her peppermint drops. She fainted, and Josephine ran for the camphor.

"Again." Josie consulted a small pocket mirror. "I suspect that it isn't her fault."

Soon after, Jan arranged to sit down with an insurance man to see where he needed protection, but Lizzy shooed the agent from his door. It was her duty to warn Jan and forestall worse to come. That's why she had come, to forestall.

She smiled brightly with the wisdom drawn from decades and told her son, himself near retirement age:

"Look, it all starts and ends with charity. It's simple: whatever you give to the needy will be returned to you ten-fold. That is all the protection you need."

"Did Dewey visit you?"

"Of course he did. He told me everything."

"I might have known!"

"Have Josie sort a pile of discards for Estella, and hide some cash within. That way, no one can say that you've grown stingy. I'd like to die with my honor intact—" This included an unbroken string of donations. "You're short on money, son? Is that why you won't tithe, as you have always done? You need some money? Why not ask? Why beat about the bush? Tell me what's wrong. I'm your mother. You know that I can take most anything, except a son who isn't ten percenting."

She knew she had some money somewhere. She didn't quite remember where, but she would look for it.

"Demand for Lizzy's Cheese is at an all-time peak—"

She spelled things out for him. "The Finkelsteins again?" she asked, to spice the day a bit.

Jan didn't argue that. He didn't even try to take the stinger from her words, though she expected that.

She saw that Josie, by the window, raised her chin. She set her own jaw firmly:

"This union stuff. It's dangerous. It's everywhere. Your workers are in danger of contamination. What will be next? Roast pig for breakfast? *Ach!* The Donoghues would like that—wouldn't they? What will be next? Stretch out and fall asleep at noon?"

This irked Old Lizzy most: that every Donoghue expected life served on a silver platter. Where was it all going to end?

"I have the gift of second sight," she told her son, who nodded. Jan saw with increased clarity that Dewey was right; the Lord and His work must come first. "I have the formula. All will be well, as long as people pay attention to the Gospel and do what's right by God. Dismiss the Donoghues. The Donoghues are trouble. And I mean trouble! Trouble! It's just like Dewey said: They've caught the union bug."

"I know."

"This country is losing its fiber. Does grain grow by itself? Do chickens feed themselves? As Dewey pointed out in church in front of everybody just last week, you used to be a solid ten percenter—"

"You plan to give the Donoghues their marching papers, Jan?" asked Josie, from the window, now stabbing with her darning needle. Hard.

"It seems I have no choice."

"Estella's expecting again."

"Another mouth to feed," sighed Lizzy.

"She needs a wage-earning husband," said Josie.

"You know who is behind all this? I'm telling you. It is the shyster lawyers. If they take their old claim to court, the shysters will get rich. Jan's in for serious trouble—"

"Where are the papers, Lizzy?"

"We had a clear agreement. We even shook hands on the deal—"

"Mom, try to think. Was it an outright sale?"

"Why, it's been ages. Ages!" What papers? She really didn't know. What difference did it make? She started sniffling with distress. "Was there a document? There could have been. I might have stuck it in my apron. I might have washed that apron. Why, in the olden days, we didn't need the lawyers. A handshake was enough, and furthermore—"

That was the trouble with the younger generation—they didn't understand. They didn't understand that, in staying on the right side of the law, there was no need for lawyering. One's conscience did all the policing.

"I handed that swindler my last two dollars, for that miserable pigeon-fouled shack! The conniver! The rascal! The drifter! He took to his heels and was gone! I never saw him again! Whereas the three of us—Herb, Jan and me, with just a mule between us, the soil below, the good Lord at our side and His fine sky above—"

Awash in reminiscence, Old Lizzy rocked herself. With Jan's help and with her dear departed second husband's help, she, Lizzy Neufeld, a female immigrant from Russia, had launched the finest wheat domain in the entire state of Kansas. Did she deserve a son who lapsed in ten percenting?

"I say it is this union business, Jan. They'll be your ruin! A bunch of racketeers and Reds!" That was the final punch line. She stopped herself, however. There was a look to Jan that she had never seen before. It was as though he stared beyond the kitchen, beyond the red geraniums.

He spoke quietly, as though to himself:

"They're asking summer wages, no matter what the season. No business can survive that kind of waste and excess. Besides, I would be setting precedent—"

"Exactly!" said his mother firmly, though she had never heard the word. She moved the rocker to the window and sat down, next to Josie. "Did you hear what your husband said? He would be setting precedent. What do you say to that? Jan has to let them go. They're troubling him. They're stressing him. Just look at your poor husband, Josie. He'll have himself a heart attack. The tension just never lets up. That's why I say: dismiss them."

"If you do that, Jan Neufeld" said Josie, speaking to her lap, "then Doctorjay will be so angry, he'll not speak to you for weeks. He will be hopping mad, now that he's married Abigail—"

"So?" Lizzy queried, looking glum, about to lose her argument. This was Jan's sorest point—what Doctorjay would say if he put down his foot and stopped the Donoghues and their extravagance. She, Lizzy, had already seen the healer hurry across the street, pretending his eyesight was failing, when Jan had waved to slow him down so he could help him choose a brand new color for his flivver.

Jan wrapped himself in silence. The drumming in his ears increased. The room was swaying gently. He felt disoriented and strangely afraid; she knew that his enormous appetite was gone.

"You won't land in the poorhouse," said Josie the barbarian, "if you give people not as fortunate as you a decent helping hand. Just as I always say to Abigail—"

That, too. All was not well in Doctorjay's patched household either. Since he had married Abigail, Doctorjay had been adrift politically and dangerously tilting to the Left. Of late, the healer went from house to house to tell astonished people: "There are two sides to every blasted story. The Donoghues are not as bad as everybody thinks. They have a point. They are Americans. Since they are frank and speak their minds, they have as many enemies as friends."

The wedding guests had come and gone, all bringing gifts and wishes. Now there was litter in the yard; hillbilly music blared from the Victrola. Odd people camped in tents beneath the trees and ate the plums that Noralee, may she rest in her grave, had nursed up from her precious seedlings.

When, after a tense meal, the bonesetter came knocking on Jan's heart one final time to beg forbearance for the rascals, no matter what the price, Jan pondered, undecided. He knew he owed his friend a lifetime of advice. Now was the time to pay it back.

"I vouch for those two boys of Abigail's," said Doctorjay, a man who always kept his word.

"They're handing out pink pamphlets."

"I'll put a stop to it."

"They're seeding discontent."

"I know. I know. They're the rotten apples in my barrel. Jan, give them one more chance. As a personal favor to me."

Jan nodded with reluctance. He knew the formula: if you put people out of work, in idleness they only cooked up further mischief.

"Thanks, pal! That will restore my household peace."

Jan, who had struggled through a sleepless night, torn between doing right and going easy, called back the Donoghues. He kept them on against his better judgment, right through the slump of a very bad harvest—which meant that he had moved the discontent on which the have-nots throve, right into his own mill.

Now tension grew around the silos and, more than once, police cars came on screeching tires to haul the scoundrels off to jail to let them cool their heads and heels. Abigail pouted, and Doctorjay fled farther from reality. In short, it was a mess.

Lizzy made sure that she visited daily. She came with a walker, but visit she did. It was clear that a serious matter troubled Jan's mind. What it was, she was dying to know. That's why she came, to find out.

"I have no choice but to suspect the Jews behind this union talk," she told him one last time.

Jan's thoughts were miles away. "I hope that you are wrong."

"I'm not. That's what the Elders say. The Hebrews have stirred up the Donoghues. That bunch of shady swindlers!"

"Mom—"

"The good life does not fall like manna from heaven. It has to be earned by the sweat of one's brow."

Josie lifted her head in surprise at the edge in Lizzy's voice. "What's wrong, Lizzy? Anything wrong?"

"You ask what's wrong? I'll tell you. A weight is on my mind." Lizzy swallowed hard and waited for that odd, disturbing ripple that, in moments such as this, would run along her spine and end up in her toes. "I feel a premonition."

"What kind of premonition?"

Lizzy wouldn't let herself be calmed. "Jan's got to let them go. The Donoghues are trouble. The Jews are running them. The Jews give them their slogans. I hate to say this, Jan, but they're chiselers. I say enough is enough. It doesn't take a genius to know that trouble's brewing. Somewhere. Life doesn't come to anyone served on a silver platter—"

"Don't worry, Mom. I'm a cautious man."

She spoke from raw, chill instinct. She and her people were this country's spine, and if you snapped that spine, the body politic would wreck.

"You couldn't ever please them. Never! Not even Herbert could. Remember? Herbert used to hire them while they were still in school to help out with the summer chores. A pointless exercise in generosity. You give them generosity—they'll ask for more and more. They multiply like rabbits, all waiting to be fed on generosity."

Old Lizzy was at her wit's end. She, who had helped to tame and build this land, was staring at a five percenter? Her children and her children's children lived and worked and flourished in the Dakotas. In Nebraska. Manitoba. Saskatoon. Ontario. Was that success, or what? And they? The Donoghues? Thrift and frugality? No. Order and decency? Never. They merely stepped up their catcalls. They agitated for a two-day weekend—they might just get it, too!

"Jan! Listen, son! You don't need the Donoghues. Let them try selling apples."

"I'll keep an eye on them."

"I say: just let them go."

"Mom, will you let me do the worrying? Are you taking the

pills Josie ordered for you?"

"A dime a pill? Not me!" A mystery elixir, that's what she took, concocted from crushed toad. Old age might be wasting her body, but surely not her spirit, which glowed as warmly and as surely as the dry buffalo chips she still remembered clearly.

"I hear," said Josephine, for her part on the warpath by that time, "the unions are gaining support."

"That's nonsense. Who said that?"

"I read the papers from Topeka," said Josie evenly, "to keep myself informed."

"If you must read," cried Lizzy, warm coffee in her belly, therefore mileage in her soul, "why don't you read those books that have a happy ending? Where everything is sorted out?"

She shocked herself with that attack, but it felt sweet. Oh, it felt wonderful! The morning was still young; the air was raw and biting; it burned Old Lizzy's tongue and ran into her stomach like a flame.

"It's still the Reds? You still are partial to the Bolshies? When will you ever learn?"

She hadn't meant to speak out loud or be so critical, but words had a way of escaping, like smoke ascending through an opening left in a dilapidated roof. "An eight- hour day, that's what they want? A forty hour week? Are you kidding me?"

"That's right. What's wrong with that? In Russia—"

Ah! Finally some sparks, to spice the day a bit! Lizzy knew enough about the vagaries of human nature to know that trouble was afoot. Big trouble. Huge. And chances were that it was marital.

She rushed to Jan's side mentally. Her instincts told her clearly: here was a weary husband, worrying his head over the agitation at the mill, the rabbits' damage to the grain, the interest on his business loans, and what did Josie say? What did Josie do? She sided with the Communists and Jews!

"That's what you get," she scolded, wagging an old finger, "for putting poetry ahead of prayer. For preferring the typewriter's rattle to the hum of a sewing machine. Did I not warn you,

Josephine? Your Bolshie organizers—"

"My Bolshie organizers!" cried Josie, stricken by blatant betrayal. "What did you say? You said my Bolshie organizers?"

"The Finkelsteins are not your friends?"

"They are my friends. They aren't Red."

"I am amazed she doesn't wield a pitch fork," said Lizzy to herself. She knew what she knew, which was plenty. Now it was up to her to channel that abundant energy of Josephine's into constructive, useful channels. The Elder Dewey's basement was deluged with lady volunteers, all multipying Christian cheer.

"We have to start planning for Thanksgiving baskets! We'll send two big ones to the Donoghues. We'll hide some cash inside. We'll pack an extra basket for Estella, who has another bastard in her belly. The Holy Season is as fine a time as any—" That was the one advantage of old age: yours was the final word. "—as fine a season as they come to share your blessings with the poor."

Josie put both fingers in her ears, but Lizzy hadn't finished.

"Take Little Melly," shouted Lizzy. "A volunteer, as eager as they come. Her recipes are legend! Her hair, still hardly gray! I can still see her catching butterflies with Jan down by the river bank—"

Josie jumped up then, charged head to toe with a turbulent fury.

"Now, Josie! Josie!" Lizzy cried, elated. "Why, every time I mention Little Melly—" and Josie fell back in her chair.

And Jan! A helpless man who lived and died and never had a clue as to that source of energy that fueled two angry females. He tried to intervene, to no avail at all: "Why argue back and forth on such a fine and sunny day?"

"Right. Josie, dear, how is your calendar?"

"My calendar is full."

"The County Fair is just around the corner."

"Which one? Another hodgepodge fair?"

"You could chair the committee."

"I already serve on seven committees. I counted them up.

Now I beg to be counted out!"

"Just do your bit," said Lizzy primly. "Just do your bit for charity. Just help us spread Thanksgiving cheer."

"Me? Hah!"

"If nothing else, you could stuff Dewey's envelopes—"

"No! No, I say! Stuff envelopes?"

"Make decorations, then."

"That's where I draw the line!"

"Just take it easy. Take it easy. Let Rarey climb up in the attic to see what's in the boxes you stacked away last year—" She, Lizzy, had eyes in her head, though misty more often than not. Jan had his mill, his workers, and his worries; he did not need a labor union argument right in his well-scrubbed kitchen. "All of a sudden, I don't feel so good—" If worst came to worst, she could always fall into a faint. It never failed. It didn't now. She made the most of it. Both Jan and Josie jumped up to assist. A chair went over. Jan cried out in panic: "Mother, sit here. Sit! Sit by the window here!" And Josie cried, too: "Quick, Rarey! Run! Where are the pills the Wichita doctors prescribed?"

"The pills? The pink pills?"

"Did you hide them again? Did you take them as you were supposed to?"

"I forget if I did or I didn't," murmured Lizzy, victorious in martyrdom. "These days, my memory comes and goes. Just comes and goes. *Ach,* children!"

Why put your faith in pills from Wichita or wills left in some tackle box? She kept her medications and her documents stacked in a corner of her cupboard where she just never ever looked— except perhaps but twice a year, at spring and fall cleaning. That way, you could ignore them.

"I follow Doctorjay's instructions," moaned Lizzy, slumping. "He tells me what to do. Pure honey and boiled onions. An hour before bedtime. It never fails. Tomorrow, I'll be good as new."

"Come live with us," said Jan, now hovering. "So we can keep an eye on you."

"Yes, do," said Josie, not too graciously. "You're living here already. You might as well move in."

Old Lizzy looked at Jan and Josephine through faded, swimming eyes. She fanned herself with a napkin, awaiting contradiction. "No, no. I better not. I might be underfoot."

"Why, Mom! The very thought!"

"I may be old, but I cling to my pride as long as I can." She, Lizzy, was in splendid form. Life still had plenty of excitement. "Let go of my arm, Josephine!"

The stairs? A minor obstacle! After such a spicy argument, she was unwilling to go back to being a mere mortal.

Perhaps she'd head straight down to Little Melly's porch on this fine, shiny morning and get her all hopped up as well? "Oh! By the way. Before I forget. Your snapdragons, Josie! They do look kind of peaked—"

And with that last, fine parting shot, Old Lizzy headed to the spinster to unload everything.

Chapter 66

The teacher hovered close. "Who's plotting sabotage against the Party?"

"How should I know? I cannot tell," lied Mimi, despairing of her clumsy tongue that slung itself around Low-German diphthongs as though they were thick ropes. It was no secret to the little Pioneer that agents of the Soviet had started shadowing the twins, just waiting for an opportunity to pounce on them and catch them at their prayers.

No wonder Mimi hated praying. That loathsome habit, she decided, was worse than being pawed at by the brigade foreman, who had tried.

She loved her brothers, though, and hence she shielded them. She still looked at them with adoring eyes.

"Does anybody know," the teacher asked, not one to give up easily, "a traitor in our midst who, in the past, has had forbidden dealings with a foreigner?"

"I do not even have a clue," insisted Mimi skillfully, remembering to smile —remembering that hungry, rainy afternoon when Dewey had come visiting to settle a belated score. She still remembered him, the fat American—the wet wind blew his whiskers sideways! When she remembered him that way, she always doubled up with laughter.

His brand of Faith was anything but joy. The mystic Savior whom he served up by dipping in those burlap sacks—bypassing her, no matter what that rodent did, deep in her empty belly!—would be forevermore as far from her emotions as Siberia.

The teacher had a lot to say, and all of it was cutting. Her voice became louder and louder. "If there are traitors in our midst, somebody has to turn them in. It might as well be you."

"We all agree. All traitors must be punished."

"The kulaks are a sore on our Mother Russia's body," the teacher bellowed frantically, and Mimi smiled at that as well, with all her might, for she was sharp, her mind was full of images.

She split her soul in half. She lived in two different worlds. She sloughed off one as she entered the other. A heady freedom, an exquisite pleasure, as right as gentle rain that fell upon a lake, came to her inner world when she played someone other than herself.

She was still young, but already she knew: "What I say is only what I say. It's simply empty blabber."

She knew that when the teacher pried: "Who is still prey to superstition?" and when she, Mimi, echoed faithfully: "Who might that be? Among us, who could be so foolish?" words were just words. Just that, and only that.

She learned to have one part of her, detached, observe the other as it compromised. She was a loyal and enthusiastic patriot rooting for the Soviet cause by day and the Lord's furtive child at night as she watched silently while those at Apanlee still prayed, with twisted faces, heaving chests: "Deliverance! Deliverance! Dear Lord, let us survive!"

That's what she heard as she grew up, but her heart had grown hard as a rock. To Mimi, the Gospel meant nothing.

She watched when Natasha knelt before her last icon, and held her breath as she kissed it She marveled at Marleen, who still had Faith, despite experience—that must have taught her: "Faith is sham!"—whose voice no longer cracked. She watched the twins thumb the Forbidden Book and glimpsed how something struck—a spark so pure, so genuine it kindled a prophetic light that started glowing deep within, much like a consecrated candle in a catacomb.

All that was there. She sensed it vividly. Yet they were of the past. The future was hers to grasp tightly.

She was earning high honors in class, a choice pupil endorsed by the Party.

"If you hear someone finding fault with our illustrious government, you better come running and tell. Report it at once. Report it in full. An extra star awaits you."

"I will."

"Reporting is your moral duty. Somebody has to do it. It might as well be you."

She knew that the entire German neighborhood was shivering beneath the Party's bedraggled red banners; the hammer and sickle, the malevolent Red energy that never gave out. There was no escaping; the abyss widened daily; her family stood at the brink. A dry and bony hand was closing on their necks.

At home, her pious brothers said, while practicing their parables: "Now spread your little fingers, love. Keep still and count to five. We'll help you think of five good answers next time the teacher asks you to report—"

"If need be," said the teacher, while winding up her lesson for the day, "you, too, will vote on who will live and who will die. Now, is that clearly understood?"

She was chilling at what that might mean.

She listened to her brothers pray in furtive whispers and let their prayers seep into her pores until the trees, the meadows, and the clouds above began to melt. She listened and she disapproved in principle, but here was a bedeviled question mark:

How could those two be a disgrace to Russia?

So they had faults? She saw their faults with eyes of love. She did most anything they asked.

She ran their errands, tremblingly. That slip of paper in her pocket? A cryptic map: she clutched it in her palm. It showed the neighbors where to meet in secrecy so they could kneel as well and be replenished in the Lord.

Yet she was was proud of her Pioneer scarf. She was small, and she wanted to please. If her Pioneer leader discovered her treason, she would be cursed and abused.

When she sat down to analyze her sad predicament—to have Faith and be a part of Apanlee, or be a proper Soviet citizen, free of all inner chains and shackles—her scales tipped neatly toward freedom. She had a life to live; she did not choose to live beneath a cloud about to burst and soak her to the marrow.

All this was intertwined for the young Pioneer, precariously balanced as she stood between her need to be a child in someone's lap, curled up and purring like a kitten, and a devoted Pioneer, not falling short of Party expectations. The daily tug that pulled her every which way as she was growing up—the Party's dictum on the one hand, her brothers' fervor for the Gospel on the other—felt like the aching of her limbs, felt like the rising of the rivers swelling with the coming of the rains, felt like the grave stones of her ancestors, made out of granite, moldy now, who had built Apanlee. She almost lost herself.

She watched Larissa change.

Faith had at long last touched Larissa and made her lively and young; it briefly made her beautiful. She held the twins enthralled.

She glowed like an ember, dispensing fragrance, warmth, and light. "The Holy Spirit led me. I could not have done it alone," she readily admitted.

Ah! Hallelujah time! Let the sea roar. Let the floods clap their hands. Let the hills all be joyful together!

The twins linked hands with Mimi and told her, smiling:

"See?"

Her brothers were the Lord's own laborers, who chafed by day until the skin peeled from their palms, who frequented the hungry for the Lord by night, who met with faithful souls in darkened rooms, in secret corners, who had committed to the crown of thorns for the sake of the Savior they loved.

Her brothers said, encircling her: "The Lord is our shepherd, dear. The Gospel tells us clearly—"

The teacher said: "A preacher is a parasite. Two preachers are two parasites. As hazardous as fire."

The government inspector who showed up next at Apanlee was in a nasty mood. His little eyes roamed greedily. He told the twins that he had reason to believe some farmers in the area had sabotaged the quota yield set to alleviate the shortages of seed, now more acute than ever.

The twins stood tall. They had grown strong enough, by then, to hold their own against most any bureaucrat.

"We don't know what you mean."

This one did not back off. "Show us your ration cards."

"What ration cards? We don't need ration cards. The earth grows anything we need."

The Party agent shivered in his overcoat despite the newsprint he had stuffed into his shirt to break the blasts of winter. He spoke derisively: "Did you report your surplus yield to the newly formed village committee?"

"We meet our needs without the help of government, as we have always done."

"You criticize obliquely? Be careful with your words."

The twins just shrugged. The snoopers multiplied.

At first, they were just smug and meddlesome and talked of Liberty, Fraternity, Equality—but soon that changed. That changed! In yet another season, they looked as though they packed bees in their pockets, with stingers still intact.

They drew this farmer, that farmer aside to mock them first, then scold, then threaten, then tempt them with their offers.

"You! Let's be frank. If you help us on the kolkhoz, together we'll accomplish miracles. You'll only have yourself to
blame for what will happen next if you refuse to join. Why are
you looking pained?"

"It's our land," the stubborn foreigners declared.

That was the sentiment. Their glances seemed to say: "Why
would we want to feed a bird that's going to the block tomorrow?"

That kind of life was not worth living, the foreigners decided, and by the time the first Five-Year Plan rolled around, the
Germans had closed ranks.

You could bend them. You could twist them. You could
pinch them and harass them, but you could not break their spirit.

To walk behind a plow, to feel the richness of the soil between his toes, that was now the mandate for every German
farmer worth his name. To delve into that fount of Faith that
had sustained his forebears, that was his source of strength.

Ah! Faith in tomorrow by seeding today on the land that the
Lord had bestowed on the creed!

That was the secret plan—to keep the seed alive: a small
grain field between the tiny legal cabbage patch next to the
house and the illegal chicken coop, well camouflaged. Just
root by tiny root.

"You can't," the agents said.

Ah, no? If not today—well, surely then tomorrow.

When the detested quota agents came, someone always let
out with a whistle.

These things were not said loudly, not even among themselves, but were widely understood. Their faces seemed to say:
You have a lofty theory of social betterment. On our side, we
have the prowess of our Lord who blows His breath onto the
seed and causes it to burst.

So. Sabotage or not? Let history decide.

It is well documented, so they claim, that during Soviet Russia's early years, not many Germans could be found atop a

kolkhoz sleigh.

"A tax on the cow. A tax on the pig," the next official said soon afterwards when he arrived at Apanlee. He seemed to have plenty of time.

He rifled through boxes and drawers and dumped out one or two, but then he left, and no more came of that. Before he slammed the door, he growled: "If you think long and hard, you will discover why you're guilty."

The only thing he took with him that day was an old box containing Uncle Benny's cherished Josie-letters. As he passed through the hall, holding his find aloft as though it were a ticking bomb, behind him wafted a faint scent of Dorothy's bouquet—rose water from St. Petersburg, before it was called Petrograd.

"That scares you? Eh?" he laughed.

Outside stood an accomplice who took the box from him and stored it carefully. Natasha, watching from behind the curtains, saw that his eyes were full of milk. The cup fell from her fingers.

The Pioneer ran after him. "Wait! Wait! Whatever gave you that idea?"

She was the only one who found her tongue in time, but it is doubtful that he heard the tremor in her voice, and if he did, that he paid much attention.

"Someone around here," he said and tweaked her cheek, "is shirking work for public benefit. Think hard. Who might that traitor be?" He kept smiling at her without having a reason. She stood her ground while trembling in her socks.

He added nastily: "I know your ilk. All of you foreigners, ingrained and stubborn monarchists—"

She was so eager for his satisfaction she saw him to the gate and even opened it for him. "Look here! Look at my Stalin buttons!"

"It's us today," he told her murkily before he disappeared, "and all of you tomorrow."

Natasha shrugged repeatedly when she was told she could improve her lot by spying on Marleen.

"We are your friends!" the quota agents told her, while paying her sly compliments. "We'll make a decent human being out of you. You're as good as any citizen. It's freedom now, Natasha. It's Liberty. Fraternity. Equality."

"What is this? A grim joke?"

Could freedom buy her anything she didn't own already? She had her family. The hard, gray years had welded them; their lives were now interwoven.

"Rich with manure, the soil of Apanlee," the agents said, and let the words sink in.

Natasha pondered that as well. She listened sullenly.

The only thing she wanted for herself was this: a heated brick for her cold feet when she came back from queuing. Marleen made sure of it. "My feet hurt," she could whine, just as Marleen had done, in her own haughty days, and somebody ran for a towel in which to wrap that brick: Here, rest your legs on this fine antique stool, Natasha!

"They're using you, exploiting you."

She had nothing to say in reply. Her answers were hopelessly vague.

"Well. Think it over. Will you?"

She snorted with derision. Her nose was stuffed with so-called freedom, which wasn't worth a kopeck, and maybe even less. She had no use at all for people telling her how she could smuggle secret messages and thus improve her standing. She bristled at the thought.

"What do you say? Is it a deal? We need to have a serious talk. Why are you working for the Germans? When is enough enough?"

"Get lost. And don't come back again!"

The Party's agents visited Natasha repeatedly to talk to her about her future and the important role she could assume, if she so chose, in helping Russia to renew.

She'd just thrust out her lower lip. She wanted none of that.

They promsied they would help her build a pig sty big enough to hold two hundred sows. "It's science now," they told her.

"Nu. Nu," Natasha said.

They were a stubborn lot, like pesky horse flies, all. She knew precisely how to turn the mule. She knew the art of silence.

"Natasha, can we count on you? You could help us enormously. We know that you came from a horseless family. You're lucky. You have no class blemish, Natasha—"

She kept stalling, assessing her chances. "A litter of piglets?"

"Of course."

"What else?"

"You write your ticket now."

When they assailed her with the argument that millions had martyred themselves so she could join a state-owned farm and be the equal of her former masters, she burst into loud laughter. Was she a weathercock?

She didn't lack for gratitude, nor was she missing recognition. In the starvation years, there had been nights so cold she and Marleen had slept together in one bed, arms wrapped around each other.

"You are a loyal citizen. Is that not true, Natasha?"

"What do you take me for? Just leave me out of it."

As though he'd been Russian courtier, one agent even tried to kiss her hand.

"We need to know who's plotting to destroy our country's reconstructive efforts—"

What did he want from her? Do violence to her bunions and make her march all day behind the bloody banners? Report suspicious behavior by the terrorized people she loved?

She pointed out for the tenth time that she was family; she had her place at Apanlee; she was expected now to take a weekly bath, like everybody else—and whether she required it or not.

"I even claim the wash tub first," she told them boastfully. She walked through any door she pleased. The burdens of inequity had largely disappeared, if they had ever bothered her at all.

The agent smiled at her—a smile that did not reach his eyes. "You still don't understand. You have no choice. You must report to us who is concealing stolen property—"

She let fly a spitball or two; she had practiced a few in her time. She flew at him with many curses. She lashed him with her tongue.

"Get lost," Natasha yelled. "And don't come here again."

"I am your equal now as well," she could have said to any bureaucrat, and used her elbows, too. And no one would have argued. But this she learned, though slowly: you did not argue with the government. Not if you valued life.

Nobody spoke against the Soviet government—unless you were a fool.

The chorus of the agents' accusations never stopped. Who kept surplus potatoes hidden in his cellar? Who hoarded beans? Who seeded barley, oats, and rye?

"The Easter bunny," said Natasha. When censured and rebuked, she looked demure and dim. She just fell quiet and stayed that way, no matter what the lure.

The agents said: "You won't be reasonable, Citizen? You'll only have yourself to blame if there's a price to pay."

Four agents surrounded her soon afterwards and whispered each other their cues. They looked like four hard-bitten dogs. Over tobacco an offer emerged.

"Here's what you do. Here's what we'll do for you—" The agent grinned, for he was confident. He grinned and kept on grinning.

"What's that supposed to mean?"

"Come on, now. Smile at me. You had a son once. Right? We know a thing or two."

"What are you saying, Citizen? We know about his past.

Why beat about the bush?"

Natasha was treading with care now. Her instincts responded. The corners of her mouth pulled downwards.

"Anything," the agents told her carefully, "can happen. Anything. Just anything."

"He vanished years ago. He did not leave a trace."

"Citizen, it's up to you. The offer is good for three weeks."

Something inside her quailed. "All that is a patchwork of lies."

"If I were you—"

"All that was yesterday. Tomorrow is tomorrow." She hardly ever thought about her wastrel son, though when she did, strong fingers pressed against her windpipe until she gasped for air.

She chose to count Dominik dead. She hoped he'd fallen bravely.

Chapter 67

The government inspectors multiplied, and all were heartless with the Germans. They told them, sneeringly: "The Kremlin has dispatched us to bear a personal message. You may not like it much, but you will join a kolkhoz willingly before this year is gone."

Before they left, they checked the wash house, wall to wall. They checked the barn. The attic. Next, the cellar.

They told Marleen: "Come to the registration desk tomorrow."

Now all was ration cards—not just for bread but salt, shoes, yarn, screws, bolts and buttons.

She walked on foot into the nearest town to stand in line to register, with Mimi next to her. Behind her walked Larissa, followed at a short distance by Natasha. By then, a woman still felt relatively safe to go and ask for ration cards, whereas a man did not. To be a male from Apanlee meant being targeted for torment.

Therefore, the twins stayed home—why be a double lightning rod? It was no longer safe to let the sun shine on their faces, now that they had a blood-red check mark by their names.

By then, Marleen was nearly blind with hatred. Steadfast, she surrendered nothing. She had by no means lost the game.

"Last name?" the ration card inspector asked Marleen. The tormentor expertly launched himself. In Moscow, they noticed his zeal. His voice grew thick and menacing. He rose and stood behind her. She could not see his face.

"I'm waiting, Citizen."

"My name is Neufeld. Marleen Neufeld."

"With *umlaut*?"

"No. No *umlaut*."

"No *umlaut*? All Germans have an *umlaut*. Born what?"

"Born Fröse."

"With *umlaut*?"

The heat rose in Marleen's gaunt face. "With *umlaut*. Yes. Not that it matters, Citizen."

"It matters. Ah! It matters. That's how we tell. That's how we recognize imperialists." He gripped her by her shoulders. "Here is a chair. Sit in the middle of the room so we can see you better. So we can study you and weigh your answers properly." His thumbs lay on her collarbone. "So you're a foreigner? A trickster? Don't try to deceive me. I want you to know that my patience is short."

"What do you want to know?"

" Just how, exactly, are you harming our Soviet Motherland?"

Her hands lay in her lap. Only her knuckles whitened. She kept her voice as steady as she could. "I am not harming anyone. I was born here, in the Ukraine. So were my parents. So were my grandparents. From all I know, the Fröses have been loyal Russian citizens for seven generations—"

"How many males still in your family?" His hands were on her neck. He was massaging it. His thumbs made circling motions.

"Two sons."

"No! You don't say!"

"Fine citizens, *tovarich*. With not a single blemish on their names."

He let go of her then. He sat himself across from her, leaned back in his chair, smirked briefly, and rested both heels on the table. "Two preachers, so we hear?"

"No. Not ordained. They never were ordained."

"Look out of the window," he ordered. "Citizen! What do you see?"

"My eyes are weak."

"I'll lend you mine." His small eyes were liquid with spite. "You see the Park of Glorious Victories. Is that not right? Is that not what you see?"

"She does. She does," cried Mimi, stepping forward eagerly.

"What else?"

"She sees the statue of our Father Lenin, his image mounted on a truck."

The agent smiled at Mimi through a set of yellow teeth. "Is that a fact?"

"And my entire family," the teenager declared, her own voice thin and high, "admire him. We love him, and we honor him."

"How do we know? Where is your proof?"

The words came by themselves, for she had practiced them until they were as smooth as pebbles. This was familiar domain. "He is the man," insisted Mimi earnestly, "who spent his intellect to carry light to the oppressed—"

"That," hissed Natasha, furious, for she had taken all she could, now stepping forward, pinching Mimi, "is neither here nor there."

The ration card inspector studiously ignored Natasha. He fixed his yellow smile on Mimi's anxious face. "What else do you suppose your carrion mother sees? Patrolling the streets? Hands on their guns?"

"*Tovarich*—"

"Soviet guards, right?"

"Right."

"Armed?"

"Right."

"And on the lookout for our country's spies, diversionists and traitors?"

Marleen had doubts that she would ever calm herself enough to speak, but she said hoarsely, shaking: "We're patriotic citizens. We love this land. We always have. We always will. Not one of us ever would dream of destroying our country—"

There was a pause. Her tormentor drummed his knuckles. He tested the trap before it was sprung.

"All right. All right. Let's say that I believe you. At least I do for now. Why not? Here is another question, Citizen—" He paused to give his question added weight. "Did you, or did you not, write begging letters to a distant relative in Kansas? Her name, as I recall, was Josephine?"

Fear came in a great wave. Marleen tried hard to keep her voice from cracking. "It's been at least eight years. We corresponded casually."

"Is that a fact? What did she write about?"

"She wrote about reform. I didn't understand the details. I thought she just was being used by someone in America. She was somebody's mouthpiece. It never meant a thing."

"What do you know of her?"

"Not much. I never paid attention. She used to correspond at length with an old uncle, now deceased—"

"But you wrote back?"

"Just once or twice. It did not mean a thing."

"You begged for help. Had you no shame? When you wrote shameful letters to those American imperialists, what did you say to her? Were you and she engaged in secret plans? Did you and she hatch plans to sabotage our Motherland? Was she your uncle's ilk?"

"I barely knew this woman."

"Let's say I don't believe you."

"She was on your side, Citizen. It was my understanding that she was in favor of the Revolution—" explained Marleen. Her heart was swelling, getting thick. She caught and steeled herself. She swallowed hard and added bitterly: "She was a humanist. We had nothing whatever in common. She wrote a lot of silly letters, all meant to gladden Uncle Benny's heart. I should have tossed them in the flames—"

"Why didn't you?"

"I guess I must have forgotten."

"Did you report the contents of those letters to the appropriate authorities?"

"No. Uncle Benny kept them in a box to which he had the only key—"

"You had no curiosity?"

"No. I did not. I couldn't have cared less. She was an odd and distant relative. She loved her books more than her neighbors. She may have borne our name; she was not one of us. Her mind ran in a different groove. Besides, all this was long ago—"

"—before the Revolution set us free—" said Mimi, smiling broadly.

The ration card inspector started pulling on his mustache: "Say! Have you ever heard of quotas?"

"Of course. I know the quota chart. It's hanging in my barn."

"The quota laws are strict."

"I know."

"They are our firm, established rules. I have some excellent advice for you. Just try to do your share."

"I will."

Behind that mustache lurked a smile that simply wouldn't quit. "Your sons are on the list of people who are considered marginal—"

"That's wrong. That is unfair. My sons will gladly do their share, rebuilding Russia."

"It is no longer Russia. It is the Soviet Union."

"The Soviet Union, then."

"These days," he said, and stared hard at the Pioneer, "a proper citizen will want to do his share."

The Pioneer stood tall. To enter into combat on this man's terms would be foolish.

He started plucking on her earlobe. He loosened his belt and gave a soft belch.

"No telling what this country needs. No telling. Hear? Is that not right, my little dove? Speak up and tell the truth—"

"We all agree," said Mimi, "that we live in challenging times." She cast a sideways glance. Her mother had her own hands deeply buried in her pockets, but she could see the fists. Her mother's tormentor was snapping his suspenders. He faced Marleen at last, who could no longer trust herself to speak.

"You wouldn't want to be regarded as a wrecker, would you? You'll want to do your share? Your sons will want to do their share? Your daughter here will want to do her share? Natasha wants to do her share? We must chip in to help rebuild our Motherland. Is that not so?"

"It is."

"It's better that you understand that, Citizen."

"I do."

He kept twirling his pencil between thumb and pinkie. He spoke as slowly as he could while pulling thoughtfully on a short flint.

"Here's what you must remember: if your output falls short, your twin sons will be held accountable." He spun around. He started hurling charges. "If you speak up and tell us all, they will be spared. Well, are you ready to confess?"

"Confess to what?"

He started blowing smoke rings. He said, his eyes on Mimi: "What do they look like, your two brothers? What is their physical description?"

"Tall. Blond. Blue eyes. Impossible to tell apart. As alike as two peas in a pod."

"A steady gait? A firm jaw and an honest brow?"

"Yes," said Marleen. "Now that you mention it."

"Don't try to anger me. Don't think I can be easily confused. I have it from good sources that your two sons are secret spokesmen for a cult—"

Marleen's tongue curled itself against her palate. Her shoulders slumped. She muttered hoarsely: "We've covered this already. I don't know what you mean—"

"Your sons don't qualify for ration cards, regrettably," he told her, tapping lightly. "Just so you understand that. Your sons are classified as parasites. Two worthless parasites, that's all. Without significance to our glorious nation—"

Plunk! went the rubber stamp, and left a bright red smear.

The agents shouted angrily: "Don't argue now! This is a criminal investigation. If you as much as look like running, we'll open fire. Now, is that clearly understood?"

"We have established," said the government officials, for example, to Hans Friesen, one of Marleen's most trusted neighbors, "that you, your sons, your grandsons, your father and your uncles are documented traitors to the Motherland—"

The German farmer stood before them, shaking. "I never once—" His roots in the Ukraine had grown into the very bedrock of the land his great-grandfather had claimed. "I don't know what—"

The agents had a lot to say, and none of it was pleasant. When they were finished, nobody spoke until the agents jeered:

"Why are you lying, Citizen? We came with documented proof."

"What proof?"

"Five years ago, you wickedly salted away a whole pig." They started shouting, viciously: "Confess! Admit your guilt. Admit you are a saboteur. We'll find out soon enough."

Before the week was out, a toady pointed a stiff finger to a cattle train and said to the whole Friesen family: "Siberia will teach you respect."

They were the first but not the last. In years to come, by the hundreds and thousands, they vanished. The Germans all vanished. They vanished.

Everywhere in the vicinity of Apanlee, the grain inspectors climbed atop the roofs and peered into the chimneys, looking for evidence of criminally hidden grain. They ransacked the cellars as well as the attics. They stripped down the wash house. They combed through the barns, looking for kernels hidden in the straw. They dumped out every drawer. Their voices grew louder and louder.

"Arrested for suspected sabotage," they told a German farmer whose name was Hannes Voth.

"But why—?" asked Hannes Voth. Above his brow, an anarchist's knife had gouged out a deep scar. He was still young, not yet fifty, but terror, ruin and grief had made of him an ancient invalid. He was half-blind by then and almost deaf, but still he heard and saw, and what he didn't hear and see he started to imagine.

A toady took him by the arm: "May Comrade Stalin live to be a hundred. We know you are a spy. We know that for a fact."

The victim raised a feeble argument. He stammered; his conscience was clear. He loved his country, Russia; he wouldn't ever harm the land and its inhabitants.

"Shut up!" The guards knocked him down, but he struggled to stand. The grain inspector had a camel's nose above a boastful smile. He started shouting loudly: "It's now official, Citizen. There's nothing you can do. We have your confession, all spelled out already. The only thing we need now is your signature. Don't give us any gall."

The hapless farmer tried to reason. "How can I be a spy? I never left my acres—"

The agent seized him by his beard and started pulling hard. "Don't you remember, Citizen? As though it happened yesterday! You wished us ill. You sabotaged morale. You indulged in seditious talk. In the name of Joseph Stalin, you are arrested, Citizen—"

"Not even in my dreams," the German farmer argued, terrified, "did I have a seditious conversation—"

"Then what about your sons?"

The words froze on the victim's lips. His heart sank to his heels. It turned so quiet that you could hear him chewing on his tongue. "My sons?"

"That's right. Your sons. Don't you still have three sons?"

In happier days, his wife had given birth to seven sons, each healthier than the other. He had three left—three youngsters in their teens, not even old enough to shave. The rest were dead and gone. One son lay in a shallow grave somewhere, a victim of the civil war. Typhus had swept away two more. A fourth had died of hunger.

"—where are your three remaining sons? Where are you hiding them? Behind your hoarded grain? This moment, we demand an answer!"

"There is no grain. It's true. My word is solid granite—"

"We'll help you," said the serpentines. "All of you people, saboteurs and royalists! All of you, German swine! We'll help you to remember!"

The blows of rifle butts and cudgels brought out the first, who cowered underneath a bed as though he were a cur. It was a wintry afternoon; the agents made short shrift.

They took the youngster by the elbow and walked him down the street; no one saw what happened afterwards and, worse, none dared to ask. He disappeared and was not seen again.

He was the first, that anguished day, but by no means the last.

"Now. Has your memory returned? Where are the other two?"

The German moved his lips, but not a word came out. His fingers jerked as though they touched live coals. His face looked like a coast, ceroded by invisible waves. "Take me, instead. I'll follow willingly."

"Do we need carrion? You're old. What use have we of you?"

The agents whispered to each other. This went on for a while. "Don't say we didn't warn you," the grain inspector hissed, at last, surrounded by his underlings. "We're writing a reminder to ourselves to check on you periodically. We will discover before long where you have hidden your two sons, and where you're hiding grain—"

They found the second the next week, hiding in a neighbor's attic. They took him outside, barefoot. They backed up the truck in which they had come, and started the engine, which rattled. They leaned the shaking boy against the barn.

"Now's the time to speak and tell us of your father's treachery," they coaxed, but not for long. The first shot sent the youngster to his knees. The next tore up his belly. The third hit well enough so that he crumpled and lay still. This happened in broad daylight, as many people watched.

The father heard the crackling of the shots, inside the house, where two men held him, buckled, on the floor. The grain inspectors came back in and stood him upright, several times, much like a shock of wheat that wouldn't hold together.

"Now. Has your memory returned?"

The German scanned the faces that surrounded him. Not one of them showed mercy. His thoughts flew into disarray. "It's true. I hid some grain. I now confess. I swear the only thing I ever did was try to feed my family. I know now that was treason—"

The agent had a row of upper teeth, all large and yellow and decayed. He wore a self-satisfied smile.

"See? There you go. You didn't act alone, did you?"

"Nobody else—"

"You stashed away your grain? Who helped you plot your crimes? Who helped you hide your harvests?"

"But I—"

"It's up to you," the grain inspector said. He leaned against the door frame to scratch his back befittingly. "There's still one left. You have a week. Who else was plotting to destroy the Soviet recovering economy? If I were you, I'd think that answer over carefully."

Then they came for the last. They arrived a few minutes to midnight. They pulled the fifteen-year-old from the attic and led him out into the orchards, hands tied behind his back.

They said: "Two minutes. That is all."

They revved up the engine again. At that, the German farmer Hannes Voth, once prosperous beyond a farming man's most fearless dreams, a model citizen by all accounts, confessed that he had sabotaged the harvest.

The lesson was not lost on anyone. Amazing stories spilled out tales of wholesale espionage, of counter-Revolutionary plots, defeatist conversations and terrorist connections. Some openly confessed to being spies, and others to spreading corruption.

Not a few now admitted that they had plotted wickedly to blow up mines and factories. There was no end to it.

It was not wise, even a slow-wit realized, to trifle with an accusation—it grew by what it fed on: arrests and more arrests. The files grew fat and fatter. The ranks of the Germans grew thin.

These were bitterly desperate times for Marleen. She stayed in the background and kept her head down—relieved in a sick, twisted way that the firing squads in prison courtyards in every major town did not yet aim and rip apart her own sons' pulsing hearts.

The terror had fallen on somebody else. There was still reprieve for her sons. The local censor still smiled on her daughter, Mimi, a splendid Soviet Pioneer. And Mimi still smiled back.

Investigators came repeatedly to Apanlee, with crow bars and with dogs, to search for hidden grain. They stalked through the entire manor, tracking mud through every room. They stomped their boots across the wooden floors of Apanlee and cried:

"A hollow sound. Where is the grain? Where is the grain?"

"No grain," Marleen told them repeatedly, but still they climbed into her attic. They rummaged her stables and rifled her pantry. They even leaped into her cellar and dug into the brine where Marleen kept the gherkins she had harvested with luck and skill despite a tardy spring.

They shouted themselves hoarse: "Where is the grain? Where is the grain?" exchanging telling glances.

They searched the barn and the abandoned chicken coop, running their bayonets into the mildewed straw. The searchers hectored angrily: "The grain. The grain. Say, Citizen. Where did you hide your grain?"

"There is no grain," Marleen kept telling them, but they took bench marks of the chimney in her parlor room and checked behind the double window frames. They swarmed throughout the orchards; they smashed the dishes in the summer kitchen and left the pieces on the floor. Wherever they discovered a suspicious-looking site, in went the crow bar, poking and probing.

"Confess you fed it grain," they hollered even at Natasha, while slashing at a rooster's crop with knives that glittered in the sun. "Confess you are a traitor, saboteur and terrorist. Explain the why and hows—"

They sat down in Marleen's kitchen to thaw their toes out by her fire. "We're here to discuss serious matters. Well, are you ready to confess?"

They used long sentences to taunt, humiliate, and threaten. They started blowing smoke so thick it was hard to see their faces.

"We know a thing or two. We know most everything. Confess! You harmed your Motherland. Help us unravel your son's crime when they hid grain in bottles in the water—"

The afternoon turned gray, then black.

"We know they've hidden the grain. We know they've slaughtered livestock. How can you refuse us? Out with the truth! Why be so secretive? Could it be your sons were waiting for high prices in the spring? By covering for them, you make yourself a thief. A saboteur. A criminal. A counter-Revolutionary who's robbing our glorious Soviet state!"

"But never once—"

"We know how you disguise yourselves, you traitors! Why be so stubborn? Why be cross? The New World Order has arrived."

They went at her, hammer and sickle.

All the Party agents were soon in a dangerous mood. Their voices grew louder and louder.

"Speak up. Who else? Who's hiding in the bosom of your family? How many females? Altogether?"

"My daughter, Mimi. Five stars of merit to her name—"

"Who else?"

"This woman here. Larissa is her name."

"A relative?"

"No. Strictly speaking, no."

"What's that? A trick? You think that we are easily confused? It says here that she has your name. Therefore, she must be related. Speak up. Confess! Is she a relative or not? Spare me your boastful history. Who else?"

"Natasha, over there. A former serv—"

"My mother," whispered Mimi, now pulling the investigator's sleeve, "has some peculiar quirks."

A glint came to his eyes. "Is that a fact?"

"All of her thoughts are nebulous," reported Mimi expertly. "She sits with her head in her hands. She fantasizes lavishly—"

He tried to pull the Pioneer onto his knees. "Aha! Now we're getting somewhere. Now we are getting nearer to the truth. She's not a worthy parent? She makes you say things you'd rather not say? She makes you do things you know you shouldn't do?"

The Pioneer smiled prettily while raising one eyebrow and winking at him. "Why would I give away my secrets?"

His hand massaged her thigh. "Well, try. It cannot hurt to try. Why don't you tell me one?"

"She isn't harming anyone," said Mimi. "Trust me. She's living in the past. Believe me, Citizen. Her memory is dim. Her mind is like a sieve."

"She has forgotten how she plotted to embezzle property belonging to the State?"

The Pioneer was not deceived. Her head was tilted to one side, coquettishly. "I can be trusted, Citizen."

She shrugged him off expertly while sliding off his lap. "Now, listen. Here's the plan—" She shifted eagerly from foot to foot. "Just count on me. I will report to you. I'll keep an eye on her."

The toady stared at her. "You are alert and well-informed? How old are you? When was the last time you reported a suspicious relative? How many traitors, all in all, have you exposed so far?"

She grinned as broadly as she could. "Is anyone above suspicion? Including you, *tovarich*? "

"That's neither here nor there," Natasha said, who saw with her third eye. Now light and fire flashed in Natasha's veins as well. She started cuffing Mimi.

The Pioneer paid no attention. She winked at the interrogator: "I eavesdrop on the side."

"You could be useful, girl," he muttered. "Why don't I have a word with you? Alone?"

She was talking so fast that her words ran into each other. "I can be trusted. Ask. Ask anyone. In my brigade, I am a member in good standing. I take my orders from the Party. That's all I am allowed to say. You can depend on me. I know a thing or two."

"Well. Tell me this. This woman here? Natasha? Why does your mother call her a servant? There must be some compelling reason. Is she still being victimized?"

Marleen burst into laughter. Shrill. Natasha ducked, then lurched.

"Nobody dares exploit Natasha," Natasha trumpeted. "I'm now a liberated citizen. In fact, one of the best! Let that be clearly known."

The agent slammed the table with his fist so that the ink pot jumped. "Where do you sleep? Still in the fodder house?"

"By choice."

"Out with the truth! What is your pay?"

"They never paid me. Never!" explained Natasha eagerly. "They never have. They never will. I'm just as good as family. They treat me equally. Last week, I claimed the wash tub first before—"

"Do you sweep floors? Do they leave all the dirty work to you?"

"Just the family wash. Just that—" She glanced at Marleen for approval.

Marleen looked as though she were standing in ice water up to her armpits, chilled to her marrow, threadbare but proud. "It's true. She still does the family wash," she said clearly. She stripped her daughter's clutching fingers from her arm. She struggled down a strangling lump. "She's one of us. We treat her well. She treats us well. We have never exploited her. Never! Is that not true, Natasha?"

"*Nu. Nu.*"

"We always gave her choices. Why, even in the olden days when she was still a lowly chambermaid—"

"But you should see her now!" the Pioneer broke in. "She's making a name for herself. She walks from room to room and doesn't even knock."

"It's true!" Natasha smiled expansively. Ah! What a family! "I even slam the doors!"

How things had changed! Now they were putty in her hands. They were no longer stingy with her cast-offs. There was a fine umbrella, for example. In former days, Marleen would have held onto it, no matter how Natasha bawled. "I have it now," Natasha boasted, beaming. "It's my umbrella now."

The toady focused on Natasha. "Do you have relatives that you can call your own?"

"A son. She had a son." Marleen was fighting specks of light that danced behind her eyeballs.

"We know. His name was Dominik. We know the last small detail, and therefore—"

Natasha jumped, arthritic feet and all, into the middle of his sentence. She wrung her hands and started wailing loudly the moment people mentioned Dominik. "I take the blame. All. All of it. When he was small, I should have swaddled him more tightly—"

"Let's get right to the bottom of this matter. How did this woman treat your son?"

Marleen could not be stopped. She jumped up from her chair.

"You want the truth?" she shouted. "I boxed his ears when he was small. I should have lopped them off—" She looked like a woman demented.

"Aha! The truth at last! Now you are showing your true feelings. You didn't like him much?"

"Why should I have?"

"You brutalized, exploited, and abused your loyal servant's only son?"

"A hero of the Revolution, Dominik!" Natasha shouted, desperate. Marleen fell back into her chair, exhausted. "We are living in unnatural times," she said weakly.

"Natasha," argued Mimi, her own voice straining now, "used to be proud of her fine son. I vouch for that. I kept a notebook with remarks. To this day, she will brag how Dominik fought bravely. Regrettably, he's dead. We heard he was condemned to death for wounding a high officer. Natasha burst out sobbing—"

The Soviet agent scratched himself luxuriously—his lice gave him no rest. "What if you're mistaken?"

Marleen's white face was crumbling. Natasha, too, recoiled as though she had been struck.

The Pioneer pushed to the foreground, eagerly. "Out with the truth," said Mimi. She seemed no longer young. There was an edge to her young mouth the agent could not fail to notice. She told the scoundrel, leaning forward: "Look here. Why keep on playing cat and mouse? You have a file as well."

He savored every word. "He's dead? You think that Dominik is dead? That's what you think? That's what you hope? Well, you're in for a surprise. He escaped, I'm very pleased to say. He's alive and heading this way—"

"He is? Oh, *bozhe moi*. That is good news. Where is he now? What does he do?"

"The right arm of the Soviet," said the inspector slowly.

Natasha crossed herself in front of all. "Alive? Oh! Holy Mother Russia!"

"A proven Party man. Replete with uniform," the agent finished slowly. "Why should I keep on barking at you folks when I can keep a dog?"

Chapter 68

The bucket brigades came racing, as did the fire trucks. Bright yellow flames leaped out of windows, while the neighbors leaped into their trousers as shouts went up the length of Mennotown:

"Fire!"

"Fire!"

"Fire at Jan's mill!"

It was a spectacular sight, a spooky night and a prophetic arson few Mennotowners would forget. Invisible hands threw fistfuls of sparks. The wheat dust, in seconds, became an inferno. The heat exploded the roof. The wind sat, howling, in the chimneys. The flames kept leaping through the embers. Burning shingles flew in every direction, and smoke bulged up toward the moon in mushroom after mushroom.

The night guard made it out through a window he knocked out with the toe of his boot. He ran over the roof, slid down to the ground, behind him his trailing suspenders.

"Fire! Help! Help! Fire!"

For hours, the air howled and sobbed and hooted and whistled and wept. Hundreds of window panes cracked. Red beams of light kept fingering the sky, which glowed first purple, then yellow, then red, as if the sun were about to come up. The shingles on neighboring buildings ignited. A strangely persistent eastern wind, that smelled of uprooted earth, spread the heat and fanned the flames which seized upon the chicken shed, then jumped onto Jan's stables.

The fire burned five of Jan's packing sheds and fourteen brand new barracks, where extra bags of wheat were stacked. A newly-built silo collapsed. Now the roof of the tool house was gone.

The fire spread to Jan's and Josie's property. It collapsed in a shower of sparks. In stunned silence, Jan's neighbors watched his pride and joy burn down and wondered what he'd say and do once he had caught his breath and rubbed the soot from his old, red-rimmed eyes.

Jan spoke at last, still staring at the glowing embers, and here is what he said:

"The Lord is warning me. I never let myself be rescued and redeemed." An odd, queer light lurked deep within his eyes.

"I've been my own worst enemy," Jan told the night. Loose folds of worry pulled his face into a mask of helplessness as his life's work lay at his feet—a sorry heap of ashes. He turned and faced his wife. "What did I sow? What have I reaped? All is finished. Everything is gone."

She reached for him in an instinctive gesture. "Come on, Jan. Come with me. I'll make you a hot bowl of soup. I'll get you something decent for your stomach."

He brushed her hand away. He staggered slightly, and then he turned and fell.

She bent to him, astonished at seeing him fallen. "Jan, please. You don't feel well? What is it, Jan? Here. Take my arm."

His tongue was slurred: "It's all my fault. My fault. My fault."

She helped him to his feet. "You're not yourself. Tomorrow you'll feel better." She wrapped both arms around him. "Here is my shoulder. Hold on tight."

Jan struggled free of Josie. When he could stand again, he leaned, exhausted, against a blackened wall. "I sowed myself some dragon's teeth," he said, his voice a stranger's voice. "And this is the result."

"Here. Careful. Watch your step."

"I never gave due credit to the Lord."

"You're tired. In shock." She gently took his hand to soothe a bulging blister. "Don't we survive in good times and bad? We can rebuild. It's just a silly fire."

He said, a cruel edge to his voice: "You do not understand. A chicken's not a bird, and a woman is not an accountant."

"Jan?"

"You just don't understand. You never understood."

"Sit down here. Catch your breath. Take all the time you need. I'll stay with you. I'll wait."

"Wait? Wait for what?"

"For you to catch your senses."

"It is too late. Too late."

"What are you saying, Jan? We have more money in the bank than anyone I know. We have more land than anyone can use. We will rebuild. We'll work from a clean slate."

The fire had excited Josephine as though she had made love. Her words tumbled over each other. Here was a challenge; this was her fight; she would go as to war, with a heart that was shouting with joy at the challenge.

Jan stared at her. "It's too late." He took his watch, put it to his ear, and listened. "The time for that is past."

"There's always yet another season," said Josie helplessly. "I'll stand by you. We'll find a way tomorrow—"

"And who are you?" he asked, a total stranger now.

"Jan, what—"

"Without my hard-earned money, can you find your nose in the dark?"

Her hands flew to her lips. "You're not yourself." She struggled down her panic. "Here. Let me fasten that shoelace."

"First thing in the morning," Jan ordered her, in a voice she didn't recognize, "you send for Dewey Epp. That's an order. Hear?"

"Whatever for? You aren't poor! Don't let yourself be panicked. There's always next year's crop."

"Do you know what the grasshoppers did last July? The soil is full of eggs."

"Your grain will sprout anew. Nobody I know grows such abundant crops—"

He shook his head. He looked as if he were drunk. "Shut up!" he said. "Shut up!" His back was curved against the wind, which kept on blowing and hooting, and as he struggled on and down the street and straight into the bed that Lizzy vacated in haste, his mother noticed, too: a phosphorescent light had settled in Jan's eyes.

The decades fell away from Lizzy. She dragged her quilts down from the attic. She packed Jan into pillows. She was beside herself.

"Here, take my apron, Josie. Don't dawdle. Hurry up. Don't stand there, staring out the window. There's dishes in the sink."

"A good, long weekend rest will do my husband good," said Josie to herself, and quietly did the dishes.

Monday sneaked by, and Jan was still in bed. He refused her the smallest of smiles.

The neighbors came to take a look and offer their assistance. They gathered slowly, one by one, and sat around the stove to speak with reverence of Lizzy's hospitality.

"This, too, will pass," said Josephine, and kneaded still more dough.

Tuesday arrived, and Jan's face was still ashen, his temperature high. When all her patience was exhausted, she said at last: "Jan, let me call a doctor."

His mother made short shrift of that. "A cup of chicken broth."

"I think Jan has suffered a stroke."

"Of course not," said Lizzy, and made sure that another rooster lost his head. A Sunday chicken, fried just so, would help her son to rally; he was strong; he was an enterprising man. Charred lumber? Gutted harvests? He was a whiz at fixing things. Jan would replace the burned-down buildings, one by one. She had unending faith in him; there was nothing that Jan couldn't do. He knew precisely how to cope with manifold misfortunes— grasshoppers, jackrabbits, unseasonable rains that made the crop rot in the fields, stray cows, all that.

"Be sure you take your Ready Relief," she coached Jan every morning, her faith in Doctorjay intact.

Soon, Josie itched all over.

"Run, Josie. Hurry! Close the door. Don't let the dung flies in—"

"Come Jan. Let's take a walk. Just you and I. Here, take my arm. Let's get some sun. A brisk walk will do wonders—"

"Rest and warm milk," his mother ordered curtly.

"It's just the shock," said Josephine.

"A bag of sand right on his abdomen," said Doctorjay who visited periodically. Doctorjay never neglected a patient. His tonics still wrought the most marvelous cures. Each afternoon, come rain or shine, the bonesetter came chugging up the road in his beloved flivver to slap Jan on the shoulder, as in the olden days.

"Just keep your chin up! Hear? You're sicker than a dog. You're whiter than a sheet. Keep your old chin up, chap! It's not as if the walls of Jericho came down! Now, scat, all you females! Just leave him be and give him time to heal."

The moment he arrived, Old Lizzy glued herself to Doctorjay's squat heels. "Tell me the truth. Will he get better soon?"

"I have nothing but hope to report."

"Don't spare me, Doctorjay."

"Nothing but hope, Lizzy. Nothing but hope!"

To Josephine the healer said, when out of earshot of Jan's mother: "The good Lord only knows."

"Who's out there in the kitchen, Josie?" Jan asked, leaning

on one elbow.

This was one of her catty days. "Why? Can't you guess? Your mother. Your sister. And Lady Prayerful."

"What are they doing, kitten?"

"Having their morning kaffeeklatsch."

"Come sit here by my bed. Give me your pretty little hand."

He reached for her, but she withdrew. Her face was taut and hard. "You mark my word. They're going to stay til noon."

"Can you spare me ten minutes?"

"I'm busy. Can't you see?"

"I have to have a word with you."

"Not now." He tried to catch her eye, but she would not relent. He caught her by her fingers and pulled them to his chest. "Your hand, a small and dainty butterfly."

"Leave me alone."

"Don't. Josie, not like that! Don't be like that. They're merely catching up on what has happened with the neighbors. A lot has happened in the neighborhood since yesterday—"

"Those three," said Josie, choked, "are thicker than thieves. Thicker than thieves. That's all I have to say."

"So let them. That's their joy."

"They're plotting and scheming against me—" Her head ached, her ears were ringing, her appetite was gone. "They're cooking up stories about me. They are having a ball when they claim—"

"Look, are they hurting anybody? They're gossiping. That's all. Just let them be. Don't be uncharitable. Before noon, they will have tired each other—"

"But they're sitting in my kitchen. I'm trying to fix lunch."

"It's not your kitchen, Josie. It's my mother's."

"They nibble me to death. All morning long. Day after day. Walking down memory lane—"

"I know. I know. Just try to be more patient. We are my mother's guests. She can have all the guests she wishes. You won't get anywhere complaining."

"You're telling me?"

"You're very bright," he said. "But there are things you just don't understand. There's comfort in nostalgia. It feels good looking back."

She set her jaw. "To each his own."

He looked at her. "We've been married decades now. It's time we had a talk."

"I said not now."

"When, Josie? You're avoiding me. There's something of great urgency I must discuss with you—" He tried to sit. The room careened. Pain pounded in his temples.

But Josie's nerves were at the snapping point; she said, her own voice breaking: "I feel sick in the pit of my stomach."

"What is the matter with my little Josie—"

"If you must ask, you do not want to know. Let go of me."

"Now is as good a time as any. We must have a long talk. I never told you, Josie—"

But she was burning with resentment stored up by weeks of tedium. "You know what they argue about? Suspenders, a quarter. A Butterick pattern, a dime—"

"—I thought I was safe. I thought I could gamble a little. Beyond the boundaries of prudence—"

"Which mold to use for candles! The schoolmaster's cold! The needs of Miss-Goody-Two-Shoes's canary. The various cooking stages of a rooster. I am not kidding you!"

"Josie! Josie! Pay attention! I can't add up my losses any more—"

Her eyes snapped sharply into focus. "Jan, what in the world do you mean?"

"I took too many risks. I played the Hebrew game."

"Just what are you talking about?"

"I'm telling you: I'm finished!"

"As soon as the insurance agents are done with their assessment—"

"We have no policy. I never took it out."

"What? But why not?"

"I did not think I needed it. I knew that Dewey was against

it—"

"Why, Dewey, that dull maggot!"

"Shh! Don't! He was convinced that prayers were enough."

She stared at him. "You mean to say—"

Jan was perspiring heavily. He took a trembling breath. "—and now I don't even have the cash to pay a filing fee to start a farming bill of sale—"

A lifelong struggle fell away. The words came by themselves: "But you have me. I can learn how to balance the books."

She sat down by his bed. She put both arms around him. Inside her chest, a gale was tossing balls of fire. She felt as rich as though she had just visited a bakery where all was warm and clean. She said with a small laugh: "You mean to say your dollars are no longer magic?"

He listened to the beat of raindrops falling slowly on the roof. He smelled the strong odor of ashes.

"I played the market, Josie. Now I'm poorer than the poorest pauper. I lie in the dust before God."

She looked at him, her orphaned heart aglow, and knew: "This is the moment I've been waiting for. I've spent a lifetime waiting for this moment."

"You listen to me, Jan—" Joy leaped to the tip of her tongue and started coursing in a soft and molten current. She thought her heart would burst—that heart of hers, unclaimed and chaste despite so many years, now swept by a torrent of feelings.

"Jan? Are you serious? There's nothing left to hold us here? So let us leave. Let us start over. Just you and I and Rarey. We aren't poor! We can't be poor! For see? We have each other. How can two people such as you and I and our little son be poor? "

"You just don't understand. Right now, the Donoghues have more cash than I do."

"So what? Let's leave. The three of us. Go somewhere else! Let's go to California. I've learned to type. I'll help." She felt drunk with the prospect of freedom. She had never felt richer than now. "Why, Jan! You are talking to me! You are finally talking to me! We'll manage. We'll make do! Why, it was just a little fire, Jan, and maybe a small stroke. That's all. A puny little fire. A silly little stroke. First thing in the morning, I'll get us a map. I'll study opportunities for us in California!"

That night, she cried from happiness until sleep stole her senses.

The snow shrunk to clumps. The clumps finished melting. And Jan still lay in bed or else sat by the window.

He sat there, staring at the rain, without a word, for hours. When he tried standing, he groped at the wall for support. The minutes passed so slowly it seemed to Josephine that time was standing still.

She met the healer's eyes: "It's getting worse?"

Doctorjay blew his nose. "You want the truth? Here is the truth. Jan looks exactly like the broken bones of Christ. What worries me is not so much his body as his mind. His mind is like a glass of beer without the extra sparkle."

The summer came and went. The weather turned wet and then cold.

Still, Josie clung to hope. Jan would see things her way.

Soon, she was clinging to that hope as though it were a life raft.

She discussed all her plans for leaving with young Rarey. They talked when all the lights were out. Instead of sleeping soundly through the night to help a young boy's bones solidify, he and his mother talked.

The world smelled of decay.

The weeks turned into months.

The months became a year. Josie's hope ran through her fingers like water.

"As soon as Jan has licked his cold," said Josie to a friend in Wichita she visited as soon as she could free herself from bedside duties, "we'll call the masons and the carpenters."

"Sure. Sure. I know a Hebrew I can recommend. He'll cut you a fine loan."

She did not mention California. "I thought we might enlarge the house and add on a study for Rarey." Her bedside duties strained her more than she admitted even to herself, for Jan continued to be querulous. He was no easy patient: he wanted this, he wanted that, he kept on pushing her around until she felt like screeching.

"I need to feel useful," he said to her just yesterday, in an accusing tone of voice, as though his being helpless was now her fault as well.

So let him be useful, Josie thought, in any matter fit.

Details. Improvements. Sturdier doors. More modern windows, with good, strong hinges in the middle. Three stories high. Plus attic.

"Jan has huge plans. He will fit window frames into the structure," she told her friend, who still looked skeptical. "He'll hoist a brand new roof."

"What's wrong with him, do you suppose?"

"Nobody knows."

"What do you think?"

"This never-ending bedrest makes him sick," said Josephine, now drumming with her knuckles. "His mother hovers over him. He needs to get up. Move around. Get the blood circulating in his toes. His limbs are numb. His—" She checked herself. "Don't tell a soul. That man lost more than just his eyebrows and his lashes—"

Her friend raised both her eyebrows: "No! Really? You don't say!'

"Yes. Not that it matters now."

Sarcastically: "You are a lucky woman."

"Yes. Yes, I am."

Of course she was. She couldn't wait to see Jan leave that bed, start puttering about, get out from under Lizzy.

"He always spent too much on me—" she said to all her friends, as in the good old days, and hoped they'd cluck their tongues. She also said that to her enemies, of whom she had as many.

Old Lizzy had her firstborn in her pocket. She turned her kitchen drawers inside out for special healing recipes. Her eyes were dim, electricity dear, but she kept looking. Looking. Maybe if luck was on her side, she'd find that document the Donoghues still fussed about; that would cheer Jan; she knew it would cheer him a lot. She could have thrown a switch, but she did not: she lit her oil lamps everywhere.

"A penny saved, a penny earned," said Lizzy.

Jan did not contradict her. He smiled a shaky smile and stroked his stubble chin. He looked as though he meant to cross a river but didn't know where to begin to wade.

Little Melly came visiting daily. She came in through the back door, not bothering to knock. She brought a spoon, a towel, several extra pairs of socks, as well as a half-finished puzzle depicting her idols overseas: Their Royal Highnesses, the Princesses Elizabeth and Margaret.

"Here, Jan," she coaxed coyly, settling herself by the window. "I started it. You finish it. Forget the fire. Divert your mind with cheerful thoughts. Let's see what you can do—"

Jan, having fought a rasping cough all night, smiled wanly at the spinster. "I owe you, Little Melly. Had you not been so adamant for us to buy the fire trucks, the arson would have been much worse—"

He settled down to fit the pieces of the puzzle depicting England's future queen. The spinster flushed with victory.

Soon, Little Melly came and went three or four times a day— a wide, devoted shadow. She helped Jan start a scrapbook depicting details of the devastating night. She came barefoot, her shoes in her hand. She brought a brand new puzzle every week to help Jan pass the time. Jan's mind did not recoil when touching hers. She sidled up to him and stayed.

The rains skipped Kansas in the year that followed next. The sun baked the earth to a crisp. The harvest was iffy at best.

Then came winter. The farmers pulled down the ear flaps

and turned their collars up. Now, March. Next, April. Through Lizzy's open window panes wafted balmy May. Jan missed the second season's start and did not even notice. He swallowed his syrup and peppermint drops. He couldn't tell between present and past, but he could easily define the difference between Baptist and Methodist and point out with examples that both of them were devious and, therefore, dangerous.

All that was thanks to Dewey. The Holy Spirit was as nourishing as mother's milk, Jan had since learned from Dewey. The preacher bled Jan's pride with exhortation after exhortation from the Bible to make sufficient room for Faith. "A life without our Savior Christ," exhorted Dewey skillfully, "is like a supper without salt—"

Every Sunday after church, Dewey came churning up the road, clad in his fraying Sunday tweeds, looking for a shady spot to park the yellow flivver and have a little chat, a little restoration prayer with Jan Neufeld.

"The herds are perplexed," read Dewey to Jan from the Bible. "Look Ye for His pasture—"

Jan listened carefully. He nodded heavily at every solemn word.

It took but little effort on the preacher's part to take possession of Jan's broken will. Jan needed Dewey Epp. The beauty of the psalms restored his mind to a precarious balance. Without his weekly share of Dewey's Daily Thoughts, he felt disoriented and afraid. He felt as though he'd been a tomcat that had its whiskers burned away.

Josie watched Rarey sitting by the window, idle and motionless, anemic and forlorn. She felt her heart contract.

She tried diverting tactics. "Just do your homework, darling."

His talent couldn't be ignited. She watched as Rarey scribbled something on a slate, but it was evident he couldn't concentrate. Unspoken words hung in the room like fog.

No sooner had he written down a sentence or a number, than he tried to rub it out. At last he spoke. "Mom, what's a stock market crash?"

"A what? I haven't the faintest idea. If you don't know the definition of a word, you have to look it up."

"My dictionary burned up in the fire."

"I'll buy you a new one. As soon as we go home."

"You aren't going home," said Lizzy evenly, while sticking out her chin, as brown and brittle as an onion leaf. "Not while Jan is still sick."

"Your father's sick," admitted Josie, stroking Rarey's hair with trembling fingers. "We have to stay at Grandma's. For just a little while. I know it's crowded around here; you want your privacy. But just as soon as—"

Old Lizzy's chin grew even longer. "You're welcome to stay here, my darling little one. It makes your Daddy happy to have his Mom take care of him; it makes her happy, too."

"I know," said Rarey, squirming.

"Grandma loves to have you here. She loves to ladle soup into your poor sick Daddy until her spoon scrapes the bottom of the caldron. Go in and have a talk with Daddy—"

"Yes. do," said Josephine. "Go in and talk to Daddy. Tell him what's on your mind. Ask him when we are leaving, finally, for California—"

Outside, the asphalt shone with rain. A thin but penetrating wind began to whistle forcefully.

"Mom. What's the matter with my Dad?"

"It's nothing, Rarey. Really. He'll soon be well again. It won't be long." She tried to comfort him. "Listen. Just listen to that rain! Have you ever heard anything like it? And here it is not yet November."

Tears strangled Rarey's voice: "If he adds two plus two, he might get three. He might get five. Mom! What's the matter with my father?"

"It's just an old garden variety cold. I promise you. Before the year is out, we'll have our privacy. I promise you. You mark my word."

She knew it was a lie. Defeat lodged in Jan's spine.

Chapter 69

Things were bad, and getting worse. First the stocks plunged, then the brokers, falling to their deaths from high-rise windows onto the sidewalks of New York. Banks slammed their doors and rammed them shut. Wall Street was in a panic.

Jan leafed through Rarey's dictionary. The flames had singed it at the edges, and many words were lost. Stock market crash? The dictionary didn't say. It was a brand new phrase, as yet to be defined. He started with the A's and ended with the Z's, and when he finished, he could not remember, precisely, what it was he sought to learn. All was a hazy blur.

Across the prairie, mill after mill began to shut down. Grass grew through cracks in the asphalt. Nobody knew how to climb out of the puzzling and painful Depression.

Business everywhere fell off, even on Broadway and Main, where the Jews sold their furs and their pearls.

Wages sank to unheard depths.

Taxes shot into the sky.

Another spring arrived. The weather stayed sullen. Jan's fields lay deep in brownish water. A late frost, coming from nowhere, turned them to sheets of ice. That kept the winter wheat from breathing, and long before the preachers started sprucing up their sermons about the Lord's resolve to test the Faith of Mennotown, Jan knew that yet another harvest would be lost.

He tried to keep his mounting debts from Josie, although at every opportunity she tried to buttonhole him to get the latest figures. She prodded him and pushed him and would not give him peace: "Jan, something vexing on your mind?"

He longed to tell somebody: "My net is only half of what it was last year." Arms folded, however, he told her: "Stop digging, Josie. Do."

"Of course," said Josephine. "Sorry for troubling you. Why don't you take a hike?"

His flivver sat unused, just gathering bird droppings. It needed care; the clutch had been slipping; the radiator boiled; the engine sounded sluggish. But where to find the cash?

His farm equipment needed major overhaul—but where to get a loan?

"If you would let me help, I'd help," said Josie. "You know I've learned to type."

But Jan just shook his head. "Type what? Type invoices?" Nobody had the extra cash for binder twine, much less for sacks of seed.

"So suit yourself," said Josie sharply. "Don't say I didn't ask."

She closed the door so hard the handle came off in her hand.

Lizzy kept vinegar towels on Jan's burning head all through that saddening, worsening year—tiptoeing back and forth as quietly as she could, fussing and nursing as best she knew how in her old-fashioned, time-proven ways.

Another fence fell into ruin.

Where Lizzy used to keep her butter tubs, now spiders spun their webs.

Lizzy could not imagine her son might succumb. Just yesterday a man of awesome energy—a man who made square deals, loved sports, did more than his share of charity work—and now he couldn't shake a cold?

She buttoned him up to his neck. Her heart just broke for him.

She laid down the law: "Seven glasses of milk. Every day!" To help him out, she stretched her household pennies. "Stop it now, Josephine. Why wash your hands three dozen times a day?"

An extra piece of soap was now a luxury few people could afford. But Josie wouldn't be appeased. "It's dusty around here. The dust is simply everywhere—"

"Then sweep again," said Lizzy, while trying out an awkward recipe that called for linseed oil instead of butter. "The broom sits in the corner."

Jan couldn't raise his spirits no matter how he tried. He lacked the strength to come to the simplest conclusions. Josie owed the grocer, the butcher. She put a cardboard insert in her shoe to reinforce the sole. She covered acorns with soft cloth, thus fashioning her buttons. She wore her dresses inside out—and every stitch she wore was made by hand from discards. She brushed her teeth with salt and bought the cheapest cuts of meat, but when it came to gifts for Rarey—brushes, paper, books, supplies—that's where she drew the line.

She still had her nose in her books. Before she even finished one, already she reached for another.

As far as Lizzy was concerned, a book was an aversion. "Some people always find the time to read, no matter what the time of day, no matter what the weather," said Lizzy, speaking sharply.

"If it upsets you, then don't read," snapped Josie, for her part.

"Looking for solutions between covers never got you anywhere," said Lizzy, sounding grim.

"That's your opinion. Merely your opinion." Josie, too, was growing grim, not only in her looks but in her attitude. Whereas in olden times, she gobbled anything that was in print, now her beloved penny dreadfuls left her cold; romantic books fell from her listless hands. Her world was gray on gray.

Around Jan's favorite recalcitrant, Old Lizzy tried to hold her tongue. She knew that unpaid bills lay like huge boulders on Jan's chest. His debts were crushing him.

"You are my bedrock, son," she told him many times, to give him confidence. "There's nothing you can't do."

From the time that he was twelve years old, Lizzy had relied on Jan. She knew he would search long and hard to find a way to square his obligations.

Jan sold a choice stallion, which helped, but not for long. He rented the one piece of land still unencumbered, down by the sluggish river, not good for anything but grazing.

He counted on the money from the lease, but the Depression went from bad to worse; the neighbor who had meant to run his goats there, defaulted on the payment. Jan had to take it back.

"Try squaring a circle," said Josie.

"That, too," said Jan, starting to shake uncontrollably, "is easier said than done."

Jan shipped his last grain load to Wichita, only to learn that the price he obtained didn't cover the freight.

He stood, forlorn and shivering, watching the trains pass by. He saw that they were empty. He stood and watched down by the bend where, once upon a golden time, he and his giggling puppy love had put their pennies on the track and watched them being flattened. Now if a train arrived at all, it wobbled sluggishly, at half the speed, while he stood there and watched.

His heart was empty as a cave, for Josie wouldn't smile at him; she refused him the tiniest smiles. It was as if all feelings had come to a standstill, along with the mills and the trains.

Another fence tipped sideways.

His daughters' children brought their fishing rods to be repaired and to make Jan feel useful. He looked down at his strangely paralyzed hands.

Months passed; Jan didn't get better. He seldom went upstairs, where Josie pounded on her typewriter and Rarey kept his brushes.

It was warm in Lizzy's kitchen; why go upstairs where it was drafty from a broken window? He meant to fix that window, as soon as he could spare the cash.

He helped his mother do the dishes and puttered in the pantry, doing this and doing that, until Lizzy, with a pained expression, told him: "Forgive me, son, but I grow weary of the tension. Don't do that, please. It makes me itch all over."

Jan's eyes no longer held her glance. "What do you mean? Do what?"

"Re-stack my pots and pans."

"I didn't know I did."

"You did."

"I'm sorry, Mom. I'm sorry."

"All right! All right!"

"Mom—"

"Go take in a talkie," said Lizzy. "Take Rarey, and go watch a flicker."

"The newsreels make me dizzy."

"Here. Take your coat. The talkie starts at two."

Jan went, for there was nothing else to do. He sat, forlorn and stony, and listened as the audience whistled at the mustached man from Austria who tossed his forelock from his eyes. The screen was draped with swastikas. The flags snapped in the breeze; the streets were black with throngs. The German air ships swooped and dove. The Führer raised his hand in a salute, and people pulled their caps. He sent a wave of fury through the audience and caused enormous traffic jams. His voice reverberated through the speakers strung out across the trees. He shouted into several microphones at once.

He pointed a stiff finger and shouted that he would shine the light of certitude on Germany; he would expose the traitors and connivers.

To forestall bankruptcy, Jan put three of his last remaining parcels up for sale—land he had set aside to deed to Rarey as soon as he would want a homestead of his own.

That measure wrung his heart. He kept wiping the sweat from his arms, face, and neck—but this was an emergency; he had no other choice.

He offered it to several Jews with whom he'd traded in the past. He still had patriotic feelings; the shame of going to the Jews with hat in hand was almost more than he could bear, but after having brought himself to go that far, against every instinct in his bone, Jan realized with shame and bitterness: the Hebrews walked away.

There was now a growing and festering mood: people blamed them for the Depression. The widespread argument now ran: You couldn't ever trust a Jew to help you in a pinch. They sold you two left shoes and claimed that was the latest fashion. Some people called that chutzpah.

The Hebrews in the universities still spoke of betterment for all humanity; their claim was they pitied the dull, the obscure, and the poor, but they destroyed the middle class, as far as Jan could tell. To wit: they huddled over secret anagrams, and what that meant was anybody's guess.

Jan visited with three neighbors at the garden fence, who voiced the same concerns.

"Go look for Josie's Finkelsteins," one said, not even hiding malice. "Only the Levis have money left over."

Jan wished himself a hundred miles away, but duty was duty; it had to be done. There was no other choice. He started looking for a usurer to underwrite a loan—and look he did, all afternoon. In vain.

The only thing he found was dust and wind that swept in gusts through all the dirty streets of Wichita. The windows of the Levi stores were empty, with spider webs collecting in the corners, "For Sale" signs plastered on the walls. Jan felt, as he walked down the empty streets, that his heart's blood was leaking from his boots.

He tried to share that odd sensation when he came home at

dusk. He told his wife: "I was panhandled by a friend."

"Who?"

"Who? Never mind. No need to spread his shame."

"What happened?"

"He asked me for a loan to fill his flivver tank. I didn't have a dollar left to spare."

She stared at him with hungry eyes. She knew this rankled most—that helping others was no longer possible.

"I used to think that, in America, if you worked hard, plenty would be your reward." His hands lay inert in his lap. "I used to lavish help on neighbors wherever I saw them in need—"

"Of course you did," said Lizzy from the window. "You will again. You'll pull out soon. Your neighbors count on you to help them in a pinch."

Jan let himself be packed into his mother's quilts, but not before he said: "Blow out the light now, Josie. We have to save on fuel. Come. Let me hold you, kitten."

"Not now."

He pulled his knees up to his chin so terror could not leap upon him like a leopard.

Most citizens of Kansas, by that time, saw eye to eye with Henry Ford, and Jan did, too, now that his world was upside down: Ford's bogeymen had crooked noses, greedy eyes.

Not even Lizzy voiced objections when this was mentioned openly, right in her well-scrubbed kitchen. "Where there's smoke, there must be fire," said Lizzy, and knew that all agreed. "You draw the line somewhere."

She added that she was no "bigotist". She was fond of that word.

"No racist feelings here," said Lizzy. "But on the other hand, it makes you wonder, doesn't it?" She watched the bobbing heads.

She had adapted to okays, to electricity and telephones, but she had never even once conversed at leisure with a Hebrew. She kept a discreet distance. She did not even shop at five-and-tens, unless it was for Rarey.

She could not help but see what everybody saw: the Jews had lots of cash, no matter what the season.

But sharing, no. Not they.

Their furtive glances never rested anywhere. It was as Dewey said: they had a murky history. They hankered for the Holy Land and dreamed of taking over Palestine. That was their secret wish.

"They are the Devil's tools," Dewey had preached just the previous week. Without mincing his words, he announced that the Antichrist had already been born, intent on devouring the world. It was merely a matter of time, claimed Dewey, until the devil carried out his threat and started gobbling up the globe. "Just go and take a look at Wichita," said Dewey, "and draw your own conclusions."

The begging bowl was now a common sight.

Stale bread sold for a nickel, but no one had the cash.

Before another year was gone, established merchants, one by one, succumbed like swatted flies. Many homeless people slept in doorways and on the benches in the park. Hundreds prowled the alleys in their matted coats and muddied boots, grubbing through mountains of garbage for morsels of discarded food.

Along the railroad tracks on Twenty-First and Broadway, gray transients huddled in shacks they had constructed of cardboard, fruit crates, and blankets. Many slept in packing crates, and some in empty barrels. Hobos stood elbow to elbow, their backs hunched to the wind, in line for a warm bowl of soup.

"Fine soil for the Gospel," said Dewey. He knew from past experience that nothing helped a good awakening to Christ like a hot bowl of onion soup. He resolved to cut in on the action. The papers called it "Dewey's Dole", and it became the model for the state. Overnight, charity had grown into a thriving business, a mighty and controlling industry. Whoever wasn't scared of paperwork became a civil servant, and that's what Dewey did.

Soon, Dewey's food bank ran full steam, and people came from everywhere to let themselves be fed while being rescued and redeemed to turn a brand new leaf.

Twelve relatives poured from a van that broke down right in front of Lizzy's home. The wind, they claimed, had blown them out of Oklahoma.

These were times to band together. Old Lizzy shelved her goiter problems: family was family.

"Let's double up! Let's double up! Here. Try my pumpkin pie!"

It was no longer ham and eggs, rather turnips, onions, parsnips, and carrots. Old Lizzy didn't mind. She loved good company; it helped her pass the time. This was her home; a guest was always welcome. Times would get better, surely.

"Stay for a week," she said at first, and Josie fluffed the pillows. And why not, meanwhile, settle down for an extended chat and do the best you could?

Her Oklahoma cousins, thrice removed, were glad to thread her needles. They made a bit more work for Jospehine, what with the extra toweling, but then, work never hurt a body.

A month went by, and Lizzy said: "Why, stay another month, what is another month?" And, soon, she said: "Just stay until the rains return. Don't even mention leaving."

From morning till the sun went down, the relatives sat placidly in Lizzy's crowded kitchen, and talked about the good old days, when life was spare but good.

"It's not just a matter of doing, but doing without," they loyally bolstered each other. Assorted neighbors would join in, agreeing, for nothing could shake their convictions: the good days would be back. The past was dim, the present troublesome, the future a huge question mark. You clung to memories.

Old Lizzy was content. She was preparing for the grave and made no secret of the fact, but in the meantime, here was her family—she still right in the middle! What more could she have asked?

Many of the little baby boys and girls she had helped to life with Doctorjay's assistance long ago were parents and grandparents now. She knew them, one by one—knew all their quirks and oddities and weaknesses and foibles. She shone with happiness when yet more company arrived.

Her feet turned cold while sitting; her breath, at times, grew short—what with the dusty winds that blew and blew and would not be appeased. The doctors Josie called on her behalf, despite Jan's worried frowns—for every penny had to stretch!—looked somber and scribbled prescriptions.

They said to her: "More vegetables. Less *Griebenschmalz*," but when they left, she scoffed at every word. When Josie wasn't looking, she threw the fancy medicine into the sink and relied on the powers of prayer and camomile tea.

"What if those pills snuff out my mind?" she argued to herself.

She was content to dabble with the trusted remedies that Doctorjay left on her sill, next to her red geraniums. Her mind was still magnificent, her memories intact. Years vanished, but memories stayed.

Remember how we swapped those roosters to improve the size and color of our eggs? Remember the Electric Nineties? Remember how we were afraid at first to throw that switch? And slept with light all night?

Upstairs sat Josephine, still pounding on her typewriter, which made Jan's headaches soar. When she said "California," he thought his head would split.

Jan could not put his land into a suitcase and take it somewhere else. While his family slept, Jan kept on pacing. Pacing. His mood was black and heavy. His earth still lay untilled; he hungered for the soil, enough to drive him mad. He longed for the potato blossoms Rarey loved to paint—first white, then blue, then pink!—but even if he planted his potatoes, which was a monumental chore, then who would dig them out?

Jan had no money left. He couldn't hire help. Cash was in short supply. Five years ago, he had employed a hundred field hands easily and sent the overflow to help his daughters' husbands. Now he could barely pay for axle grease—a quarter for a pound.

The family watched silently as Jan scanned the "Help Wanted" ads.

He sat by the window, hunched over the *Wichita Eagle.* Each morning, he studied the fine print, line upon line and letter by letter, still hoping against hope to find a place in the economy where he could use his skills for other people's betterment and still keep an eye on the soil.

He even hitched three rides to Wichita, because fuel was dear now and hard to obtain. Broken and bleeding, that's how he came back.

He had a laugh that Josie did not recognize. He sat there, shivering, with bluish lips. But still, he kept on laughing. He laughed and couldn't stop.

She said without turning around: "What happened to your coat?"

"I gave it away. I gave it to a homeless man. He was about my size—"

She kept tapping her foot with impatience. No stranger to mood swings was Josie. "What do you mean, you gave it away? That was your finest garment. It cost you an arm and a leg."

"He was a wheezing windbag. He said he had no address—"

"You gave away your coat? So a stranger could walk around beaming?"

"You just don't understand. You don't. You do not understand."

She shrugged and said no more. The country shivered in the grip of something vile and menacing and ominous that no one understood.

Chapter 70

Natasha learned from Dominik, when he returned to Apanlee, his chest ablaze with decorations, that Comrade Stalin would bring lasting peace, prosperity and progress.

"And to that end," declared her son, "I am in charge of Apanlee. Does anyone object?" He gave the twins such an eyeful of hatred that they stepped aside without words.

Natasha's jaws snapped open. Her eyes grew round with alarm.

"All this to satisfy a grudge?" Natasha asked, but only of herself. Aloud she said, drying her hands on her apron: "What is the meaning of all this? Answer your mother now!"

"Use your imagination."

Her eyelids started quivering, for what she saw could not be put in words. She followed him, determined, as he strode whistling through the halls of Apanlee and knuckled the ancestral portraits: *"Donnerwetter! Donnerwetter!"*

The Pioneer took Marleen's elbow gently. "Come, Mother. Please. There is no point in standing in his way."

"There isn't," Dominik affirmed, and winked at Mimi, venturesome, while sprawling in the kitchen. "Here, feel my shirt. Feel the magnificent material."

He helped himself to several young potatoes still steaming on the table while grinning at the Pioneer. He liked her from the start, deciding on the spot how to make use of her.

That's how Natasha's son returned—in charge of the Apanlee harvests.

He hung his sheepskin on a nail and leaned his rifle in a corner. He dropped his backpack in the middle of the floor and said what he had come to say.

"We will remake the universe. Out with the old. In with the new. It's now the New World Order."

"I know you," said Marleen, still standing in the door. "I've known you all my life. There's nothing I don't know."

"There's nowhere you can hide," he said to her, in turn. "It's better that you understand that."

She did not drop her gaze. She quietly said: "I do."

He had practiced his menacing stare. Malevolence belched out of him like lava. He left no opportunity alone. "Just you remember that."

"I will."

"Good, then. To start, why don't we call a village Soviet meeting? We might as well start now."

The transfer of the land from private ownership to Comrade Stalin's custody turned out to be a brisk, efficient fifteen-minute matter. The village Soviet witnessed it. The fog rose from the soil. The afternoon turned black.

"We have no interest whatsoever in compromise," said Dominik. He lavished praise on every aspect of the Revolution. He declared that his task was to double the Apanlee harvests.

He told the crowd that had grown thick outside: "We all know beggars can't be choosers. I hope that you agree."

By then, there was hardly a struggle.

"We might as well shake hands," said Dominik. "I need you, and you need me. Let's start over with a clean slate. Why don't we let bygones be bygones?"

It gave him pleasure to observe the twins were burning with affront. "Right here," he told the village Soviet, and watched him dip his pen in Uncle Benny's marble ink pot. "Right on the dotted line."

"That's right. Right here," replied the village toady, blotting the paper, letting the pen wiper slide into his pocket after tugging briefly at his beard.

"That's done," cried an elated Dominik. "My, how the world will change! How we'll be engineering global human betterment!"

"Here's to our brand new, scientific, pig-producing program," declared a sodden Dominik while climbing on a chair. He looked as though he were running a fever. "The past is the past, and forgotten already. So let's drink to the future. Why not? I need you to be on my side." "Bottoms up! Bottoms up!" his drunken cronies howled.

"The future has arrived."

"We'll make traitors walk barefoot to Moscow!"

When the cheering died down, he had this to say to the twins: "I have good news for you. You will be in charge of the pig-tending brigade—" His gaze slid slowly to Larissa's neck. It lingered there as though to say: "Soon, we will have a feast."

He preened himself in front of every mirror. He told Marleen at every opportunity: "I take my orders from the Kremlin. Knock that into your German head." He also said: "For every sow, a separate stall. For every boar, a bucket full of barley."

Marleen wore a look as though stunned by a blow of such force that it numbed all her nerve ends at once. But she kept to herself; she backed into a silence as thick as fog.

She knew that Dominik would heed no clock, no calendar.

A sort of twilight settled on her face and stayed there, hiding her. She was the kind who listened to her thoughts.

She never argued back. Her nerves were taut with rage. Let not the right hand know about the left!—that was her motto now.

He gave her a wink and a slap on the back. A bean stuck to

his chin.

She saw no need to be obedient to his whims. She knew that shouting would not till the fields, and cursing would not milk the cows or carry fodder to the horses.

But Dominik puffed out his chest and laughed right in her face. There was no dimple on his chin, but he was in fine fettle. He said it first to her and later to the neighbors: "You'll thank me soon enough." And then he added slyly: "Don't say you weren't warned," still laughing to himself.

"Double lightning! Double lightning," prophesied Natasha darkly, but Dominik picked up his mother jauntily and hoisted her into the air.

Natasha was the only one at Apanlee who showed no fear of Dominik. At every opportunity, Natasha told her son: "I want no part of this."

She found a pillow for his stomach, for soon she realized his mounting quota worries gave him a lot of gas. She mediated, meanwhile. She did the best she could.

She had a hidden ledge on which two icons stood—one for her son, one for the twins; she prayed for all of them. Natasha had broad shoulders for the yoke on which she dangled her two buckets. She balanced them precariously. She stepped in front of Dominik while Apanlee was sighing in the wind. She warned him he was pressing his luck.

"Get out of the draft while you can. There's work to be done in the fields. This won't be like handing out pamphlets."

He rolled himself a cigarette. He had a ready answer. "Whatever needs to happen will be done. It's for our Motherland."

Natasha kept a civil tongue while talking to Marleen. She explained that her son was a man of importance, an official of weight at the Party.

"All else might fail," she told Marleen. "I'm still his mother. See? He'll listen to his mother."

As days grew into weeks, she told Marleen repeatedly: "Just keep out of his way. I know how to sweeten his temper."

She kept her eye on Dominik, as she had always done. The Kremlin? Moscow? Comrade Stalin? She picked no useless argument.

"Don't spit into a well," she said to him, relying on time-tested proverbs. "The day will come when you will have to drink from it—"

"There's freedom now. I can do anything I please."

"Don't push your luck. The Germans know the secrets you'll soon be needing, son—"

"They will do anything I say."

"Don't count on it."

"The Revolution evened up a score. And not a day too soon."

She was carefully picking her way. She would not let herself be cowed by Party schemes and rules. "Sure. Sure. As soon as every rooster learns to whistle," Natasha said, and thus had the last word.

Freedom was now at hand, Natasha knew, which was just wonderful—so much of it, in fact, there was overflow.

It meant that she could speak her mind at every opportunity. It meant that she could do that now. Therefore, she said to Dominik: "Don't let their faces fool you. Make sure your luck holds out."

She gave him many handy pointers. She was his mother. That sufficed.

"Don't lose your head," she scolded Dominik, but he was on a roll, and nothing stopped him now.

She lingered by the stove. "Now listen to your mother, fool! You cannot fix a broken egg—"

"Perhaps not. But I can slurp the evidence—"

"And give yourself a case of indigestion—"

"I am in perfect standing with the Party. I am a dedicated patriot. That's all they need to know."

While frightened neighbors groveled at his feet, Natasha brandished her big broom, and chased him from corner to corner.

Shortly thereafter, a truck full of government workers arrived from Berdyansk. The first to jump down from the wagon was Shura, as vulgar as a whistle.

Shura carried papers verifying that she was a trusted and respected proletarian. Her voice was rough and thick. Her hair looked like a beehive.

"You, there!" she squealed, while fastening a mean eye on Marleen. "Don't stand there, gawking wastefully. You will report to me. I am the new fowl brigadier. I'll be in charge of doubling egg production." She had a cold and used her sleeve. She had watery eyelids and a coarse tongue, but she was charged with an amazing energy. "Come here! Hold out your hand so I can ink it with a number."

Natasha could tell that this woman lacked breeding. She remembered her finest society manners.

"Who's she? No doubt she grew up among quarrels and blows," she said to Dominik. She took the harlot firmly by the elbow and announced. "You can sleep in the straw in the stable."

"She's having my child," said Dominik slowly. "It will sleep in the cradle that was denied me. It's she and I, from now on, who'll fill the nursery."

Shura proudly wore the blood-red ribbon she had earned for her political activities, having been a noted agitator in the days of Civil War. She never missed a May Day procession.

She told Natasha soon thereafter that she had lost three brothers to the proletarian struggle. She spoke of her three martyred siblings in a vague but patriotic way.

She said she lived to honor them. They gave her rights nobody else possessed. She kept rubbing her knuckles with spittle.

"They sacrificed. We follow in their footsteps. They did not die in vain."

Natasha answered carefully. "The quota laws are strict."

"For every drop of blood, a sea of blood. Such is the balance sheet."

Natasha paused at length before she asked: "So? What is

your conclusion?"

After thinking for several minutes, Shura threw out her chest and, flicking at a dead fly that had fallen from the sill, proclaimed: "Here's what I think: if you work in the barn, you better get used to the smell."

Natasha had a ready proverb of her own: "Every day holds a sunrise and a sunset."

"Hah! Wait and see!"

Natasha kept on peeling her potatoes. "I must be dense. What are you saying, Citizen? What are you telling me?"

"See this?" Shura paused, then pulled a notebook from the shelf. "This is a list of do's and don'ts. It settles every argument."

"Dethroned but not defeated," is what Natasha said.

The steps of Apanlee were jammed with people, and more came streaming down the goose path to learn the New World Order rules from Dominik who strove for an appeasing mood. Natasha ran for chairs.

"Come here. Sit down beside me," he offered, belching loudly.

"We will get by with what we grow," the Germans said in turn.

"Look. What's the point of arguing? We have a Five-Year Plan. I need you, and you need me. I'm giving you plenty of warning. You will work for the state if you wish to continue to eat."

Night after night, he surrounded himself with his cronies, who were a noisy lot. They drank boisterous toasts to the Red Revolution, to the Hammer and Sickle, to Lenin, to Stalin. "To friendship among all the nations," they shouted. "To the World Revolution!" they roared. "Bottoms up! Hey? Bottoms up!"

They drank to the country they would reconstruct, now sunk in a sea of red banners.

"To the future! The future!" they sang.

"We'll be revamping everything."

"We'll put our most productive workers in the paper."

Said Dominik, at intervals, still hectoring the Germans: "We'll make a showcase out of Apanlee. If you cooperate, you'll have no problems whatsoever. If, on the other hand—"

In days to come, his smile was slanting more and more. He modified his boasts.

"Look, let's be friends instead of enemies. I'm just a little peg in a vast scheme. It isn't me you have to fear. Who knows who'll soon be feasting on your marrow?"

He did not notice that the planting season slipped away. His cronies stayed and stayed. Night after night, they drank until they grew weary.

They cheered the city labor squads expected in a convoy who were mysteriously delayed. They drank toasts to the milking brigades about to be scheduled; they toasted the vegetable crews about to be formed. Toasting Yuri and Sascha who stood, silent statues, and watched it all happen, they drank hearty toasts to a four-season grain.

"Bottoms up! *Nu?* Bottoms up!" roared an inebriated Dominik. "The night is still young. Who's talking about going home? I will not hear of leaving."

"We'll make a happy world for all," insisted Shura, too, who had not yet improved her manners. She talked with a mouth full of food. "We are all equal now. Dead are all class distinctions."

Shura made a racket when she ate. She told Natasha many bloody stories. Some uncouth joke was always tickling her.

One morning, she sat there in the sunshine, giggling to herself. She seemed unable to control her mirth. "Some people may not like our ways, but then, so what? So what?"

Her life and times had made a stoic of Natasha. "You're right. So what? Good question, Shura. Excellent."

Shura spit through a gap in her teeth.

"Don't make me furious. I know you take their sides. Who knows them better than you do?"

"That's right. I do. Just you remember that."

"I freely criticize myself for being much too lenient," claimed Shura soon thereafter, and laughed until her belly ached. "Catch me their biggest, fattest rooster."

"No rooster, Citizen."

She started shouting lustily: "Tomorrow, Dominik will be expecting guests. They are important Party comrades. I need that rooster to impress them. I want that rooster! Now!"

Natasha squared her jaw and said: "Shout all you want, but shout at me; there is no point in shouting at Marleen; she does not have a rooster."

"I'll squash her like a louse," yelled Shura. "I'll hang her from the ceiling by her heels."

"Look at the smoke that rises from her chimney," Natasha pointed out. "It doesn't even curl."

"I need that rooster, and that's it."

"You better listen. Citizen! You listen to this toothless peasant. Marleen is proud, but she is no one's fool. Where would she hide a rooster? A rooster makes a ruckus. She can't afford to draw attention to herself."

"A pampered settler sitting on the country's richest soil, and does not have a rooster?"

"No rooster," lied Natasha, while thinking of the laying hen she had helped hide, still worth at least ten eggs.

"I have it from reliable informants that there exists an extra bird at Apanlee. I know that for a fact. What will the Party think? Where is she hiding it?"

Natasha started wheedling. "Can every rumor safely be believed?"

"No rooster?"

"Well, a hen. All feathers, skin and bones."

"Ha!" Shura cried triumphantly. "The truth prevails. We must investigate at once."

"It's just a skinny hen, too skinny for the pot!"

"Be sure to tell Marleen to have it plucked for me," yelled Shura, in the know.

There was no end to it.

Chapter 71

Marleen stood upon the blood-soaked earth of Apanlee and watched what happened next. The government told Dominik how many pounds of cheese and butter to deliver, but did it tell the cows?

His first totals fell short of the quota.

Her glance turned into beams of steel when Dominik tried covering his bafflement while boasting broadly to his cronies: "It may be difficult at first, but all we need is time. The future will bring peace, prosperity and progress—"

She told him evenly: "That's what we hope for, Citizen. That is our fervent hope."

"What? Are you mocking me?"

"We have no disagreement, Dominik. All of us hope fervently for lasting peace, prosperity and progress."

The grain procurement plan that Dominik had slovenly drawn up did not impress the twins, although what came out of their mouths was not the language written in their eyes.

"When it comes to the future, Dominik," they said to him,

sarcastically, "nobody has your ingenuity."

Admitting that he needed them to help him with his quota lists was anguish magnified. "They'll make any confession I please to dictate," he boasted to his mother. "We have the means to make a deaf-mute speak. They'd better understand that."

"Yes. I suppose so. I suppose so. The moment when that rooster learns to whistle you slaughtered just last week."

"I know they will."

"If you say so."

"I do."

"And who made sure your limbs grew straight? You fool! *Durak! Durak!* Why don't you listen to your mother?" Natasha spread her huge, rough hands. Natasha was ashamed. In fact, her shame was grim. Her memory was not yet dim. She dove to the root of the matter.

"What have they ever done to you?" she asked with genuine astonishment. "Why do you hate them so? If you would only treat them properly—"

"You ask?"

"I do. When I was young, I might have made mistakes. The fault was mine. I made mistakes. Why punish them, instead?"

"So? Let us profit by mistakes," said Dominik, and winked. He sprawled in the family tub. "They're imperialist spies. I know they are plotting and scheming."

Natasha warmed his towels by the fire. "Remember: they know how to rescue your harvest."

He soaped himself from head to toe. "We'll teach them a lesson. It's time they learned a lesson they are not likely to forget."

She watched him, thinking canny thoughts. Her son was her son; he was without conscience, but he was still her son. That was the bottom line. Natasha liked to keep her irons in the fire. She understood self-interest. It never hurt to pour cold water over sizzling coals. Therefore, she said to Dominik: "I'm glad you are making a name for yourself. Still, do you need to shout so? They're human beings. They have pride."

He laughed so hard he almost strangled on his words. "How often do I have to tell you? A cat dislikes a dog."

She heard that laugh and ran to tell the twins: "Be careful what you say. He knows how to wring a confession."

This was but a family quarrel. If she took sides, it would make things much worse. She clung to all of them with a defiant loyalty. They were the only family she had.

Soon it was clear to everyone: The unifying element at Apanlee was Baba.

"Let's say that you've been cautioned," growled Dominik, after he had assembled the entire neighborhood to give them a fine scolding. "This is a state farm now. The rules have changed. You hear?" He now unrolled a scroll that looked like a map of the village. His eyebrows grew bushier and bushier.

"Splinters must fly," he let it be known, "when trees are chopped down. We're chopping down trees. We're chopping down forests, in fact."

He knew they were blinded by hate. The frown on his forehead was etched. He recognized defiance. He would make sure that it didn't spell defeat. He stopped them in the middle of their proverbs. "Don't claim you weren't warned."

They merely stood there, shuffling.

"Heroic workers," he announced, "are going to receive appropriate rewards. Defeatists, saboteurs, and shirkers, on the other hand, will have a choice: Siberia or heaven."

He smacked his lips and closed his eyes. A strong wind came from nowhere and whirled the leaves about. A cat shot up an apple tree, its fur on end with terror.

Marleen said to Natasha: "My sons, whose hearts are brimming with the Holy Spirit, are shadowed at each step."

Natasha had no ready answer. She, too, would listen to the tread of terror on the cobblestones of Apanlee, and knew that when they came and took this one, that one—good neighbors, every one!—a hush fell after they left.

Thus disappeared a widow's only son. This happened the following spring.

Louise, whose maiden name was Hansen, was distantly related to Marleen. Somewhere in bygone years two cousins had married and had fused the clans of the Hansens, the Penners, the Harms, and the Dycks. In better days, their offspring had been numerous as beetles in the spring, but then the Revolution came and put an end to progeny—all poor Louise had left was just one timid son. He was a meek and waxen fellow, but still the apple of her eye. She loved him more than life. She surveyed every girl she knew and pushed them in his path.

The Soviet agents came for him. They pulled him from deep sleep. They walked him silently behind the lilac bush Louise's grandmother had planted lovingly when she first came to the Ukraine from Northern Germany.

They said to him while he still rubbed the night out of his eyes:

"Confess you are a saboteur and traitor."

He reached back, grasping at a branch. It was a lilac twig, rich with the sap of May. The branch snapped in his hand. That was the only sound before the bullet flew. That's where he fell, another nameless victim, and did not rise again.

"*Tovarich*," said Natasha to her son, to let him know she understood the rules. "This letter came this morning—"

Dominik took it from her and straightened all the creases. He said without looking at her: "How am I supposed to triple the crop? How? How? Will someone tell me how?"

Natasha watched him stealthily. She stuck with her instincts; she had rehearsed them well. She saw the glint of fear in Dominik, though he was now a man who carried great weight in the Party.

She cuffed him playfully and grinned from ear to ear. "I don't know why, but the twins come to mind. They have a sure touch with the kernels."

From his desk, he picked up a thick sheaf of papers. He spoke to the wall and the ceiling.

"They want their travel papers, do they not? They want to leave the country?"

She raised her chin, alert. "A travel paper is more precious than a nugget."

He started chewing on a hangnail. "That's good to know. That's excellent to know."

She jumped with both arthritic feet into the middle of his thoughts. "That might be just the lever that you need. It's whom you know that counts. You have a lot of friends. In highest Party quarters. You're brilliant, Dominik. What's more, you are in charge. You don't need a production gap. They need to sleep at night and not lie staring at the ceiling."

"Go on."

"If they believe that they can get their travel papers through your friends in highest quarters, they'll help you with the crops."

"You think they will?"

"I know they will. Just leave things to your mother."

"You're sure?"

"I'll put in a good word for you. Don't push them out into the rain. Let them sleep in the attic."

"All right. But only for the season."

Natasha ran to tell Marleen. "The unused west wing is still yours to occupy in any way you please. If you keep to yourself and try not to offend—"

Marleen was not deceived. "How is he going to triple the crop?" She smiled her thinnest smile.

"You'll help him," said Natasha. "And not another word."

"So! Let them bite themselves until they bleed," cried Shura next, her face a fiery red. "Let's send them to the tundras of the north. Let's let Siberia rattle their bones."

She kept shouting to vent her resentment: "If you claim that they are innocent, I counter: 'They are guilty!' We'll fling them to their graves—"

This anger was Natasha's opportunity. She started shedding light.

"I speak of far-off days. Those were not ordinary boys. Ah, yes! Fat! Lightly freckled! Fantastic shadows, memories! They had a sure touch with the rye—"

"They're underfoot in my own kitchen, constantly. We're not yet done with them." Shura looked as if she were caught in a towering rage.

Natasha's voice took on a singsong lilt. "Look. There's a middle way. If you divide the building lengthwise, Shura—"

"What? Never! I said never! I want them out! I need my elbow room."

"They wouldn't bother you. They're down to their last kopeck."

"So?"

A silly smile sat on Natasha's face. Her nose was red and shiny. "Take Marleen, for example. She isn't any threat. She isn't any trouble. She turns her ration cards this way and that and can't see a way out."

"Ha!"

"I'll talk to her. I'll tell her that you claim the wash tub. She can wash in the outside rain barrel."

"And her towels, too! Hear?"

"All right. Of course."

"Make sure she understands that."

"I will. Don't shout. In turn, you share with her your samovar. Don't be pigheaded, Shura—"

"I want all her quilts," yelled Shura. "Tell her, Natasha! Now!" She began to spit venom and spite. "We don't need Germans underfoot. They show contempt for what we're trying to do. I want them out! I want them out and gone!"

"They can sleep in the back chamber, then?" Natasha busied herself with a task. "Or maybe even the attic? It's empty. Full of spiders. The rest of the house will be yours. Let them keep the attic while you keep the rest."

"No. I said no. The barn is good enough," decided Shura angrily, and kicked the premium piglet she had installed beneath the bench in Marleen's summer kitchen. It left its droppings on the floor and squealed at everyone.

This was a taxing time for Dominik. He learned that he must argue everything. Their excuses were many; his output grew leaner and leaner. Before the year was out, his bloodshot, angry eyes fixed coldly on Marleen.

"They will listen to you. Your word carries weight around here."

"I don't know what you mean. My farming methods are old-fashioned. The future means nothing to me."

He turned to Mimi next. He knew she sided with the government. Her backflips were precision. She wore her fiery cap with pride.

She said to him, keen on the rules: "Forget about my mother. She's useless, Dominik. You're on your own. You have a lot of ingenuity. Use it to your own benefit. The Party counts on you. The Party will reward you."

"Your brothers, then? What might I trade with them?"

The Pioneer glanced swiftly at Larissa. Larissa's eyes glazed over, a tremor ran along her spine, but she said not one word. She simply sat there, silent and demure, while struggling with a sock of Dominik's that had a giant hole.

Soon afterwards, two panting government inspectors came to check the quota yield. They wouldn't go away. Their patience was beginning to run short.

Natasha kept wringing her hands. She watched them prowling through the neighborhood, searching everywhere for hidden grain, testing with an iron rod for loose spots in the earth.

"In a nutshell, details! That's what we need. Details! *Tovarich*! Dominik! Who's in charge around here? Why can't you keep up with your quotas?"

"Just give me time—"

"There is strong proof of sabotage. Right under your own roof! What do you have to say in your defense, *tovarich* Dominik? Someone somewhere must be punished. It might as well be you."

When Dominik was walking through the silent streets surrounding Apanlee, he knew that his footsteps cast fear. He soon began to keep a notebook, and every time he saw a group of Germans, he scribbled something furtively.

They knew that he hated them all. He knew that that was mutual.

He stared at the twins as though they were strangers. They stared at the barns, at the rust-covered tractors without saying a word. He knew forbidden thoughts were sliding through their minds like lances.

"Well, when it rains, it pours," the twins said to each other. Their eyes no longer met. Each had a lot to hide.

Natasha had a lifetime of experience at squeezing joy out of a desperate situation. Each quarrel that Shura and Dominik started, she finished.

"Marleen asks permission to grow her own pig," wheedled Natasha the following week.

"A pig? Did you say pig? The Party frowns on private pigs."

"Forbidden in theory. Allowed in practice."

"No! Never! Not a pig!"

"A piglet. That's all. It's high time you plant your potatoes."

"If she owns anything the Party disallows, she'll be regarded as a wrecker. Piglets are disallowed—"

"She'll feed it dandelion greens!"

"What's next? A private cow?" yelled Dominik.

"A pig. That's all. I swear that's all. Perhaps a bucket, too? Do you want a potato harvest failure? Can you afford that, Dominik? The Party has your file."

Dominik snapped sharply to attention. "As if I didn't know."

"Where are your seed potatoes?"

"Out with the truth. Have they found out the special shipment of the seed potatoes didn't come?"

"They have. They have. And so have all the others. Your wife has the screech of a raven—"

"Are they spying on me? Are they laughing at me? Blast

them to smithereens!"

"They heard your troubles through the wall. A private piglet is a meager price to pay for a potato crop."

"No! I said no!"

"What will you do if the potato crews arrive, dispatched by Comrade Stalin, and you have no potatoes with which to plant the fields?"

"Hush! Not a word!"

"Don't you hush me! Who rocked you through the night when you were feverish? And who looked out for you when you were small and quarrelsome?" She had rehearsed this well. "You listen to your mother! You let Marleen have that piglet. Now! Don't give me an excuse! They're useful. They know how to grow fat potatoes from peels. What is a little piglet by comparison? I'll talk to her. I'll trade you their potato secrets if you will let her have that piglet that's messing up your kitchen. She's got to eat. She'll make it fat, and in the meantime, son, make sure you keep your cool—"

In the following weeks, her wheedling grew louder and louder. "Don't you hush me! Who took your side against the twins? Who fed you jam behind their backs? Do me a favor, will you? A puny cow, that's all."

"I can't. That's too great a risk. I can't afford a blot on my record."

"The season cannot wait. One measly cow. As a personal favor to me."

"I could be shot!" hissed Dominik. "For advocating private property."

She flew into full combat. She started shouting in his face: "A party functionary needs a harvest. You know what happened to three foremen in a neighboring kolkhoz? They marched them to the sand pits. They shot them, one by one."

He started shouting back: "She has a secret file already that's growing thicker by the day. She used to write those Josie letters to rally help from foreign interventionists. "

"I fear for you. I weep for you," Natasha wailed expertly.

"No! I said no!"

"Who swaddled you ten times a day when you had diarrhea? What is a set of horses in return for all the pains your mother suffered, bearing you? It wasn't easy giving birth to you. I might well have died!"

"You said a cow! Now horses, too?"

"They're driving a hard bargain."

"No. No. And no and no!"

"If you don't listen to your mother, your mother will be broken-hearted, for Stalin's commissars will come and they will shoot you dead because of quota lags!" Natasha may have lost her youth—she hadn't lost her tongue. At every opportunity, she lashed and bashed at him to help him fill his quotas. Oh, *bozhe moi!* And pretty soon it will be time to seed new corn, and after corn comes barley."

"It's April, son! You hear? By this time of the year, your father's corn stood three feet tall. You haven't even seeded."

He shook her by the shoulders. "A *schweinehund*! A trickster and exploiter!"

She shouted back: "Who, Hein? A splendid man! A huge and gentle beast!"

"He stole your innocence!"

"I gave it willingly!"

"He used you. He exploited you!"

Why! You ungrateful lout! Three piglets, that is all! You listen to your mother!"

"He never once stood by my side when I was small and barred from feasting at their holidays—"

Natasha yelled defiantly and slammed the door so hard that all the rafters shook: "Ha! Many times! Believe me, many times!"

"Not even once!"

"By your two dirty ears he picked you up and kissed you smackingly!"

But in the end, all was in vain. It was as Dominik declared: a cat dislikes a dog. There was no compromise.

Thus, after having been evicted from her homestead altogether by the pointed finger of a bull-necked commissar who had a camel's nose and stank of onions and wet rags, Marleen moved out of Apanlee.

She did this by degrees, and not without a struggle.

"You don't need a production gap," she said to Dominik before she disappeared, for she had patented her worth. That's how Marleen moved out—head high, jaw locked, and every muscle taut.

She left her home the way a fighting general breaks off battle, resisting, inch by inch. She first moved out into the corridor, then farther down the hall into a narrow pantry, then even farther back behind a thin partition she erected in the barn and, in the end, into the drafty edifice, once occupied by Ivan and Natasha, the hut where Dominik was born.

"He cannot even grasp," Marleen said to Natasha, "how little he can take away!"

Her shoe soles were in shreds; her elbows were frayed; and her skirt had three holes—but oh! her jaw, her stubbonr Prussian jaw! That jaw was chiseled from granite and sharper than ever, now locked in place as though a dead bolt had snapped shut.

Natasha helped her·push the bulge of bedding down the hall. "Here. Easy! I said, easy! Don't forget to come back for your grandfather clock. Every day holds a sunrise and sunset."

Chapter 72

A first-generation homestead, belonging to the Friesen family, just down the road and to the left of the untidy Donoghues, fell beneath the auctioneer's hammer. To the good folks of Mennotown, it felt as though a guillotine's blade had fallen on an honest and innocent head.

The Friesens were as fine a family as ever there lived in Kansas. Ever since the days when Mennotown had been a frontier town, they had led exemplary lives. With them, it was the Ten Commandments to the letter from the cradle to the grave. Their hallmarks were forbearance, stamina, thrift, diligence, persistence and endurance. Their children and their children's children had helped put village after village on the map. And though the Lord had blessed them lavishly and given them not just necessities, but telephones and flivvers, they never stepped outside the norm—at every "Stop" they stopped.

"It's hard to grasp. That kind of life can end in poverty?" said Jan, and let himself fall heavily into his wicker chair. "Where will it end? What's happening to us?"

He knew: in charity, the Friesens had few rivals. If there was need in someone else's home, they reached into their pockets. They gave as much as they could spare, and often twice as much.

Jan had avoided thinking of the future—beyond next day, next week. He could no longer do so now. The wolf was at the door. He looked down at his hands.

"What is the matter with our country? How can this be? The clothes on their backs is all the Friesens salvage out of a life of honesty and thrift?"

It was incomprehensible.

Doctorjay dipped deep into a hidden kitty and came up with a fistful of dollars no one knew he had still stashed away. He bought the Friesen farm before the usurers foreclosed, which was a stroke of genius, and neighborly besides. He bought their inventory, too—all of it, lock, stock, and barrel. He did that without wasting words. His mustache bristled with the challenge. His oldest son, a licensed dentist with an enameled name plate next to his own, no longer drilled teeth; he recommended quick extractions which went for half the price. Between them, they had pooled their savings.

"Once you're on your feet again," said Doctorjay to the despondent farmer who looked as if his eyes had turned as stony as the dark side of the moon, "I'll let you buy it back."

Soon, Doctorjay took over parcel after parcel from his neighbors.

Three sons-in-law came visiting. They circled Jan like three determined birds, and in the end the bravest said: "It's about your mortgage, Dad."

"Leave things to me," said Jan in such a voice that they could say no more. They left, discussing in hushed voices the tragedy that had befallen their most highly esteemed leader.

He watched them grimly from the window, and knew what they were saying: "Jan is a changed and different man." He knew that they were right. Before his illness laid him low, he would have started to rebuild before the embers died.

When Lizzy asked: "Jan, are you going somewhere—?" he

said he didn't know.

"You need more rest, Jan."

"That's it. Rest."

"Just give it lots of time."

Time? Jan had nothing else but time. Time weighed on Jan, each minute like a bar bell. An hour was a mountain. A day seemed an eternity.

Jan yearned for corn with firm, fat ears, for barley that swished as it fell. He longed to rake and bind and stack the grain of yesteryear, but the doctors kept shaking their heads. The Wichita doctors that Josie had summoned, this against every instinct in his bones, had warned him, again and again: "Bedrest! Bedrest! Old fellow, can't you see what you are doing to yourself?"

There was the daily walk, meanwhile, to pick up everybody's mail. Jan did that each morning at nine.

Next came a slow walk to the park. A slow stroll to the firehouse. He peered in empty windows. He studied the signs: "We're firing—not hiring." Many door frames were broken or sagging.

On his way back, he sometimes stopped by Little Melly's porch because she didn't scatter high-flown phrases, she said things in plain English.

"It is a shocking thought," said she, "that so much toil can end in poverty."

It pleased him that she stored his words. She echoed his opinions. She was as comforting to Jan as old and well-worn slippers. "Come sit here. By my side. For just a little while? So you can catch your breath?" She snatched his hand. She had even tried some palmistry on him by studying his calluses. "Your troubles will soon end."

She said to Jan: "Here. Take my chair to sit on. Why don't you stay for supper?" but he replied: "No. Thanks. I can't. Is it true you are taking in boarders?"

"Despite my age and rheumatism, yes."

She knew, like no one else: a penny had to stretch. She shopped for everything according to how durable it was and not how good it looked. Her pantry had no sugar left, but she had no complaint. She might still go to Wichita to finger wares in stores, but the Depression taught her self-control; she always put them back.

"The soft days are over. Right, Jan? The lavish days are gone?"

His thin smile held no joy. "Yes. You're right. The good old days are gone."

She studied him obliquely. Here was old dirt to pay. She, Little Melly, well remembered how, any time it struck her fancy, Josie used to visit far-flung relatives in Winnipeg or Calgary or even as far as Vancouver, and never mind the Coupon Clipping Afternoon or Dewey's Indian Mission. And now?

Jan's Josie walked around with cardboard in her soles like everybody else, but did she help scrub Dewey's church? No. Did she stitch quilts to aid his Vagrant Mission? Hardly.

Jan said to Little Melly: "It breaks my heart. Last night, I heard her cry."

"Tears," said the spinster firmly, "are sent to us to wash our eyes so we can better read the Ten Commandments." She laid it out for him: the Lord was very, very angry, with the good and with the bad. He made the weather fickle. He manifested his displeasure by ruining the crops. Now that it was agreed by all the world was steeped in sin, why didn't Josie let herself be rescued and redeemed? Dewey would gladly lend a hand, if only Josie asked.

Jan took a feeble stand. "Well, don't we all know Josie?"

"Yes, don't we know she has an awful monkey on her back?"

No longer did Jan's Josie look as though she'd stepped out of the pages of a novel. Both elbows were now frayed. When Dewey talked of Jesus Christ—what Christ could do for Josephine—she covered her ears with her hands.

The previous year, wheat prices had dropped sharply, surged once, then dropped again. The weather had destroyed the winter crop as well. Good farmers everywhere, industrious and loyal, all of them having struggled on their homestead ever since the days of dark and bitter wheat, now found themselves in court, then left their farms with not a penny in their pockets.

"We must vote in the Democrats next time around," said Dewey now, who always, in the past, had voted straight Republican. "I guess the last election was a blunder?"

This was the newest fad. The Methodists were getting into that, into the risky business of switching votes and siding with the have-nots. The bonesetter was into that. Now that the crusty healer had hitched himself to Abigail, switching parties didn't seem so odd.

Doctorjay went checking up on politics at Dewey's Dole and recognized three business friends from Wichita with whom he had made deals in better days, when money was as plentiful as daisies in the meadows.

What he encountered shocked him to the core.

Here stood his counterparts, enfeebled and defeated, resigned to fate and accident, in line with panhandlers and vagabonds, while Dewey, Archie at his elbow, helped them to put their souls in order before he let them help themselves to slices of stale bread. The bread was green and moldy at the edges, but Dewey said: "Still edible!" His yield was rich. Ten sinners in one day!

"Our Congress in paralysis?" said Doctorjay to Dewey in hopes of sparking a lively argument. He had brought Abigail along, who tied her handkerchief around her neck instead of wearing it, where it belonged, deep in her left-hand pocket.

"No! You don't say!" squealed Abigail, to reinforce her husband. "For once, the little people in this country get a chance?"

Dewey merely glared at Abigail. That one was still the kind that tried to make men blush. She had smooth skin and costly tastes, and Doctorjay had change to spare, which was a miracle, considering. He lavished it on Abigail. He was agog with Abigail.

"God is your only hope," said Dewey sourly. "Just put your trust in Him. The sins of pride and vanity must go. They must be rooted out."

"The union people claim this time around they will elect a

Democrat," boomed Doctorjay, and winked at Abigail. He now was shaving twice a day. They were seen holding hands.

"There is no way to stop modernity," mourned Dewey.

The healer, checking up on Jan so he could sound him out on politics, took one of Lizzy's towels, spread it across Jan's chest and, putting his big ear upon it, listened carefully.

"You're getting stronger, Jan. I am an optimist. Something good is bound to happen. A fine solution will turn up. Within four weeks, you'll be as good as new. Maybe you, too, should vote the Democrats into the White House? What do you say? At least, there's money still in Washington. Look how they're spending it. It cannot get much worse."

Jan sagged a little from a hearty blow delivered for the sake of sentiment. "I am too old and useless to change my voting habits."

"You old? You useless?" cried a stricken Doctorjay, and slapped Jan's shoulder with such force a little puff of dust rose up in the air. "Don't give me your excuses. Just stop that nonsense! Stop it! I order you: just cut it out! Another week in bed is all you need. Just take my word for it. Raw carrot juice! Before this year is out, you'll sprint down that long road again just like the yearling that you are. Right, Josie? Josephine?"

"I wish you wouldn't wink."

"Who, me? I never wink. Right, Abigail?" Already he was on a roll, oblivious. "A man can't live on air and on surmises. Stick out your tongue, old fellow. Here. Step up, Jan. Right this way. To the window. So I can study it. See? There you go. Your tongue is all right. Your tongue still looks like forty—"

"It's not his tongue," said Josie, furious. "It's his attitude. His spirits."

The healer chose to stay the course. He gazed at her attentively. "I'm twelve years older than your husband. And look at me. Still going strong. Ask Abigail about last night—"

"Stop it," said Josie, beneath her breath. "Just stop it. Stop it. Stop it."

"What did I say?"

"If you must ask, then you don't need to know."

"To spruce your marriage up a bit, perhaps you should take Abigail into your confidence?" He tickled her under the chin. She practically took off his scalp. She spilled her coffee on herself. Her hands were shaking badly. But Doctorjay was Doctorjay, banking on his instincts. He blew a cloud of smoke into her eyes, for he could not leave well enough alone:

"Say, Josie! Did you hear the latest joke?"

"No. And I hope I never will."

"It comes straight from the horse's mouth."

"So? Spare me, Doctorjay."

"From Henry Ford himself. Here's what he said. He said: 'If I had the money, these days, would I be driving a Ford?' Pretty funny? Huh? Is that a joke? Or what?"

"A joke that splits my sides."

"You used to laugh at Ford jokes," pouted Doctorjay.

"I did? I can't remember."

"I have a joke for you," said Jan. "Here goes. What is a Hooverflag?"

The healer scratched his pate. "A Hooverflag? Beats me."

"Try harder. What's a Hooverflag?"

"What *is* a Hooverflag?"

"Pockets turned inside out. Ha-ha! What is a Hooverwagon?"

"Jan, no idea. No idea!"

"A gasless flivver—dragged by mules."

"Say! That's funny! That is funny!"

"Yes, isn't it? What's Hooverville?"

The village healer sobered up. "Enough. That's taking things too far."

You had your pride; you leaned on that pride. You couldn't find a slum in Mennotown—not yet!—unless you counted in the Donoghues who were a world apart. You flew the American flag, no matter that the paint was peeling badly on the trusty wooden pole. As long as you had that, you still had hope and trust. A Roosevelt had done well once—another Roosevelt was rising fast, according to the dailies, and he was fond of sausage, beer and babies.

Most farmers felt that way about the Democratic candidate who promised boosts for the economy. These were resilient folks; that was their hall mark; belt-tightening was nothing new; they knew how to do it. They'd done it before; they would do it again. The Lord was just testing their fabric.

"No matter what," said Doctorjay, "we'll stick it out and, in the end, emerge triumphantly." There was still pride in battle on the prairie. So what if, temporarily, you scraped the bottom of your kitty? It only strengthened your intentions.

"In Hoover we trusted. Soon we'll be busted," the faith healer philosophized.

"What's that I see," gushed Little Melly. "A brand new pair of shoes?"

"That's right," said Josephine. "I needed them. They were on sale. I threw away a pair last week because they showed my toes."

"Two dozen bushels of good wheat to buy a single pair of shoes," sighed Lizzy.

"Not counting the laces. Not counting the laces," said Josie.

"Sooner or later," prophesied Jan, not even smiling at his words, "she'll overspend herself. She's bound to meet her Waterloo. Is that not right? Is that what everybody thinks?"

But Doctorjay just snorted. Waterloo was here.

Josie picked up the paper that lay on her porch, provoking a tiny explosion of dust. She glanced at the headlines to get herself riled up on wrath.

"Look here! Look here! This Adolf-what's-his-name? He's poking at the hornets' nest again. That man is dangerous. That's religion, over there. That's not politics—"

"Don't be ridiculous."

"This man and our own illustrious Elder," decided Josie, whose tastes had always run to odd comparisons, "run on identical fuel. Both claim that the Jews have cooked up the Depression."

"Maybe they're right?" Such was the common thought.

"Be fair!" demanded Josie fiercely, in search of any audience. Political matters were fuel for her feverish brain, oil on her liberal embers. She had a shrewd, discriminating eye. She had her own deep wounds. She spread her fingers wide to amplify her theory: both claimed the stewardship of God. Both knew exactly what was good for everybody else. Both had a cross they claimed had mystic powers. Both robbed you of the here and now by promising rewards in the beyond.

Which was a fraud. A laugh.

That's what she said. But that was Josephine. No wonder that she was ignored in her own family.

Jan took the paper from her hand. "Calm down. Calm down. We have our own diversionists right here. Our country's in a hopeless muddle."

She gave a trembling sigh. "I know."

"If rain does not come soon—"

"Yes. Yes. I know! I know!"

"Don't be so angry, Josie."

"Me? Angry?"

"So listen, will you? Now?"

"Can't we have an intelligent discussion around here? Besides the trouble with the land? The weather?"

"Come here. Sit right by me. Let us discuss the Führer. We must help the poor persecuted Jews in Germany? We must help Russia? Is that what you're trying to say?"

"We used to do those things. We used to be America."

"What's Russia to us? What's Germany to us? We have our troubles here. We're tightening our belts. Let's clean up our own backyard before we take on other people's woes—"

"Remember Apanlee? You used to think that Apanlee—"

"It isn't," said Jan slowly, now shuffling after Josie while she kept up her back to him, "as if they had to stay and suffer their calamities. Nobody made them stay in Russia. Nobody makes

Jews stay in Germany. When there is trouble, you just leave.
You just pack up and leave. My parents left. Your parents left.
The door is open. Why don't they just get up and leave, avoiding
all their woes—"

She swung around. She practically shrieked. "Then do what
you are advocating. How often must I beg? Let's go to California. Let's you and I and Rarey pack up and go to California."

"What on earth for?"

"There is no point in staying here. We need a brand new
start."

"Our place is here. In Mennotown. In Kansas."

"Sure! To the bitter end."

And so, that desperate, darkening summer, Jan tried to fit
together the pieces of a landscape which he no longer understood, despair beneath his eyelids, stubble on his chin.

Chapter 73

Jan had lots of time to take in rousing speeches. He took in several.

The government had solid plans, he learned, to pay the Kansas farmers to leave the soil untilled so as to save on fuel. That was a notion so preposterous it made Jan think that Dewey might be right: Who was behind the unions? Who was behind the country's worsening malaise?

Unspoken words. the Jews.

It wasn't violent or coarse. It was just there, edged in the craggy faces that centuries had carved. The Jews were Jews, the neighbors knew, and couldn't be reformed. The ancient blood of Christ could not redeem the Jews. They wanted your money to share with unworthy people, a thousand pardons, Josephine! Among themselves, they called each other liars, but linking hands, they swindled you out of your house and home.

Meanwhile, the feds had plans galore. The government assured the citizens of Mennotown via the wireless: the days of woe would end; the doldrums were a temporary phase. The country was resilient. The country would recover. The good times would be back.

Huge taxes were levied on wheat.

The farmers salted the earth with their tears. There was no sympathy in Washington for Kansas.

Stories are told of difficult days, wearisome days, which seemed to last forever. And still the drought dragged on. The future seemed darker than blindness.

The relatives watched in stunned silence as several bank officials came and repossessed three tractors that Jan had bought on credit a year before the fire.

A throbbing vein stood out on Jan's left temple. "I'll get them back," he said. "I know who is responsible. They're destroying from within."

This wasn't said out loud, but everybody knew, while watching White House bureaucrats spew lofty, silly notions: where the riffraff was gathering now, Jewish slogans could always be heard.

Jan came to that conclusion slowly. But there it was—he could no longer close his eyes; it was as Little Melly said: the banksters in New York had engineered America's demise so they could lend their money to the government to bail it out again.

He even said as much, to a round of stony faces who gathered at the Chamber.

The neighbors nodded, since he spoke their thoughts. They hadn't noticed it before, but now they noticed clearly: the Jews were everywhere. They always studied Christians with eyes of bitter envy.

What did they want? More blood.

They hid their eyes behind sunglasses. They never said: "Come. Share some bread and tea." They didn't say: "Come spend the day!" except perhaps to Josephine who still consoled herself with visits to the Finkelsteins, wasting long evenings in endless and futile discussion.

"How can you rob me of that joy?" she said to Jan, and he had no reply.

She went alone. He stayed behind. It was a dusty day. The

clouds hung very low, blotting out the sun. He was assailed by troubling thoughts and images, most all of which were gloomy.

Jan tried to focus on the inner light, but all was gray on gray.

His preacher, Jan discovered as days dragged on with no relief in sight, had a decided point.

"They are Jews from the day they are born. And that's how they die, still Jewish," said Dewey.

"There's not a single country in the world that does not hate the hook nose," was Dewey's point of view. "They push their origins of species."

Jan merely listened quietly, not up to any argument. Whether this was truth or merely rumor was very hard to tell, but logic made you leap to the conclusion that people so consistently, so universally disliked across the span of centuries must have brought that hatred on themselves.

The sun beat on the prairie brutally. The dust blew hard all summer. The worries of the grain belt deepened. The Oklahoma relatives stayed on.

Each Sunday, Dewey preached. The faithful hung their heads.

That, too, was part of the old covenant, part of the pattern of seeing one's life go around in a time-proven, time-tested loop. Once more, the Lord was testing them, but He was on their side. Regardless. Old Lizzy never doubted that. The covenant was hers.

She might be poor in copper pennies, but she was rich in certitude. Love and devotion for her Lord were welling in her heart. The Lord had never turned His face away from her. Why would He now? No way.

Life was a hurdle and a chore. A quarter had to stretch. You argued the greengrocer's prices. Keeping the gas meter down was a challenge.

From April to October, not a single drop of rain fell on Kansas. The rafters creaked and moaned.

Josie listened to her husband's footsteps in the middle of the night and knew: "The winds are stripping the top soil."

First died the corn as the dust clouds brought death to the plains.

The winter wheat was hardier; it struggled for a while, trying to anchor the soil, but it was a hopeless endeavor.

The wind blew hard. Dust swirled.

The thermometer soared.

Flies came in clouds and settled on the cattle.

Beans, potatoes, onions, turnips, cabbage, pumpkins, cucumbers, and melons—everything dried up. Cows went dry for lack of fodder. Laying hens stopped being laying hens.

The birds flew in panic before the black blizzards. Flivvers slid into dry ditches. Trains stalled, sometimes derailed. The train conductors could no longer see the warning signals, for all was black on black.

Each day, huge clouds of dust rolled over Mennotown, and not a ray of sun could pierce the dusty air. The winds downed several telephone poles, disrupting the lifeline of gossip. The chickens keeled over, beaks open, and died. The dogs lay, whimpering, their tails between their legs, and Lizzy's cattle huddled with curved backs and snorted with the effort of sucking in their breath.

Jan tried to ride his tractor once or twice, scorning every warning his heart would not hold out, armed with a set of goggles and a wet handkerchief across his creased, sand-pitted face, but he was back before noon.

The storm, said Jan, collapsing, just ripped the seed out of his hands, the plants out of his furrows, his heart out of his aching chest. His lungs were on fire. His eyes saw dust on dust.

He sat there, stupefied. The heat was such that it was hard to breathe.

"What's happening to us?" he asked repeatedly, to which no one could answer. The wind howled its reply.

It plucked stalk after stalk out by its roots. The dust storms came howling again, lifting the powder-dry soil in the east and dumping it over Mennotown, along the fences and into the orchards. The drifts of soil behind the beehives were higher than a man.

For an eternity, it seemed, no ray of sun broke through the flying dust of Kansas. The winds rose with the sun and died down with the sun, and all night long the Kansas soil fell down on Mennotown in spades.

A landscape bleak and bare!

It was, moaned Lizzy, coughing rackingly, the end of the world, the end of all life on this earth.

Old Lizzy was dying in earnest, surrounded by her loved ones, all visiting on Sunday afternoons despite the winds that would not be appeased, all praying with her patiently so she could stealthily pass on from life to death, from Faith to certainty as, gasp by gasp and day by day, her loyal heart gave out.

She sat silent, caved into herself, by the window, struggling for breath, moaning softly to herself so she would not disturb her grandson's aimless doodling. So let Rarey scribble maps of California while she was dying slowly—instead of sitting by her side and holding her old hand!

No one said a word.

The Hillsbury gravedigger blew in for a timely visit and stayed all afternoon, and Lizzy rose herself sufficiently to brew his coffee, coughing, and told him in detail, exactly, how to conduct his business.

"I promise you. Exactly as you wish."

She held up all ten of her fingers, though he could barely see, what with the dust that kept on swirling even in her kitchen. "Ten steps away from Herberts grave," she told him, coughing rackingly. This might be her last chance to make the most of widowhood.

"Nobody wants to be neglected, not even after death," she said repeatedly to Josephine. "I have few wishes left. I'd like to specify—"

But Josie only shrugged. It was as if a race had run its course.

There was no more to say.

Josie ran from room to room and fought the dust like a woman possessed. The day was thick with shadows. The darkness pressed against her window panes.

She tried to keep the windows shuttered, itself no easy task. She tried to seal her doors against the raging winds.

Each morning, long before the sun came up, she hung wet sheets in every crevice. And still the dust crept in.

Josie wet a kitchen towel, pressed it to her face so she could breathe easy without choking on the dust, and went out to look for mail, drawing it from the mailbox in a great puff of dust. She laid the batch beside Jan's morning coffee cup. The dust swirled all around it. She said to his bent back:

"Dewey's having a rain dance tonight."

"I know."

"Are you going, Jan? If so, don't count on me."

"Why not?"

"I still have to finish—"

What was it that she had to finish? The dust had choked that thought. Gray, choking dust was everywhere she looked: on her sills, in her dishes, on her lips that cracked and hurt.

Jan spoke up sharply then. "The Lord must be appeased."

"The Lord," said Josephine, "is nowhere to be seen."

She tried to tape the windows shut to keep the dust clouds out. She kept on wedging rags beneath her doors; she stuffed wet towels up the chimney. There was dust in her hair, dust in her eyes, dust on her tongue, dust in her soul.

And yet. What powered Josie, even then: her dream of California.

"Somewhere out there, there's California," said Josie to herself, for now she hardly ever spoke to anyone except her inner self. "It's hard to fathom, but somewhere, out there, in the far distance, an ocean still exists."

The relatives stepped up their prayers. Little Melly came over to help the good relatives pray. Together they sang and they prayed— their melodies painfully slow.

Josie kneaded her bread in a drawer so the relatives had something to eat. She kept the yeast she needed in a special Mason jar, the flour in a bucket with a lid. She tried to keep the lid shut, gumming it with tape and putty. But still the dust invaded her flour, her yeast.

When she made all those beds the Oklahoma relatives still occupied, she shook the dust off of the covers while they were busy, praying. They sapped her energy. The dust lay simply everywhere. There was dust in Josie's nostrils and gritty dust between her toes. There was grit ingrained in every finger joint, grit in her eyes, grit in her teeth.

She went to rinse her mouth each hour on the hour, but there was no relief from feeling filthy—as filthy and as helpless as she had felt in her whole life.

When Jan said: "Josie, will you please—" she said to Jan: "Shut up!"

When it was clear to all that Lizzy had finally caught a serious case of dust pneumonia and would not last the night, Jan moved his mother into Josie's bed. "Move over as far as you can."

"But it's my bed. It's the only privacy I have—"

"She needs someone to keep a careful eye on her. Just try to sleep lightly. I'll sleep on the couch."

So Josie moved over and Lizzy kept on dying. "Say something, lovey. Please. Say something," whimpered Lizzy. "Why don't you talk to me?" Old Lizzy couldn't understand why Josie wept so desperately when Lizzy tried so hard to do her best, to make herself as small as possible while she was busy dying.

In the end, Josie raised herself upon a tired elbow, saying softly: "I'll just spend the night sitting up. You can have the bed to yourself."

Jan sat in the dark by the window.

"I need to talk to you, " said Josie. "Jan, listen. Can we talk? I need to talk to you. I want to talk to you."

"So talk."

"What do you mean? How can we talk? We have no privacy. I am a stranger in my bed. I am a stranger in my kitchen. No matter where I step these days, I'm stepping on a praying mantis."

"They are my kin. They have no place to go. I cannot fail them now."

"There's always someone underfoot—"

"They're relatives."

"Why don't you send them back? It's not as if, these days, we have that much to share. Do we have any privacy at all where we can sit and talk?"

Jan shifted the weight on his heart. "I feel like a tree whose trunk has been hollowed. What have I done? Where have I sinned? I must repent, and so must you. It is our only chance."

A shriek sat deep in Josie's throat. She fought against it savagely. She managed to say this: "Religious prying is as indecent as probing body cavities. That's my opinion. Now you know."

"You are a total stranger."

"Jan, why are you sitting alone in the dark? Why don't you light a candle?"

"It costs too much."

"How you have changed."

"The seasons change. We change."

She had run out of words. She pulled up a chair and wiped across her burning eyes and tried to read his face.

"She's dying, finally," said Josie. "She's dying in my bed. I can't sleep in a bed where someone else is dying. This is my final word: get her out of my bed—"

Jan told her in a tone so cold that it sent shivers down her spine: "Tomorrow morning, eight o'clock, there's going to be a revival. I order you to come."

"Did you hear what I said? Your mother's dying in my bed—"

"It is her bed," said Jan. "You are her guest. Now hush."

"Jan, please—"

"Such battering as we've endured these past three years does not fall on the righteous. It falls on sinning souls so that they may repent. No doubt we sinned. I sinned. You sinned. We have no options left. We must repent or perish."

The silence grew and grew. Jan said at last: "And yet, I still remember you. When I kissed you, you tasted of sunshine and parsley. When I made love to you—"

"Enough."

"My love for you," said Jan, "was not a potato. Why did you throw it out the window? At least grant me an honest answer—"

"And once upon a time," said Josephine, and didn't think her heart could hold such grief, "I looked at life, I looked at love, much as a sculptor looks at marble. I was going to carve out a thing of great beauty. I was an artist once. I had such strength. I had such dreams. Your people broke my chisel. I will not let that happen to my son."

"Leave Rarey out of this. In truth—"

She felt as dry and barren as the soil, her soul as pitted as her windows. "In truth? You do not want to know the truth—"

"But I do. I cannot think of anything to give me more relief."

"All right. Here is the truth. You are like Abraham. You're cruel and unfeeling. Your God is vengeful, harsh and mean. You'll sacrifice your son as you have sacrificed your wife. For what? Tradition? Family? It's all a stranglehold—"

"There's nothing in this world," said Jan, "that's more important, next to Faith, than one's own loving family."

"So you will throw your own son to the wolves?"

"We are links in a chain. Spokes in a wheel. It's not just you and me and Rarey. It's everyone. It's more. We're kin. We're folk. We all belong together. Something is strangling us. What is it?"

"Just do yourself a favor and send those relatives away. As far as I'm concerned, they're just a bunch of strangers—"

"You are the stranger here."

"I now repeat: you'd rather throw your own son to the wolves?"

"I failed you. There's no doubt in my heart that I failed you. Yet I loved you. For so many years, I loved you and loved you and loved you—"

"Yes. By some sorry trick of fate," said Josephine, "you up and married me."

And yet another day. The worst. The sun's hard beams clubbed Mennotown. The howling winds brought ever-deepening disaster.

Day turned to night long before noon, and night became a nightmare. The soil lay thick on Lizzy's window sill, clung to her roof, crept through the smallest chinks. The earth was lifted to the sky, and then fell back on Mennotown and settled on its roofs, a suffocating blur.

It started choking everything.

It strangled Rarey's rabbits. It snuffed out Little Melly's honey bees. It suffocated Josie's last small shred of patience. And on that dark and muggy morning, finally, the dust clouds came and smothered Lizzy Neufeld. She died at ninety years of age. Her Savior did not hide from her the secret of longevity, but in the end, she died.

Chapter 74

They bedded Lizzy in the cracked and dusty ground, clothed in her finest chemise. The *Wichita Eagle* sent a reporter to tally the extended clan who stood around her grave in tears—a hundred and twenty-six souls.

The minister spoke suitably—an out-of-towner, sadly, for Dewey pulled his head between his shoulder blades and simply shook his head. This borrowed preacher, too, had known Old Lizzy well; he started coughing and then set to weeping and said he couldn't finish, and Doctorjay stepped up to Lizzy's grave and ended his sermon for him. Though his voice was gritty as the sand he felt between his teeth, the healer spoke with firm authority, and what he told the grieving people condensed the essence that was Lizzy by acclaim.

"A prairie pioneer," said Doctorjay, "has gone to meet her Maker. I vouch for this: if there are meadows in the sky, she'll always take two buckets."

Before the day wore down, Jan struggled through the dust to thank Little Melly for her support in his helpless and feverish days.

She spied him at once from her window.

"And how are you?" Jan asked, collapsing in a chair. "How are you holding up?"

"As well as can be expected." She tried pushing the cat from her lap. "And you?"

"Still that strange numbness in my fingers. The trees still sway. Sometimes I think that Josie might be right. I may have had a stroke."

"Impossible," said Little Melly, forcefully.

"How can you say that, Missy?"

A treacherous color crept into her face. "Had it been a stroke, Jan, you would not remember—"

Jan looked at her through sheets of gauze and thought: "Yes, I remember. I remember. I remember you gathering bluebells and poppies."

She looked at him through clouded eyes as well: "This old and broken man was once my sun-burned love."

"Of course. Of course I still remember everything," he told her softly, just sitting there, stroking one hand with the other. "We both remember. Don't we?"

Her nose and cheeks were red. Her hands were trembling badly. "How could we not remember? That's all that's left. Just memories."

"I am so tired, Missy."

"I wish I—" she said helplessly, and found no words to finish.

He said at last: "Let's talk about it finally. You know me well. You know that in my heart I never called you anything but Missy—"

She sputtered nonsense now. "When the Donoghues burned down your mill, you might have—might have suffered just a little embryo."

That jolted him. He leaned back in his chair. "A what?"

"An embryo. I looked it up in Doctorjay's fat doctor book."

A tiny smile sat in the corners of his mouth. "Don't try to

imitate. She isn't you. She's Josie. You are Missy. You mean an embolism, don't you?"

"I guess. Could be. It's all the same to me. It was no stroke, however. It's nothing, Jan. You will prevail. You'll overcome. You'll rally as you always do. We count on you, Jan Neufeld."

"Remember our squirrel hunts?" he said with a wry smile, since he could read her easily. "You were so little then you barely came up to my knees."

She cleared the dust coat from her throat: "See what I mean? It was no stroke. You do remember everything—"

"Yes, I remember everything."

She spoke against a wall of tears. "Things aren't going very well?"

"So-so."

"I heard you had to sell a wagon load of barley to buy your son a brand new set of brushes?"

" There was no point in waiting any longer."

The spinster's voice was out of breath as if she had been running up a hill. "That's not what I was told."

"Now, Missy. Missy. Missy."

"How is the *wunderkind*? Still stretching his own boundaries? Discovering frontiers?"

"He's gone. She's packed him off today. You know about his talent. She wrote to everybody and then some and helped him win that talent scholarship—"

"The modern Hebrew school?"

"Top-notch. Top-notch! Lord, how I'll miss the youngster! As soon as he's through junior high, she'll send him out to California—"

"Oh? California? You don't say. And whose idea was that?"

He said, after a long pause: "Your tongue is still as pointed as your needle. Oh, Missy. Just for once. Just don't let Josie be the scapegoat for all the sins of Israel." He looked at her. She looked at him, and in the end, she dropped her gaze. "Where, pray, is California?" asked Little Melly, and blew her nose into a carefully embroidered handkerchief. "No relatives live there.

What's wrong with Mennotown? What's wrong with our school? The primer, the Psalter and the prayer books are fine."

"Rarey will need more than Mennotown can offer. He is a bookish child. Besides—"

"Jan, how are you going to pay for all that nonsense?"

"Perhaps I could take out a loan—"

"She could have saved up for a rainy day," said Little Melly lamely. "Like everybody else."

Between long silences, he asked: "Are you all right? You don't look well."

"Angina. That's what it is. Angina. The Wichita doctors look grim."

"What's Doctorjay's opinion?"

"He came up with a tonic to thin and purify the blood."

"Well, are you taking it?"

"Of course."

Jan spoke into the fading day: "I failed you. Don't think that I don't know. I feel I ought to tell you. At least I owe you that. I failed you miserably. I should have looked harder to find you a husband. I made you miss out on so much. I let you down so bad—"

"Jan, no. Please. Don't. You never let me down. Just knowing you—"

"I let you down. I let her down. I loved you, Missy, but I loved Josie more." He took a trembling breath. "I was so much in love with her I didn't think my heart could hold it in. I know today that kind of love was wrong. But you—" He leaned forward, unfurling her cramped fingers. "—you, Missy, were always in my thoughts."

The spinster did not think she could survive his eyes. " I have my church. I have my duties. I belong to six charity clubs—"

"I broke your heart."

"My Savior mended it."

"You should have had ten children—"

"I have Dewey's grandchildren now. They all say their

prayers. They all do their chores. I love them all, but Archie—"
Her words tumbled over each other. "—Archie is my favorite. I
know he will go far. I look at him and know: I have to steer him
well. The Holy Spirit burns in him; he'll have to go and serve
the Lord in far-off places to drain off extra zeal. If he stays here,
in Mennotown, he'll split the church wide open."

"Let's not talk about Archie. Let's talk of you and me. I
failed you. God knows I know I failed you—"

She sighed and folded her hands: "You didn't, Jan. You didn't.
For, see? You were mine once." Her lip started trembling. "I
cannot tell you how that helps." Her hands were no longer her
own. She dropped a spool of thread. He bent to retrieve it for
her. She said to his bent neck: "What did she ever own that
wasn't mine to start?"

He stood. The words came by themselves.

"If only I had loved you half as much as you loved me, I
would have been a happy man. I wanted you to know that. Be
sure to take your tonic, hear? I better go—"

"Go where?" she asked, as they stood, face to face.

"Go home," said Jan. "Where else?"

The morning after Lizzy's funeral, Jan went to the Mennotown
Bank to apply for a government loan. Even after he made up his
mind, he kept rounding the block as though rounding the Horn,
and when he finally pushed back the door and stepped into the
building, he saw himself confronted by none other than a smirking Donoghue who sat behind a desk, on his lapel a pink Roosevelt
button.

With salary plus benefits behind his name and therefore in
fine fettle, this newly hired program agent flashed Jan a toothy
smile behind a walrus mustache.

"What's new, old chap? What brings you here? A little business, eh? Between the two of us?"

Jan knew at once: this is a man of cruelty and hatred. He told
the knave who, he had every reason to suspect, had thrown the
match that laid his life to ashes: "My Congress voted in a meas-

ure to help the farmers out. I am here to apply for the Barnyard Subsidy Loan."

The lout loved every minute. His eyes turned into narrow slits. "You've exhausted your savings account? Dear me. Dear me. How careless."

Jan wrought a meager smile that came from the pits of his shame. "Three devastating summers in a row—" He watched himself as though he watched a stranger. "I need a helping hand."

The Donoghue turned chatty. ""Don't we all wish for just a little rain? For just a tiny tinkle?"

Jan steadied himself, leaned forward, bit hard on his tongue, and endured. He spoke as calmly as he could, his heart wrung by affliction.

"I am a farmer, and in need. I need my government to lend a helping hand. I am not talking hand-outs. I am not talking charity. I want a loan. I am applying for a loan."

"You know the latest slogan? 'Sell an apple a day. Send the Depression away.'"

Laden as he was with sorrow and a headache pounding in his skull as though it were a hammer, Jan nonetheless said to himself: A punch would send this louse to Idaho. Aloud, he asked: "Don't waste my time. I'd like to see the papers."

The leftist started fingering some folders. He did not meet Jan's eyes. Three or four minutes ticked away. Here's what he said, at last, and in a careful voice:

"These days, broke farmers come a dime a dozen."

Jan's fists had gripped the desk. "I want the papers. Now."

The leftist's glance stopped darting back and forth and fixed itself on Jan's moist forehead. He gave a discreet smile. He flexed his fingers, snapping them as though for exercise, and finally said this: "Why throw good money after bad?"

"Give me the application forms. I said now. Not tomorrow."

"No, no. That's not how it's done. This eligibility business is tough. First, I must ask some qualifying questions. What are you doing, Mister, to better your position?"

"For this remark," said Jan, now leaning forward also, "you

should carry your nose in a sling."

The leftist spilled a bit of coffee on himself. "Well, now. Let's see. Let's see. No need to get so uppity. No need to get so huffy."

"I don't have all day."

"You're broke? Huh? Is that it? Your head is on the block? Well. You don't say! So. Now you're learning, finally, how other people feel. Say! Do you know that you may be entitled to some vouchers?"

"What vouchers?"

"To buy some surplus food the government stores up. At reasonable prices."

"I'm not broke. I still have land. I need a temporary lift. As soon as the weather improves—"

The grin was ear to ear. "In olden days, your money used to do some fancy cartwheels, I recall?"

"It's called the Barnyard Loan," said Jan, a study in restraint. "It's at attractive interest."

"I remember the wonderful things that you tried to do for the unfortunate people in Russia—" The agent gave his thigh a violent smack with the palm of his hand and leaned forward. "—while your own country's citizens went begging for a raise? Do you remember that? Are you still sending help abroad? Instead of taking care of your own needy folks at home?"

Jan had an odd sensation: he felt as though warm blood had started spurting from his neck. He asked between clenched teeth: "What's this about eligibility? What are the rules?"

"They vary. They vary. It all depends on how needy you are." The leftist regarded Jan as though he were a fish in an aquarium. "See this huge stack of paperwork? More than two hundred applications. Two hundred-some fat applications. I'll put you in line, but let me tell you! Forewarned is forearmed. You'll have to wait your turn. See this fat stack? Loan applications from all over Sedgwick County. Guys who all need a helping hand as badly as you do. Those hard-luck stories never stop. It gets kinda old, if you know what I mean—"

A searing headache split Jan's skull, but he had learned with Dewey's help: the task before him was humility. His undue pride and vanity had led to his demise. He struggled hard against the blur that threatened to destroy his vision. He heard the dust howl through the attic of the bank he had helped build in better days. His hands became fists. He leaned forward.

"Now. I said now."

"Let's do an inventory for a starter, shall we?" said the ruffian, all condescension suddenly. "Look, I'm here to help. Let's peer into a crystal ball. Let's see what we come up with. Let's take an inventory—"

"Inventory?"

"Inventory. Right."

"What of?"

"A list of things that you still own. Land. Buildings. Farm equipment. Livestock. All mortgaged, right? All mortgaged to the hilt?"

"Most everything I own," said Jan, a robot now, "is mortgaged. Mortgaged to the hilt. My land. My home. My livestock. My farm machinery."

The Donoghue had risen now and started circling him, feeling pleasantly giddy.

"My! My! I guess you'll have to face the music. How times have changed. How times have changed. It used to be that—"

"Now if you'll kindly hand me every piece of paper that I need—"

"Your interests and mine," the leftist told him next, "coincide in the most fortunate way. There's still that will. Contested, right? The lawyers have filed on it. But do you have the money to pay them? Advice is dear, these days. We might work out a deal."

"I don't know what you mean."

"Is there a chance at all that next year's harvest will be better?"

"If it rains before too long," said Jan, who started seeing sparks that flew in all directions, "I think I can salvage about six, seven bushels per acre. As things stand now, no more than two bushels per acre. About the same amount it took to seed the land—"

"That's all?"

Jan cleared his throat. "That's all."

"That's peanuts. Peanuts. That's not collateral. You're a cornered man."

Jan's eyes were moist with sweat. He struggled with his tongue. "I'm putting all my cards out on the table. Wheat dropped to thirty cents a bushel, and people think it might drop more—" Huge slabs of concrete kept on dropping off the walls and falling on Jan's head. Each blow caused waves of pain. "I need another year. I need a solid harvest."

"Well. Are you looking for a job? We have an unemployment roster. That might be what you need."

"I am not unemployed. I've never worked for anybody else."

"That is beside the point. Nobody is entitled for assistance who isn't looking for a job. You gotta look. You gotta do your part. Just for the record: You are now case zero-three-three-eight-eight-dash-zero-zero-zero. Funny, huh? Dash-zero-zero-zero?"

"If next year's harvest—"

"Well. That's just guesswork, at this point. Isn't it? Why guess what next year's harvest will be like? Might be as bad as now. These days, we can't depend on guesswork. That's not how it's done." The ruffian started twirling his pencil. "Let's see what we come up with. Let's see what we might do. Now that the old boys' club Republicans are gone, the rules are slightly changed. Now it's the Democrats." He flashed a toothy smile. "The Democrats are foursquare for the unions, mister. They help the little man."

Jan said with great effort: "I'm known to be a prudent man. I might have overtaxed my resources, but I have lived an honorable life. But ever since this dust began to blow—"

"If that rain ever comes," said his tormentor, and started laughing shrilly, "it's gonna rain some mudballs. He-he! Some mudballs. Mudballs! He-he-he. To count on rain is iffy—"

Jan waited for the laugh to die away. He put gnarled fists on the desk, next to the cigar cutter. "You listen hard," said Jan. "You listen hard and pass this on. I want my government to know that I fight hard with everything I have, and if that means that I and farmers like me—"

"The stars and stripes forever, right? Don't give me that baloney. How much do you owe? Altogether?"

"You don't want to know."

"I may not want to know," the Donoghue spoke softly, craning his neck and rubbing his temples, "and you, Jan Neufeld, may not feel like telling me. But now you have to, see?"

"What's that supposed to mean?"

The lout was chewing on his pencil. "See all these carbon copies? They'll pass through many hands. The county bureaucrats are tough. The state is not much better. And the feds! Let me warn you! The feds! Well, what can I say? They'll all assess your situation from every conceivable angle. They'll all want things specific. They'll want you to unbutton your troubles as a harlot unbuttons her blouse. Details. That's what it's all about. Details."

"What details?"

"The more details about your troubles you can give me right up front, the better off you'll be. Such as: what happened to your previous income?"

"You know there was a fire."

A wide grin, that was all. "I wouldn't know. I wasn't there."

Jan stared out the window. A dog slinked by outside, his back curbed stiff against the wind, its fur so matted with dust it was no longer possible to tell the original color. The agent examined himself in a mirror. Next, he consulted his calendar gravely. He stroked his whiskers thoughtfully. He spoke into the fading day:

"Look. Why not settle our private little business here and now and save ourselves a giant heap of trouble in the courts? Your land belongs to us. Your mother never bought it. It was a temporary lease. I'd like to win you over to my views. I know it was a sentimental thing with her, that piece of property on which she settled as a pioneer. But she's gone now. It's a new era. The rules are different now. For once, they favor the little guy. Let us see eye to eye—"

The silence started crackling. The leftist shifted in his seat and cast a furtive glance in the direction of the door.

But Jan was Jan, and Jan caught hold of his anger. "For fifty years, she told you no. You wouldn't listen. Or else, you didn't seem to hear. It's still the self-same rules. I am my mother's son. I guard her legacy."

"It's no, then? That's your final word?"

"You got it, buster! No!"

"Do you mind giving me a reason?'

"Because I am an honorable man. Because that land is mine."

"I know that. You know that. But do those guys in Washington know that? Details. Details. That's how the game is played."

"All right. I'll give you some details. For twenty-five years, I was the head of Mennotown. I controlled every Chamber of Commerce event. My folks will back me up politically."

"You think I am some left-wing slicker, huh?"

"I think," said Jan, and faced him squarely, "that you are as unappetizing as a runny egg. That's what I think. What do you think?"

"Here's what I think. You need some help. I'd like to help. Truly I would. But you have got to give me more specifics. How much do you owe? To whom? For how long? What are the repayment conditions? When have your barns been painted last–?"

"Not since the death of Christ."

"Do you have plans to paint them, then? Do you have cash to pay for paint? We need collateral in tip-top shape. Timetables. Regular reports. Give me a date when you will finish giving all your buildings, one by one, a brand new coat of paint."

"That," said Jan Neufeld, "is none of your damn business."

A sheen formed on the lackey's forehead. "But you are wrong. I'm afraid that's how it is. That's how the game is played. You've got to play it right. And time is running out. You've got to re-paint, and you've got to report that you did. Are you willing to put that in writing?"

"There's not a citizen in Mennotown who wouldn't vouch for me."

"I know that. You know that. But do the folks in Washington know that?"

"To hell with Washington," said Jan. The vein on his fore-head was swelling. He felt such stabs of searing heat behind the sockets of his eyes that he could barely move his head.

Through a white haze of blinding flashes his tormentor kept talking as though he were a wireless. "Look. Do I make the rules? I don't make the rules. I have to go by them. The rules have changed. He-he. The more details you give me, the better off you'll be. It's helpful if you show the proper attitude. The more details I have, the better I can work this application. Here are the forms. Lay it on thick, and I mean thick! Just lay it on the line. Now that we voted in the Democrats, we know that every-body has a chance, and I mean everybody. Everybody! Paupers have a chance. Drifters have a chance. Even whores and pimps and vagrants have a chance, as long as they are not too proud to put it all on paper. Hey, even union members have a chance. It's not like in the olden days. Not any more, my friend. Here, take these forms, and lay it on the line. Be sure to bear down hard—"

Outside, the wind did not let up. The sun was gone. The trees were coated gray. Jan started struggling with the forms.

"Don't leave out any blanks. A blank will cause a snag—"

"What is the difference," asked Jan slowly, "between hard-up and destitute?"

"Two percent. Two full percentage points. I mean, is that a scream?"

"I see."

"So you would like to qualify? Three thousand bucks? Three-zero-zero-zero? You've gotta be pulling my leg. Let's go back to a previous point. What do you have to offer as security for that size of a loan?"

"Four thousand bushels of wheat."

"Where?"

"In one of my Hillsboro silos."

"But don't you claim on Line Fourteen that your silo burned down to the ground? That you had no insurance?"

"All in all," said Jan, "I own some fourteen silos. One burned. I still have thirteen left."

"Are all those silos in your name?"

"Of course."

"Rumors about you are flying."

"What rumors?"

"That there might be another fire. If I were you, I'd think that over. Thoroughly. One of my brothers sells insurance. And speaking of collateral—how can you prove the grain is yours? It might be mortgaged also—"

"It is my grain because I say it is my grain. Nobody doubts my word."

"Oh, no?" The lout's desk was so dusty that he left finger-prints on everything he touched. "This town has many blabbermouths."

"You know me," said Jan Neufeld. "Now shut your mouth and let me finish this. My son-in-laws will gladly vouch for me. So will the Hansens and the Penners and the Friesens, and so will Doctorjay—"

"Those bureaucrats. Those bureaucrats. They'll want to verify the dot above the "i". The line across the "t". Everything. Inter-est. General taxes. Special assessments. Have you tried any-where else to get consolidation loans? If you want help, you can't conceal your books from the authorities. Just like I said: it's attitude. Let's see. Your liabilities: two mortgages. A hefty loan for farm machinery—never repaid! That debt you owe the blacksmith? Overdue! Back taxes? Due with interest! Small feed and seed loans? My-oh-my! Turned over for collection." He lifted heavy lids. "That's bad. That's terrible. That makes two minuses. The hardware company that let you have spare

tires for those tractors?" The agent suddenly leaned forward.
He kept on drumming his fingers. "Well. What about your mother's cows?"

For two seconds, there was a sharp and crackling silence as
happens before lightning strikes. Jan turned as pale as though a
giant hand had struck him in the temple. When he could speak
again, his voice was not his own.

"My mother's cows?"

"That's what this game is all about. To tell the truth, I heard
about your mom. I heard she passed away? A shame. A bloody,
bloody shame. What was it, now? The gout? She made such
wonderful *vareniki*, all smothered in rich cream. I remember her
cottage cheese dumplings. I need details about your mother's
cows to make a case for you—"

"The details are," said Jan, no longer telling his tormentor
but a sadistic universe while struggling through a cloud of helpless woe, "that I am feeding Russian thistles to my departed mother's cows—"

His mother's pride and joy! The herd that sprang from
Caroline! And now their bellies sagged, their flanks were hollow, their rib cages showed. Jan heard a small boy's tears in his
own voice: "Who'd want to buy my mother's cows?"

"Those cows will have to go. They are considered liquid
capital."

"What," asked Jan slowly, "did you say?"

"I said they have to go. Those cows will have to go. They
have to go before you qualify. There is no way that you can
qualify for government assistance with liquid assets to your
name."

"You can't be serious."

"We have to demonstrate," explained the sprightly Socialist
to Jan as though here was a choice between the paddle and no
supper, "that you are destitute. That you have run your farm into
the ground in such a way that you can't get that Barnyard Loan.
That you—"

Jan practically shouted. "But that's why I am here. I *want* that Barnyard Loan! I *need* that Barnyard Loan!"

"— that you don't qualify. We have to demonstrate you are so poor, you are so destitute, that you don't qualify for any kind of loan because we cannot trust you any more that you will pay us back."

"Of course I'll pay you back!"

The leftist kept on dusting the black blizzard from his trousers. "No, no. You still don't get it, mister. Now listen hard and pay attention. That's not why you are here. It's not the Barnyard Loan. You want a grant. That's free money, mister. You want to show the bureaucrats in Washington that you are poor. Too poor to feed your mother's cows. Too poor to feed your family. Too poor to sole your shoes. That is the only way to talk to bureaucrats in Washington these days."

Now it was ax on marrow. "Now wait a minute. Wait a minute. You mean to tell me I haven't suffered yet enough for my elected President, for whom I voted in good faith—?"

"You got it, mister! That's the game. That's how the game is played."

"What are you telling me? Some loafer off the streets would qualify? Some slothful derelict? Some lazy turkey who has never steered a plow? Who does not own a penny? Has never saved a penny? Will never earn a penny?"

"You got that, buddy! Right! They qualify. You don't."

"But I—I built this town! For almost half a century, with my own hands I helped lay out the streets of Mennotown! I cannot get this loan, you say? When every Amos, every Andy can?"

"That's what it all boils down to, yes." The leftist gave a cheeky smile. "Just any local yokel, yes. Not you. Three bucks per application."

Chapter 75

Jan cut across the vacant lot where Lizzy's sod house used to be. The gate to the corral creaked softly as he pushed it open with his foot.

"There, now," he said, his voice a little slurred. "I did not make the rules. I have to go by them—"

A giggle sat deep in his throat. He knew that it was there; he forced it down; he lost no time in getting down to business. He pulled his gun and started shooting, slowly and methodically. The cows fell, one by one. He took great care to keep the hide intact; it might still be of use.

"The evil out there, larger than the sum of good men's best intentions—" The words came by themselves. He did not know what those words meant, but they were something Josie might have said. She always talked like that. She talked in question marks and riddles.

He scanned the carcasses as though he were scanning the sea. It was as if there was someone standing beside him, and he must explain why he knew that an answer was there; he was soon to find out; a circle would come to a close.

He lowered his voice to a murmur.

"The Golden Rule," he said, "a trap. A joke. A scream. Why didn't it work out? Who's behind it all?" His throat was filled with bile. The giggle he kept fighting down rose from within as though it were a bubble. "—what do you do when all the walls are coming down? You rise to the occasion!"

That was what Little Melly used to say, her faith in him intact. She stood right next to him, and speaking from the vantage point of her neat, narrow, cramped existence, Little Melly was certainly right. He sensed her presence strongly. She had always been right; she would always be right; and he, who had loved her, had failed her.

How he had missed her loving message was still a mystery to him; that he failed her was no mystery. What was he doing with that insight? Humoring the Eskimos?

Another black blizzard was building. He trembled as though gusts of wind were blowing through his body. "There, now! That's done! I call on heaven to bear witness that the usurers won out—"

He left the still-twitching cadavers lying in the dust, plodding along the deserted dirt road, still giggling to himself at the absurdity of having tried and failed.

He crossed the railroad tracks. He had so loved them as a child because they smelled of tar and speed and progress and adventure—one train on the heels of another. The flashes in his brain lit up with childhood memories—memories like summer lightning.

"See here?" he said, and swept both arms in a wide arc. "See, Missy? What I built?" Where once a whistle stop had been— right at the spot where the old, panting locomotive always had to stop because it had to take in water—his hometown, Mennotown, now grew. "When I came here and started building Mennotown," he giggled to himself, "our government, no larger than a postal station, with just one man to guard the gates—"

He leaned against a spindly tree. He muttered to himself:

"In those good days, we knew where we were going. But now? Nobody knows. Nobody knows. We do not own the government. The hidden hand moves everything—"

He pondered that a bit. It didn't make much sense. The papers claimed the gutters of the White House had not been painted in four years; even the wooden sidewalks had been ripped away and burned. That gave him an odd satisfaction, just knowing that, in his despair, he did not stand alone.

He studied several peeling gutters as though they were the landscape of his life. "I must tell Josie that," he thought. He would ask Josie, too: "Just what went wrong? Between us?" And she would chip away his pride, as she had done before: "You ask? You treated me as though I carried a disease, when all I carried was a mind—"

He stood for a while at the corner of First Street and Main, next to a cardboard shelter. The town hall he had helped to build now looked as ravaged as his heart, as violated as the countryside. The doors were hanging from their hinges.

"Move aside, man! Move aside!" a cyclist yelled rudely, and pushed Jan off the sidewalk.

Jan stepped aside. "Sure. Sure. I'm sorry. I am sorry. I said that I am sorry." He heard himself, astonished. Here were the words that summarized his life: "I am so very sorry." He said them several times to make sure that the humility was there that he had lacked before.

He plodded on. The road was full of chuck holes. Somehow that was symbolic. Tall weeds grew out of cracks. Two taxis waited by the courthouse because there was no gasoline. One of the taxi drivers waved at him. "Hey, mister! Mister! Need a ride to paradise?"

Jan shook his head and kept on walking. "Not now," he said. "Not yet."

From a cheap, crackling radio came snatches of a song. Jan stopped and cocked an ear.

"*Easy come. Easy go-ho-ho-ho—*" Cole Porter, Josie's

favorite. The song brought on a shrieking giggle. "That's it!" he gasped. "That's it! A capital idea!"

He caught himself, steeled his spine and kept on weaving down the road. Night would soon be falling. Shortly, all the windows would be darkened, for Mennotown was short on oil, and now the county's coal supply was running out as well, and with it, electricity.

In a burst of a sudden bravado, he resolved to report to his wife. There was no nonsense about Josie. He would tell her that he had gone ahead, as he had been instructed by his government, and shot his mother's cows so Rarey could attend the artist camp. Perhaps she'd spare a smile.

He knew she would be pleased, though she might want to ply him with her pointed questions, while he would have to struggle telling her the many complicated reasons why it had taken him so long, why he had failed his mother's cows. He would tell her and slap his thighs: "The fat is in the fire! The fat is in the fire!" He hoped for her to praise his caveat. He yearned to have an audience for his story: how he had shot his mother's cows.

But even this was easier said than done.

A homeless man had rolled himself into a blanket and was blocking the door of the telephone booth with his back. Jan stood outside, his face pressed to the pane, and watched him for a while.

He shook his head with disbelief while taking in the man— his toes were coming through his boots; his face and hands were dirty. That gave the vagrant rights he might not otherwise have had? It must be so. He would not leave the booth. This world was upside down. Jan waved at him and shuffled on, forgetting about calling Josie.

He came to rest against a wall where several drifters had started a fire from the debris gleaned from the dried-out river bed. The derelicts sat by the curb, deep in a vitriolic argument.

Jan stopped to help them decide it. His chest had turned into a sea of flames, but could he let this golden opportunity pass by? The hoodlums smelled bad, but he knew they pleased God, for the humble inherited heaven.

He snapped his fingers to get their attention. "The fat," he said to them, "is in the fire, man. Is that a scream, or what?" This was too good a chance to waste. He was determined to seize it and release what was building within.

"The Socialists and Bolshies," he lectured the astonished derelicts, "have run America aground. Can you deny that fact?"

"Hey, mister! That's right! That's exactly right! If you dig deep enough, somewhere you'll find a Levi—"

"Some of my wife's best friends," said Jan self-righteously, "are Jewish. That is her one small oddity. But otherwise, she's beautiful. My Josie is astonishing—"

One of the younger vagrants winnowed. "Hey, mister! Tell us more!"

"She really is. The biggest charge that can be laid on her is that—" What was it now? Something inside his head was spinning. "Ah, yes! She cannot always tell the difference between a usurer and bankster—"

"Rubbish, your views," belched one of the old, shaggy vagrants. His teeth were rotten stumps. His trousers had a rip. In his lungs was the rattle of death. "Hey, mister! Mister! Ask yourself: is there a country in the world except America that tolerates the Jews? They hand you a free hot dog while skinning you alive."

"But on the other hand—"

The hobo tore the heel off of a piece of bread with dirty hands. "Here. Want to share with me? It's from the food bank, mister."

"Anything but anything," explained Jan to the derelict, now heating to the argument still swimming in some murky depths, "is better than the dole. The dole is not for us. We are the middle class. That's what we have to tell our senators and our congressman. That's my firm opinion. 'We voted you in,' we must say. 'And we can vote you out.' We are the ones that must tell our government: 'This hooligan business must stop.'"

"You want it? Here's a piece. It's barely mildewy."

"No. Thank you. Thank you very much." Jan was glad he

remembered his manners. "I couldn't possibly."

"I serve Socialism. So should you," the vagrant said aggressively.

"A lot of citizens," preached Jan, glad for the willing audience, "agree with you. They feel exactly as you do. Did you, by any chance, vote for this what's-his-name? The last election was crooked—"

The drifter's legs and feet were wrapped in coarse, frayed sacking. He was greedily slurping a brew. It steamed a bit and was brownish. "Crooked? Did you say crooked? What's that supposed to mean? I don't like the look on your face."

"If you will only listen, I'll explain—"

"What's more, I don't like the tone of your voice. Equality for all. Fraternity. And Liberty. That is my motto now. We'll fix this country yet!"

Jan sat down next to him. "Do you value a farmer's opinion?"

"Speak, man! Why not?" The drifter gave a wide, malicious grin.

"Anything, but anything," Jan told him in an august voice, "is better than the dole. That's what I'm trying to tell you."

"Hey, you!" the vagrant elbowed Jan. "Didn't you once belong to the Rotary Club?"

"I did. I did. At testimonial dinners they always honored me—"

"No! You don't say! I used to teach economics. Big joke, that. Huh?" The vagrant started pricking at a blister.

Jan watched as carefully as if watching a complicated operation. He rubbed his hands for emphasis: "That's what you were? An economics prof? Who would have thought? One of those fancy eggheads, right? One of those yahoos with their charts and theories?"

"The thing I resent most about you is your attitude, mister!"

"How dare you speak to me like that? I built this town. I used to awe the neighbors. Stand up and look me in the eye and tell me, man to man—" Jan grabbed him by the belt and started pulling him but found he had no strength. "Without me, there would be no town. I stood for all improvements. Why do you look at me like that? Nobody doubts my word."

"What is the matter with you, mister? You want to pick a fight?"

"Not really. No. I was just looking for a—"

"—you were just looking for a meal? Right? Just follow the arrow, man. Follow the arrow. Put your pride in your pocket, man! We're all in the same sinking boat. You've got to keep step with the times. Now scat!"

One of the drifters picked up a pebble and hurled it playfully at Jan. Here was a helpless victim, his mind just scrambled eggs.

"Get outta here! Go crawl into the earth!"

The others followed suit and started pelting Jan with little sticks and cones. They were the pack. He was alone. Here was some fun to break the day's monotony.

Jan stood there, not resisting, oblivious to their malice, fair game for any cruelty. He did not tell himself: "Their life is mud and toil and filth and ignorance. Why am I in their company? What have I done? What has gone wrong?" He let abuse rain down on him, his empty gaze fixed on their rags. In the end, they tired of their victim and their game.

"Hearty applause, that was my reward," explained Jan as a parting shot with twisted lips while leaning on the arrow. It pointed to eight words: "Soup kitchen. Address required. One free meal per day."

"That's Dewey's Dole," he told them, helpfully, in case they didn't know.

"That so?"

"Just take my word for it. I know the way," Jan told himself as though he were a stranger who had asked for directions of himself.

Jan kept on trekking on. He still felt dazed and lost. He passed by several neighbors standing in small groups on the cracked sidewalk next to the Janzen store, now boarded up as well.

"Hey, Jan! Come say hello!" They waved at him, inviting him to join them, but he ignored them haughtily.

They stared after him, fumbling for something to say, when Doctorjay came puffing up the road in his asthmatic flivver.

"*We're older now than we were ye-he-hesterday*," sang Doctorjay, offkey but with devotion, a one-man sing-along. "*But younger than tomo-ho-rrow—*"

He wore a huge Panama hat that partly blocked his vision, but, just in time, he spotted Jan, right through the pitted windshield—and, in a mirthful mood because of having run across a crony he hadn't seen in years and celebrating the occasion a little bit too lustily, he guessed where his flivver was heading, and almost ran over poor Jan.

"Watch out, you idiot! You! Watch out!"

He recognized Jan just in the nick of time and spun the motorcar around the curb at thirty miles an hour. He brought it to a screeching halt. He jumped out of his seat so he could pound Jan on the shoulder. A cloud of dust arose. The healer slung his arm across Jan's shoulder blades and yelled, a happy man:

"Look what I found! A neighbor! A companion!"

"You're rip-roaring drunk!" scolded Jan and waggled his finger as if he were Dewey.

"Forgive the aroma!" yelped Doctorjay. "That skunk had unfortunate timing. I plowed right over his tail. What a mess! What a stench! Old pal, you wanna take a ride to Wichita? I'm warning you. If you sit next to me, we'll both be stinking to high Heaven. What's one more skunk, right? More or less? Say, did you hear the latest joke about two skunks in competition with a flivver?"

"No."

"Well, then?"

"What?"

"Well, can I tell that joke to you?"

"Of course. Of course."

Oh, jeez. Now I forgot the punch line." Doctorjay looked at

Jan sideways and fell silent.

Before long, a dilemma arose. It was still early afternoon, but Doctorjay had tanked up on sufficient fire water so that the patriotic songs, never far away, now bubbled strongly to the fore. It was no fun to sing alone when one had company.

That was the reason Doctorjay took his huge foot off the gas pedal, pulled to the side, and peered at Jan suspiciously.

Jan's face was as gray as the sky.

"Onward! Onward, Christian Soldiers!" hummed the healer, unable to resist.

Jan smiled a shaky smile. "I'm just not in the mood." He shook his head and swallowed. The invisible fire was eating its way through his veins.

Doctorjay put out a clumsy feeler: "Cat's got your tongue, Jan? Anything wrong? Don't be a pessimist. It's just one bank. One measly bank. You're a man of reputation. You can go someplace else."

"How did you know," asked Jan, now snapping sharply to attention, "that I just paid a visit to the bank?"

This was not one of Doctorjay's perceptive days. He was too busy struggling with the songs that kept on leaping to his tongue. "You know this town. Word gets around."

"It does?"

"Well, don't you know we have a lot of blabbermouths?" belched Doctorjay, who knew no inhibition.

Jan's voice was murderous. "What do they say?"

"Cheer up, old chap. Cheer up! Admit defeat for once. What do the neighbors say? They say your credit is exhausted. Whose fault is that? Your own. Who chaired the Hoover-for-President-Club? You! Didn't you? Where was your judgment, man? In Hoover we trusted. Now we're busted. Say, Jan. What's that? What's bulging from your pocket?"

"That," said Jan Neufeld, "is a gun."

Something sat grinning between them. It sobered Doctorjay enough. He cleared his throat. "You wouldn't be so foolish, would you? You aren't courting nonsense, are you?"

"I just picked off my mother's cows."

"You did? What made you do that, Jan?"

"Well, as the song goes," Jan told his old friend, facing him, "Easy come and easy go."

"I bet you anything," cried Doctorjay, now rallying through fog, "that next week will be better. Next week will bring strong rain. July will break the drought. I smell the clouds already! Remember all those bumper crops? Your name will go down yet in Kansas history. . . "

"I worked for history," said Jan. "For more than half a century, I worked, believing I was making history. I tried to build a decent town where I could raise my children. I worked until I thought my arms were going to drop off—"

"I bet you my last quarter you will have wealth again with a Capital W. Come fall, your land will be bursting with kernels." A sly triumph sat suddenly in Doctorjay's red eyes. "Say, buddy! Listen! Listen! If I were you, you know what I would do? I'd go and try a limber shot of liquor—"

He put an old friend's hand right on Jan's knotty nape. He started rubbing with his thumb to soothe a hurting muscle. He practically moved himself to tears with sympathy.

"Look, now's the time. Old buddy, now's the time! I know the perfect hole. I have a nose for parlors. That stuff is balmy on the brain. There's nothing like it, Jan! What are we waiting for? Look, I won't snitch on you. Noralee would kill me from her grave, and Abigail will, too. She'll be wild is what she'll be! And Josie? Why, she'll be madder than a March hare!"

"If Josie only—"

"Right. Right, Well, never mind her. Nothing ventured, nothing gained. That's what I always say. Just try it, buddy, will you? It will do wonders for your spirit. Wonders! It'll take the edge off any worry. Just take my word for it—"

Doctorjay was snoring softly with his head next to his tumbler. Jan still sat straight, although the ceiling swayed.

"Look, Daddy," said the man behind the counter carefully. "This guy here? He's had it. He's snookered. Thoroughly. Did he come in with you? It's almost midnight now. I think I better call a cab—"

"This is my lifelong friend!"

"No! You don't say? This old lush here? Say! Aren't you the leader of the Hallelujah crowd?"

Jan slammed his fist so hard that all the glasses rattled. "Ha-ah! That's me! I'll have another serving of your giggly water."

"I thought so! See? I thought so! I knew you the moment you and your buddy here weaved in. Look, mister! Here's the door. I don't need your kinda trouble. Be good, now. Be nice. Take this old chap here by the collar and get him off my premises. Why don't you leave now? Right now? I don't need the police. Spare me your kinda trouble—!"

"I said," roared Jan, " that I want yet another drink! I want another drink this minute!"

"Give me that gun. I said give me that gun!"

"That is my gun! You can't have my gun!"

"There now. There now. You want to sit on it? Go right ahead and sit on it. Just you be sure it doesn't make an extra hole where you don't need it, right? Say, mister. Is this the first time that you ever had a drink? Are you a teetotaler? That's what your buddy claimed. He's always bragged he'd win that bet. He didn't make that up, did he?"

Jan snickered to himself. "He won it, and I lost. I lost. I lost."

"Naw! Shucks! Come on! It can't be all that bad."

"For fifty years he badgered me," Jan whined in a small voice. "He badgered me and badgered me, but I held out! I never once gave in! I had strong principles. Can you believe it? Fifty years? I mean, is that a scream? You don't believe me? Why do you look so skeptical? I don't like that smirk on your face."

"I believe you. Mister, I believe you. Sure. Why not? Anything you say."

"Then why—why are you looking at me like that?"

The man behind the counter took Jan firmly by the sleeve. "It's time to call it a night. Just leave, I said. Leave by the side door, will you? I'll try to sober up your friend on my old couch."

"I wanna sing," shouted the bonesetter, reviving suddenly. "You wanna sing with me?"

"Sure," said Jan, slurred, and tried to put his arm around his shoulders. "This is my friend. Don't anybody touch my friend."

"Just one more song," decided Doctorjay. "*I get a kick out of you—hoo—hoo—hoo!*"

"What a fine song!" shouted Jan. "Say that again? Again?"

"*I get a kick out of you—hoo-hoo—*" Doctorjay started sobbing, totally drunk, head rolling on his shoulder. "I wanna die. Why don't you let me die?"

The bartender, taking Jan's elbow, tried steering him out the door.

"See that hotel across the street? Ten stories high? Maybe they'll let you sleep it off. Just tell them who you are. Tell them you come from Mennotown. That name's still good for a few miles. Maybe they'll give you credit. Just don't fall out the window, mister—"

Dewey was just about ready to close out his bean-and-celery day when he looked up and saw Jan standing in the door, barefoot and muddy, head to toe, both shoes on a stick slung over his shoulder.

"Jan," Dewey cried, "what are you doing here this late? Did Josie chase you away with a broom?"

"Just visiting. Just visiting." A mad gleam lodged in Jan's left eye; the right was closed and turning purplish.

"Here, have a cup of good, strong coffee," shouted Dewey as if Jan couldn't hear. "Come in. Come in. Sit down. I heard the bankster turned you down? That's a shame, Jan. What a shame. Watch out! That coffee cup is hot!"

"Who told you that the bankster turned me down?"

"Word gets around," said Dewey loftily. "There! Did you burn yourself?" Dewey flared his nostrils expertly and sniffed.

"Say, isn't that the giggly water that I smell? Jan? Jan, you didn't! What will the deacons say? Here, let me help you. Sit down. I said sit down! Here's a hot bowl of soup for you. I'm just about ready to call it a day. We close at midnight now, what with the added numbers. Say! Isn't that fantastic soup? Just go ahead. Here. Be my guest. Let me put something healthy in your stomach for a change—"

Jan fell into a rhythmic chant. "Fan-tas-tic soup. Fan-tas-tic soup."

"That's Little Melly's recipe," said Dewey pointedly. "Thanks to her recipes, I get excellent press for my work. Oh, that reminds me. That reminds me. There is a fellow from the *Eagle* still fixing to come by—"

Jan started spooning soup. Curtains of cobwebs, thick with dust, were hanging from the ceiling. Between spoonfuls he managed to say: "Can I just hang around a bit? I can't go home like this. I think I am a little soused—"

"That's putting it politely."

"Don't tell my wife. Do me a favor, will you? I can't face going home. Say, this old cup of soup is really, really excellent—"

"Say what you will about the Democrats. They don't skimp on the vegetables."

"You can say that again."

"See that odd fellow over there?" whispered Dewey. "Just yesterday, the richest man in Hillsboro. And now? Not one red penny to his name. That's earthly vanity for you. You draw your own conclusions."

"You're right. That's earthly vanity—"

"I still remember him. A cheapskate. A real cheapskate. Had all those silver dollars stacked away, but stingy with the hat. No ten percenter, he. Not even five percent. And now? Just look at him. See how the Lord will force humility? Jan, are you sure you are okay? You want another ladle? Here, let me have that bowl. I'll fill it up again—"

"I'm fine," said Jan. He forced down waves of nausea. "I

beg of you. Don't tell my wife. She'll draw the wrong conclusions."

"She always does. She has her theories."

"I don't quite know what happened. I think my cold forced
me to look for warmth. That's why I tried the giggly juice—"

"A cold," lectured Dewey, not one to miss an opportunity to
steer a sinner right, "can turn into pneumonia. And pretty soon
to death. A terrible disease. Take dust pneumonia—"

Jan's tongue had turned into a snake. It reared its head and
hissed: "Shut up! Shut-up-shut-up-shut-up!"

This outburst startled Dewey Epp. "Compose yourself! Compose yourself!"

Jan all but shrieked. "Shut-up-shut-up-shut-up! Shut up!
Shut up about my mother. Shut up about my mother's cows—"

The feeding hall was crowded still with beggars. Three or
four craned their necks. They pressed close on the steps and
outside and watched as Dewey pulled his lower lip into a pout
and started blowing steam as though he were a locomotive.

"Well, pardon me! Pardon me if I managed to step on your
bunions! What did I say to make you mad? I didn't say a word!
You lost your bet? Is that what's eating you? Some people never
learn. Well, sober up. Admit defeat for once. You lost! Now
take it like a man. Would you mind giving me a hand? Here's a
broom. Just start with the entrance. You think this is a picnic?
It's hard to feed these bums! Hard work, the credit always be the
Lord's! But they're learning, man. They're learning. They're
learning to take themselves to their Savior for comfort. See that
latch over there? Just push it shut, will you? It's time to call it a
day. My hemorrhoids are killing me. Man! Have you ever seen
a dirtier place? Just sweep behind those barrels, will you? There!
Thank you! Thank you very much! That ought to do it for now!
Let's call it a day. The Lord will find a way. Why be a worrywart?
Stop worrying! Things will pick up. Now that we voted in the
Roosevelts, they'll fix the business cycle. They'll stabilize the
currency. There now! That ought to do it for today. Except for
the lists. We still have to finish the lists. I've got to keep those

lists, you understand? Account for every penny? You know how it is. You know what those bureaucrats are like. They always want details. This eligibility business is tough. They want accounting in quadruplicate. Oh, hi there! Hi there! Come on in! Come in! I didn't think you'd make it—"

A reporter stood in the door. "I'm looking for a guy named Dewey Epp. Epp as in E-pee-pee."

"That's me!" laughed Dewey. "Hey! Say! Is that a rhyme? Is that a rhyme? Ee-pee-pee!"

"Too late to take some pictures?" the young reporter asked.

"No. Jan, do you mind?" The preacher fished a pencil from his apron. "Here. Put your name right on this line. Right on the dotted line, I said just put your Friedrich Wilhelm there! Those bureaucrats are tough. They'll all want things specific. There's nothing like good press. It keeps the nickels raining—"

"Just what exactly," said Jan slowly, "are you saying, Dewey Ee-pee-pee?"

"Well," pouted Dewey, much annoyed. "You had your bowl of soup at government expense. Did you, or did you not?"

Jan forced the words. "You don't mean that! You don't!"

"Well, Mr. High-and-Mighty!" cried Dewey, piqued, and blew his allergies with vigor into a flowered handkerchief that Little Melly had embroidered recently, without an inch of wasted thread. "If you don't like my way, why don't you take your handouts from the Methodists and Presbyt—?"

That's when Jan's heart exploded. That's when the bullet flew.

Chapter 76

The jail guard blew his nose by using thumb and index finger. He smelled of soap suds and wet rags.

"Say! Is it true you shot a preacher? To tell the truth, I've often felt like doing that myself. The stuff they lay on you is drivel, nothing else—that's what I always say!"

"What day is it?" asked Jan, and put trembling fingers to his brow. His body ached all over, but every shred of memory was gone.

The guard gave Jan a little shove. "What day? You mean what date? Say, mister: are you daft?" His daily arrestees were barefoot vagrants who merited no more reflection than an unpleasant epidemic of fleas, but this arrest was different; it jolted him agreeably. "It's August first, man. August first. What did the preacher do that made you mad enough to pull a gun on him?"

Jan had the odd sensation that he addressed an audience to whom he must account. "He said to me: 'Here's the abacus. Now go ahead. Compute the measure of your losses.'"

"Come on. Move—will you? This ain't the Hilton, mister!" The guard wiped his nose on the sleeve of his shirt. "Move along, now, mister. Move along—"

"—the measure of your losses. And when I did, he climbed up on a chair to get a better view."

The guard gave out a hearty snort. "That's how they are. That's how they roll their nuts, if you know what I mean. By voyeuring your misery. You got a family?"

Jan shook his head. "Not any more." The air was stifling hot; the sky above was ink.

"Now drop your pants. At your age, no need to be squeamish. Here, raise your arms. It's just some powerful insecticide. Just as I said—this ain't the Hilton, but, on the other hand—man, listen! Chin up! It isn't all that bad—"

While Jan stood, shivering, obeying, the guard was prattling on.

"At least you got some shelter at Uncle Sam's expense. At least you'll get three meals. I know some folks who get themselves in trouble just for a place to sleep. Well. As they say. Here! Let me help you, mister. You look as though somebody said about you: There stands the cad who has betrayed us all!"

Jan flinched as though he'd been hit. "What did you say? How can you tell?"

"Just guessing, man. Just guessing." He steered Jan by the elbow. "This way to the hellhole, if you'll pardon my French."

Jan steadied himself as he moved. Along both sides of the narrow corridor ran a thick platform with a rail; he saw a rusty washing trough built into a niche in the wall. He stopped and said apologetically: "If you don't mind, let me just wash my hands—"

"No time for dawdling, mister—"

The key turned twice. Then it was dark. Jan leaned exhaustedly against the wall; it was warm as an oven and sticky with moisture. A light bulb swayed forlornly.

"Could I please have a glass of clean, cold water?"

"Less fluid, less need to empty the bucket," the guard spoke through the slit and sauntered down the hall.

Jan sat on the cot for a while, a numb and patient pauper. A pail without a lid sat prominently in the corner, smeared at the edges with dried excrement. A small, grilled window to his right outlined a sky without a single star.

"Here," said the guard, returning. "I changed my mind. It isn't much. It's just a bite. A piece of turkey and some bread. Look, try to get some solids in your stomach, mister—"

"I'm not that hungry. I'm just cold."

"Sober up, man! Sober up! You might as well put something in your stomach."

Jan wrapped himself in the thin blanket that lay at the foot of his cot. The prison guard watched for a while. "Are you nuts? It's stifling hot outside—"

"It is?" Jan kept trembling as though stricken by violent fever.

"Dog days of August, man! Dog days of August!" The guard felt a surge of pity. He was fishing for something to say.

"Hey. Let me cheer you up," he said at length and scratched himself with gusto. "You need some cheering up? You want to hear the latest? They say the picture of a girl in a white hat jumped from the wireless straight up into the inside of a plane. Can you believe a thing like that? I'm telling you. That's progress. Progress with a capital P—"

As if resisting an unwelcome current, Jan clung to the frame of his cot. Some unseen, growing force seemed to be pulling him into a black and swirling hole. He said in a barely audible voice: "I no longer belong. I want the good old days. I want no part of progress."

Even before the break of dawn, Doctorjay turned up at the jail house, parting the air with his powerful fists. In tow were Jan's six daughters' husbands, four neighbors with dangling suspenders, two relatives from Oklahoma, young Rarey, and Mennotown's three councilmen.

The group surrounded Jan, who stood defenseless and bewildered. No one knew what to say.

Doctorjay kept clearing his throat and finally said, in a voice choked with woe: "Will you ever forgive an old donkey like me?"

Huge tears were welling up in Rarey. "I've broken all my brushes. I've been a pampered baby for too long."

Jan's sons-in-law pressed closer, creating a protective wall. "Dad! Don't you worry. Don't you worry. The neighbors all came running! We've put up every penny of your bail. It's all arranged already—"

The Oklahomans lied: "We've come into some windfall money. We'll pay the bond. We'll put you up in the hotel, with just one guard outside."

The councilmen spoke in one voice: "You'll be alone. No one to bother you. Your lawyer is already on his way—"

Jan stood, ringed by his relatives and friends, and said when he could speak again: "I want a top floor room."

The congregation, gray with sorrow, buried both—the Preacher Dewey first, and then Jan Neufeld, the man who founded Mennotown, a sorry suicide.

A sackful of tears for the preacher, and for Jan Neufeld this: a hushed, apologetic eulogy delivered by a Unitarian. The dead man had been popular, but even so, it proved impossible to find a willing Elder. The town was in deep shock—but still: a suicide was a suicide and could not properly be called by any other name. It was a shock that rocked them like an earthquake. There was no way to summarize the depths of the disaster until the Lord spoke up.

He spoke to His people with howling and whistling and thunder and lightning and buckets of raindrops that lasted a day and a night. When finally the Lord fell silent, the dust bowl was gone. The earth would renew. The terror had come to an end. While Doctorjay still fended off reporters, the black winds slackened and diminished. Horizon to horizon, the sky turned soft and smooth. The roofs of Mennotown lay glittering once more. The rivers overflowed. They say that not a trace of dust remained in all the state of Kansas.

The rains brought such relief that for three days the stars and stripes snapped in the breeze in gratitude, and somewhere in the distance, a radio blared to passersby that happy days were here again. Again.

As the faithful gathered in the church that Jan had built for Dewey Epp, Mennotown lay flush against the earth, awash in blinding sunlight, the first time in three years. It was a sparkling day. The long-expected miracle had happened: a soft and gentle rain had silenced the tornadoes and made the brown earth willing to accept Jan's loyal, broken bones.

The people watched the rain and knew the Lord wept over Jan, as He wept over Dewey, and now they felt that they could, too—weep over both, with equal grief. And weep they did, and that felt good. When finally the rain was spent, when all the tears had fallen, the clouds outside looked fluffed like Lizzy's legendary feather beds. The sky was very blue, and smelling like clean laundry. The boiling haze was gone.

"Let us not judge but understand," the Unitarian now intoned while standing on paper-thin soles, uncertain of heaven and hell. "For only as we understand our fellow man, can we be understood—"

He pulled out a poem and told them of things that were not of this earth, while the mourners kept dabbing tears from their eyes and casting cold glances at Josie.

The sanctuary was packed, but all hung back, preferring the rear pews. No one was willing to sit next to Josephine, whose husband had seen fit to hurl his broken heart past seven rows of blind, cracked windows, down to the sidewalk, with a thud.

The papers, busy with the tragedy, had claimed, in smarmy words, that chances were the giggle juice had pulled the trigger, that the Depression was at fault. There was no doubt: She knew a deeper truth. She was dressed in her suffragette yellow.

Prying eyes were rifling Josie's face, but she paid no attention. It was as if her husband's death had let her lean her cheek against a slab of marble to feel its smoothness and its strength. It was as though she, too, had knelt beside a crystal spring and washed the night from her red eyes. She looked as though, once blinded, now she saw.

"Suffering is like a filter," the Unitarian proffered next. "It purifies all thought—" He started speaking gently of the glory of a sunset and the stillness of the night. As many mourners yesterday had listened and heard the eulogy for Dewey, so now they did for Jan: in fact, subtract the third and fourth rows where the progressives perched, stiff with self-consciousness, their glances in their laps, subtract the differences in sermons, the mourners were the same.

And yet, the universe had split apart, revealing the abyss.

All eyes were glued on Josie. She looked like a bird that had stared down the mouth of a cannon. She sat there, a slim, ramrod woman, erect in the very first row, and to her left sat Rarey.

She held the youngster's hand. Now and then she whispered something in his ear that made him struggle even harder against the tears. Behind them, two rows of the pews were completely empty. Her closest relatives sat in the third. But she was not alone, for to her right sat Doctorjay whose face was almost purple, and he was staring straight ahead.

He sat as close to Josephine as he could scoot inside a church and not risk snickers for his boldness. The mourners, like a wall, had drawn aside as he stalked in, now sobered to his bones. He paid nobody heed. He plunked himself right next to Josephine, and there he sat, and there he stayed. The congregation blanched.

At intervals, the widow turned full face to him and smiled a grateful smile. Her wonted wealth of words had flown from her bold tongue. She sat upright, as though at attention, as if her ear were cocked.

The impact of the shock had altered Josie's face. The mourners clearly saw the grief and rue and anguish in that well-cut, aging profile, the total disbelief. She was bracing herself for what now was to come. You could tell: she had finally used up her luck.

"He was much loved, and will be missed," the Unitarian said, and Little Melly, well-practiced when it came to shedding tears, at that point started leaking. Her parched heart, too; it counted, too; it cried out for some heartfelt release. She watched the widow through the tears that kept on welling up beneath her lowered lashes. She fumbled for her handkerchief. This was as sweet as honey, as bitter as quinine. She took her time to savor every nuance. There was no special hurry. Dewey was no longer there to shake a warning finger, but that Josie's punishment was overdue was very clear to Little Melly as well as everybody else.

The spinster had gone to her knees to seek guidance the previous night, and now she sat and waited. And to herself she said: "Her measure has run out."

Little Melly was as drained as any bride at last allowed to leave the wedding bed. She sat in the next-to-last row. She had helped bury Dewey, whom she had raised, her junior by seven years, and she had wept for him, adding her share to all these heaving sobs around his open casket, up front and in full view.

Jan's casket stood alone. Laid out in splendor, true!—but closed.

"Give us the strength to accept the things we cannot change—" the Unitarian said, passing the Good Book by and claiming, merely sideways, that Jesus was a noble man and Jan's beloved model, without admitting even once: He was the one and only Savior without whom life and death lost all design. All Unitarians were like that.

As Little Melly sat and listened to the garbled message, she slowly grasped at last what she had struggled all along to comprehend: it took a tragedy of this enormity for Josie to come to her senses, and thus, in a round-about way, prove Little Melly right.

"—to change the things we can, and the wisdom to know the difference," the Unitarian preacher sorrowed. "Let the bow in the Archer's hands be for gladness, for as He loves the arrow that flies—"

434   Ingrid Rimland

The spinster's face jerked violently at the assault of unaccustomed thought. Her flitting glances settled on the healer's checkered tie which seemed to strangle him, restricting his Adam's apple. It hopped around in protest as though it danced the jitterbug. His bushy eyebrows bounced.

"That's Doctorjay," thought Little Melly, with such a surge of gall she briefly lost her place within her prayer book. "He can't leave well enough alone! Not even now. He's always been her champion. Why can't he, just for once—?"

And it was true. It was unbearable. The bonesetter looked desperately ill-at-ease as if a fly were sitting on his nose, and yet he showed resolve. There was a somber will. There was such fury in his face that it made Abigail, who sat with several of her own far in the back, chew on her lower lip and fumble with her collar.

The healer didn't move. He sat there, next to Josie, and Little Melly sensed he had the constitution of a bull. It was so quiet in the church a fly could just have zipped around and landed anywhere. She saw it very clearly; she was that overwrought. She longed to swat it with her prayer book. There was no fly, of course; her mind imagined it. The rain had washed them into the gutters. She wanted to reach out and smack it hard and cause a small explosion, to ease the tension in the church the Unitarian had brought on, but she sat rooted to her pew.

"—so He loves also the bow that is stable."

Little Melly's bosom started heaving with emotion. Finally! Oh, finally! The focus was on Him. Up to this point, she wasn't even sure if those were Gospel words or someone's watered-down opinion.

"Let us now sing," suggested Archibald, and rose out of his pew. The Unitarian was wrapping up, and Archie took his place to fill in for his father and give Jan his good-bye.

"All right. All right. That's it!" He gave the Unitarian a helpful nudge right down the steps and launched himself into protracted amens. His good eye was glassy and cold, like a bird's. His bad eye was swollen and closed.

There was a moment's silence, and then the faithful rose and started filing past Jan's casket, while Archibald commenced to sing:

"Von der Eh-he-herde reiß mich los,
mache mei-hei-heinen Glauben groß—"

The congregation joined obligingly, the service drawing to its close. It was a fitting song to close a funeral, expressing keen emotions. The relatives kept rubbing at their eyes, and Little Melly knew: that tested song contained enough bad memories to hurt Jan's widow like the blazes.

Out in the sunshine, Josie stood, alone. The faces around her were wooden. The papers to foreclose the homestead were now on file in court. Jan had been king on Appian Way. Now he was dead. All earthly power was in vain. His kingdom would be blown to bits. You could already sense it: the Donoghues were fingering their cash.

The banker now stepped forward. He told the widow, as they stood upon the steps of Dewey's church that Jan had built in better days when money still was plentiful: "My patience has run out." He told her, loud enough so that the farthest row inside could hear: "A week. That's all that I can give you. Believe me. The matter is out of my hands. Here is your carbon copy."

Her voice was cold and even: "You do what you must do."

"The paperwork alone is eating up our profit. If I were you, I wouldn't count on anything. This week alone, the bank has had nine foreclosures. "

"She has one friend. That's me," said Doctorjay, now stepping up, his eyes two narrow slits.

"You've got to have the money, buddy," said the banker. He clasped both hands in front of him as though he were a priest reciting litanies: "Cash, man! That's where it's at. Jan Neufeld was indebted to the hilt. Three lifetimes wouldn't be enough to repay all the money he borrowed. You've got to have the cash. To pay the bank. To pay back taxes. To pay redemption fees."

The folks exchanged grave looks. If glances could have

murdered, that banker would have had ten thousand arrows in his back.

"There's no free wool with which to make your breeches," the banker said, and turned to throw his parting shot right over his left shoulder. "Don't expect any favors from me."

All through the night, Josie hunched over unpaid bills by the light of the kerosene lamp, for the utility had sent a man to cut off electricity. She worked with concentration. Now dawn was breaking gently. The sky was coloring slowly. It would be a sun-flooded day.

Rarey huddled at her feet, clad in his striped pajamas. He never left her side. His mind was spinning with fatigue, but he refused the couch.

She bent to him. Her heart just melted at his sight—his tousled hair, his narrow shoulders. She wrapped both arms around him; he buried his face in her lap. Both sat in the parlor in silence.

At long last, Josie said: "No matter where I look, it's like curing one illness with the help of five doctors. If I rob Peter to pay Paul—"

"We'll find a way," said her young son. "I don't need private lessons."

"No, darling. No. I'd like for us to leave. If we stay here, you will have to shoulder a load that belongs on the back of a man. The bankster and the Donoghues will put us out of business."

"We'll manage, Mom. We're family."

"I don't think so," said Josie.

In the slow-breaking dawn, the twelve-year-old looked up. He was so pale he was translucent. "I'll take a paper route—"

She could not help herself; the words kept spilling out: "What did I ever want of life? I wanted for your paintings to be as colorful as anemones. How could that have been wrong?"

His head lay on her knees, his arms were wrapped around her tired body. He lifted a determined chin.

"There's Doctorjay. He said he'd find a way—"

"He's a good friend, but he's not a sorcerer. He'd help us if he could, but Doctorjay has not an extra penny to his name. His fortunes, too, are shattered. And now there's Abigail. He's thrown in his lot with Abigail."

"Don't worry, Mom. Please, Mom. Don't cry because—"

"I am not crying, darling. My tears fell years ago."

She filled her lungs with morning air, and something deep within stopped trembling.

"I'm looking at realities. No matter where I look, I can't see a way out. I cannot keep the farm. Let's focus on your talent, Rarey. Let's leave with heads held high. Thank God that your sisters are grown. They don't need me. They never did. They have their husbands, their families, their embroidery and their *vareniki*. It will be you and me and your fine talent, Rarey. I knew from the beginning you were special. I will let nothing, no one steal your talent. You are bright; you confounded the Mennotown teachers."

"But, Mom—"

"Here's what I see: I can try to rescue your farm, or I can try to rescue your talent. I cannot do both. I don't have the strength to do both. I have to decide. I want you to help me decide. I'm not an alchemist. I can't work miracles. I am no longer young. Were I still young, it would be different. But I—I missed so much. I should have learned to run a farm, to run a business. I asked to learn. Right up until the eve of bankruptcy I begged your father daily—"

A lifetime filled with offering her gifts to hostile minds and hearts! She caught herself and swallowed down what crowded on her tongue. Instead she said:

"The Donoghues will get the farm. That has already been decided. There's nothing we can do. They'll get a grant. They have their fingers in the nation's kitty." She steeled herself. "The best that I can hope for is for a little pocket cash. If we sell everything, we can repay our bills. We'll walk away with honor. We'll walk with heads held high. Let's cut our losses, Rarey. It's

better late than never. We'll find another home. We'll go to
California."

Her young son's body clung to her as though he were a burr.
"We can't do that."

"Ah, but we can. We can. That's what I'm telling you." To
the ends of the earth she would go! The words spilled from a
well she had dammed for so long she had forgotten how her feelings could rush, surge, sing, shout with wonderful release. "It's
not about today! It's not about tomorrow! It started years ago.
And all because my heart was speaking in a language all its own!"

It now was almost day; she didn't even notice; she turned up
the wick; she poured herself into her young son's eyes, for it was
now or never. The shackles of a lifetime fell away. "Had I not
grown, I would have fit in nicely. But I grew. I wasn't a man, but
I grew. I kept searching for meaning, for knowledge. Your father did not die a torn or broken man because of me. And not
because of you, my darling. Don't ever think that it was you.
Don't ever for a moment think it was because he could not pay
your lessons. He didn't even die because he ended on the dole.
Not even that! He died because he overstepped his boundaries.
He fell in love with me and stepped out of the herd." She filled
the last cell of her lungs with air and said: "He loved me! And so
what! Fools love. But intelligent people admire."

Her son was staring at her now, unblinking, but she had more
to say.

"That's what it's all about. Respect. Not love. Respect. And
admiration! You have two choices with the herd: you're either
brutalized, or else you learn to brutalize. Chiefly, you brutalize
yourself. Listen! I wish you were older, but I can't hold back.
Your father and I were young once. We weren't married then,
but we were very much in love. Your father held me in his arms,
and I was shimmering with life. I had no choice. I said: Yes.
Yes. The wind kept on ruffling his sheaves—"

The years fell away. She was fifteen again, and there was
molten lava in her body.

"My feelings for your father on that day were deep and strong

and true. I thought that I was beautiful. I longed for admiration.
I longed to lose myself. Of that, there came a child. A little boy.
A little miracle. I loved him so. But they had only darts. Their
poisoned darts flew every which way, and some of them went
deep. Some went so deep that they became a part of me, a scarred
and poisoned part of me, and by and by, I lost my radiance—"

"My father—"

"Your father? Your father? I could have been his, for the
asking. I was there, in the palm of his hands. At first, he just
laughed. But soon he stopped laughing. The herd made him
stop. At our wedding, I couldn't wear white, for the clan kept on
scolding: 'Black sin. Oh, black sin.' The deacons? They couldn't
forgive and forget. And soon he couldn't either."

She stared into the sunrise, but all was not yet said.

"I wanted good things for that child. History. Geography.
Music. Sculpture. I even asked for algebra—"

When she could speak again, she told her last-born quietly:
"He was your brother, Rarey. He died in a freak accident. The
child conceived in love became an icicle. And people said: 'That's
punishment! You brought it on yourself!'"

She sat there in the glare of golden morning rays and could
not stop herself:

"From porch to porch, the rumors flew, and when I needed
comfort, I got just poisoned darts. Just darts. Just vicious, poisoned darts. No matter what I did, his people said: 'Poor Jan.
He's hooked. She has the devil in her eyes.' There is no compromise in Mennotown. There is no middle way. They are no better
than the worst of cannibals. They will devour their own. Look at
that sunrise, darling. You wonder who has made that sun. They
say the Lord. The Lord. The Lord. And yet, that kind of sunrise
leaves them cold! Don't ever count on Him. Their Lord feeds on
their cookie-cutter natures. Unless you have that cookie-cutter
nature, too, He won't be on your side. Is there a loving God?
Hah! What a joke! What a sick joke their preachers have dreamed
up. I was forever after grubbing through the rubble."

"My father—"

"Your father was a pious man. Nobody argues with that. He lived a decent life. At least he tried! He tried! But look at what he missed. How he missed out on life! And when his farm goes on the block, tomorrow, and you're left without a penny, you watch and learn your lesson." It ran through her mind like a nightmare. She knew that, tomorrow, the headlines would holler. She turned to Rarey fully: "I'll do what you wish, but I know what I want. And here's what I want—"

She cupped his young face with warm hands and spoke clearly:

"—I want you to learn to sketch better and better. I want you to bring home a girl with black curls. I want you to add to your life huge splashes of color. I want you to plump up your heart with strong dreams. I want you to choose your own friends. I want you to think your own thoughts. I don't want to see you with the herd, the Deweys and the Archies and their ilk—"

"Maybe no one will come tomorrow," said Rarey, choked, a helpless child.

"Just never fear," his mother said. "You have a day to think it over. But mark my word. Just mark my word. They'll come. The smell of blood will travel with the current."

Chapter 77

All hope was riding on the healer. Those who knew Doctorjay were sure he would send every scoundrel packing if he had to forge hard money from thin air. He was the only man to put the bankers out of business, make mincemeat out of them. A show-down was expected, the likes of which made even Archie's glass eye gleam, and everyone was fixing to be there.

A farm auction was an occasion; it always drew crowds. Jan's farm, defenseless on the auction block, was an event few people who could travel would have missed.

Now all the relatives were gathering in groups where they indulged in soggy, emotional reunions. Some had drawn up long lists of things they thought they could afford; they shared them, comparing motley items. Even those who had no money what-soever to spend on windfall bargains had come out of curiosity, taking it all in.

Prospective bidders for farm machinery arrived in buggies from as far away as Hillsboro. Excited lookers-on spilled out of tattered flivvers and gathered on the lawn. Two chartered buses came from Wichita, and people had to push and shove to find a place where they could watch the action. The lawn was black with visitors, fingering this item, then that, pulling watches from their pockets as if they couldn't wait, greeting one another with trembling hugs and kisses as if the shock of Jan's demise had made them into long-lost friends, finding comfort on each other's shoulders. Fence to fence and gate to gate, the people kept milling about. Even a Catholic priest had arrived in a black cylindrical hat, and now was sifting through Jan's recreational items, chiefly his fish lines and hooks.

Careful cash customers, all!

"Let's see now what we have here," announced the auctioneer, launching a warm-up exercise. "All right, now! Folks! Move closer, fellows! Ladies! Closer! Let's let the community spirit run high!"

The throng solidified. People moved elbow to elbow.

"We want to send Jan's little lad through college, right? Let's not be stingy now. What have we got here? Look at this! Two duckfoot cultivators. A rotary rod weeder. Three harrows in excellent shape except for this one little—"

At that moment, Josie stepped out of the house. The dog started growling, just hearing her step. She knew that the neighbors stood ready to take her apart; she kicked a footstool hard and sprained a toe and didn't even flinch. She still had the devil in her. She wore her sparklers in both ears. She carried a large chunk of chalk and started marking items.

She marked them, one by one, to set the proper floor. Her eyes were wide open, unblinking. A nickel here. A quarter there. She moved with surety, as though she still were in her prosperous days, replete with parasol. Pride and vanity had ruled her since she came to Mennotown, and now she let them know: no law can make me stay!

Why give her enemies a pat?

She knew there was no mercy. The people she had fought since she could think and speak—as was her wont, all metaphors and similes—would carry everything away: the stove with its embossed nickel trimmings, the staggered kettles, sifters, funnels, knives and measures. The frying pans. The skillets, pots and cleavers. The reaping hooks and wagon irons. The sickles. Flails. The grindstones. Ladles. Flints and axes. Everything.

"Let's go ahead," she said loudly, as though she gave the sign for her own execution, defiant to the end.

She calmly went about her work, chalking numbers up to make the auction easier. Her eyes surveyed the lawn where everything was piled to be inspected and appraised. All would be auctioned off and carried away, as she and Rarey stood and watched. The lion's share, she knew, would go to Doctorjay for storage in his shed, for that prime pickings would go to the healer was already a foregone conclusion. Not that he needed anything, except for sentiment. The Depression had come like a frightening earthquake and had affected Doctorjay like anyone else. He was too old, in any case, to go back to plowing the earth. But he would surely want Jan's antique iron plow, to donate it to the museum that he and Jan had planned to build, as soon as the harvests improved. Maybe the Russian scythe as well—worn, thin, and dented now?

A dimpled hand lay on her sleeve. "How are you, Josephine?"

Josie's face grew tight with dislike. She cleared her throat. Her voice was glass on glass. "Good morning, Cousin Melly. And how are you today?"

"I meant to call to offer my condolences," sighed Little Melly softly, "but being only human, like everybody else, I couldn't bring myself to call. I bet you didn't sleep a wink, what with your debts and all. If you had only listened and taken boarders in—"

Little Melly had come to partake. She was there to take in the drama. She was prepared and fortified, in hat and white, striped socks. She'd given her two braids an extra-careful combing, anchored a pink bow, and ironed fifty pleats into her skirt. She quivered like a bowl of pudding.

Josie threw her own glove into the ring. "Is this your finest hour?"

Little Melly shook her head, troubled but forgiving. "Whatever do you mean?"

She understood what made for peace in Mennotown. She didn't have to lift her voice, she was adept at setting an example. "Don't talk like that, my dear. It's really not becoming—" Taking in the auction crowd with a sad and misty eye, she added ruefully: "I thought no one would come, what with the scarcity of cash. But look at this. Just look at all the people." With a hefty little heave and a proprietary air, she settled her broad hips atop a bedroom dresser.

"Ah, my," she sighed. "Who would have thought that it would come to this—" Her lips twisted into a smile. She could restrain herself no longer. Her legs were dangling in the air; she was ripe with anticipation.

"I want to bid on her sewing machine," she announced to the people around her. "I might as well make sure it's mine before somebody else takes off with it. I saved my money by taking in boarders. I have plans to put that old Singer to excellent use—"

Despite her lowered lashes, Little Melly could see clearly: a neighbor's jaw fell low with disappointment; she had wanted that sewing machine for herself.

"At least she'll get a decent price, Josie will," she added charitably. "I'll do that for Jan's sake. I owe him that. Some people have forgotten, but Jan and I—we used to go way back! Way back! For his sake, I'll bid just as high as I can—"

"You look as guilty, Little Melly," said Josie with a smile as crooked as a legendary street in San Francisco described in one of Rarey's books, "as if you were about to rob someone's apple tree."

But Little Melly just said: "Pooh!" and smiled forgivingly. She gently dropped her gaze to show she bore no grudges.

"Why not me, Josephine? Why not keep things of value in the family? I want that box of yarn. That set of bobbins, too. At least then you can come and do your mending in my home. As often as you like—"

There was no ready comeback to that parting shot, and Josie

turned her back and walked away with Rarey by her side, still skinny by Mennotown standards, sidestepping several relatives who were eagerly digging through chisels.

"Hey, Doctorjay! Hey-hey-hey, Doctorjay!" The crowd broke into applause.

"Me-he-hellon pulled the whistle—

Hoo-hoo-hoover rang the bell—!" hooted Doctorjay, and never mind his age!

Even from the distance, you could tell: one drink had led to another. The dog yelped once, then cowered. The cat shot up a tree. Archie came flying to throw open the gates—as wide as he possibly could. All heads turned right as if a swivel moved them thus. People stopped shuffling and fingering items.

"And the co-ho-hountry

went to hell—"

A brisk tail wind was propelling Doctorjay, and sparks flew liberally from his mustache as he came slithering around the corner in his flivver. The tires screeched. The motorcar went "whooosh" and Abigail, who had come early to post herself next to a pile of special fishing rods to make sure that her sons had every chance to do their pick-and-choose, let out a bleat of terror.

"Wa-ha-hall Street gave the signal," bellowed Doctorjay, and the crowd took up the chant at once: *"—and the cou-hou-hountry went to hell—!"*

The Donoghues fell into edgy snickers. They started swaying with the rhythm and the lyrics of the song: *"—and the co—ho—hountry went to hell!"*

The healer was magnificently drunk. He scattered people left and right as if they were just chaff. He ruddered through the crowd while looking for a chair onto which he could climb for the sake of still better surveillance. His chin was thrust out; his Adam's apple danced as it had danced in church, at Jan's sad, somber services.

"Now hear me out! Now hear me out!" howled Doctorjay. Determined he was; combative he felt; no one would stop him this morning! It was clear he was livid with rage. The *Wichita Eagle* reporters kept pushing and shoving to get a better look. "My turn! This is my turn! You're in for a blistering sermon. I'm preaching today! I'm preaching today! But first things first!"

At that, he drew Jan's pistol from his trousers and shot a hole into the sky. "Our country went to hell! Is that the American way?"

The Donoghues ducked expertly. The banker flinched as though he had been hit, and his heart dropped into his trousers.

"Is that the American way? To knock somebody down? And then keep hitting him? And hitting him? And hitting him—?"

The healer was a beast that day, beside himself with grief. He headed straight for Josephine, who stood there, in high heels. His smoking pistol in his hand, now roaring like a lion out of Africa, he headed straight for her and put an iron arm around her heaving shoulder as though she were a harlot and he an eager dolt. He swung himself around and all but lifted her out of her heels and her pretentious stockings.

He fixed the crowd with a stern look and spoke in a voice that held murder.

"Well, now. Speak up. Why are you here? Are you here to get something for nothing?"

The throng retreated visibly. A faint went as good as unnoticed. The newspaper man snapped picture after picture. A timid oldster, hard-of-hearing, commenced to stroke his shedding beard and tried to cup his ear.

The healer took the widow by the shoulders and started spinning her as though she were a top. "Take a good look at her! I said take a good look!" The veins in his neck swelled like strings. "You people are Americans," cried Doctorjay, this in a voice so charged it could have detonated dynamite beneath a barrel filled with kerosene. "This is a damsel in distress. This is your fellow citizen. This country does not kick a person who is down! If someone's down, you help him up! You help him up and dust his trousers! That's what you do! That's what you do! Do you need me to tell you that?" His gun was waving angry arches.

"Bring me," demanded Doctorjay, as if he were a Southern Baptist instead of just a loosey-goosey Lutheran who shunned salvation still, no matter what the urgency, "old Lizzy's Russian Bible. Bring me the Bible she brought all the way from Apanlee—"

You never saw Archibald scurry so fast, right through the hostile crowd.

"Since we just buried Dewey Epp," gasped Doctorjay, his voice a somersault, as if this were a lark, a comedy, as if this were the happiest of occasions, "he cannot boot me out of church. Can he? He-he. Chiefly he can't since I have never joined—"

The banker's face told all: this isn't going to get any better.

"See that? See that?" barked Doctorjay. He plowed into his pocket and brought up a handful of change. "What am I holding in my hand?"

"That's money," acknowledged the banker. From the crowd came an uneasy hoot. The banker's eyelids started twitching. Robert, the postal attendant, recovered his grin. Frankie, the grocery clerk, craned his long neck to get a better look.

"What kind of money, mister?" demanded Doctorjay and looked just like a Hottentot about to scalp the banker and have himself a feast.

"I guess—I guess it's honest money," the bankster stuttered feebly, and wiped across his brow. Wet patches formed under his armpits.

"Hah! Right you are!" roared Doctorjay. "How can you tell? An overdue patient just paid up his bill. Is that a stroke of luck, or what? I feel like bidding lavishly. I'm bidding this dime here on Lizzy's milk buckets. A dime for the buckets that started it all. A silver dime for Lizzy's buckets!" He kept waving his pistol about.

A neighbor tugged him by the sleeve. "You can't do that! The floor is set. The widow herself set the floor. A dollar and a quarter for six buckets—"

"Who says I can't? You say I can't?" tongue-lashed a beet-red Doctorjay. "This is America! America! This is God's country, folks! In God's own country, don't you know? A citizen can do exactly as he pleases? That's what my good friend Lizzy used to say—"

A ground swell of voices replied with a sigh. The healer pulled his checkered handkerchief and vigorously blew his nose.

"Those were her buckets, folks. I see her still, as if it happened yesterday. She sat there on those dented pails amidst the weeds of prairie land—"

The people hushed at that.

"—and started showing off with not a penny to her name: 'I'll have the fattest cows! I'll have the strongest calves—!' She came from Apanlee. She wasn't common folk. She came from bookish people, steeped in all kinds of knowledge. But once she came to Kansas, my good friend Lizzy knew: 'We can't be both. Let us, therefore, be pious rather than poetic—'" His jaw began to tremble. He started sniffling noisily. "She said: 'We can't be fancy here. We must lead useful lives. I'll set a fine example.' Her special qualities just radiated out from her without the benefit of schooling. A sack of potatoes, a gunny sack filled to the seams with dry buffalo chips—those things, to her, were poetry. When she produced a loaf of bread—why, that was symmetry! That's what I call perfection! Her chickens multiplied like algebra. God rest her gallant soul."

His voice was quivering with agitation; he stared at Josephine who fought with a constricted throat. He spoke again, this time in his finest High German:

"Her tulips? Every color of the rainbow. She didn't need a brush and easel. See over there? That naked spot? That's where it all began. That's where old Lizzy's sod house used to be. That was before the Santa Fe hauled in the fancy lumber with which Jan built the house. Debtfree. That was before the banksters came and put all values upside down and told him bad was good and black was white and paper good as gold—"

The crowd stood there, in silence. A few had taken off their hats.

"—you listen, Josephine! You think you must be first in everything? She was ahead of you, first class in every way. She was the first to own a hand pump by the sink—next to a wooden drain board!—and when that hand pump squeaked, the angels sang in harmony. I heard them harmonize. The angels sang when Lizzy mashed potatoes. Believe you me, the Lord hummed right along. And when she graduated to a cistern, she thought she had it made—"

Huge tears were rolling down his cheeks and fell into the grass. All eyes were riveted on Josie.

"I looked at her and knew: this is a queen. She's aristocracy. I put my doctor shingle upside down; she quietly set it right. She always paid the grocer. She never belittled Annetta. She melted down her past and helped me get rid of my hymen!"

"Your hyphen!" whispered Josephine, convulsed with her emotions, red as her own geraniums.

But Doctorjay was swinging now; he paid no heed to Josie. Her and her fancy words! He was swinging his speech as though swinging a child by its heels.

"She had a son. I know. I know. Don't interrupt me now! I'm not yet finished, see? You say she had a dozen children, if you count those that died too soon and those that moved away—" His voice was crackling with emotion. "She loved them all—but Jan! Jan was the apple of her eye. That youngster was her favorite. How she loved Jan! She thought she saw the seventh wonder of the world. She honored him, and she respected him. She stood behind his chair to watch him eat—that was her happiness. She loved him more than life itself because she knew: 'He loves the soil. Within that freckled fellow sings the blood of generations—'"

The crowd had hushed. A few reached for each other. They formed a chain of human hands.

"While he was still a boy, with hardly any mustache, he looked for soil no plow had ever touched, and when he found that soil, it was as if he'd found a bride. I watched him as he hauled the harvests, a wheelbarrow full at a time! That boy knew deeper joy than any king on any throne, just sitting on his haystack, just shouting to the world—"

Something within Doctorjay turned stony then, and barren as a desert. He struggled with his voice until he held it firmly in his fists.

"He, too, was unlearned," he added, facing Josie fully, and there was pain and shame and anger in his face the likes of which she'd never seen in her entire life. "But what of that? Do you judge love by text? Do you judge manhood by a comma? There was no time for schools. Who would have fed the herds? Who would have tended to the cows? From inside him came knowledge. From ancestry. Without the benefit of books he was the one who first converted everything. To steam. To gasoline. His crop varieties—the envy of the nation! He said to me once, shyly: 'My children's children will yet claim the universe—' He spread his arms across his family much as an eagle spreads its wings. Jan knew as no one knew: without a sense of duty to his family and to his soil, a man is not a man."

Little Melly had, by then, collapsed into herself, dissolved into a flood of ready tears. She felt as naked as a new-born sparrow in the spring while memories of forty years ago commenced to swirl like dervishes. "He was my love," she told herself. "He should have been my man."

She knew the picture Doctorjay was calling forth; it was her property; she kept it framed and dusted it daily, next to her stomach bitters. Every time she looked at it, a thrill ran down her spine. She looked with swimming eyes at Doctorjay to hear him say that now, but Doctorjay just took her spinster heart and broke it right in two as though it were a pretzel.

"And you! You listen, Little Melly! Don't look at me like that! I read you like a book. I know you would have specialized in motherhood. That would have been your calling. You were pretty and pink in those years! You had an ample bosom! You were rosy and shone like a ham! You would have thrown yourself into domestic life as Josie never did. But see? He didn't choose you, Missy. Why not? Go ask yourself why not. I'll give you one good reason. Because his blood ran strong. He craved a worthy partner. You didn't see that. Josie did. So he chose her. Not you. And you? You joined the Hallelujah choir so everybody said: 'Oh, look at Little Melly. So wronged, and yet so brave!' But on the sly, what did you do? You turned into a telephoniac! You were like a mosquito: you pricked, and you drank blood. That's what Jan understood and loved in Josephine: The fairness of her soul. She stretched her arms beyond the boundaries of Mennotown, as you did not. That's why. Jan looked into her dancing eyes and put himself in mortal peril. We saw it flickering—that small, forbidden flame. We should have stepped on it—"

Now it was Josie's turn. He set to pummeling her savagely with words stored deep within. "You, Josie! It's your turn. You were a daffodil, and we just common dandelions? That's what you thought? We were just common folks? With scars and warts and calluses? And you were different? Better? When you came here to live with us, when you fell to the floor and started screaming, I should have pulled you upright by your braids and doused you then and there! I should have had your wisdom teeth extracted on the spot! I stood all ready with my pliers, but Jan— Jan held me back by my own belt and said: "She's just a child. She's just a little girl. Only the sky is as pretty as Josie.'

"But he was wrong. You weren't pretty then. You aren't pretty now. You're selfish, Josie! Selfish! Life isn't gloss. It's duty. There's nothing pretty about selfishness! Your wrinkles all run right to left, not up and down, as nature likes its wrinkles. You people! Look at her! Her husband showered her with status. At testimonial dinners, he seated her above the salt. Did he not feed her well? Did he not cherish her? She was the first who had a home with electricity. She was the first who had a telephone, a double laundry tub. And she? What did she do? She launched a thunderbolt against his groin as though he were her enemy. He loved her, and he married her. And she? She wounded him with disobedience. She took all her housewifely duties to town. She had no business typing letters for the Finkelsteins—"

He turned to Josephine directly: "It wasn't that he was a

man, and you were just a woman. That wasn't it at all. It wasn't
this suffragist nonsense. It was the end effect. It was the end
result. Had you shown him respect, that would have made him
ten feet tall. That would have made him happy. How often did
I hear him say: 'Blow out the light now, kitten!' with longing in
his voice. But you? You hung his manhood like a rooster from
the ceiling by the heels! That's not the way to treat a man who
gave you all he had—!"

He took the widow by her shoulders so that she faced the
neighbors, a thick, united cluster.

"You face your music, Josephine. You bridle your sharp
tongue. You listen to what I and others have to say. You hate
vareniki? You do not like our diphthongs? You say you hate our
songs? You've despised us from the time you came here, with
the devil dancing in your eyes. You wounded us at every opportunity. You saw an enemy in every relative you met. The
Finkelsteins are fancier than we are? They're smarter than we
are? Ha! Phooey, Josephine! We're sturdier than they are! Our
roots go deep into the earth. Where is their grain? Where is their
Apanlee?"

They stood in a circle, all holding hands, all humming with
emotion. But Doctorjay had not yet finished with his sermon,
and finish it he would.

"When we used poor and stilted grammar, you cast sarcastic
glances, Don't think we haven't noticed. Don't think it didn't
hurt. Had not Jan loved you so, we would have put a stop to it.
A woman should appear in print but twice: when she marries;
when she dies. But you? How often were you in the paper, on
spiked heels yet, next to the Socialists? We have been patient
with your notions. Our patience has run out. You make an inward resolution to reform. No more inflammatory talk, you hear?
Out with the jaundiced arguments about corsets and curls and
self-esteem! Now is your opportunity to change, as Dewey always said—"

He placed his searchlight there.

"And Dewey! Dewey Epp, whom I raised from his soggy

diapers. The preacher whom we buried yesterday was not the smartest man who ever walked on Appian Way. In fact, he was a fool! But see? He was cheap, and he, too, had his place. He was cheaper than the police, and he kept our town spic and span. The peasants used to say way back in the old country: The mightier Thou are, God, the greater the tsar's joy. I often looked at him and saw his face was small and mean and understood why you disliked him so. So Dewey was a dullard? Perhaps. What preacher isn't dull and boring? They bore you right out of your tree. But look at what he proffered! The Sermon on the Mount! The Ten Commandments, Josie! That's what it's all about. Good neighbors living within range of one another so they can help each other without words in times of greatest need. You never knew that, did you? When Dewey hounded you, as many times he did, it did not mean you shouldn't have some fun. What's fun? All people are entitled to some fun. I like some fun myself. But don't forget: fun is a feather, while pride is a boulder. A boulder! It anchors you to everything that's right. It keeps you down; it steadies you and keeps you from the riffraff and the rabble—"

Heads now turned left, to face the Donoghues, backed up into the wall, for clearly, they were next.

"What? Can't you take a joke?" one mumbled timidly before he slunk away, the others following, toe over heel, but now no stopping Doctorjay. He did not fail his neighbors' expectations.

"And you! You there. You owe your life to Lizzy! I see her still the night that you were born—she sat there with a towel in one hand and a pot of coffee in the other, waiting up all night with me, just sitting, watching, praying. And when you finally came out, she turned to me and said: 'Their heads are twisted to the left, and something within them is broken.' From the cradle, you were trouble. Heels first, that's how you arrived in this world! That's how you live. That's how you'll die. That's trouble! I mean trouble!"

He had to stop to blow his nose and dab his eyes once more,

but he was not yet finished. He finished them as well, albeit in absentia, and shook an angry fist:

"She sat them down and gave them plenty of advice. Was it her fault they did not heed her words? They stepped in every chicken dropping and then they ran to Washington, complaining of the stink. She listened to their woes and came up with a number of solutions. I watched them through the years, and don't tell me that I watched only Abigail. I know all their shenanigans. Life on a silver platter, right? Not while I still have breath left—"

Doctorjay sucked in a deep and trembling gulp of air and dropped onto one knee before Jan's little son:

"You, Rarey. You are last. Your father was a citizen. He built a fine community. He came here before Mennotown was Mennotown, a place so small you couldn't even find it on a map. Just dirt roads. Nothing else. He kept long hours at the mill. He didn't ask for handouts. He didn't claim he was entitled to free meals. This country lied to him. The banksters said: 'If you play by our rules, the rules will serve you well.' That is some joke! Some monumental joke! His dream betrayed, his pride in shreds, that's how your father died. This country broke his heart. This country is no longer pretty. Someone stole its core. Don't ask me how it happened. It's all mixed up with dynamite, Karl Marx, free love, and curly hair. The bread these hucksters eat, your father grew. The town he built, the crooks and hucksters own. The people he elected run someone else's show. Whose show? Not mine. Not yours. And not your father's either. They will not serve us well. Let's not let our enemies choose all our enemies for us!"

He caught himself. He spoke as though to himself:

"And even I. I was his friend, but was I vigilant? I'm weeping over someone whose murderer I am. What did I do to help him out? I should have been his comrade. I didn't see his pain. I lusted after Abigail. While his strong farmer's heart was breaking with the betrayal of it all, I told him flivver jokes! I asked him to chuckle with Amos 'n Andy. Jan wasn't asking for the moon. What did he need to pull himself out of this pit his own elected leaders dug? A wife who was a wife. A friend who was a friend. A town that was a town. A bankster with a heart."

He faced the banker now, down on his knees, with Rarey in his arms. "This is Jan's son. When he began to work for usury, no longer paying cash on cash, you put his pecker in your pocket. He could have made it through the dirty decade with just a little help from you. Your interest crushed his bones—" The healer placed his hand on Lizzy's Bible and trumpeted through tears: "So help me, dearest God in Heaven. You gave him this land. The banksters won't take it away."

And then he stood.

"See this? That's all the cash I have. Exactly fifteen dollars. This is my show. I'm bidding seven dollars here on that fine set of plows—"

The auctioneer retrieved his voice. "No! No! You can't do that! The floor's been set at twelve—"

"I can't? Who says I can't?" The healer's voice was booming like a cannon. He pointed his beard in defiance. "Don't tell me what I can and cannot do! I voted in this government. And I can vote it out. You mean to tell me now I have no speaking part? I'm bidding seven. Seven dollars! On second thought, I'm bidding six. And as I look around this minute, I can see that my good neighbor, Peter Friesen, thinks he's bidding five—"

The farmer Friesen gulped and sputtered. "Upwards! Upwards! The widow needs the cash!"

"Is that a fact?" hissed Doctorjay. He started fingering the trigger. "Don't you, too, feel a secret urge to bid four greenbacks on Jan's plows?"

A sheen sat on the farmer Unruh's forehead. "I guess I do," he stuttered, his eyes on the gun, his beard full of tears. "Four bucks for the entire set of plows—"

"Well! Fancy that. Now there's two of us who feel like bidding downwards. Might there be three? What? Brother Penner?"

The farmer Penner cleared his throat. "Two-fifty," he said hoarsely, and wiped the tears out of his wrinkles. "Jan once lent me an extra mule when mine broke an ankle in one of the ruts—"

"I'm topping you. I'm bidding two—"
"One-seventy-five!"
"One-fifty—"
"One."
"Three quarters—"
"Fifty-"
"Fifty one! Fifty two! Fifty taken!" cried the auctioneer, thick perspiration forming on his upper lip.

The bonesetter was howling now. "We're on a roll! We're on a roll. Jan's threshers? Splendid threshers! Four bucks for the entire set?"

"Two-fifty!" shouted several people from the crowd.

"I see it's catching on!" trumpeted Doctorjay. "I see at least two dozen people who have caught on to what this day is all about—"

"Three fifty—" cried the banker, shrilly. "That was the floor. We did agree there'd be a floor. The widow herself said—"

Doctorjay turned to the banker and said sharply: "Sit down, you toady, and shut up! or I'll cancel your membership in the Chamber of Commerce. Downwards! Downwards, Christian Soldiers—!" He pointed both thumbs to the floor. "That's how we're bidding today!   I don't bid upwards on this brand new, shiny day and don't know anyone who does."

"A dime on that fine, pretty chest," announced a young mother, a baby nestling in her arms. "Hop down, Little Melly! This minute. Get off Josie's chest."

"A penny. A penny once. A penny twice. A penny taken for the chest—"

That is the splendid story, repeated to this day. Thus went the auction backwards, as far as it could go, and Josie, too, much like a mare in front of an abyss, stopped right in time. And started walking backward. Right there. It was magnificent. In Josie's soul that day, the story goes, a bitter struggle came to rest. She put away her angry arrows. Had Lizzy known, she would have been so pleased—that, in the end, Jan's widow learned her lesson well and settled down to Mason jars. Like everybody else.

When all was said and done, the bonesetter said in his thickest tongue: "Vell! Finally! Ve haff our country back."

The coins piled up in a small heap next to his smoking pistol. He turned two red-rimmed eyes, as if they were two searchlights, on Jan's young son and said: "Come here. You do your numbers, laddie. You help me count, will you? If we believe your mother's boasts, you've got a brain. You've got the quickest mind in town—"

The count turned out to be exactly fifteen dollars.

"Fifteen dollars? You don't say! That's what a good man's lifetime work is worth? How my good Noralee would have rejoiced. She always tried to get the best of Lizzy—" The healer dabbed his lids. "Now she is gone. And Lizzy, too. And I will die tomorrow. And, in the meantime, I have Abigail to occupy my time. She'll eat me out of house and home. I'll have my hands full keeping up. Here is the cash. It's yours. I'm not a farmer, Rarey. I do not need your father's farm. If you permit me, son, I'll sell it back to you—"

"Doctorjay, I don't have fifteen dollars. This cash goes to the bank."

"Why, in that case," said Doctorjay, "I'm sure our bankster here will want to do a little business with you by giving you a line of credit at reasonable interest that won't eat up your soul!"

The banker gulped three times and muttered something sounding like collateral. The healer took the banker firmly by his collar:

"No usury in Mennotown. No monkey business here. No hanky panky in quadruplicates. His father's name is plenty of collateral—"

The banker dove into the crowd and disappeared to hoots and hisses, coattails flapping. The healer squatted next to Josie's son so that their eyes were level, and here is what he said:

"You listen, lad. You listen hard. You're in this for the long haul. You think you're you? You aren't you. You're but a tiny morsel. You are so small you, too, will come and go. In the blink of an eye, you'll be gone. But on the other hand, you're tall. Because you have a history. Because of Apanlee. You came of honorable stock. Your future is already charted. The business of America? It's now your business, laddie. You're young. We're old. We all count on you Rarey. You put away your easels until the work is done! You put your shoulder to the wheel and shove! You include yourself in! Is that understood? Repeat after me: 'I include myself in.'"

Rarey spoke softly: "I include myself in."

"Hand me the liquidation papers, Josephine."

They say she pulled her mirror. They say she took a good look at herself, and then she looked around, and what she saw were faces of a thousand friends, and all of them were open. Naked. Smiling.

And Josie said: "Hand me my travel papers."

She tore them up. She threw them high into the air. The Kansas wind blew them about. She stopped herself just in the nick of time from hurling her young son into vast space without that pride that was imported out of Apanlee to hold him back and pin him down and give him solid moorings. And everybody knew: the soil of her soul had been plowed. The seeds of pride would grow.

Those who are still alive remember it as if it happened yesterday. They'll tell you with emotion shining in their faces: they walked toward each other—the lone and stubborn heretic and the solidified *Gemeend*. Bareheaded, they stood in a circle around her, holding hands, breaking into a favorite hymn. And many eyes were moist. The earth was theirs. The grain was theirs. The sun was theirs as well, on loan from the Lord in the sky. It was still hanging there, eternally, a glob of gold amid the boundless sky of Kansas that shone its rays on gladness and goodwill, and even Little Melly gave a little hiccup, high and shrill, and summarized it all: "Will you now join our quilting bee?" and Josie gulped and said: "I will. I do. You have my solemn word—"

She had not cried for more than thirty years. She started crying now. Her tears started falling like raindrops.

Had there been cannons somewhere, they would have thun-
dered their salute. Had there been fireworks, they would have
flowered in the clouds. Where one world ended, another began.
From that day on, her excesses were gone. She changed, and for
the better. From that day on, she bought for durability. She gave
when deacons knocked. She took up Lizzy's butter churns. When
someone came to ask her for a cookie recipe, she shared it willingly.

You hear this story still—in Kansas, in Nebraska, in Winnipeg, in the Dakotas. They swear she said that sunny, fragrant
morning of the auction: "I will."

She said: "I do."

She said like Ruth: "Let Thy God by my God. Thy people be
my people—"

Not in so many words, of course—for saying that out loud
took time. Getting rid of her poodle took time. Getting rid of the
Hebrews took more time, for she'd grown used to them. But best
of all, the story goes, not ever did she sin again against the spirit
of the times by storming the Rotarians.

Lebensraum! - Book III - Chapters 78 - 125

Reviewed by Michael S. McMillen

Of all America's foes in all of her wars, no enemy has been more vilified for so long as the Third Reich. Every now and again, someone wonders why.

If novelty enhances a novel's appeal, Lebensraum! - Book III should be a bestseller. The sections dealing with the Second World War will strike many readers as the literary equivalent of a photographic negative. For a change, the Nazis are wearing the white hats.

While writing this review, I came across a relevant quotation from *Founding Father* by Richard Whalen: "World War II was the liberals' war and they are understandably determined to uphold their version of its origins with all the formidable political and intellectual resources at their command."

Since the early 1940s, Adolf Hitler has been the West's Villain for All Seasons. Books, plays, movies, "docudramas," and television series feature Nazis and Germans interchangeably in the stock roles of archetype of evil and scourge of mankind. The only time National Socialists aren't portrayed as goose-stepping demons is when they are cast as hyperpunctilious, heiling buffoons.

In Lebensraum! - Book III the reader will find no such caricatures of the German Volk. He will find instead an army and a people fighting fiercely to preserve their own race, a nation stung to the core by an all-destroying, internationalist foe.

It would be petty to object that Lebensraum! Book III fails to present an objective moral study of Hitler and his Reich. As a novel, the focus of Lebensraum! is not statistical analysis of the motives and actions of its characters. Lebensraum! is not a comprehensive history of World War II. The story is, however, rooted in fact.

History attests that there were people during the Second

World War who welcomed the Nazis as saviors and heroes. The German pioneers of Lebensraum! who had once grown prosperous under the Romanovs are their representatives.

When one considers the nature of Stalin's gulag state, its goal of yoking all its subject under collectives directed by a central committee in Moscow, one can understand that the people crushed under its iron boot might have looked upon the armies of the Führer with grateful anticipation.

Lebensraum! - Book III gives us an exciting and heartbreaking glimpse of one people's moment of vindication against a comprehensively brutal engine of oppression. After the hellish terror unleashed by the Soviet revolution, Justice cries out for vengeance from the skies – or from the earth.

Young Jonathan, who escaped from the Soviets and found his way to Germany, grows into a loyal soldier of the Fatherland, and is among the Landsers who reclaim – albeit temporarily – Apanlee for its rightful owners.

Eventually, owing to overextension and strategic errors on the part of the Fuehrer (e.g., his refusal to permit retreat) the Wehrmacht is driven back by the Red Army, now counted among the Allies. One of the tragedies stalking the stoic German survivors is that those who could have helped defend them, side instead with the beast seeking to devour them.

The remnants of the Neufeld and Epp clans in the Ukraine are unable to understand the world's indifference to their suffering. They cannot imagine that the rest of the world is infected with the same notions of international collectivism as the Soviet state.

They are utterly baffled and mystified when America, the land of Liberty, which received their own kin not so many decades earlier, joins forces with Stalin and his Reds.

When people are faced with such an inexplicable fact, they seek desperately to satisfy themselves with some kind of an answer. Lebensraum! records accurately the answer that many fixed upon: international Jewry.

The objective reader will bear in mind that the anti-Judaism expressed by some characters in these novels is not an invention of the author. The reader would do well to note that most of the main characters bear no animosity towards the Jews or anyone else. They simply wish to be left alone. Moreover, at one point, young Jonathan starts to tell what sounds like an off-colour story about Jews and is quickly chastised by Heidi, the woman who had rescued him from the streets. She explains that some of the good people with whom she had traded are Jews. The point, I believe, is that although bigoted anti-semitism unfortunately existed in Germany and elsewhere, it has nothing to do with the desire of the Germans for freedom and living space.

For centuries, the Jews had been viewed with suspicion throughout Christian Europe. This is not fundamentally because they happened to be adept at trade and finance; these functions are vital to an economy and constitute nothing inherently dishonourable or exploitative. Marked by their refusal to embrace the cross and creed of Christ, the Jews were frozen out of the circle of production by the economically fastidious (and sometimes woefully ignorant) Christians, and they became the exchangers, lenders and middlemen. Not surprisingly, many succumbed to the temptations inherent in such preoccupations and came to regard the people whose money they managed as convenient nuisances– profitable in the collective but of little consequence individually.

Marxism views the mass of men essentially the same way – and excoriates Christianity to boot. Socialist mythology sees its chosen people – the proletariat or working class – scattered and dispersed across the world and mistreated by bourgeois, primarily Christian, society.

Many Jews became the willing spokesmen and penmen for this new global ideology. Many were archly sympathetic to its call for a strictly secular state that would tear down the crosses and churches in deference to dreams of futuristic fraternity and equality.

Marx promised a far-off Utopia to all men in exchange for a radical break with the individualistic, nationalist Christian past.

The proverbial wandering Jew became in many instances an ambitious booster for both the international banker and international bolshevik. The apparent contradiction in this union of banksters and rowdies continues to mislead the unwary to this day.

Ingrid Rimland has described the concomitant growth of these two forces vividly and dramatically in Lebensraum!, particularly in Book III. Her picture of an America slouching through the Roosevelt years convinced of the gospel verity of the New York Times is not a flattering one.

Nevertheless I, as a patriotic American who believes in the founding principles of this nation, applaud the author for penning so blunt a satire of her adopted land.

America has often been described as a country with a great and eager heart. Sometimes her eagerness does her no good: the willingness to believe the glowing and deceptive dispatches from the Soviet Union; the reflexive anti-Germanism imbibed freely from the media outlets of the era; the gullible surrender to state welfarism, so long as it is buttered liberally with prattle of "compassion" and "tolerance."; the sheep-like acquiescence in the quasi-religion of received propaganda concerning the nature and extent of German mistreatment of the Jews during the war.

All this – what one might dub a pathological obsession with acting out good intentions – is symbolozed by Rarey Neufeld, who goes enthusiastically off to war to kill his German brethren for Uncle Sam (and Uncle Joe). Book III ends with a touching letter to his wife from this genuinely good man, who is killed in the waning hours of the war by anti-aircraft fire from his own German cousin, Erika.

World War II was a disaster for everyone involved. Nevertheless, the corruption and self-hatred it fomented in the USA and Germany contributed to the unthinkable rise of the clumsy but vicious and deadly Soviet Empire.

Some claim to see in the political fall of the unwieldy beast the death of Communism. Such people are sadly mistaken. Communism today reigns and runs rampant on American college campuses and in the nooks and crannies of government both here and in Western Europe.

Today "internationalism" has become "globalism" and the UN has replaced the Red Army as the socialists' army of choice. I say here in sorrow and in anger that this very trilogy that I am reviewing will probably be banned in some of the "democracies" that helped defeat Hitler and prop up Stalin.

What God's plan for this weary world may be, I do not profess to speculate upon. I do assert, however, that the political ideas and ideals that the world needs have already been formulated - and were once put into practice for nearly a century - right here in America.

It's here in America that Ingrid Rimland's trilogy is being published. If America does not speak out on behalf of the rights of man and for the unhindered pursuit of truth, who will?

Ingrid Rimland has spoken out again - eloquently and clearly. Those who do not share her vision of America are free to disagree and to criticize.

Those who care to join her in this literary quest for Lebensraum! will find a good story well told. What more can you ask of a novelist?